Sun Silly
by Aace AaBright

A financial gift from the sale of each copy of Sun Silly will be made to these charities – Victims Center (United Way) and Together We Rise (a college fund for foster teens). In my heart, I know this is where the greatest joy from writing Sun Silly will come from.

Love Life & Laugh,
Aace

© 2020 US.Copyright Office

Cast of Core Characters

VeeLee VonVouge:

Anglaia Clinton:

Lara London:

Adamina-Rose Clintin:

Aarontino Jackkson:

Chapter 1

VeeLee sipping on sunshine

  THE ALARMS IN MY HEAD BONE STABBED AT my ears, pinching off the hint of a dream? My eyes danced for a time beneath the calm darkness of my eyelids then sprung open to the pain of the stinging night air. I coiled into a sitting position and wiped at the fog of wet breath on the glass until I could see through the smudge of the car door window. It was a drunken man shushing the bottle he had inadvertently kicked. He was pushing down the noise with both hands as if asking for mercy, his eyes bulging from his face like a stepped-on goldfish. That is when our eyes connected in a dance of the damned, and my heart stumbled to a stop. With a groan similar to that of an engine straining on a weak battery, my heart wrenched tight then jolted into a rapid crescendo of African drums thumping wildly in my chest. The man staggered like a zombie in my direction.

I knew the door was locked but checked it anyway, just in case. He tapped on the window with his unkempt corkscrew of a fingernail and said, "Hey!" There was no other option but to be terrified.

Go Away! I silently screamed to myself.

I was required to answer to adults, even ones dumbed by liquid drugs. We had known every other drunk in the K-sea area, my mom was a stripper and part-time waitress—a magnet for guys like this one. Just as I was about to wake her from her passed out crouch in the back seat, a horn honked. The man gawked over his shoulder to see the taxi, spewed some cuss words in my direction he thought my look deserved and surfed away on a clumsy wave—leaving a line of barf behind on the pavement as he went.

I was accustomed to nights like these. Mom had us living this way since dad committed suicide. Some nights she would leave the club with a man, and I would be left to fend for myself. The sound of silence would always be my preference, my friend. Being alone was not the end of the world, yet despair would manage its way into my thoughts in the form of a random pity-party but knew I couldn't take too seriously. *Remember VeeLee, feelings are visitors, it's better not to marry any of them. Tough times make tough people. Lara's voice echoed through the jelly of my brain.* Followed by the subconscious voice of Christopher who constantly reminded me that we shared an organ, a heart. He liked to make me feel it, sometimes the heartbeat would take off like a racecar for no reason or seemed to move around in my chest like a baby in the womb.

Silence my magic pill, it proceeded me in my daily walk and forged a strength strong as steel, my personal reality, my personality. A molded expression of resoluteness ran the smile off my face most days, vowing not to look into any mirror directly as it would give my ego energy to complain. My adopted facial expression was much easier to use than telling people to leave me alone, although there were weak moments where my words could not shape mean, tough thoughts correctly, and this face of mine betrayed me as a kind soul.

Mom would not replace the alternator, and we had to push-start the car all the time. The trunk of the car usually had a plastic-wrapped case of bottled water and some assorted canned goods like beef stew and mom's favorite, cheese curls—the messiest snack ever invented, along with a mound of trash bags filled with our crap. There were pillows and blankets we used when it was cold or cracked the windows in the summertime where I wished on every star in our galaxy for a breeze—when the car battery was completely dead, I knew fate would have me playing patty-cake with the hot hands of the devil. There were a few times where the windows were down, and I didn't have the keys or battery juice to roll them up, a perfect scenario for a thunderstorm to jump out of the sky without notice. Not only was the witchy wind, licks of lightning, and explosions of thunder scary, but as everything inside the car got soaking wet, it made me feel like worthless scum.

Who could ask for more? Right! My attendance at school was horrific, too. I missed first block regularly. If mom had a bad hangover, she'd say, "Screw it! Read your books, baby boy. Momma's sick today," and pass back out.

Weekends and summer break were the hardest to deal with when we were homeless—I was always amazed by the number of gawkers that passed by the car and conceitedly pretended to push the clouds higher into the atmosphere with their eyes, not wanting to look or see something glaringly wrong in the world. Becoming part of a time-consuming or financial solution would be too much to ask—most smudged looks I received were repetitive and easily dismissed.

It was a guessing game when or if mom would return to me when the club closed. Most often, I'd have to wait until she sobered up at some Joe's house and was able to come back to get me and the car. Most often we were at the mercy of some horny drunken man she most likely had met for the first time. It was completely random—nine or noon? I never knew. I would end up pacing around the parking lot in between the books Lara from the Trueman Library had recommended. Books that graced my life with alternatives, but not quite a safe refuge, as the weight of them in my backpack slowed me down when I needed to move fast.

I learned early on how to make myself invisible and avoid drawing attention, especially when police officers patrolled the area. If they found me, mom and I would go through tons of drama at the police station, where we could be kept for hours before released. Mom hated social workers and law enforcement passionately—she was always in trouble for something. As long as I had batteries for my flashlight, I was somewhat content. I could hide beneath the blankets and read, entertained and educated by the wily minds and wonderful worlds shared by amazing authors.

When mom didn't get dragged off by some man's billfold or muscles like tonight, she would be passed out in the back seat of the car. I learned to use the seasons to my advantage over the years, a morning ritual of rolling the windows up in the summer and down in the winter, so she would get up sooner and get us to a shower and food.

There had been a drought of new dancers at the club lately... mom preyed on them, especially the young and naïve. On a good day, it took about ten minutes for mom to convince the tenderfoot that life had managed to keep them apart all their lives, that they somehow had beat the odds and were now besties—mom would then invade the new girl's life and home with her poor me song and dance, clinging on to the residence for as long as possible... eventually they all found instant peace the day they kicked us out.

The drunken stranger who had kicked the bottle earlier had me wide awake now, and I could do nothing else but mull over my thoughts. Maybe prepare a speech I'd someday present to a gathering of curious souls.

Maybe I'd say something like, "There are but words presented in the English language to derive my understanding and the basic meaning of all things. Spelling out our spells in a line of words that generically substitutes for life's explanation, to include creating every problem we want to have. Everything is only words. To be clear, there are other languages and symbols one might wiggle their way forward in various ways to forge Aristotle's golden mean. That glorious alchemy of virtuous meaning. Where all noble truths merged into the happiness of our next breath, constantly kissing the darkness of death. One colossal consciousness of ultimate virtuous knowing...

"And yes, virtue is simple. It's the strength or essence of a thing. In a paraphrastic way, the highest virtue is not conscious of itself. It is every known thing's magic. When you breathe, you do not praise yourself for being virtuous in breathing and giving yourself life. If you have beautiful green eyes, you do not praise yourself for growing the most bravura jewels on earth that entertain colors and forms. You may say they're just pretty eyes but seeing is the true miracle of eyeballs— it's like the healing medicine of a plant, its strength, its virtue. Numbers too clearly scream truths. Screams magic. The past and future are simply thought streams of illusion. Dreams lurking for an emotion to gallop upon, hormones that give life to feelings—"

Maybe someone would like a speech like this one day? Dunno, but I will always be grateful for the friendship and tutelage of Lara London. She seems set on making me a *learned* man in the future. My brain has hoarded the collected thoughts of many great minds, which I now gallantly use to explore my greatest fascination of all: the sun.

My beloved sun is very hot, reaching temperatures of fifteen million degrees Celsius. The sun is so large that one million planet earths could fit inside it. And it continues to get hotter the longer it burns. And yes, in a billion years, the earth will become a blackened chunk of floating space charcoal. Human life will one day end on this planet. Until then, we human beings will be required to hunt energy on a daily basis.

For the past three years, I have absorbed as much of the men I admire as possible: Isaac Newton's calculus, Hipparchus of Nicaea's trigonometry, Muhammad ibn Musa Al-

Khwarizmi's algebra, Euclid of Alexandria's geometry, Galileo Galilei, Albert Einstein, and Stephen Hawking's astronomy, theoretical and modern physics. Orders of operations and formulas were exciting to watch until they became rudimentary or otherwise boring.

 To me, mathematics became similar to looking at a color spectrum. Once you know blue is blue, it's not very impressive to tout blue all day long. I wanted to find answers to my questions and solve some mysteries of my own. Not come up with the known answer to someone else's numbers and riddles. Fun for a while and impressed my schoolteachers, but I lost interest in testing. The best math one can learn is the answer to the future cost of choices made at any random moment. A daily calculation tilted to the good is exactly *the* correct method to avoid life's infinity of random *problems*.

 Mom snorted as she jostled around in the back seat, trying to find a more comfortable position. Her breath and uncommonly foul-smelling feet were making me nauseous as usual. When we lived in the car, my bedroom was in the passenger front seat. When I reclined the seat back to sleep, mom's butt was a foot away and pointed directly at my head, when she farted, the fragrance of inner dead was not worth the act of breathing. It was like inhaling a sickening contagion meant to kill me.

 Tonight was one of those stinky nights. I rolled the windows down and got out of the car so that the night air might suck the majority of the stench from the inside of our makeshift motel on wheels. At school, I, too, had a reputation for smelling funky when we lived countless days in the car. I could actually become repulsed by the smell of myself too, and knew it was an issue. My schoolmates enjoyed being as rude to me as possible concerning my hygiene or stale clothes.

 Mom could not legally drive us places after work anymore. She had too many drinking and driving offenses. The last offense was a bit outlandish as we were sleeping in the car and a female police officer mom had insulted the week before nailed her for a DUI, mom was completely wasted and had access to the car keys. The charges stuck in court. One more time and she would be jailed for at least a year, or most likely for as long as the law allowed—the Judges in K-sea did not like her. She had met them all at one time or another.

Unavoidably, I became a risk-taker like my mom by driving the car to a safe spot close to school without a driver's license. When possible, I would try to get to school an hour early and follow Mr. Watts, the janitor inside after he unlocked the back door. For some reason, I felt like I needed to sneak on the tips of my shoes down the school hallways to the gym for a quick shower. Don't really know why. It may have been due to the embarrassment of my explanation to school authorities should I be nabbed for loitering. I think Mr. Watts knew what I was doing, and I was grateful he never caused me any trouble.

I pushed on the car door until the dome light went out and eased myself onto the hood of the car, placed my hands behind my head, and relaxed against the windshield. I laid there spread-eagle and watched the stars winking. It made me smile as my vision collected the vast space between the things in space. The soul of K-sea had settled down to a soft eerie quiet, rendering a few faint wayward sounds in the distance. The traffic had hushed, and the city was at rest—boring or not, I began to think of more numbers. Couldn't help it. It was a habit.

Nikola Tesla's discoveries and his hint to the numbers three, six, and nine were captivating. But for me, I realized that true magic exists in the numbers thirty-seven and sixty-four, especially when used in scientific equations. Tesla's universal understanding of energy is so mind-boggling that if I could spend one day with anyone who ever lived, it would be him. He fathered alternating current and truly wanted to gift the world with his Wardenclyffe Tower—a power station that would have created a free wireless power delivery system for all… incredible thinking that came from a man almost a hundred years ago, ideas that will most likely be suppressed forever due to worldly money matters. A most audacious gesture, nonetheless. Fortunately, a great deal of the wireless principles has been adopted in the communication arena as Wi-Fi, cellphones, and computers.

With similar concepts, I intend to capture the sun. I just need to learn how best to package and market the most potent energy source in our universe—food. Those awesome little chunks of sun we toss in our mouth and eat. I will most likely challenge grocery stores and put a great deal of the medical and pharmaceutical industries out of business, giving spinach, seaweed farmers, and beekeepers a huge raise.

Is a job or a day's pay worth a day of life? Should I run and hide from the preeminent fight of pill-pushing doctors and powerful folks of fake food factories. How much would a billionaire pay for a day of life? I ask myself.

My approach will be much different than Tesla's. I will overwhelm the nation and world before the wealthy can react and steal my ideas. Only the powerful can fight the powerful, long gone are the days where the power of people was a realistic campaign. Tesla's work and futuristic thinking continually blows my mind… he adamantinely believed that it would one day be possible to photograph thoughts, making our minds a picture book we could hold in our hands and head. Sometimes I'm grateful he didn't figure that one out. Yet thoughts are little energy fields, things that have a life of their own and kill the majority of the human species in one way or another. Negative thoughts are ornery critters that will tuck themselves into an organ or meridian system and create one of twenty-five thousand diseases the medical field hopes to profit from.

These thoughts at two o'clock in the morning were becoming heavy as they jump atop my eyelashes, making it hard to keep them open. It's time to get off this car hood and get some rest.

I curled up into a fetal position in the car seat and skimmed a few more thoughts, without a doubt knowing this sort of life disgusted me and motivated me to engage in solving complex matters. I would someday create an extraordinary life. Thoughts of my future made my mind explode and pause in noble silence at the same time. So far, I have two very good scientific formulas to test in a scientific laboratory. I have committed them to memory so that they will never be left or lost in a trash bag somewhere.

My mentor, Lara London, feels I would do well to consider politics. She has gone over many of the great and not-so-great leaders of the past, and whole-heartedly believes there is no
greater power on earth, yet I enjoy learning scientific models much more.

In studying physiology—how the human body functions—I have noted that the entire liver replaces itself every ninety days, and a cup of lemon juice can aid in its detoxification, giving the organ a helping hand to perform over three hundred functions, making the entire human body healthier. Yes, lemons. It fascinated me to learn that the vast majority of negative thoughts like to hang out in the liver as well, which the key fix there is forgiveness and a few secrets I'm learning about the sun.

Lara also thinks that a good magnet rubbed across the skin, love shared from a happy heart, fifteen rigorous sweat-producing minutes of exercise, and of course, a daily cup of fresh lemon juice in the morning is the most potent magical medicine prescription on earth. I agree with her and would only add my future Sun Silly pill.

"Huh. What. What?" mom mumbled, "Go to sleep, baby boy. Make sure the doors are locked," she said aloud when I woke her with the light and click of closing the car door. She quickly passed back out after another round of tumbling about. The rotten air was gone now, and I might, in fact, be able to go to sleep.

Chapter 2

The dance of Anglaia

MAYBE IT WAS THE DREAMS? SHE WAS driven to shape me into her snooty little identity—a daughter that most resembled her. She was Mother Earth in her own mind and obviously created me by her damned self—a modern-day immaculate conception had somehow reoccurred, and she was the only one who knew about it. Thankfully, I was born a girl, or she may have named me Jesus, Jr—a name she called me most days, anyway.

She wanted a prissy little prom queen—which I could totally pull off—but that's beside the point. She needed to be known as the mother who raised the greatest child on the planet. Sarah's child! Constantly pushing me into a place I didn't fit—similar to giving a cat a bath in a hot cup of coffee. *Try if you dare, Mother.* Like a lioness, I purred at the thought of a good catfight. Sometimes—most of the time—my mother, Sarah, needed and would be reminded of this simple fact. Repeatedly. I had a way of wrapping words in my attitude and unleashing them like a great, angry hurricane goddess. My storms could be quite volatile and did create a bad day for anyone who pissed me off.

My name Anglaia, which most people jacked up. It is pronounced "on-glay-ah." The name is from one of the three graces, daughters of the Greek god, Zeus. My grandfather, Jacob Clintin, had a statue of the naked ladies on display in his home. The girls had cute bodies, but I found them awkward to look at when I was a young girl. Stories of Sisyphus and the farmer's almanac were grandfather's general mix of conversation, which had me leaning more on my father, Bruce, and his hippy, laid-back approach of how to live my life.

We were the Clintin family, and yes, there was no end to the puns, jokes, and BS that came with such a last name. Should the two families be put in the same room together, it would be agreed—no relation! Healaray was a badass, accomplished political woman, and I knew I got some residuals out of the name deal, especially with adults who simply heard my last name. I knew most of them were doing abridged geography and genealogy in the back of their heads, trying to rationalize a family possibility. It was fun to let a stranger's mind wonder. If I was asked, "are you related," I would shrug my shoulders, leaving them to answer their own question...

It was getting late, and I was beyond tired. The fresh smell of clean sheets made me smile as I lay thinking of what tomorrow might bring. Then scream one echoed down the hallway, stealing my thoughts. "There her ass goes again," I said to myself, shaking my head side to side, wallowing a crater in my pillow. It was like listening to the same song or watching the same movie over and over again, year after year. Scream, wait nine seconds, scream two. Then a wave of light would pour into my room through the cracks around my door.

My father, Bruce, would now be gently speaking to her and holding her close. Father never lost his temper when it came to my mother's dreams. But I thought it was complete and utter nonsense. The main nightmare lasted for two minutes and two seconds, the most frequent dream she had. Some sucked more than others and played on longer if Father was sound asleep. The dreams entailed on and off spurts of heavy breathing, moans, and jibber-jabber. Her body would contort and twitch like my dogs did when they slept. These nightmares were no longer her own—we all suffered her hillbilly childhood.

The family and doctors had determined the catalyst to these dreams and other fits of insanity were the combination of her sleeping pills and red wine, which did not mix well. I took it upon myself to be as helpful as I could by pouring out every single bottle of red wine I found. Sometimes I couldn't get the damn cork out, so I'd toss the whole bottle away.

We would war over wine bottles and sleep. When I found her fishing out the bottles from the trash, I knew I had to change my strategy and took the bottles out to the back yard and smashed them on a huge landscaping rock I had named "Mr. Rocky Wino." I couldn't help the rock was a damn drunk. "It had to have wine, Mother," I'd mock. Needless to say, she didn't purr about my purrfect solution.

I would never claim to be related to those idiots in her dreams, ever. It was about the only thing we could wholeheartedly agree on. My mom's side of the family was basically off-limits. When the subject came up, I'd sincerely tell everyone who asked about her family that she was given up for adoption at birth—end of story. Her nightmare usually involved her running and trying to get away from something. Shadows that came alive in the dark. From the blackness, a cold torment danced in her mind when she let down her guard. Drifting off to sleep was not a simple involuntary act. It required medication. Mother has yet to tell me what happened. All I know is that when morning came, a plume of red blood spiderwebs crowded into her swollen eyes and made my head hurt to look into them.

    I really try to be an interesting girl, participating in all the interesting activities where I could be noticed, like cheerleading. Truth was, turning sixteen was all that was on my mind these days. Everything else about life really sucked—especially my mother's rules. Today was a typical routine day. Father dropped me off at the mailbox and drove the Hummer around our home to park it the garage. I entered the front door, slinging the mail in the general direction of the coffee table. "Anglaia, you could stop and say hello to Mrs. Matches. We were just talking about how well you're doing in high school," Mother said, cooing like she had her vibrator set on pulsate.
    "I might if you will stop wearing those open-toe stiletto shoes. Your toes look like gnarly mutated tree frogs sucking for air—those are some fat, disgusting toes, Mother."
    Thanks for punching my brain Mother. Absolutely disgusting! So glad I got grandmother's cute hands and feet.
    "Not good! Not good at all... Hi, Melissa," I said rolling my eyes like loose marbles in a shoebox.
    Father snorted in the kitchen as I joined him. I think my new retort tickled him as his keys rattled across the countertop. He had many to choose from over the years.
    We had just gotten home. Cheer practice went long, and I was cranky, tired, and hungry. I pushed the one-minute quick-set button on the microwave, traversed back into the front room, and snatched their bottle of Moscato wine and dashed out to give Mr. Rocky Wino a drink.
    Melissa gasped and then blurted out, "What the..." as I left. I didn't see a sleeping bag and knew she wouldn't be losing

sleep from the aftermath she was helping to create. "I paid for that, you little—" Then her lips tightened and cinched closed.

"Bite me!" I said.

"Anglaia, mind your manners, young lady. Bruce!" Mother said sharply.

Father gave me *the look*. "Anglaia… do not do that again," he grumbled, and we kind of smiled at each other.

"Okay father… Sorry!" I said loud enough for the whiners in the sitting room to hear.

I know if anyone has my back, it's my amazing father!

"Melissa, I have more wine if we need it. That child of mine… Geez," Mother said.

Melissa Matches was here for old people talk time. She had been my mother's best friend for as long as I could remember. They usually didn't talk—they gossiped. Probably more than my girls and me. I know one thing for sure—my friends would never sniff each other's armpits when a new deodorant came out as they did. The Matches always seemed to be around. They even came on one of our family vacations, and we sat together in church—which drove my father and me nuts.

It seemed we could not get away from them no matter our tactics—which involved shenanigans from time to time. Melissa's husband, Mike, was a northern motormouth with a Northeastern Basston accent. He never shut up and absolutely knew everything, just ask his wife who thought she had lassoed Albert Einstein! It looked like the conversation I cheerfully interrupted was most likely more serious than I could have known. Being tipsy this early in the day wasn't going to make matters any better, though. I did know that.

"Enjoy your evening ladies."

Why are adults so annoying?

I *did* allow them to keep their half-full wine glasses, and yes, I expected a thank-you for saving the day, but I wouldn't hold my breath.

Father aimed his voice toward the sitting room, while glancing at me, "Sarah, did you say Melissa was here?" We smiled at each other again, and that was the last I heard as I pulled my soggy burrito from the microwave, grabbed some chips and salsa, and went to my bedroom, slamming the door.

I flopped on my bed, turned on some music, and eyeballed the picture of my awesome grandparents. Grandfather's home was situated conveniently on Table Lock Lake in Bronson. A tourist destination in the Midwest in the state of Mizzeree. He was the moneyman, the green-stream, or lifeline that anchored and shaped the family's attitude and personality—just kidding. Truth be told, Grandmother was the breadwinner by far and away, but Grandfather was in charge. Sort of. He was the man, anyway.

Grandfather, Jacob Clintin, came from a line of dairy farmers. A three-hundred-acre farm passed down the line for a hundred years. Grandfather absolutely hated it. He would tell me stories of going to school smelling like cow piss, and that in the winter it would snow so deep he and his brother had to walk on top of fence posts barefooted for six miles to get to school. The farm was located between the towns of Sycamore and Rogersbill, fifteen miles south of Queenfield, Mizzeree, where we lived.

Speckled across the farmland were many Amish families as well, who intended to squeeze the land for the best living they could manage without modern convenience. The women wore long dresses of one color, and the men wore white button-up shirts, black pants held up by thick leather belts, and black suspenders—most of them wore black hats and had bushy sideburns. Me and the body hair of men simply did not get along—it creeped me out. And yes, my church is usually praying for a plethora of my sinful vocalizations already. Amen. People judge me—, I judge people. *Fair* is *fair*! Really don't care.

My grandfather had mixed emotions and many stories about the Amish way of life too. Especially the Hossfly family that owned the farm adjoining his childhood home. "If we could only pick our neighbors," he'd say. Which included the Nitzenslobbers who currently lived next door.

The thing he said he hated most about dairy farming was the never-being-done part of seven-day workweeks. Working life began from the time you could lift a bucket of feed. It was a lifestyle where you were always ten things behind—something always needed to be done or fixed. You were never done or off for the weekend, that was silly talk, he'd say.

Grandfather Jacob was also a Mother Nature guru—through and through. He always had a nutshell prospective dancing around in my ears. Many years of knowledge crammed into my brain in a matter of minutes, especially when it came to his opinion of my *teenage attitude*. "Not a church girl, Grandfather," I'd tell myself, even though we went a couple of times a month. I did learn to roll up my tongue and comments when he was around. Grandfather Jacob had no problem spanking my ass if he deemed it necessary. My personality had been adjusted about ten times so far.

It was hard for me to believe Grandfather didn't share my father's sense of humor when it came to me respecting my elders. I was greatly troubled when my parents just watched and said nothing when he bent me over his knee. I still remain in utter shock to this very day! I felt Mother should have been the one bent over his knee. She deserved it more. She should have been spanked at least a hundred times by now, but never was. She waited until we got home to throw her fits.

Grandfather once told me that when ducks fought, they would shake their tail feathers afterwards signaling the end of their anger. That anger didn't ruin or rule the rest of their day or life. His duck lesson was, "Have the fight. Win or lose, shake it off and go on," followed by his hilarious, Boogie-Woogie-Shake-n-Bake-Duck-Butt dance. Watching that old man shaking his ass as fast as he could just made me laugh till my stomach hurt. He was right. Staying mad was stupid. But staying mad was easier for me. I couldn't help myself by just letting go. I liked a good fight.

When Grandfather Jacob inherited the farm, it went straight on the market the very next week. His only brother, Tom, had died in the Vietnam War. Uncle Tom, who I never met, hated the farming life, too, and was looking for any way he could to leave the work camp environment of the dairy farm. But things didn't go well for him. His ticket out simply sent his soul elsewhere.

Shortly after the sale of the dairy farm, Grandfather Jacob hit the jackpot. He put five-hundred thousand into Ooogle's IPO stock, and the rest is history. He ended up marrying his investment broker, Adamina-Rose, who is my grandmother.

Her name was as rare as her florescent-orange hair. Her name meant "red of the earth" and was the feminine of the first man ever—Adam. She legally added the hyphen to her name. It was not her given name. Hyphens were unpopular in the days of Abraham, Isaac, and Joseph around the time she was born—a million years ago. Old people can be very annoying.

Grandmother Adamina-Rose was a striking redheaded-ginger who always seemed to maintain an uncommon deep-bronzed tan. She commanded the wandering eye, most of the time deliberately. She walked somewhat stiff-legged with the bounce of a ballerina—full of grace and elegance. She had a twenty-five-thousand-dollar smile, literally—porcelain veneers top and bottom, front to back. Grandmother could conjure up a genuine belly laugh on the spot to any conversation that involved money. You could never take or find a bad fossil—every picture I found of her looked as if she and the camera lens were rigged, a magic setting that could be adjusted to beautiful.

Grandmother's family was tied to the old Historic Route 66 crew that fled west to escape government control, taxes, and the lure of gold in them there hills. The gold was really to be found in opening banks and financing every man's gold-digging dream, including the gal gold diggers who packed up kids or whatever they had and chased the dreams of finding that lucky man who dug the hole in the right spot. That is what some members of our family root did—finance dreams with interest, to be more precise. She grew up in Sun-funcisco, Key-la-fornee. Her parents were banking executives with ties to the Ralsten, Walls, and Farbo Families, and had been for generations.

Grandmother Adamina-Rose was a west coast girl through and through. Her old surfboards hung on the walls in the game room, along with great pictures of giant waves. She graduated from Samfort University, business finance her major. Her childhood and college days were filled with sunny beaches and beautiful people who knew success and how to make black numbers of a bank statement and investment portfolio look like a bouquet of flowers.

She could have anything or anyone she wanted in life and for the most part, did. Always motivated and smiling a happy smile. She lived a full, successful life with great expectations for many years to come. There were bits and pieces she passed to me over the years, offerings she whittled off her memory totem pole here and there and became more in-depth as my hair grew. Some, my little ears revoked instantly.

Chapter 3

The pulse of VeeLee VonVouge

  THE MORNING SUNLIGHT RIPPED THROUGH the dark night time sky— a numb night with no near-death drama tales to chronicle. Surprisingly, mom was an early riser and I was a light sleeper. I heard her begin to rustle around in the back seat, when she asked, "Are you awake?"
  "Uh-huh. Where we headed?"

"Thought we'd stop by the Stop & Save and grab some burger stuff and try Tammy's first, maybe she'll let us in? If not, we can go to Ranger Park and you can be a good baby boy and grill us something to eat!"

"And then what?"

"I don't know baby boy…. Maybe I'll drop you off at a friend's? I gotta a busy night: It's Saturday—you know the deal."

"Can you take me to the library?"

"Why. Just so you can keep learning from them philosophies, givin' you more woo-woo ideas?"

"Philosophers Mom. They teach you how to master thoughts—how to create the blueprint to our own master philosophy. How to understand the meaning of life."

"See. Crazy talk. I guess. I'll drop you off and here's ten bucks to get a cab to the club when you're done—come to the door and get the keys from Rosco."

"Okay."

Childhood programming was, at times, difficult to look away from. As was the negativity I experienced when put together with my mom's boss, Aarontino. He was from Key-la-fornee and all about the business of making my mom—and others like her—his business. He was part owner and managed two five-star fine-dining restaurants named A-Rose.

A-Rose was one of six five-star restaurants in the K-sea area, which was an enormous amount of competition for a fine dining experience. I had mopped floors and helped the dishwasher clean the nasty grease traps in the kitchen many times over the past four years. I wasn't officially on the payroll but was handed a wad of cash on occasion. Sometimes it could be three in the morning before Mom and I would get off and be able to go home, that is, if we even had a place to squat. Here lately we slept in the car. I was typically called on by Aarontino when A-Rose needed a little extra elbow grease before big city inspections—inspectors were treated like gods by Aarontino. The beloved inspectors determined whether he kept his glorious stars.

He preached the Michelin system nonstop when I was working at A-Rose, putting me under extreme pressure, as if the future of his family's restaurant chain depended on the job I did. The happiness of the staff—mainly my mom—and all his wealthy patrons were counting on me.

Aarontino and A-Rose did not seem like a good fit, in my opinion. He seemed out of place there, like a white whale in a goldfish tank. There was a gentle demeanor that came across from time to time, although I think he was ill-prepared for the heaviness and stress of running such a high-end business that involved knowing laws and entertaining snobby rich people.

Aarontino became an entirely different soul when the sun went down. Becoming the leader of a cult who aspired to have the pampered taste buds of his guests explode in celebration. Aarontino and Chef Beerbabe were both arrogant and difficult to be around when the lights dimmed. My main job was to stay out of sight and out of the way. Everyone was on pins and needles when A-Rose was feeding. For the workers, it was like being on a dangerous street where all the streetlights had been shot out.

We called them Halloween streets, and there were many of them in K-sea. If you stopped your vehicle for any reason, masked monsters would separate the occupants and steal everything, to include the car wheels if they looked good. If the occupant resisted, it was a sure beatdown. Pull a gun, and a person would be shot dead on the spot without hesitation. Poverty didn't have feelings—people didn't matter to gangbangers. A moonless night made matters worse on a Halloween street—an individual would always remember the meaning of finding themselves on the wrong side of town. Most often, it was a very traumatic experience and required a hospital visit.

My mentor, Lara, had given me countless hours of advice and conceptual monologues to evoke when it came time to deal with thugs, Aarontino, Chef Beerbabe, and even with my mom, for that matter. In most situations, Lara's guideposts and pointers were very effective, with the exception of someone raising their voice toward my mom. At that moment, my thoughts stopped, and action of some form would boil in my heart. It may have been for survival reasons, unconscious in nature, but I would always try to defend her as best words and a puffed-up chest would allow.

Aarontino and Chef Beerbabe were a walk in the park when compared to the crew mom worked for at the strip club. They were mean, tough, and violent men every day of the week. When I successfully deflected the attention away from Mom and onto myself, every single one of them, high-class or no-class, would go crazy on me—or as Lara would correct me and state, they were simply being unconscious and had issues adulting. I usually mentioned that it was not a good idea to assault my mom or a minor, that the city was full of lawyers who would love a chance to go after a business owner or a chef whose bank account had something in it. Thugs would just laugh at me.

Aarontino had only been in the city for five years but seemed to know everyone, a variety of people who came from every background and walk of life. He could have folks from a Halloween street come after me if he wanted, and that would be that. I had a few bloody noses in the past that I felt could have been connected to him. Nobody talks on the street.

Lara introduced many ideas into my mind. Her favorite topic seemed to be about great human beings and excellence. Rulers, kings, presidents, military men, philosophers, and philosophies. The light and shadow cast from the mountain of yin and yang. Spiritual gurus like Confucius, Gautama Buddha, Jesus Christ, Watts, and Tolle would balance the scale at the end of the day.

She seemed to want me to know about the affairs of the underground Deep State society and its impact on the world. That there was an elite organization out there that was beyond top secret—and who, according to her, ran the world. To me, it was the only thing that made me feel she might be living in a world of make-believe. She ornately described the Illuminati folks as the "Nine Kings of the Nonagon" or otherwise abbreviated as K9 during our conversations. I listened intently, for no other reason than to be close to her. For all intents and purposes, she was my only slice of sanity.

    The vibration of her voice was a symphony of heavenly sound that made me happy. Even going over the twenty-three pairs of chromosomes was exciting; her X chromosome of the forty-six was my favorite. Although, sex and cellular respiration were a bit dry when it became scientific. Being a virgin, I had no first-hand knowledge of the matter of sex, but instincts told me that my first sexual experience had to be with a girl who made me feel like Lara did.

    The foreign terms of the Nonagon—a nine-sided building with nine levels, each run by a king based on tenure—was still great fiction and unbelievable to me. "All world governments were ruled by K9," Lara said without batting an eye. I could tell she wholeheartedly believed what she was trying to share. Even the leaders of our great and most powerful nation on earth were under the ever-watchful eye of "big brother's daddies," she'd joke. We all abided by the grand game rules, whether we knew about them or not. They made the rules and laws. "Dollar laws," she coined begrudgingly. If my regurgitating her lessons and adding my own research spin would impress Lara and kept her talking, so be it! I'd do it! I wanted to feel the symphony her mollifying voice for as long as possible. It was how I healed.

Chapter 4

Anglaia's family clay

GRANDMOTHER RECENTLY SHARED AN olden college secret the one where she made love to a black man named Giovanni Jackkson. He was a six-foot-six sex god with an Italian name, full of muscle and bedroom swagger. She recalled how she felt kissing his fleshy, weighted, wet lips, and the feel of his silky skin. How in the bedroom she had held onto him for as long as she could, but when he got really excited, he was too powerful to control. All a woman could do was hold her breath and smile. It was unfiltered, but yeah, might need a minute, Grandmother.

I remember asking her why she didn't marry Giovanni if he was so great. Hell, if she would have chosen Giovanni, I would not need to spend so much time getting a tan. She said he had many college girls to entertain back then. Most of them were madly in love with him. They thought and believed he'd come around to rewarding their financial and physical contributions on some glorious day in the future. They'd catch Giovanni and get the ring.

In college, Giovanni managed a strip club and enjoyed the perks and power he found there. He was the son of a professional athlete, and everyone wanted to get to know him, score a free ticket to the games, and rub elbows with the son of a famous man with money. He had the eye of many women for various reasons. He studied business, and Grandmother knew he would be very successful.

Every story of Giovanni Jackkson usually ended with some disclaimer. He was slick as wet ice and smooth as Beethoven's Moonlight Sonata. Women were simply business—a business that made him a great deal of money. The word *love* in the bedroom was easy to say but wasn't allowed in his heart. He had told Grandmother it would be similar to a drug dealer using his own poison and becoming addicted to the product—a choice that was always the beginning of the end.

"He was just a season, after all. I'm a ginger and uniquely overqualified in the bedroom myself," Grandmother snickered wildly on the topic. Her eyes told a different story, though. An occasional tear fell hard to the floor like a dropped bowling ball, which was very weird to me. For now, it was the version of her memories she wanted me to hear. I could feel others may find us down the road. The wild college days where she went to the clubs and beaches in Los Andsoless, Sunfuncisco and other hotspots along the coast was like watching an award-winning movie of recollection. Perhaps a pre-college recruitment ploy? It might have been her concern of me extending the bloodline in the future? Don't know. Don't care.

She did actually know celebrities. They called her phone and kept in touch now and again. Most didn't matter on the silver screen these days, but it was impressive, nonetheless. Sometimes I'd daydream and wondered what my life would have been like had I grown up in Key-la-fornee. How much different would my life have been from growing up in Mizzeree? Anyhow. I do my best to make the Midwest the place to be. That's how I roll.

In time, I hope to know the whole truth about everything—not really, but she likes it when I say that. For now, Grandmother's travels had landed her in Bronson. Not quite a shipwreck, however the sounds and smells of the salty ocean called her back to Key-la-fornee at least a dozen times a year. Initially, she came to Mizzeree to enjoy a change of pace at her time-share on Table Lock Lake and to watch the music and magic shows in the Bronson area. She first fell in love with how far her money could go and opened five branches of her investment counseling firm in the state. She met my grandfather Jacob and fell in love again.

Now that we were at a Giovanni Jackkson level of communication, I was learning more. Sometimes the conversation was more akin to an earache, but the knowledge of my family history, however unfortunate to my rather-nots, was going to be shared by the older folk—like it or not. I could care less, but they felt I needed to know—"*bite me.*" was usually my response! We were at a crossroad—she had my undivided, full attention. This granddaughter wanted a new car for her sixteenth birthday.

I was, however, a pretty good old-folk conversation escape artist. I tried not to be too fascinated or shocked and frequently disappeared indefinitely when I made a break for a bathroom run—. I did enjoy sharing some of our talks with my girlfriends, who giggled uncontrollably with bug-eyed excitement. I did sense there was much more to Grandmother's stories than her million-dollar smile suggested. The rendered glitches on her face and the random tears that licked at her eyes told on her, even when she tried to play it off by laughing too hard.

Her mother, Charlotte, my great-grandmother, was a cash queen, too, even after the financial crash that hammered the banking industry. She had lost three-quarters of her net worth and could still smile at the end of the day. I could not ever remember meeting her, but there were fossils to prove she existed and held me once. She wasn't near as photogenic as her daughter, my grandmother, but did project a sassiness and strength.

Great-Grandmother Charlotte was enraged when she learned her daughter had fallen in love with a man so far away in Mizzeree. Grandfather Jacob became a constant battleground. Before that, they were sociable as far as their mother-daughter relationship went.

Great-Grandmother Charlotte could not imagine being a part-time grandmother and adamantly forbid such a dumbass, selfish choice. After all, Adamina-Rose had the pick of so many heartthrobs up and down the west coast—educated, wealthy young men who came from affluent families. It made her mom sick. Literally. Charlotte had gotten so worked up at the wedding that my grandparents had to delay their honeymoon for two days and be at her hospital bedside. She had given herself a mild stroke. If I had been there, I would have told her, without a doubt, to bite me.

Great-Grandmother Charlotte was a New Dorker from New Dork City—an east coast chick that migrated west. Apparently, she enjoyed living on the west coast, but her personality was very matter-of-fact and boldly intolerant. Her nature was hostile and condescending according to my grandmother, more so after the wedding.

She intended to make Grandmother pay for choosing Grandfather Jacob and for moving so far away. "A country bumpkin farm boy? Really?" was my grandmother's translation. Scandal and mystery surrounded the death or disappearance of my great-grandfather, Cleo Ray, as well. He was married to Charlotte.

Being a prevalent cog in the banking industry, there were high stakes and ominous connections to some nasty, disgruntled folks who usually went outside the boundaries of the law when they lost tons of money. When bankers came knocking for payments owed, sometimes it got ugly.

Rock star lawyers settled most matters in the courtroom. Some matters of money simply became an earmark for murder. Great-Grandfather Cleo Ray disappeared while on a business trip to the Swiss Alps. I was told he had a dry Mojave Desert sense of humor and was hard to get along with, too. He wasn't' fooled often, but Charlotte managed the impossible.

Great-Grandmother put herself through college by moonlighting as a bartender and singing at a few upscale venues near Watchadone Square Park in Moonhattan. She graduated from New Dork University (NDU) with bachelor's in finance. She never told him of her means to success, as she always dressed so classy and played the role of a sophisticate. The biological clock was spinning on Grandfather Cleo Ray, who knew he needed to copy himself and have children soon if he was going to.

When they met, he was in his mid-thirties. He fell for Great-Grandmother's long legs and the tease of her sassy essence. Some thought his death might have been about the seven-digit life insurance policy. Not a logical conclusion if Great-Grandmother couldn't cash it in without a body which, to this day, has yet to materialize. The name Cleo Ray is on the headstone with Grandmother Charlotte, but there is no day of death etched on it. Maybe he figured out how to cheat the end of time. Guess he gets to live forever now. Good job, genius!

I could care less about Cleo Ray. He and Charlotte are as dead to me as my mother's hillbilly-ass side of the woodpile. Blood transports oxygen, that's it as far as I'm concerned. I'm not connected to relatives who don't make my life better. I have all the family I need or want. I like things just the way they are. I'm told both of my great-grandmothers died before I was five years old. They died of cancer, and that's why there is such an emphasis on living healthy. Microwaved burrito, anyone?

When it came to eating, I remember spending summers on Table Lock Lake, riding sea-doos, and going on occasional fishing trips with my grandfather. I personally think fishing is a dumbass hillbilly pastime, too. It drives me insane to watch a fish being skinned alive—then *yummy*, we get to eat them later. Oh boy. Yippee. It literally gags me every time. It requires some serious mental gymnastics for me to eat freshly caught fish. Most of the time, it will remain on my plate. I will always think the process sucks. I won't eat fish sticks either.

There was something magical about riding in the most expensive fish and ski boat on Table Lock Lake. The boat motor was huge and powerful—it sliced a deep gash into the body of sparkling water and hissed like a cobra, the column of water shot twenty feet into the air, following us like a scorpion tail situated between two soft, rolling waves to either side. I did like the quick suntan opportunity—my true desire for being on the lake fishing with my grandfather. I fished in my swimsuit and had no interest in holding a fishing pole. When we stopped at his fishing spots, I would roll around on my towel on the back deck and work on my suntan. Riding on the boat and listening to Grandfather was fun enough for me. The more time on the lake I spent, the darker my skin got, the better I looked in my cheerleading uniform.

It's all about making your memories and living your life. That was the secret to life in Grandmother's opinion, and I tried my best to embrace that perspective. Always remember she would say, "Life is not a possession, it is a function—your heart beats or it doesn't. Each day you wake, try to become the most beautiful flower the world has known, and show your full bloom every day you can, Show your true essence—hopefully, one of happiness, joy, and love." A bunch of gooey garbage I could hear on Sunday at *The Assemblage*, if you ask me.

I'd say I most likely got my looks from Grandmother, minus the red hair. More than one person has told me was a cross between Litney Spheres and Henafur Annason—a hot blond thang, I guess?

Formal education was the flag Grandmother waved the most and could yap endlessly about going to college. Basically, I had no option. She and Father had already argued about what college I would attend.

I didn't know ghosts were in the business of making babies, but that's the story of my mom, Sarah. She didn't talk about her family, and most of what I knew came from a bossy bitch who I didn't want to hear a word from, anyway. I just wanted her to leave me alone and get her own effing life. Seriously. When I did want to ask Mother something, she would be in her twenty-year college closet mode trying to get her Ph.D. thesis done. Her "do not disturb" mode.

She was a perfectionist and egomaniac. You could never capitalize or make bold enough the great ME she had idealized herself to be. She was way too important to notice her daughter or anyone else for that matter. When she did awake from her illusions, *Imperious of Earth*, and wanted to pet me like a puppy, I'd growl and snip at her because it felt similar to gargling with broken glass soaked in tobacco spit.

To those on the outside, she was beautiful, educated, and successful—someone who was doing everything perfectly. No one could praise her enough—she gorged on compliments. Not to mention, Ms. Goody-two-shoes carried forty-five extra pounds she could not seem to shake off. Guess my birth was to blame. It was my great pleasure to remind her as often as I could. "Doughy douche-bag" was one of my favorites. Thing is, she was so full of herself that only people who heard my comments were offended. She was never listening, anyway. It's probably why Father didn't get overly excited when I went on one of my "go to hell, Mother" rants.

My father, Bruce, started his own business from the ground up, and I knew it filled him with happiness. Make no mistake about it; I was the brightest twinkle in my father's eye, yet one did not have to look hard to see he truly loved and honored my mother. He would be with her till the end of time. He trusted her. Far removed from his parents' ideas of what he should do with his life, it came down to him starting a meat-packing company.

It was nowhere close to the financial returns Grandmother Adamina-Rose had hoped her son would achieve. She took every opportunity to reteach him better business plans so that he would make more money. He took it about as serious as he did with Mother meddling in the bookkeeping of his dream.

Grandmother constantly showed him accounting strategies and tax write-offs—her native tongue. She tried to prepare him to take over her investment counseling company after Father graduated from college—he had other ideas. She wholeheartedly wanted to hand over the helm of her multimillion-dollar business to her son. Father wanted nothing to do with it. His creation was simple and fulfilling, and that was that. He intended to live his own life the way he wanted, and that's exactly what I intend to do as well. IT'S MY LIFE.

Father had the means and aptitude to have gotten his college degree from Samfort if he wanted to, and still argues with Grandmother to this day that math is math—the number nine at Samfort was the same number nine in Mizzeree State University. He would say that if you wanted to revolve around the skeleton of someone else's dream in the corporate world, your alumni would matter and could affect your marketability and earning power.

Money was not what made Father tick. I was what made him tick… okay, and Mother and his family and friends, too. He did, after all, have a hippy-like laid-back demeanor. Nothing really affected him negatively. Whatever came, he just seemed to accept it like a relaxing Buddhist mantra—ohm or something. I sometimes wondered if his brain and heart even had—or could create—negative emotions. There were times I would lose my mind with Mother, and he would just watch with a blank stare. His head slowly moved like tree limbs swaying on a soft breeze. He was my awesome father. The best.

Some of my girlfriends had actually fallen in love with him. They wouldn't be asked back over to my house if they made cheesy comments about him. He was all mine. Grow up, chicky-poo, and bite me!

His meat-packing company was called Top Chops, Inc. For a meat-packing company, it did very well. To me, it was about like fishing, though. It made my stomach sick to see death up close and personal. There was way too much blood and gross slimy parts and stinky stuff. Sometimes I had to go to Top Chops with my parents and hang out. One thing was for sure—my ass was *not* hanging out in the freezer-like atmosphere of the packing line or working for that matter. I had much better things to do on my phone or sitting in Father's giant office chair at his desk, screwing up his computer. Letting me hang out with my friends at the mall would have made everyone happy, but *no* was most often the answer.

Father had twenty-five well-treated workers—a crew who could accomplish uncommon results and busted their butts for him. When Mother came around being nosy and pushy, the workers' morale plunged dramatically, and the atmosphere fell cold as the meat freezers. It would not shift to sunshine until she left the building. She had fired four or five people in the past, and everyone knew the deal—just smile and be pleasant until she became bored and left. She had her own office next to Father's. She was addicted to going over the financials. She would scrutinize every dollar—she literally asked the same annoying payroll questions every single Friday.

For some reason, Mother couldn't wrap her head around owning a business where employees made a good living as well. As the owner, Father tried to explain it was better to pay overtime or even double time to loyal workers who had experience than to pay health care and benefits to a larger workforce in hopes of controlling individual income. "We pay our *people* and we will pay them well," he often said. That was his chill-out line, and for some reason, it shut her up.

One of the things my father hated most was a layoff or letting people go. It was a serious matter, one he tried to stay ahead of by being smart in the first place. Good people would always level the playing field of a turbulent economy. "People will take care of the people who take care of them," was one of his favorite quotes. "Everyone wins," he'd tell Mother, which usually made her roll her eyes.

It was the time of the month when Father held his Texas Hold 'Em poker tournament, a card game where the best poker hand won. Run out of poker chips, and you were out of the money. They okayed the game on the first Saturday of the month. The Clintin home was invaded by a dozen of Father's friends and transformed into a gambling hall. Most of his friends rode motorcycles, but none were outlaws. It really seemed to annoy the neighbors in our neighborhood, though. The bikes were loud, and the noise seemed to strike fear into the peaceful surroundings. It seemed the neighbors were more interested in creating the Hollywood possibility of being robbed and tortured perhaps. It was an imagined story that had the potential of making the local news. We were continuously stopped and questioned by our overly concerned neighbors, so-much-so Father stopped mowing the lawn and hired a lawn service.

The twelve guys came with two hundred dollars in tow. Play began at one o'clock sharp. If life took a player elsewhere, they still had to pay the winner of the day one hundred and contribute one hundred to the December pot, which the top five players in points would play for. One hundred points were given for a first-place finish—fifty points for a second-place finish—twenty-five points for a third-place finish every week.

If the police came by due to a neighbor's complaints of motorcycle noise or suspected gambling, the card game was deemed a charitable event, and the winnings would be donated to a charity of the winner's choice. One of the players, William, was a police officer, which puzzled me for some time. I didn't think policemen were allowed to gamble. He was nice to me, and that's all that really mattered. Sometimes William would show his badge, and that was the end of any questioning by law enforcement.

Ten thousand dollars went to the winner in the December championship, second place received fifteen hundred and third received five hundred. Not a bad way to jumpstart Christmas. It was enough money that the players did take it seriously, although the conversations were usually relaxed and fun and somewhat educational.

The card game was a guys-only event. "No wives or kids allowed" was the sort of unspoken agreement. If I was bored, I would let them know it was my house, though, men or not! There are poker rules, and then there are Anglaia rules. Trust me, they knew my rules from the time I turned five years old.

I could get them to laugh when I thumped my chest with my right fist and then pointed to the ground with my index finger chanting, "My house!"

"Whose house," they'd reply.

"My house," I'd repeat.

I had made the bikers into cheerleaders—not an easy task! It seemed to tickle my father hearing his buddies cheer with me and laugh their asses off. "Word-of-caution. Do not try this at home. I have serious chick-charm, and *you*, most likely, *do not*," I'd tell Mother or any other want-to-be Anglaias out there.

Other than my father, Frankie was my favorite player who came over to play. He was muscled up, had tattoo's, and just had a badass presence. He and Father were classmates from the beginning of time. Frankie chose the military option out of high school and deployed to Earrack and Offgone-is-stand several times.

He was now in Queenfield, which must have seemed like watching grass grow. I'd say, from what I knew about him, his life now moved like pond water compared to combat. The craziest thing is he now worked for my father. It would be as odd as Grandfather singing in an opera. It just didn't make sense to me at all. A wild, powerful man cooped up in a meat processing plant. Yep, I don't get it. But I do feel safe when Frankie is around.

We lived in the Midwest in the city of Queenfield, in the state of Mizzeree. The state of Arkinpaw was to the south and Eyeway to the north. The major cities in the state of Mizzeree were K-sea to the northwest, and Saint L's was to the northeast. Queenfield was near the bottom of the state and the hub of the local area, with several well-established towns surrounding in every direction—Oatzark, Flixa, and Rebubblelick, to name a few of the bigger communities close by.

Chapter 5

VonVouge's voyage of violence

  MS. LONDON WAS IN HER LATE TWENTIES when we met. She looked like she was a high school student in a mentoring role. Her youthful tone had yet to leave her face. Her attire was uptown professional with a hint of hippy. I could never correctly pick the way she would present her hair—braids, ponytail, up, down, in a bun, or, my favorite, naturally flowing locks pouring over her shoulders and straight down her back. Each style received my full attention.

I knew the best time to visit the library was around four-thirty in the afternoon. I could sometimes catch her in workout attire headed to the gym. Seeing her in her stretchy yoga pants was like hitting the lotto. Realizing this four-thirty pattern on Tuesdays and Thursdays, I think she knew it was like my call to prayer. If I missed, she would comment the next time she saw me. I could never control the boyish grin that followed once my eye found her.

Ms. London's beautiful face and sexy body had no chance of competing for my heart of hearts. When it came down to love, I was deeply in love with her intellectual depth. Lara knew everything! And she seemed to love teaching me all she knew from A to Z. It amazed me when she could find a book she hadn't read in ten years and go to an exact page to show me in black and white what I wanted to know or what she needed me to learn. It blew my mind every single time. Her magic stimulated my synaptic sparks into the most supreme Fourth of July firework show the recesses of my mind could allow. She made genetics, the Fibonacci series, frequencies, math, psychology, and physiology fun to understand.

I took a deep dive into the systems and functions of the human body and the figure eight of circulation. The glorious physiology of lungs—breathing seemed so fascinating when she went into detail. I remember her telling me that every drop of blood in our bodies is pumped by our heart and oxygenated by our lungs every minute. The breakdown was eighty-three gallons of blood an hour, two thousand gallons of blood a day. The human tube, as she referred to a person's body, was nothing more than a straw that was kept alive by the consumption of the periodic table we ate, absorbed, and eliminated. The most baffling elements were vitamins, water, and salt. If stretched out, the mouth, stomach, and intestines all the way to the anus was simply one long tube with a hole at either end.

Knowledge, to me, was a person's ability to recall other people's best guesses articulated by language. It seemed everyone remembered what they wanted to remember. My thoughts seemed so basic and not a big deal at all, but my teachers and friends thought I should have already invented a pill that would double the human lifespan. I had my ideas about capturing the sun and hoped I would not be burned in the process of creating it.

Lara was my main motivation, though. Spending time with her was the utmost turn-on ever. I knew there were a hundred million awesome single women in the world. If it were a possibility, I would choose Ms. Lara London without pause every single time, no question about it! Thinking about introducing her as my wife, Mrs. VonVouge, was childish, but it tickled me when alone with my thoughts.

During my visits to the Trueman Public Library, Ms. London would take the time to talk to me like a concerned friend—one with fortified boundaries and a seriousness that would not allow me to enter the realm of dreams and fantasy that a typical teenage boy going through puberty might experience.

She taught me how the mind worked by sharing the great minds of the past and the truths they had found. Reading put me on the fast-track of understanding, even the true meaning of one's life. It was curious to me how I began to crave her voice and wisdom more than the thoughts of watching her walk the isles of the library in hunt of a book. She allowed me to lag behind on some days, but most often, we were side by side.

My favorite people to learn about were Nicola Tesla, Einstein, Leonardo Da Vinci, Hippocrates, and a touch of Darwin. Most of my independent reading was on psychology, modern science, anatomy, and physiology. Lara was beginning to shift our book list to philosophy—Plato, and the like.

Toozoolee was my best friend, a Polynesian kid with long, thick, wavy, jet-black hair and golden-brown eyes. He was a quiet person who rarely raised his voice and kept to himself. He was mysterious, and people always asked me what his deal was. Why did he keep everything to himself? They needed to figure him out for some reason, and when they couldn't get the scoop, they wanted to know about him even more. As best friends, he asked me not to share anything with anyone. I agreed.

We lived in the same rundown apartment complex most of the time, in between Mom's new man-of-the-week routine, where we temporarily moved in with the so-called "great guy." But Weston was the worst of all. He taught me how to hate. Even though we got away from him almost two years ago, it hurts as if yesterday. I did not *ever* think mom was going to listen to me when it came to Weston—she was head-over-heels in love with him. Weston made it very clear that it was his home and his rules from the very start. A place of fear and terror and pain.

Weston Wickit was Hollywood handsome—dark, Italian skin with dull brown eyes that I couldn't look at directly. He typically wore a white wife-beater tank top, gold chains around his neck and wrist, a large-faced gold watch, blue jeans, and square-toed cowboy boots. He had tattoos of skulls all over his arms, a roaring lion on his right chest, and large gothic letters spelling out Death Dealer, which was arched like a rotated half-moon and stretched from shoulder-to-shoulder across his entire back. He was covered completely with ink, as were most of mom's men. He was probably six-foot-two tall and well over two hundred pounds.

He would not leave me alone, which was all I wanted. I could not simply stay in his spare room that had no bed in it and read my books. I had to be in the front room of his trailer watching him drink and cuss the TV for hours on end when mom was at work stripping or at A-Rose. I will never forget the first beating. Weston gave it to me for not rinsing off my plate and putting it into the dishwasher.

He grabbed me by the arm and dragged me into his bedroom, ripped the belt from the belt loops of his jeans, and told me to pull down my pants. I said no. And he swung the belt as hard as could across my arm and back. It stung like a million stinging ants were inside my shirt attacking me. He snarled his face and groaned his evil words to drop my pants, all the while whipping me. I was in shock. I was in pain. I was scared. I thought I was about to be killed.

Weston had gone mad and finally overpowered me and had me in a headlock, squeezing my throat so tight that I couldn't breathe. "Are you going to obey your elders?" He squeezed tighter. "Are you? I will teach you not to disrespect me in my house!" Weston yelled directly into my left ear.

"Yes!" I cried.

"What?"

"Yes," I said in a choked voice. Weston played this control game, repeating, "Are you? What?" for at least ten more times. It seemed Weston liked choking me. Mom picked him because he was a hardcore gym rat with giant muscles. I first thought to fight him when I said no, but the headlock stole my will. Weston then let me go and said, "Drop 'em, boy!" I did, and he spent another twenty minutes spanking my rear end brutally with his belt. I didn't want to cry but couldn't help it. After a while, I couldn't feel anything. I had gone numb, but the sound alone had a terror in it.

I told my mom the next day when I woke up, and she said we have to respect Weston's rules, which made him smile. She said, "He will teach you how to be a man." The beatings came regularly for any reason at all after that. I hated living in Weston's tin can. I hated him and his worthless neighbors who did nothing, either—I could hear their TV and music, so I knew they could hear my beatings. Mom would get mad at me if I complained of my spankings or that he walked around nude. "Are you trying to get us kicked out of here and back on the streets?" she would say. "We got it good here," she would say.

He acted like a nice guy to me when she was around and would completely change when I was left alone with him. They sat around kissing and playing with each other as if they were making a triple-X-rated adult movie. Sometimes Weston would go watch her strip and bring a dancer home to share and party with until the sun came up. That was the only time I could get in some good reading. We were too far away from Trueman Library to exchange my books. I had read all three many times—they were past due. Most of the time, I had to lay on my side to reread because of the bruises.

The frequency of his senselessness increased, and Weston was becoming addicted to the headlocks and making me drop my pants. He was becoming sadistic with the impulses of a destroyer. He finally did it when mom was home, and I just knew she would come to my rescue and take us far, far away—but she didn't. She was pilled-out on hydrocodone, and whatever it was I saw Weston drop into her beer. Most likely, the date-rape drug Rohypnol or Ecstasy. He continued with his habit of me and started to drop his pants while he spanked me, all the while playing with himself and slinging slime on me. It made me sick and embarrassed.

On day mom, at last, felt the spankings were too excessive and threw a two-minute fit until he dragged her by her hair into his room and spanked *her* with the belt. He groaned the same evil words I had heard a million times. She screamed bloody murder, then must have cried herself to sleep.

I knew this had to be the final straw. He went nice again the next morning, and she blew it off. "I love him," she said to me later on that day. Going to school was the biggest challenge because the hard, wooden chairs hurt my bruises, and I refused to shower after gym class because I didn't want anyone to see my butt and back. I was being made fun of by thirteen-year-olds. They could be just ruthless as Weston.

Weston treated mom like a whore, slapping her around even more when his brother Dusty and other moron friends came around. He would pull mom's shirt up or skirt up, grabbing her boobs or privates in front of them. They all would laugh at her, and she played along and laughed back, which made me more upset as it only encouraged more abuse. It then became another of Weston's habits. He kissed her hard and licked her face in front of me, tossing her on the floor and holding her down until she stopped giving him any attention, got really mad, and threatened to move out.

The first time mom told him we were leaving, I got really excited. Then it just became a part of their game. Weston had a laugh that was sin itself, loud and haunting. I was petrified of the sound. It made me sick. Mom just laughed her party-on laugh, which only fed Weston's narcissistic ego. Mom ignored everything he did, acting helpless. I couldn't help but say under my breath, "You're such a dumb-dumb, mom."

The sober day finally came when she tried to pry my head loose from his chokehold, and Weston shoved her across the room. She fell into the end table, and the lamp crashed onto the floor with her. I was struggling to breathe. Mom came back to help me. Weston backhanded her in the face, and her lips dripped fresh blood down on my face. Weston smiled and yelled at us.

Mom grabbed her phone, and the bouncers of the strip club showed up fifteen minutes later. Mom let them in, and they tackled Weston. Two minutes later, the police showed up thanks to his helpful neighbors. The bouncers barely had time to mess Weston's hair up. Let alone give him what he deserved. I didn't care, we were finally free, and my legs, butt, and back would finally heal. I was grateful he had not mounted me.

After all the charges were filed, and the men were hauled off in handcuffs, mom dug out some empty trash bags from under Weston's sink, and we filled them with our things. She destroyed what she could, and I grabbed his neatly coiled belt from his dresser and tossed it into one of the trash bags.

"Why do you want that?"

"I don't want him to hurt anyone else with it."

It was late when we parked in front of the Tanner Apartment office, our energy completely drained, and conversation unnecessary. We would be moving back into the heckles of the ghetto, which made me happy. Didn't know which apartment number it would be this time, but I knew I could expect bare wires, missing light bulbs and light fixtures, the toilet and refrigerator might or might not work, cabinets would be missing doors and shelves, and we would have to make due with raggedy furniture that looked as frumpy as the miniskirts mom wore in the cold of winter. There would be holes punched in the gang graffiti-painted drywall, which I would try to repair and paint if we were there long enough.

I was always baffled by the fact that street gangs and bikers had to have their stupid symbols like the government did—flags of fortune they waved around to intimidate the hopes of helpless citizens. I personally found it unbelievable that a person had to fear a handkerchief, a jacket or uniform patch, a head-sweat bandana, or the color of a t-shirt. It was how the dollar bill world worked. It disgusted me just as much as Weston. But if for no other reason, I learned the lesson of freedom. It was my early Christmas gift. Most likely the only one I'd get this year. Mom turned off the car and radio, and we both quickly fell asleep in the car.

My friends and the Trueman Library were again close by. Life was getting better. Tina was the apartment manager and did not like my mom. They had cussed each other out a hundred times over the years. I think each time we left, Tina prayed we would never return. And now we were back—pathetic and full of bruises. Tina rolled her eyes again when we left her office with the keys.

As soon as we unloaded the trash bags, I asked to go see Toozoolee. Mom quickly said yes. She needed rest. I navigated through the Tanner complex to my friend's apartment and knocked on his door. He answered, and we went to his room and talked for a bit. I divulged some of the craziness that had happened while I was gone. At first, I think Toozoolee thought I had learned to tell wild tales while I was away—so when I showed him the black and blue stripes on my back, he said we should go find this guy and cut his throat. He got mad for me. It made me feel better that he was truly on my side.

I asked Toozoolee if I could borrow his bike so I could ride to the Trueman Library. I had some overdue books and really wanted to see Lara. He reluctantly agreed. It was his pride and joy, and the only good thing he had. He never let anyone ride it but me.

I slung my backpack on and pedaled as fast as I could standing up. I could not sit down—it was too painful. When I arrived, Lara was just about to get in her car and leave. A minute later, and I would have missed her. "Lara!" I called out.

She looked and smiled. I pedaled up to her, "I'm back at Tanner!"

"That's great news, VeeLee. I've missed you." My teeth were tickled by the sun as I smiled sheepishly. Lara glanced at her watch.

"I'm really late on these books. I'm sorry."

"Maybe we can make a deal." She smiled and continued, "I need just a minute, VeeLee." She grabbed her phone from her purse and called off her lunch date with some lady named Kylie and said, "We shall and soon. How about tomorrow? Same place. Same time... Sounds good." She hung up and motioned for me to take the lead as I pushed the bicycle.

"Shall we..." I said and grinned some more. Lara smiled her friendship all over me as we walked down the sidewalk and to the entrance of the Trueman Library. I placed the bike in the rack and locked it. We went inside the glass double doors, taking a direct path to Lara's office. I gingerly eased into the chair, putting most of my weight onto my left but cheek. The right one was too messed up.

"Are you okay? I noticed you were walking differently, and when you sat down... well, it didn't look normal."

"Mom picked another scumbag. Well, let me rephrase that—*the* worst scumbag on the planet. A guy named Weston."

"What happened? Did he hurt you?"

"I'll be all right."

"VeeLee VonVouge... *Did he hurt you?*"

I raised my shirt again. Her eyes suddenly pooled with swirls of tears, gravity began jerking them from her eyes. She stood up and moved to the window with her right hand covering her mouth. Looking out the window and back to me, then back out the window.

I didn't know what to do but apologize. "I'm sorry. I didn't mean to make you cry."

She seemed overwhelmed by emotions. "Okay, okay," she said quickly and forced out two fast breaths of air as if she were about to lift a fallen tree. She slammed her arms down to her side, turned around, and came back to her chair. She sat in silence for a few seconds to collect her thoughts and dabbed at her wet eyes. "Now. Please tell me what happened. I need to know who did this to you."

"Mom's boyfriend," I answered as if I had the power of a worm. Lara picked up the phone and dialed a number. "Kylie..."

"Yeah," I heard her say.

"Could you have Timothy give me a call? I need some help, please."

"Of course," Kylie said. I could hear her voice from across Lara's desk. It was crystal clear and full of support. I felt as if I was now in no-man's land. "Is it important that you need to speak with him soon?"

"Yes. I'm afraid so."

"Will do, Lara. Talk to you tomorrow, my friend."

"Thanks, sweetheart. You're the best."

Lara put her phone face-down and wrinkled her nose with a sniff of air. She was as mad as Toozoolee. This was the first time I'd ever seen her pissed. I would have never thought it possible. She had always been so sweet and kind. It was not the reason I came, nor my intent to upset her. I was worried about the overdue books and the fact I had missed her. Then I thought of Weston—the huge crazy man. There was no way I wanted the most wonderful soul I had ever know to be hurt, too. "I don't want to tell you, Ms. London. He will beat you. He is really big and the meanest monster I've ever met. Please stay far away from Weston. Seriously, he will beat you," I said with the same terror I had relayed to my mom about the man.

"VeeLee... do you want this man to keep hurting other people?"

"No..."

"Well then, help me get him!"

"You don't understand. He has muscles like a hulk, and he will beat us both. I cannot take him yet. He's too strong."

"I understand what you are saying, VeeLee. This Weston guy is a coward. I want to show you that knowledge defeats stupidity ninety-nine percent of the time. I have no fear of this dumbass. I'm *a librarian*!" She opened a drawer on the side of her desk just to slam it shut out of frustration. Lara was angered and serious. "Please, VeeLee. Let's get Weston together!"

"Okay. But I want you to know I'm completely scared to death, Ms. London!"

"It's going to be okay, VeeLee. We will team up on him!" Lara smiled sweetly at me, and my heart filled up with good feelings.

"They took him to jail last night, and we got away."

"That's great. What's his last name."

"Weston Wickit."

"This is going to be so easy, VeeLee."

I believe you. I wanted to tell her that I loved her so much!

I wish I could have actually said the words out loud, but suspected she could feel the vibrations of my soul and read my mind. I had never shot a gun, but I was ready to go to war. Lara had inspired me, so-much-so that I couldn't hide my tears from her as I recounted the definition of hell.

Hell-on-earth was located inside a mobile home park on the north side of K-sea—what I called Weston's Tin Can of Torture.

I was watching Super Woman in action. In a matter of minutes, she had contacted five people over the phone while simultaneously pounding on the keypad of her computer, connecting others to aid in the effort. It was so impressive I could hardly believe it was all for me. She was making everything happen lightning fast—all to help a nobody kid with a backpack filled primarily with free overdue books.

It wasn't long before I was scared again in a different way as she called children's services, and we went over the details again in their office. When mom was sequestered to join us, she cried out her story, and pictures were taken of us both. Everyone was sad. Lara recommended an attorney who was even bigger than Weston. She was the highest order of librarian. In my heart and mind, Lara was the Top Librarian of the Universe. Men in Black be warned. Lara was a badass. She was my greatest friend.

It was explained to mom that Timothy did some pro bono work as a lawyer, and she wouldn't have to pay anything, which helped her make up her mind to follow through with putting the latest love of her life behind bars. Weston had managed to terrify mom, too. I also knew the power he had over her. If she were given a chance, she'd probably have us back over there if he yelled at her loud enough or when she was sufficiently drunk or stoned. There was no stopping her from feeding the voices of her unquenchable desires. She loved her drama, and I loved my momma.

As the months hitched a ride on puffy clouds, Timothy beat Weston up in the court of law. Weston would glare at us while on the stand. Mom's bouncer friends had come a couple of times and would stare back at him. But nothing like what Timothy did. I think Judge Sam Shorts enjoyed the intellect and approach of Timothy's arguments during the trial.

One morning Timothy's opening remarks stared with, "So Mr. Weston Wickit, what exactly does a coward have for breakfast in the morning? Eggs and bacon sprinkled with beating a woman and helpless child? You disgust me, Mr. Coward," he said, showing pictures of me and then of mom. He slammed his fists down on the table. Weston glared at Timothy. The jury shook their heads in disgust. They brought out the bottle filled with the date-rape pills noting that the bottle had Weston's fingerprints on it. Timothy shook the bottle at the jury, making a rattlesnake sound.

"This coward needed these little pills to rape a tiny woman. You are a real tough guy, aren't you, loser?" Timothy ran up to the stand and looked Weston in the face, shaking the pills. "In fact, the coward couldn't take on a real man with all his two-hundred-twenty-five pounds. He had to beat on a thirteen-year-old boy. What a coward." Timothy said and walked away, repeating, "What a coward!"

Weston lost it and cursed back at Timothy. Judge Shorts quickly silenced Weston. He was not in physical pain, but he was getting hurt back. The jury took twenty minutes, and Weston was gone for twenty years.

Timothy and Lara gave me a victory hug in the lobby. Timothy went on to explain what the *'since of Lee'* meant in the courtroom, that it was impossible for the letter of the law to cover every violation of the law. It meant that sometimes even a strict judge like Sam Shorts would give an attorney what's known as equity, evenhandedness, or fair play when it came to vile men who committed vile crimes. Lara ended by saying, "VeeLee, it is so easy to defeat ignorance with knowledge. I hope you understand this now."

"I do, Ms. London."

"Alright. We won," Timothy said and put his hand on my shoulder. "Thanks for being a courageous and strong young man. Best wishes to you in the future, VeeLee. If you ever need help again, just let me know, my friend," Timothy said, and we left the courthouse, going our separate ways.

Over the next few weeks, Mom was increasingly annoyed that children's services were all up in her business. They expected her to work on a parenting plan. "I'm so tired of them up my ass all the time. The effing court case is over," she would say to me. We got a lot of help, food stamps, and allowed to pick through the shelves of donations—pots, pans, clothes, and such. Mom could have even gone to college if she wanted to, but didn't, so I didn't really see the major problem she was making it out to be.

Lara had stood up for me. I had learned a lot surviving Weston's hell. My mom was clueless and most likely always would be. When mom needed attention from others, she would gloat that she put the bastard in prison. "No man hurts my baby boy," she'd say. I let her have the spotlight but knew the whole truth. It wasn't long before she hooked up with another loser. I was lifting weights regularly with Toozoolee and did push-ups constantly. My soft shell of boy skin was being molded into the war armor of a gladiator—a man.

Lara was right—knowledge did conquer stupidity. The monster man had been conquered with words and not caveman violence. Yet, I forswear that if Weston crossed my path in the future, there would be a greater justice imposed. "My turn" kind of justice. Right or wrong, I needed to return his belt.

Lara was a superhero. My hero. She was a *librarian*, after all. I loved her for a million reasons.

Chapter 6

Anglaia's emotional hiccups

  LIKE MY GRANDMOTHER, ADAMINA-ROSE, I, Anglaia, was not a huge outdoors type. Bugs and reptiles really freaked me out. I had no control over them, and that was not cool. The Oatzark mountains were the breeding grounds for a plethora of inhuman creepy crawlies that loved to insult me every chance they got. My grandmother kept a fully stocked, supersized, first aid kit at the ready. I was always under attack and stung or bitten by something nearly every time I visited.

Most of the time, I just stayed inside their mansion. I'd probably had a thousand mosquitoes zap me on the football sidelines this year alone. Grandmother said it was my blood type. O-negative blood was sugar to mosquitoes apparently, and my fear hormones were a magnet for every hate-filled cold-blooded creature. Why? Why? Why? I simply call it BS and had no problem telling God to bite me.

I attended Horseshoe High, the so-called preppie school of the four high schools in Queenfield. A-list movie stars, doctors, lawyers, and many wealthy people had graduated from Horseshoe High. It had an Ivy League college feel to it. A sense you could feel when walking the modern-day halls. The high school had been renovated with modern updates every four years or so, but for some reason, they kept the old folk relics, class of nineteen and grease-head fifty-five fossils continued to adorn the walls. They looked like old ghosts someone had managed to permanently nail to the wall. It was more like visiting the morgue to me because most of the goofy people were already dead. If I were in charge, they would all have to go bye-bye. The trophy-cases of past championships were just cluttering up the halls and should have been recycled into some outdoor faux statue of me or something as unique as me.

During my freshman year of high school, my goal was to be selected into the feared Glue Crew. It was a private crew that most everyone knew could be a legit pain in the ass. The faculty of teachers and appalled students alike did resist and otherwise outlawed the Glue Crew gang, and had every year for the last fifty years. There would always be internal policing needing done, especially these days, where teachers had been stripped of the almighty equalizer. Stories grandfather shared of teachers having troublemakers grab their ankles and enjoy the attitude adjustment of a black paddle wrapped around their butt cheeks. Grandfather's hand was bad enough, but a good paddling would probably straighten out rude, idiotic behaviors of teens these days.

The population of bullies, pill, and pot pushers were still the primary targets. They could expect their wall lockers, backpack zippers, and the like to be under the scrutiny of Batman's ever-present eye, thus our symbol of the Glue Crew. Of course, I was accepted into the group. I think they knew better to say no. We would deal with every form of moron that failed to mind their manners. We ensured they paid some determined price for their stupidity. Currently, if I identified and marked someone, he or she could expect to encounter the time-honored tactics of the Glue Crew, punishments that had been passed down for millennia at Horseshoe High.

They inflicted every manner of suffering, such as taking off visiting school's car windshield wipers, super gluing keyholes, or leaving puddles of sticky goo for people to step in and spread everywhere possible. It was part of the gig. An automatic two-week suspension and reparation for all damages were the baseline punishment handed out by the school, and in extreme gluing, you would be expelled altogether. Small infractions were usually overlooked—crime-for-a-crime was punished by the Horseshoe High principal without delay. The upperclassmen might want to fear the new crop of freshmen— we were badass'. "Fear the Glue!" Seriously.

I met my bestie and love of my life, Danielle Vanderhouse, in third grade. Our mothers became okay friends. We went to the same church located in Oatzark called *The Assemblage.* I felt inclined to believe it was simply a meeting place for coffee and a tax write-off for the wealthy as there were more Lexxuses and Cadilblack Escapades in the parking lot than anything else. The best part was that I got to cut up and hang out with Danielle. We disappeared into the youth group for a time and would later join the adults to hear Pastor Dom Spindle go from Genesis to Revelations, respectively, giving the congregation the righteous feeling that they knew every word of the Holy Bible.

When November rolled around, it would be random sermons tilted toward holiday giving and great cheer. There was always some form of security around the church as well, most likely protection from disgruntled family members whose deceased had decided it best to buy their way into heaven, leaving the church everything they had.

We girls thought it would be neat to hear our Pastor announce his net worth before passing the offering plate. His money bags were attached to a wooden board that helicoptered up and down every aisle. It was the primary method of collecting money here at *The Assemblage*, but the preferred method was to go to the office, give a credit card number, and pay ten percent automatically. I don't think I'll ever forget Pastor Dom's face when we tracked him down after a service and asked him what he thought of our idea of transparency. Thankfully we were not Catholic, or we most likely would have been sequestered to the holy box and be required to confess that we were smartasses. Private jet fuel was expensive. Duh.

Danielle was the most beautiful, sweet soul I had ever met. We were sister-like, except that our bubble baths as kids turned a little kinky as we aged. I knew every inch of her petite body and had kissed every skin cell that unfolded from head to toe. She returned the kisses completely. I envied her brilliant black hair, an iridescent tinge of black pearl. Framed by this black veil was an angel's face—not a single fault. She had the most stunning artic, light-blue eyes in the world. They simply beamed. I remember when Father caught us going down the hallway of my home, headed to my bedroom giggling our asses off. I was telling Danielle to tickle my titties. Father startled us by saying, "Goodnight, girls!" We put our hands over our mouths and laughed some more.

Father apparently told Mother who came into my room five minutes later, stating there would be no titty tickling, and that Danielle needed to sleep in the guest bedroom. She was embarrassed, and I was pissed. Danielle called her mom to come and get her. When my love left, I said to my mother, "I hate you, bitch!" and slammed the door. The next day at school, we told our story to the tribe, and we all laughed so loud that the entire Horseshoe High cafeteria stared at us.

Occasionally, we would sneak off to a house party on Friday or Saturday nights to break the boredom. Most were lame and uneventful, with the occasional Tarzan versus Rocky fistfight. Drunken cavemen performing in the greatest accomplishment most of these idiots would ever know—the art of healing when they sobered up. Perhaps the spoils of taking the slut that your drunken friend had slept with the night before were worth going to war over. Who knows?

I had Danielle, and there would be no rent to pay from us. We were there for the entertainment, not the drugs, and we had a place to sleep. Most girls who had to take this lifestyle seriously really had no other options. Drug use and rebel partying had burned their bridges. They were outcast teens who were poured into a lonely, painful, harsh, and unforgiving world. They knew exactly how to pay the rent.

You couldn't trust any of the party hoes. They would set anyone up in a heartbeat. Lying and stealing was the first thing they mastered. Tears of cuteness could quickly turn into the nastiest cartoon super-villain you ever met. It was sad to see some of these girls completely taken over by meth and heroin. They usually overdosed and died very young or got caught up and went to prison—and of course, had to pay the rent.

They knew how to get their fix. Being in a *clique* made it easier. Usually, it meant sex for drugs and a corner of a room to sleep. If they were cute enough and played the game right, they could hop in someone's bed. Most of the time, the last thing any of these girls wanted to hear was, "it's time to pay the rent."

Officer William Huttson, the police officer who played at Father's poker game, called them bad actors. I didn't worry about bad actors, though. Between Father, William, and Frankie, these punks would have a very bad day if I had to make a phone call. I know grown men, just saying.

Danielle and I had a blast stirring up the parties. We knew most of the gang, the cool kids, and they knew the deal about us. We came for fun and laughs. If people were too serious or stupid—we simply left.

Some of these houses were very rough environments, though, especially for two young, sexy girls like us. We were playing these games our freshmen, sophomore, and soon to be junior years of high school. Our parents definitely would not have approved. Some of the garbage we came across at these houses may have contributed to my affection for *Mr. Rockie Wino*—drugs and alcohol made people suck and very ugly.

Even though I didn't make the front line in cheerleading my freshmen and sophomore years at Horseshoe High, life, for the most part, was an awesome experience, just like me!

Melissa was over visiting with Mother again as always. They were in the sitting room discussing the noble charity of parenting and the advantages of foster care over adoption.

Melissa could not have children but loved them. She wanted to give her life more meaning and migraines for some reason. Perhaps they did need alcoholic beverages. From the two minutes of noise my ears translated, Melissa seemed to feel adoption was probably too permanent. The better choice, for now, was to explore the foster parent option.

Melissa's husband Mike, the pudgy northern native with the heavy Basston accent, had the ability to annoy my father, which was hard to do. His never-ending know-it-all prattle earned him the nickname of Migraine Matches. He was also one of the twelve who played poker with my father, simply by virtue of being married to my mother's best friend. Mike had no idea that the other poker players had secretly voted him out, but Father had no choice but to let him stay. One of Mother's demands. I planned to give the eventual foster child the Matches chose to parent a pair of earplugs for their birthday gift. Mike was a mouthy and obnoxious turd.

I listened long enough to feel my burrito coming up and had to make my move. I had to get my laptop so it was now or never. As I plowed through the sitting room I said, "Foster Parent. Really Melissa…"

"OUT!" Mother said and pointed in the direction of my room. I shook a smile from my face and stuck my tongue out as I left. Both shook their heads—annoyed as a chained chihuahua.

Before I realized the months of the calendar were snapping by, the end of my sophomore year slapped me in the face. On a tormented Tuesday, the spirits of hell got together and decided to say hello. Danielle was spending the night. These days, we didn't even ask for permission most of the time. The evening was winding down, and we settled into bed. I was holding her, running my fingers through her hair, and we were chatting beneath the soft orange glow of the Himalayan salt lamp. We had the radio on at a decent decibel in case we got to making too much noisy-noise.
She then whispered, "I'm pregnant."
I continued to play with her hair as if I had not heard what I thought had just stabbed me in the ear. Danielle then completely broke down and cried deeply. She knew me better than anyone other than my grandmother, Adamina-Rose. Maybe I needed to be more tolerant, more understanding. Maybe I created this by cursing at church in our youth group last Sunday at *The Assemblage*. The gentle moments of sweet love ground to a halt, and my fingers froze in place. And I started repeating what she said in my mind.
I'm pregnant... I'M Pregnant... SHE'S SAID SHE'S PREGNANT!
"You cheated on me? You, ho *bitch*!" I said.
I coiled my legs up like a praying mantis, planted my feet into the small of her back, and kicked her off my bed with all the force I possessed. She made a series of thumps when her body collected itself on the floor. Her head, hips, elbows, and knees sounded like a heavy bag of potatoes colliding on the aluminum floor of a box truck.
"You need to leave, Danielle," I said. I felt like a captured warrior princess, my hands tied behind my back, and God himself had taken form before my very eyes, took the

sharpest of swords the size of the Empire State Building and hot as the silly sun, and run me through with it. I was in shock and stunned by a foreign pain I'd never known. It was a deep hurt.

She called her mom crying and left my room with her backpack. I looked outside my window with blurred vision to see her sitting on the curb under the streetlight. Twenty minutes later, she hopped into her mother's car. My eyes and lips were swollen from painful confusion. I had no control over their radical movements. My lips had never quivered before, and I didn't like it one bit. I knew I was the first she had told. Her parents, baby daddy, and Horseshoe High had *no idea.*

We had spent all day together, and she had just said how much she loved me—we were in the process of getting cozy in bed. Wow! I did not see this one coming. There had not been any signs, hints, or feelings she was being deceitful. She had reached pro status, an official bad girl that managed to fool me. A cowardly text might have opened the door to a painful discussion where we could torment one another.

We still would have been over, but we might have been able to wiggle our way through her being prego together. We had been best friends forever. Betrayal in this way had to be handled harshly and directly. I could care less about her damn details now. I'm Anglaia Clintin, after all.

It made the end of our sophomore year very awkward at Horseshoe High. Toward the end of the football season, I did make the front row of my cheer squad, facing the fans and trying to wear my pom-poms out for a football team that was getting better—they won half their games.

I had completed driver's education class and was given a new Mustdang GT for my sixteenth birthday. Thanks, Grandmother Adamina-Rose. It was breast cancer pink with a white racing stripe running down the middle of the car from the hood to the back of the flared trunk. The pink rimmed wheels were awesome. I loved my Mustdang. The interior was a custom white winter land package—everything was white as snow and expensive. The custom radio was a dream—loud as hell.

My sixteenth birthday was the best ever. Word must have gotten out about my upcoming birthday gift. Family and friends I had not seen in years came for the party. I loaded up on how I was a spoiled brat and how lucky I was. I agreed that life was great. My newfound freedom in the form of a hotrod did make me smile. Yay for Anglaia. Bite me, Danielle!

I had seen Danielle off and on at *The Assemblage*—what looked like a tiny Asian woman who had stuffed a hippopotamus under her dress. She was sitting with the baby daddy. He was actually someone I knew. We had talked about him before and agreed he was a redneck jerk.

He would be a junior next year at Horseshoe High, too, and drove a jacked-up monster truck, played football, and stocked shelves all over Queenfield with cola products after school. It blew my mind she actually brought Beau Panderson into our church. It was bizarre seeing his arm around my girl. I felt like going over there and kicking his teeth out but favored sending them my magical Houdini finger along with generic smiles of pure hate. Hopefully, they'd be happy together: *not*.

Really though, kiss my ass. *I don't care*. They made me want to SCREAM—so I did! Right in the middle of the Sunday sermon at *The Assemblage*. At least fifteen amens rang out across the congregation.

"Damn it, Anglaia," Mother said. She smacked my leg, leaving a red mark that could be seen through my pantyhose. I could tell I scared the crap out of her, followed by Mrs. Perfect being embarrassment to heaven and beyond.

Maybe her nightmares were about having me for a daughter? Grandmother snickered at all of the attention. Maybe it was time for Grandfather's Boogie-Woogie-Shake-n-Bake-Duck-Butt-Dance. She would just have to get over it. I was pissed.

Chapter 7

Waves of the ocean—days of life

TOOZOOLEE, MY BEST FRIEND, MADE A solemn pact that we would always look out for each other. The rundown apartments had every manner of scumbag living there, and I was sure a few Westons were lurking in the shadows. The main problem was that people didn't talk in the hood. It was the law there. So, the fact that I did talk could cost me if mom kept telling our story to everyone.

At the Tanner apartment complex, nine-out-of-ten of the air conditioners poking out of the windows blew hot air when turned on or were purposely left off because people had very little money to pay higher electric bills. Occasionally, Toozoolee and I would hang out in the mall to beat the heat.

Sometimes, we would visit the American Heartband Theater and watch plays like *Shakespeare Abridged*, and *Rockin' Christmas*. There were unforgettable casts from New Dork City and beyond. The theater tickets I usually won from the Trueman Public Library book club run by Ms. London.

Toozoolee was as good a person as I'd ever known. He was as honest and loyal a friend as they came, not to mention a legitimate athlete, as well. He was slowly getting his tribal tattoos put on. They morphed across the right side of his chest and right shoulder. His tribal art looked impressive. It made me consider getting some, too. They were very expensive for a teenager and were put on in the kind of tattoo parlor where age eighteen and his parents' consent were not needed. Not that it mattered. He would not be denied. His ink was of great importance to him. I always decided against it when the time came to actually do it.

We often hunted work together, scanning connecting neighborhoods for construction dumpsters. We would find out who was in charge and volunteer to help clean up the trash and debris, making fast cash rather quickly, sometimes a couple of hundred dollars each. Toozoolee also washed dishes under the table at various restaurants, as well.

Toozoolee was very particular and only allowed Rork to do his tattoos. Sometimes it would be a couple of months before he could get a seat in Rork's chair. It did not seem to bother Toozoolee one bit. Two brothers ran the tattoo shop from their basement in Indipundents, Mizzeree, just off Trueman road. The tattoo parlor was pretty rough around the edges. Not just anyone would dare to enter.

There were high hopes for the Academy High School football team. I would have been on the field a lot in my junior year. My teammates were bonded like Spartans. We had found a love for one another and the sport of football. The competition was at a high level and taken very seriously at Academy Highschool. For most, it was the closest thing to family we had. Our coaches molded and scolded us into a team—one with a winning record for the past nine years.

Our coach, Coach Easthood, had swagger and a unique way of reaching each of us. It started in the summer with somewhere positive to hang out. The field, film, and weight-room were places where most of us had to be run off at five o'clock. At the beginning of every season, the schedule and *the board* would be unveiled, which was a bigger event than Thanksgiving, Christmas, or New Year's.

The Board would be unveiled every Monday before practice. It was covered with a black blanket sewn together like a huge pillowcase with our mascot, the *Dirty Bird*, emblazed in gold at its center. The cover was shimmied on and off reverently by the team captains. Coach Easthood's weekly message, the list of the starters, our opponent's key players, and plays we had to stop, and the key plays we had to make were highlighted. And most important of all, we had to see the *letter* Coach Easthood had sent to the opposing team. He always wrote the opposition a spirited letter, addressed to their coach. Sometimes we would get a letter back which would be tacked below ours. If a letter came back from a team with a good record and the verbiage of their coach had any hint of being disrespectful in it, we could really get fired up and make them pay dearly on the football field—Friday nights under the lights. I loved football.

We had the Berry brothers—twin towers of uncommon power and agility who were simply playmaking nightmares. Their dad, Lewis Sandburg, who was in prison for murder, thought it an excellent idea to give them the same first name as did a professional boxer back in the day, thinking perhaps it might be helpful if they ever had issues with the law as he'd had. Berry Alpha was first born, and Berry Omega was the end of Wanda, their mom's delivery woes. That is how everyone kept them straight. Their true names were Berry Sandburs, both of them, exactly the same as their identical look.

The twins played with dynamo athleticism and would bedazzle those in attendance. We all agreed they could walk onto most college teams and start without a playbook. Simply snap the ball. That was all that was needed. They were that good. I thought I might have been good enough to be the starting quarterback for any other school—not a chance at Academy.

The twins were excellent athletes, and I was nowhere close to being at their level. I had slept in their house many times, though. Our moms knew each other. Berry A was number nine, our quarterback. Berry O, number six, our running back. Every once in a while, they'd trade places, or sometimes Coach Easthood would let me take a few snaps to confuse our opponents. I was number three, a slot receiver for a few trick plays and *the* starting free safety on defense. Toozoolee was number fifty-five, middle linebacker, a hard-hitting headhunter.

I was probably closer to Berry O, as he seemed to look out for me. Berry A was cocky and more self-centered, but I considered both friends. Their older brother Reggie, three years our elder, was an entirely different matter. He hated my guts and roughed me up every chance he got. My skin color was a big deal to him—a well-known tuff guy on the streets. The police came three cars deep when they had to come and pick him up.

I felt I owed the Sandburg family a great deal for trying to help me out when Mom screwed up bad enough to get locked up. I did my best to avoid Reggie when I stayed there. It seemed he checked every room every night to see if I might be over. He had a bully mentality and was addicted to pestering me, nothing like Weston, but it still sucked that there were so many mean guys in the world. Neither one of the twins wanted to deal with him either, but when they did, they did it together, and it got ugly.

I did my best to fit in and not cause problems. Having a place to sleep and a bite to eat was priceless. But after a while of good intentions, everyone got restless and needed a break from me living with them. I wasn't their responsibility, and I had overheard many adults reprimand my mom on the subject.

K-sea had offered me much in the lines of a street education, as well as formal knowledge published in the books I had read. I knew about people—what made them tick in respects to the extent words and my youth would allow. I knew I was at a slight disadvantage in life concerning the environment and culture in which I was raised. It was glaringly clear I had an intimate relationship with the harshness of inner-city life. Everything was a personal perspective and temporary. I had seen bad choices and the complicated existence they created. For now, it was go-time. I had a few years to position myself for success, and that was the only option I gave myself.

My mom, Jillie Jo, on the other hand, was simply a disgrace. Bar hopping was Mom's idea of a day off, and she habitually slept with any young drunk guy she could lure into a bed. I didn't know if she knew where her actual bed was most of the time, as she would be gone for days at a time. She couldn't keep a normal nine-to-five job and maxed out every credit card she could get her hands on. She was in trouble for writing hot checks, missed court dates, drug and alcohol charges, and others I'm embarrassed to mention.

Truth is, she was basically a giant scumbag who I dearly loved. Most of the cash she had was peeled off sweaty dance floors featuring a pole and gloomy lights. She had no problem stealing from anybody. Young, old, male or female—everyone was fair game. She would seduce them with batting eyelashes, giggles, naughty words, and aggressive body suggestions. Once she had them in her web, she grabbed everything she could and disappeared before they knew what hit them. Some never learned and continually came back for more. Being called out or caught red-handed didn't bother mom at all. It was part of the game—her habit. Mom could put her hands on a complete stranger, and they would be naked ten minutes later. Years of this disgusting, anything-goes behavior had me racing in the opposite direction.

My dad had shot himself in the head—perhaps his idea of a Thanksgiving gift—and of course, it was important to him that we had a front-row seat to the show. Not sure if my memory captured it correctly, but I'm sure he had us sit on the couch, put the pistol to the side of his head, and said, "I'm done!" then pulled the trigger. Mom's screams scared me more than the loud noise of the gunshot. That is the day I think mom changed into the person she is today.

There would be no child support coming in to help out on the bills. Just my mom's luck, and she constantly reminded me of this fact. We did qualify for some state assistance and moved from place to place due to Mom's reputation for writing bad checks. Tanner always let us move back in for some reason. And I probably slept in a car more than any child in the state of Mizzeree.

We were masterful escape artists. Within five minutes, we could have our trash bags of clothes and three small tubs of worldly possessions packed and gone. We usually had no choice but to head back to the rundown Tanner apartments, located just off Indipundents Avenue. If Mom's mail did catch up to her, there would be at least nine different addresses on the envelopes, some I did not remember living at. Mom rarely opened her mail. "Too stressful," she stated.

Aunt Janie and her daughter, Kaylee, occasionally come by to do what whores do. They were a stew of witches who got together to share laughs and lies. Particularly fabrications that estranged men from their money. The one thing you could bank on was they were thieves deep as bone marrow could get, deceitful con-artist maggots whose tempting smiles and erotic bodies would take all they could take from anyone, anytime.

Sometimes when they sunbathed, you would almost feel they were taking the sun's love instead of receiving it. It had been a while since the hat-trick of clowns had been together.

Mom said the duet had found a man in the boondocks who owned three houses and were most likely "after his shit," as she put it. He was apparently a nice guy, but whatever.

Mom had a nightlife that no good man could come to grips with for long. I, too, had to let any notions go that she was interested in anything other than her method of survival. I, personally, was so thankful for the day I chose to replace her with books. Smells of sour breath from alcohol and cigarettes, weed, stinky feet, and the stench of her sex sludge disgusted me. Compounding matters was the constant insult of loud noise. "We're partying, get over yourself," Mom would say. A shower and silence would have made a huge difference in my mental constitution. The life she had chosen for me seemed an ever-expanding constellation of selfish rudeness.

When it came time to move out and relocate, she usually stated that the guy had changed too much or was another damn control freak. When she decided it was over, she could not just leave the man. She always had to destroy something personal—pictures of his kids, a favorite cup, or the screen of his TV. Sometimes she even ordered me to get involved, which annoyed me because I didn't want to get charged with a crime. Typically, I was asked to erase everything on his computer, stating there were most likely compromising pictures that needed to be deleted and help her tip the refrigerator over on its side with the doors open, laying to ruin as much as possible. We had to make him pay for giving us a place to live, however temporary. If there was enough time, the dude's place would get seriously trashed. Seemingly, it eased Mom's suffering. "That'll teach that jerk," she would say and laugh in an eerie hollow howl.

It seemed she would have a chance at a normal life when she met my dad, Robert VonVouge. They married after high school, and Dad soon took off for military basic training. Mom birthed me soon thereafter. We moved around a lot during the eight years Dad served in the military. It was a loop in time that eventually took us back to K-sea after he was kicked out for failing a drug screening.

Dad was never the same after the deployments. He didn't seem to care about life in general. He had managed to alienate what few family members and friends he did have. Work was not a high priority. He would work for temporary agencies long enough to pay the rent, electric bill, or fill his wooden cigar box full of marijuana. Dad just wanted to be left alone. I didn't enjoy being yelled at, so voilà, we came to a mutual understanding.

Mom got nothing from the Smith family when they died. Everything went to their only son, who had nothing to do with them the entire time they were alive. Mom sold her soul to them, taking them to a million doctors' appointments, helping them with their errands and bills, thinking it would pay off in the end. She was wrong again, which made the reality of her world even heavier and more annoying for me. It was plain to see they were using her, but she had her own ideas—they would reward her someday, she just knew it. She was wrong, wrong, wrong. She then pumped her hurt out onto the world.

I knew others who had it much worse, so I made it a point not to whine. Mom sure was trying her best to catch up with weirdos and be crowned *Queen Crazy*, though. Perhaps a title would settle her soul. There were plenty of horror stories on Indipundents and Prospect Avenues that put things into perspective for me. K-sea was an old spirit and had seen it all. Our visit to this city was nothing more than the hands of a wind-up clock ticking away. The hands would wind down to a stop, and eventually, death would rule the pointing pointless.

Today got complicated quickly when I was picked up by children's services. She was locked up again, and it looked like Mom would not just be there for a quick visit to catch up with her old jailbird friends. Unfortunately, it looked to be an extended stay this time. She might actually become chemically unpolluted for the longest period of her adult life. The charges she caught were going to change everything for both of us. Usually, I stayed with Toozoolee or the Berry brothers when she went to jail. It was embarrassing, but something both families were accustomed to.

This time the State of Mizzeree Children's Services was seriously involved, and there would now be the caseworkers' highbrow overwatch to contend with—a plethora of newly imposed rules to follow. I knew it was pointless to write mom letters or try to talk to her on the phone as it simply reminded her of the freedom she was missing out on. She was being wronged again, and communication with me would be too bothersome. I was free, after all, and she was not. Over the years, she handed down a book of pointless rules that she usually made up on the fly. Rarely did any of them make a bit of sense. It was in my best interest to focus on my breath and send my thoughts into realms of the lively words of mostly dead authors. That's all I had control of at the moment.

Typically, when she was bailed out by Aarontino, her boss at A-Rose, it wasn't long before her life patterns inevitably recycled back into the only way she knew how to exist. She most likely would have to lower her standards of life after this incarceration. She would be much older when she got out. No one would pay money to watch her older body dance. Although, it would be somewhat easier to start over or flop down at some lowlife's place, as there would be no teenager to drag around. I would be an adult and on my own when she was released.

It would be years before the wind would move the wad of dirty paper, my mom, Jillie Jo resembled. The streets would be a bit cleaner for a time. I hoped she might find some peace along the way, but I sincerely doubted it. I knew she was in jail, soon to be prison, and was blaming dead people for her troubles—her parents, adopted parents, and my dad. It was an ignorant conclusion that she completely identified with.

I tried to educate her on how the mind worked, but the noise in her head was too loud. I could not break through. She could not hear my words or have the ability to listen and understand what I was trying to share—notions I had learned in books Ms. London had recommended.

When I amassed the great minds from the assimilation of study, the information seemed best explained by using my *Field of Snow* analogy. I told her to imagine her mind patterns. Her thoughts were likened to a field on a hill covered with deep snow. The first time you walked down the hill through the deep snow, each step was very difficult. The more you used the same path, the easier the steps became, just like a person's thoughts. Eventually, going down the same path would become effortless, like putting on roller skates, and you could whiz downhill on snow-packed ice with no effort at all.

The more you thought of the same thought, the more automatic it became. Change from this easy path or mind pattern would take a lot of determination and hard work. The first steps in a different direction would be tough steps through deep snow to start with, but a new path and a new life would be worth it. It would be worth it to start a new, healthy way of thinking and living a healthy life. It could all begin with *one... tough... step...* in a new direction. She would just look at me and say, "Aww, VeeLee. I love you, baby boy." It usually took five minutes to transition the conversation back to how horrible her life was.

Her wrists always ached from pole dancing, not to mention she would have an array of bruises from head to toe. There was never a shortage of salty words to convey how demanding her bosses, Richard and Aarontino Jackkson, were. Richard was a disgusting soul of rotten pus to me. I avoided him and his moron crew at all costs. He was no Weston, but I detested him completely and wished him death by heart-attack every time I looked across his lustful eyes.

Aarontino, on the other hand, had homes and restaurants in K-sea and Saint L's, which he constantly traveled back and forth to, making Mom's other boss at the strip club, Richard, mad as hell when she left town with him. If I was ever asked, "No one's business," was the answer Mom wanted me to convey. Aarontino was very impatient and harbored light disgust for my friends and me, postulating on numerous occasions he wasn't a fan of kids these days. Aarontino was tall and in great muscular fitness, wearing suits and always well-kempt. He was always heavily doused in a European cologne called Frederic Malle. Admittedly, I loved the scent. He had a lot of money.

Sometimes I would alternate my stories to my mom. Sometimes I used the pickle story to try and motivate her when she was down and extremely negative, which was every other minute. She would tend to throw her entire day away when the slightest thing would go amiss, sending her into tantrums that resembled epileptic fits.

I'd say, "Mom. Imagine you were snowed-in in our apartment for two weeks, and all you could think about was Famous Carl's double BBQ steak-burger on the other side of town. When the snow cleared, you took off to get that steak-burger. On the way, you received a speeding and seatbelt ticket. After waiting in line for an hour, when you finally reached the counter, the attendant put up a sold-out sign in your face. You flagged the gentleman down who had purchased the last burger, told him your troubles and offered him triple the price. He agreed, and you now held Famous Carl's burger in your hand. As you raised the burger to take the first bite, a *pickle* fell to the ground."

I would then ask her, "Would you now throw the entire burger away or enjoy the rest of it?" I was trying to show her that the rest of the day could be delicious if she did not let a *pickle* mishap steal her whole burger—steal her whole day. Most of the time, she responded in surprise as if it were the first time she had heard the story. I knew I had told her dozens of times, but I think she flushed her memory down the toilet every morning. One less thing she would need to remember.

Nearly all her bad experiences were connected to a person, and if she could see them as a dropped pickle and let the situation go, she might be able to enjoy the rest of the day. "What a pickle ordeal," or "what a pickle-head," I'd say. I told her these stories many times, but they never seemed to sink in.

Her memory truly wrinkled my forehead, and, for the life of me, I couldn't understand why I was responsible for trying to re-raise my mom. I truly sucked at it on purpose, knowing no human on God's green earth was coming to challenge my parenting skills or take the job over for me.

It was no secret I had misguided feelings for Lara London. Her intelligence was beautiful and made my heart smile. She knew everything. If it were not for her enthusiasm and inspiration to the written word, I would have been gobbled up by the negative environment where I lived. The positive side of K-sea had found me. Lara held the light and shined it on me, which turned me on in every possible way—my mind, eyes, heart, gut, and, dare I say, balls. Swamped by teenage testosterone, I'd shift into a hot mess every single time I saw her.

The books Lara checked out to me were exactly what my mind hungered to know. She didn't intentionally try to turn me on physically—I don't think she did, anyway—but her legs and butt were firm and amazing and perfectly shaped. When she sat talking with me about an author or subject, she'd have her legs crossed. With the skill of a fire juggler, she took the heel of her foot from her high heeled shoe and balanced it on her toes, exposing most of her foot. It was my eye-candy-cocaine watching her shoe dangle in the air.

My catnip-kryptonite came from scanning her yoga-fit legs, and the shiny gold anklet only exacerbated matters when it dangled around on her adorable ankle. It really drove me nuts. I loved her in a million ways for a million reasons. But Lara had drawn a bold, dark line in the sandbox I dared not cross. She had a particular look that needed no words when I thought to be creative. Anything extracurricular was out of the question of reality. I was confounded and unable to arrest my mind. I reluctantly grappled and inaccessibly daydreamed in every manner about Ms. Lara London.

My caseworker Connie stated Queenfield would be a three-hour trip. I offered little small talk and think Connie liked it that way. Driving seemed to stress her out. We never really seemed to connect on any level— at the end of the day, she made me feel I was simply a paycheck.

There would be people and familiars of K-sea I would dearly miss. It only took twenty minutes for my hometown to fade from sight behind us. My hometown already felt a million miles away.

Ms. London, as she required me to address her, was at the top of the list. I was thinking of the day we had met. It was at a book fair at my school. I was in Middle School at the time. She was from the Trueman Public Library handing out free books, the sort of books she had deemed suitable and educational for youngsters. It was clear I had to find the most extravagant gift box my mind could create and put my thoughts of sweet Lara away for now.

Chapter 8

Horseshoe High

      I WAS TRYING TO WRAP MY HEAD AROUND everything that had happened. My eyes burned with a fire that even teardrops couldn't cool. Negative news had found me, and I was faced with greater problems to solve than trigonometry and thoughts of losing a beautiful, intelligent friend along with my football family.

      My great test now is to find the ability to survive in an unknown environment and evolve into a new state of being, and hopefully, a favorable existence. I have been placed in the foster care system over the summer of the beginning of my junior year of high school. So, all that I know and dream of will all have to wait for now as the car wheels of my caseworker roll me to my new foster home in Queenfield, Mizzeree. This is day one of another dropped pickle in life.

I was riding shotgun with a stranger I hardly knew. We were crossing the Mizzeree River, and I was watching the water dash in and out of view between the bridge posts that flashed across my eyes at sixty-five miles per hour. I was leaving K-sea, the only life I knew and was comfortable with. The sound of tires lulled me into a trance as if listening to a duet of lost treasures of dueling cellos—deep and full of mystery. My memories sloshed around like ice cubes in a half-filled crystal glass. This was the coldest air-conditioning I had experienced all summer. My legs advertised multitudes of goose pimples. Wearing shorts may not have been a good idea.

I most likely would return to my childhood haunts someday. However, today, I had to make a pit stop in the ever-expanding universe. I was on my way to Queenfield, an unavoidable mud puddle in my life, and I had no choice but to go through it.

"We'll be there soon, VeeLee," my caseworker said as she drove the remaining leg of Highway 13, crossing over Interstate 44.

My eyes widened at the sound of her voice. It caught me off guard, startling me. We entered Queenfield at two-eighteen in the afternoon, and I scanned the cityscape for no apparent reason. It would be rude to doze off into another round of mental melancholy. It was tearing me up to leave what little I had in K-sea. Making new friends was not my strong suit, but knew I would need to. It was simply an aggravating process of life. I planned to stay in touch with my hometown crew best I could. I was to meet Mike and Melissa Matches today and tried to focus on my demeanor. I hoped they would be somewhat normal.

Connie softly pumped on the brake, hung a left onto Battlefront Road, then a right on Dazzlefield. We pulled into the Horseshoe High parking lot and parked. Connie looked in my direction, and I grabbed my backpack and unzipped it, pulling out two books from the over-stuffed backpack. Thoughts of Lara crept in. I already missed her.

It felt a little odd getting down to business so quickly without any foreplay, so to speak, but Children's Services and my foster parents wanted me to get the best classes I could. It was the first day of enrollment at Horseshoe High, and huddles of kids dotted the premises inside and out. Connie passed my school transcripts and case file to Melissa, who seemed to be feeling just as awkward about our new arrangement and first introduction to each other.

"I'm VeeLee," I said, offering my hand. She came into my space and lightly hugged me. Connie watched me as if I were a pit bull that got off its chain. Her phone was primed for a 911 emergency. It struck me funny how some adults changed so quickly in the company of other adults—fortified in fakeness.

"Okay. It looks like the front door is that way," I said and pointed in the general direction. I slung my backpack over my shoulder, thinking to myself with a deep breath, "Let's do this."

I thanked Connie for being so kind as to agree to return the books to the Trueman Library for me. She, without hesitation, hopped into her car and drove off as if stressed about the drive back to K-sea. I shook my head, watching my only connection to my homeland disappear. The books she was now in possession of were decent bits of information from Aristotle that any lawyer might consider when it came to arguments in court—he never lost one.

Aristotle's greatness and supreme knowledge were never to be fully known—his library was destroyed by morons. He would have been an interesting person to have known in person. He learned from Plato, who created the first college. Plato learned from Socrates, who invented philosophy. A badass trio, in my opinion. My greatest fascination with books was words and the interpretation of meaning by the human mind.

Knowledge was truly the ultimate equalizer for anyone in need of change, understanding, and in search of the meaning of life. Utter intelligence was lent down for centuries by complete strangers who took the time to document that intelligence for the benefit of others. No judgments of the readers or listeners were a consideration. To me, the gift of the written word and the notes of music were all the same. Gifts.

I had a very painful introduction to Horseshoe High as I had to get all the inoculations. My shot records had not made it down with my file. My counselor seemed to be overworked and somewhat stressed. She drifted in and out of my voice, tapping the keyboard of her computer several times frustratedly before it would accept my class choices. Most of my curriculum selections seemed to surprise Melissa. "Can I play football, Melissa?" I asked.

"Don't know, can you?" She laughed. "I'm sure Mike won't mind."

I asked my counselor for the coach's name and contact information. She reached across her desk, licked her fingertips, and pulled out a flyer for me. I wanted to get my hands on the playbook and practice times. I might even become the starting quarterback for Horseshoe High and lead the team to some amazing victories. Football was a great passion of mine—the only sport I was interested in. I turned some heads last year in the K-sea area, even with the great talent there. *Queenfield competition should be much easier*, I thought to myself.

Melissa paid a few more fees and abracadabra, we were finished at the school. We simultaneously closed the car doors of the red SUV that still had the temporary paper license plate taped on the back glass. Guess she had now reached soccer mom status.

Melissa believed Mike would allow football if my grades didn't suffer. In my mind, that was a joke. The tidbits of recycled words and equations at the high school level came easily to me. Now that I was in the state foster care system, I also had the opportunity to take some college-level courses free of charge at the local technical college, basically double-dipping. Unlike my mom, I planned to make use of the opportunity. But being in a live contact sport like football was the adrenalin boost that sent every cell of my body into ecstasy.

It was obvious by the tone of her voice that neither Mike nor Melissa had ever played sports or were interested in them whatsoever—just a hunch. It might have been a good thing to have put her on the spot before she had more time to think on the matter. I don't know what the final decision will be, but for now, I was signed up to play. It was my stress outlet—my happy place.

We were now en route to my new squat, the place I'd lay my head for a while. Mike was at work, a union job where he made parts for farm equipment. Melissa had taken off work to pick me up. She was a registered nurse at the Medical State Prison that once housed the New Dork City mob guy, Fawn Gonedee. It was located right in the middle of Queenfield. Melissa was giving me the scoop about the prison hospital on our way to her house. She said the prison didn't seem to bother the locals much, which was a bit surprising. It had opened in 1933 and housed a thousand inmates.

We pulled into the laid-back neighborhood where the Matches lived. It was just off Dazzlefield Street, no more than two miles away from the Horseshoe High. I remembered how it felt good each day after walking nearly four miles to get to my old, crappy, stale-carpet, bug-infested, rotten food-smelling Tanner apartment. It was a great accomplishment getting through the rough and tough areas of the K-sea projects on a daily basis, not to mention extremely nerve-racking when I had to run for my life or fight.

In time, folks got used to you being around. Occasionally, all you had to do was run the fastest. Sometimes it simply was impossible. There are some fast-ass dudes in the hood. On a bad day, you just had to take the black eye, lose the contents of your pockets and your backpack, and go on about your business. Some days it was impossible to avoid negative contact. Putting up a good fight now and again was part of getting respect. Girls of the hood were challenged equally. No one received a free pass.

The street taught you when you could fight back. Everyone knew that on any given day, you could get shot, and nothing you had on you was worth a bullet. Nearly everyone was packing heat. People were in continuous communication and knew each other as one giant dysfunctional family. If you were passing through or visiting, you would never know the years of neighborhood history. The survival of family and friendships in these areas had always been challenging. The bonds were strong, and they looked out for one another when it came to strangers in the area—most of the time anyway.

My new place in Queenfield seemed chill and had a calm, laid-back vibe to it. I smiled at Melissa as we exited the vehicle and headed inside. She smiled back. The house was a brick, one level, with an extended two-car garage—a very basic place with an average yard. I was grateful.

We entered the home, and Melissa began explaining the layout. Her voice was somewhat uneasy as if giving out secrets to a treasure map or handing the keys to a thief. She may have felt a little awkward being alone with a strange young man. I could not be sure, but I tried to steady my voice and not give her reason to become skittish and send me away on day one.

Melissa seemed to be a go-along-with-the-crowd type of person in her late thirties. She was dirty blond, short in stature, and had a kind disposition—churchy. We chit-chatted about the house rules which Mike would go over again later when he got home.

I was relieved that there was not a delivery room filled with expectant family members and friends waiting for my arrival. Cake and ice cream, noisemakers and balloons to celebrate the Matches on their firstborn sixteen-year-old. I was getting the feeling my junior year in high school was going to be a new positive season in my life. I knew my thoughts controlled my actions and was the only way to make it so. Here we go, Queenfield! I'm here.

"I feel it best to wait for my husband Mike to go over the boundaries, expectations, and our hopes for you, VeeLee. Just know we feel blessed you are with us. Hearing it twice might get annoying," Melissa said with another smile.

"I understand, Ma'am. Makes sense."

"You can call me Melissa."

I had no other option but to send a smile back. She showed me to my room, and I thanked her. I was getting a little antsy and paced around the bed, stopping at the window to watch cars pass by. The room was decent in size with the smell of lemon.

Two pillows sat atop the bedspread at the head of the bed. The bedding was a fluffy white blanket with a multi-colored quilt neatly folded at the foot. A dresser—that I had clothes enough to require only one drawer—pillared cattycorner to the closet door. A fresh coat of blue paint—which looked last minute as there were runs and dabs on the door trim and baseboards—covered the walls. It was nonetheless a nice gesture when I recognized the effort.

It had been years since I had been around an adult male full-time and could only hope he was not going to make this arrangement hell. I would not be taking any more spankings nor dropping my pants. I didn't intend to be a rebel or disrespectful. I just hoped Mike's personality was flexible enough to engage. At the moment, I had a victory over street life. I was in a safe environment.

The door of his old pick-up rattled shut, and Mike walked into the house. He barreled through the door as if he had diarrhea, and his dog had just given birth to nine horses. He looked into my room wild-eyed and introduced himself. He told me to relax, and we would get to know each other after he showered the funk of his factory day down the drain.

I could faintly hear the Matches chit-chat for a short time. Then there came a pause. Their muffled tones went silent and I assumed they would have me front-and-center at any moment. Then the doorbell rang. Mike tromped to the door and opened it.

"Hello. I'm Lara, down from K-sea," she said. When my ears heard her voice, my entire body froze in pure attention. The familiar click-click, click-click from her high heels echoed on the tile floor until the sounds distanced themselves into the living room, located at the other end of the home. I was in a state of confused shock.

I tried to stretch my ears as far as they would go, yet I could not make out their conversation. I was excited and utterly confused at the same time. I didn't know whether I should bolt out from the shadows—introduce and infuse myself into the mist of the moment—or allow the adults to finish and patiently wait for them to sequester me at their leisure. Not knowing what was happening was driving me nuts.

I turned the doorknob slowly with the dexterity of a bank robber on the dial of a combination safe and gently cracked the door open so that I might vaguely eavesdrop. My interpretation would not suffice as I still could not make out the words. So down the hall, I crept.

"Thank you for coming so far to help us. My wife Melissa and I hope to give VeeLee the best opportunity we can," Mike said.

"I'm sure you two will do fine," Lara said.

I pulled my shoes off and sneaked ten feet further down the hallway and stiffened into an alert sentry. All my senses were amped up and maxed out. The conversation went back and forth for about forty-five minutes—the main topic being of the Nonagon and my potential recruitment.

The conversation was delivered at an adult depth and tone, compared to the light generalizations she had poked between my ears in the past. The things Lara was describing to the Matches were business like. *Am I dreaming?* I asked myself. I still did not believe in the Deep State, Luminaries belonging to a secret society, or a shadow government. I listened with great attention.

Lara told the Matches that I was the brightest set of eyes in the line-up, and my test scores were through the roof. She told them that I had overflowing qualifications and responded to her cues in the exact manner the Deep State was searching for. She said her job sucked when she had to deal with matters involving my mom and her tribe of scumbags, but the world and the Nine Kings would soon be in need of a fresh bag of blood and brains.

Even kings died. Most replacements were descendants of a king, someone who knew the rules and the workings of the Nonagon. An individual who could be trusted to maintain the order of the Nonagon and the world. Occasionally, a king had no offspring, or the children were not suitable for the post. They would be made into a librarian, president, senator, or governor.

"This is the reason an outgoing president is given his own library when leaving the Oval Office. It is the only secure way to keep in touch with the Nine Kings of the Nonagon. The Nine Kings possessed the supreme knowledge and the ultimate power on earth.

"Make no mistake—the Nine Kings do rule the world. They are the secret puppet masters behind the scenes everyone wants to put a face to. The shadow government, some say, is a dark force or Deep State that has control over all human life on earth. Two kings are from the United Plates, one from Eagleland, one from Hermany, one from Shinela one from Rushduh, one from Sweetdan, one from Indeehuh, one from Mixipoo, who had ousted the king from Geepan five years past.

"VeeLee was handpicked by me," Lara said.

"We didn't hear any of this in our foster training program," Melissa said.

"Yeah, this feels more like the Queen of Eagleland dropped off a prince for us to raise," Mike rattled off.

"Yes, my honey, we didn't realize our child to raise would be so important," Melissa said. Mike bobbled his head with a cheesy grin.

"It's imperative to maintain the progression of VeeLee's evolution. There could be very significant consequences imposed against each of you should you decide to inform anyone of this conversation or otherwise hinder his development. He has been through enough," Lara said.

"Oh, goodness! Mike, my honey," Melissa said. Her tone was soft and searching while rubbing on Mike's hand.

"Look. I made the call to the president on September eleventh and told him to proceed as the Nonagon had directed. I can make another call to deal with cold feet if need be," Lara said.

"No, no-no-no. We're fine. VeeLee will be fine. Everything is fine, Lara," Mike said.

Lara went on to explain how war was business and that the contractors were handpicked and paid. Many people would die. At the end of the day, there are nine men in the world worth a trillion dollars each, and you will never see them on any Fortune 500 list. Mike repeatedly tried to interrupt and take charge of the conversation to no avail. Lara knew exactly how to instantly silence him, which took Melissa by surprise.

Lara added parting words to the conversation, and I snuck back into my room, softly closed the door, and lay on the bed to wait. Mike walked Lara out. Then a knock rattled my bedroom door. I stood up, walked over to the door, and opened it. I wasn't sure if I had fallen asleep and was dreaming, but my eyelids needed the blur rubbed away. We sized each other up, shook hands again, and he asked me to join him in the living room so that we might get to know one another better.

For the next three hours, it was a special report issued by Mike "The Jabber Jaws" Matches. It took every ounce of restraint I had in me not roll my eyes. Not to mention, there was a mild stench undulating into my nose. Even though he just showered, he had a burnt rubber scent pouring off of him. It became clear he worked in a toxic environment. The smell crashed into my olfactory bulb, making me want to use my thumbs as corks and shove them up my nostrils while holding my breath. My thoughts went back to when he first arrived home with his filthy clothes covered in grease and gunk.

They were good people, it seemed, with good intentions. I was lucky in many respects. Their obliviousness to roleplaying parents was refreshing. They seemed to be genuine when they relayed intentions of being there for me twenty-four-seven, which made my knees move unintentionally on the chair. It was easy to see they were good and would be good for me. They informed me of the basic living arrangement and that we'd be going to *the Assemblage* in the morning to hear Pastor Dom share the Holy Word of God.

That was really not what I wanted to hear, and I would mount an Aristotle-style rebuttal when I better understood their mindset. I could ill afford to muddy the water on our first day and start complaining about my disregard for piety beliefs. It was not in my best interest to establish an environment of conflict and negativity. A battle would be waged and won later, just not today.

Melissa went to put dinner together, and Mike and I watched some television. I listened to him commentate on every commercial and the evening news, and I was getting that gnawing Weston rub of basically being forced to watch TV, bringing forth a remembered angst. I hated television. I was missing the solidarity of a book and didn't plan to engage in TV marathons of ridiculous programming very often. I could not see a best-bud kind of friendship brewing and would not fancy being an autophile to muse his ego.

Dinner was a game of peeping-Tom and of course, the nonexistence of silence. Mike told himself jokes that only his belly-fat jiggled to. He was a chunky, balding man, with an abnormal shrub-brush looking mustache. It was hard to imagine Melissa kissing him with that cactus looking anomaly on his face. His blackish-brown eyes almost grown together were framed by thick-lensed, black-rimmed glasses, scarcely separated by a tapered snout that flared into two trumpets at its end.

His voice would not be lost in a crowd, with a monotone yet high pitch, delivered in a fast cadence. Basically noise. I had seen versions of Mike at various schools and the hood before. I knew he would have been the sort of kid that made life hard on himself growing up. He was most likely a momma's boy, the variety that needed all the attention the world had to offer. Any form, negative or otherwise, was accepted. "May I ask a favor, Mike?"

"Sure, VeeLee."

"Not to be rude or disrespectful, but I enjoy reading and learning. So would it be alright if I didn't have to watch TV in the future?"

"My goodness, no. That's not a problem at all, is it my honey?" Melissa interceded.

"Not at all," Mike said.

Chapter 9

VeeLee enters Anglaia's world

"GOOD MORNING, MELISSA" MOTHER SAID as Melissa, Mike, and a teenage boy filed into the pew and sat next to us.

"Good morning, Sarah," Melissa said.

The choir began singing. Pastor Dom followed with a service on good and evil, light and darkness. Nutshell, darkness instantly flees from light. He gave the light switch in a dark room scenario. Once you flip the light switch of Christ on in your heart, you have nothing to fear—darkness or evil cannot exist in the light, and it must leave that instant. *Not hard, people*, I thought to myself, *Turn on the frigging light and be happy. You don't have to have a new Mustdang to make you happy like me, but it helps,* and laughed to myself.

Grandmother Adamina-Rose and Grandfather Jacob sat next to Father—a bunch of old people listening like they were hearing the last good words ever to be spoken. After the service, we puddled together in the atrium for coffee to go and quick introductions. The kid my age was named VeeLee VonVouge. He was now living with Mike and Melissa. *Good luck with that one, dude.* He would be attending Horseshoe High, and Melissa wanted me to show him around the school and introduce him to my friends.

I could not stir that into my cup of wanted to. *Not happening* was the bottom line. My Mustdang was calling me, and I didn't want to hear Mike's voice, who was warming up. It was fun to watch Grandfather Jacob's face turn red with some form of sarcasm. Humor would have to wait. I was to meet a few of my friends from the cheer squad for lunch and drive around jamming to our favorite songs. My way of shaking off the Sunday fear cloud of religion.

"We have half a lamb and the trimmings. I expect all will join us," Grandmother said, looking directly at me.

"I have plans, Grandmother," I said.

She made the face that needed no words. I huffed as if it mattered. *I'm getting so pissed*, I thought to myself. School and its demands were just around the corner. My summer was almost completely over, and now I had to drive thirty minutes to Bronson, watch the waves on the lake, and listen to old people talk about a million things other than me.

At least my friends appreciated me and knew how to treat me. They were not rude and did not constantly cut me off as if I was a two-year-old. To make matters worse, Mother invited Melissa. Invitations that wrinkled Grandfather's forehead on a regular basis.

"VeeLee, you can ride with Anglaia if you like," Mother said. Again, as if I was a two-year-old and had no effing option of who could ride in my car. VeeLee smiled at me to make matters worse.

"Dear God in Heaven," I said and took off, weaving through the church crowd at full prance, hoping VeeLee would somehow get lost. But no—wonder boy was on me like a fast-break race to dunk a basketball. He was sticky like an angry glue-crewmen at Horseshoe High. I headed to my car at full tilt and dialed the first of my friends to change our plans.

I slung the "wait" finger in VeeLee's direction and hopped in my car. VeeLee waited outside as I talked to my friends. I cracked the passenger side window, "VeeLee, please do not lean on my Mustdang. The paint is very expensive," I said and rolled the window back up. Five minutes or so later, we were moving down the highway.

I made sure the music playing on the radio was loud enough to avoid any form of chit-chat with him. I could care less about one damn thing he had to say. Most mothers would not be putting a strange boy in the car with their daughter. Mine, though, was in a hurry to replace all memory of Danielle and the way I chose to love. Hopefully, Grandmother would give Mother another after-church earful of preaching.

It wasn't as if I had not encountered such a girl before. The universe must have hiccupped and dropped this salty soul directly into my life. I was not impressed with her immaturity. She was physically beautiful and arrogantly ugly at the same time. I could live without the sour shadow that surrounded Anglaia Clintin. Blue-eyed, Barbie-doll hard-bodied blonds with perfect bleached white teeth and dark tans could be found just about anywhere.

Each time Anglaia downshifted the engine into a roar and passed someone she knew with her car, she would say, "Giddy-up, Mustdang," waving goodbye to them as we passed and chuckled to herself. We traveled through the city of Bronson and now zipped through some gnarly countryside roads that had me clutching the door armrest—white-knuckled at times. About the only time I saw a smile on her face was when the car screamed around the sharp curves.

I could tell she knew the lake roads well. What wasn't a blur was Mother Nature at her best—speckled colors of flowers and birds and thick green wooded mountains. I did enjoy the feel of her car, but if she didn't chill out soon, Mommy and Daddy would be paying for a ticket, or worse, we might be getting scraped off a damn tree. After all, Anglaia had one entire year of driving experience. So, yeah, I was terrified.

We arrived at Anglaia's grandparents' home, and it almost felt like I was about to meet someone famous even though I had already met the owners at church. It was Gatsby for sure, framed directly into the Oatzark Mountains. A Colonial Revival with a Spanish barrel roof. The orange slate smiled over the white European stucco. Large, wooden, arched windows to include stained glass swept generously across its exterior, maximizing the flow of natural sunlight.

Giant white pillars of Roman descent endorsed the presence of power. If there was one feature that stood out most, it would be the mansion's main entrance. The ten-foot wooden French doors must have weighed a ton each, aged and awe-inspiring. They most likely came from a dismantled castle of a long-forgotten king—a New Dork auction acquisition perhaps.

The residence was affixed to a ten-acre, well-manicured, emerald green lawn that was held in place by huge stone yard art in every manner scattered throughout. A blush of beautiful tulips, saffron crocus, parrot's beak, and yellow-purple lady slippers lay in patches here and there. Rare, blue-green jade vines mustached across the top of the late bloom of rhododendron.

The great dwelling was perched atop the highest elevation of any nearby home. Nosy-noisy neighbors nor rising water were a concern here. On a good day, I most likely could throw a rock and hit the lake—a hundred and twenty-five yards or so. Table Lock Lake looked as if it had been beaten down by the hot summer sun. Crocodile-looking rocks and stumps lined its banks. Otherwise, the waves were inviting, and it seemed to be an exultant lake with, "bet you didn't know," kinds of stories to tell.

In simple observation, the home was positioned to view both sunrise and sunset, which made me wonder how long they surveyed the lake to find this perfect view? A road snaked around and vanished down the hill. I assumed it would lead to a beach or boat-slip.

Anglaia nippily made her way to the keypad of the front door and disappeared like a cold spirit manifestation. I stood there on the cobblestone driveway—akin to a five-hundred-pound pumpkin floating in a mud puddle. It was hot—August hot—and it quickly became clear I was overdressed in the foreign church clothes we had purchased late-night yesterday after my welcoming speech. Clothes checked off the long list of items that included a new toothbrush, a bar of bath soap, shampoo, school supplies, and a watch.

Sweat pooled underneath my button-up shirt and slacks. I managed a few undecided steps, kicked off the Sunday slippers, and found pause in a patch of grass, grateful my feet had stopped cooking.

The caravan soon pulled in one after another like an FBI raid. Car doors opened, introducing the click-click of the ladies' high heels and heavier clunk-clunk sounds of the men. There were six cars in all, and the mansion went from zero to twenty people in two minutes—from silence to sounds of indiscernible noise.

The men peeled off and made their way around to the back of the home with loose shorts and flip-flops in tow. I followed as if in a herd of migrating buffalo, feeling I could soon face a crocodile-infested river and be torn to shreds. If only Toozoolee, Berry Alpha, or Berry Omega were here with me, my disposition would naturally move as a more powerful presence. As it was, though, I would have to create a new voice with a collection of strangers that didn't seem to notice I was among them. They shuffled inside to change and grab an iced drink or cold beer.

Mike and Bruce adjusted the pool umbrellas to better shade the area. The mutterings of Mike rode our ears like a bucking bronco. Bruce seemed to take notice of me and asked the typical introductory questions. He lent a nod of welcoming acceptance. His dad, Jacob, the homeowner, was more standoffish and reserved but did send me a halfhearted acknowledgment. He eyeballed me over for cracks and concerns.

"Anglaia," Grandmother said as dishes clanged together, sounding like a busy restaurant.

"Coming," I said.

No sooner did I round the corner into the kitchen, than Mother snatched my cellphone from my hands, like a hawk plucking a fat chicken from the yard. She put it into her purse, and my life was over for the rest of the day. The thoughts of going gangster on her crossed my mind, and I wished she would stop being such a control freak.

"Sarah," Grandmother sweetly said.

"Adamina-Rose, these phones have become like baby pacifiers to these kids these days. She spends hours on this thing. You should see our phone bill," Mother said.

I could tell Melissa was lying in wait with a barrage of support in the form of a bag of words she wanted to beat me with. I knew when they had me cornered, I would pay for giving *Mr. Rocky Wino* a drink of their wine. Not to mention being thrown together with this VeeLee kid. Maybe they had hired him to watch me—to ruin my life. All I knew was their plan wasn't going to work. They sucked, and he sucked louder. Bottom line, I didn't know him at all and didn't *want* to know VonVouge. My world was perfect before he came, and would remain perfect as I did not intend to share my life with him. No, thank you. Not happening.

"Bite me," I said and went outside to sit on Grandfather Jacob's leg. I kissed his sweaty cheek and was poked by stubble that annoyed me further. So, I went back inside. It was too damned hot, anyway. I went to my other room, the one in my grandparents' home, and put on my swimsuit, a cute tank top and shorts. Then I grabbed a towel on my way back outside to cool off in the pool. Just as I was about to peel off my clothes and jump in, my father called to me.

"Anglaia, would you go ask your grandmother for a pair of guest swimming trunks for VeeLee, please?" Father said, making his way outside. He and Mike were the first barelegged old people out in the sun. Father had the garden hose out, cooling the concrete off a bit. I was about to have a massive fit if I had to do one more thing for anyone, especially this stranger who was getting on my nerves without trying.

I rolled my eyes to the stars hidden behind the light of day and back into the house I returned. I grabbed the most ludicrous looking swimming trunks and ancient shirt on the shelf I could find. I swept back onto the scene like an actress in a dramatical play and flung the clothing in the general direction of VonVouge, similar to delivering the mail to Mother. I hoped he might complain so that I could rub his nose in my crappy day with some sharp words.

"Anglaia," Grandfather said. He didn't like me mistreating guests. I wasn't even allowed to address Mike's whiney wiles at Grandfather's place, which I thought was ridiculous. I could have seriously shut him up if they had let me. Grandfather was not much fun when annoyed. The truth was, no one really wanted to be outside—it was effing *hot.* The air-conditioning inside felt awesome, but my beloved grandfather loved being outside, no matter the season. It was the old country boy in him.

Most likely, the reason he paid extra to have cooling elements installed for an especially cold swimming pool. It was an extravagant pool that boasted four fountains spraying from its corners and gold lights that looked like you were swimming in honey at night. I had to admit it was badass. Grandmother would eventually take charge, hopefully before anyone got melanoma or sun-burned, and sequester everyone inside for an early Sunday dinner.

Once VeeLee grabbed his shorts, I said, "You can go into those woods down there and change if you want, foster boy," and pointed.

"Anglaia!" Grandfather groaned.

I surely didn't want Grandfather's belt stretched across my hindquarters. I knew I was pushing his boundaries but could not help it. The light came on inside my head, and I decided to chill. VeeLee was not going to have a seventeen-year-old spanking story to share at Horseshoe High. No sooner did my hostile attitude rapture into an out-of-control drama queen, I—with great effort—transcended into the bloom of a rose, a sweet cheerleading sweetie-pie. I had a Mustdang and smartphone to maintain.

"Sorry, VonVouge," I said. He picked up the swimming clothes and cut his eyes at me as if to say he would dearly love to push me into the pool. We all heard giggles coming from around the corner of the mansion, and at last, my lioness pride had come to my rescue. We were four teenage-girls strong, and for the first time this day, I was getting happy.

The four of us became a brood of rafting ducklings. Mother and Melissa sat poolside, soaking their feet in the opposite side of the pool, enjoying the mist of the fountain. They were chirping away about VeeLee's arrival and how Melissa thought she was going to like the parent role and that he seemed to be a good kid. My girls replied with eww every chance they got.

Being cheerleaders, we did use some of the time to rehearse some new dance moves, jumps, tumbles, and stunting component ideas, which were easier to practice in the water… except when we got water up our nose. It was mostly a gossip session, and we shared matters of great Horseshoe High significance—most of the topics were in whispers and giggles.

VeeLee casually came back outside in the clothes I had hoped would make him look like a giant dork, but for some reason, he made them look cool, "making retro-style popular again" sort of thing. He sat back down in the crooned wrought-iron wickerwork sun chair and fanned his eyes across the pool. Suddenly he drew in a long breath and yanked his shirt off, exposing a lightning bolt scar running down the center of two gorges of large chest muscles. His heavy feet slapped one after the other onto the concrete, sounding like he was wearing scuba flippers.

He ran to the edge of the pool, jumped high into the sky. VeeLee curled into the pike position, touching his toes then straightened back out, entering the water without leaving a splash. This was when I determined it sucked hanging out with cheerleaders. When the pool gave birth to VeeLee's head, my girls clapped and went effin' crazy.

Like a herd of alpha-males, Grandfather, Father, and the other old guys slung their shirts and flip-flops aimlessly, performing cannonballs all around VeeLee. This energized the party and received an even louder ovation—this time, I had to join the vibe. We were all laughing and blabbing away for a time.

An hour or so later, Grandmother called out to us, "Alright, everyone. Time to get cleaned up and have dinner."

VeeLee exited the pool with his dripping wet, youthful, and somewhat muscled-up body. It was clear that he was in good physical shape. He had strong, shredded arms and abs, thick thighs, and a cute smile, according to my girlfriends.

I had never seen my peeps blink their eyes so fast. Each one must have been taking a million photographs of him in their mind. Melissa may have straight hooked VeeLee up. I don't think any of my girls would have a problem introducing and showing him around Horseshoe High. But it sure as hell won't be me.

My mind swirled on the day's events as we made our way back to Mike and Melissa's—my new home. The headlights jutted through the night-covered road, the lay of the land swallowed up by the dark night. Similar to the contrast of my life, only days removed. Melissa listened to Mike justify his previous statements of the long day. As if hearing them for the second time would make them make better sense, it was nothing more than being lashed yet again with his lip whips. Mike was a gladiator in a clown suit, deathly serious about his opinion. Even when he was right, no one wanted to hear it— he could come up with the cure for cancer, but no one would be able to listen long enough to take Mike's mouth serious.

My belly was full of delicious lamb, perfectly cooked over an open fire pit with spices unknown to me, sautéed veggies—dessert was something called pannacotta. It was a sweet vanilla cream with a mushed red berry liquid drizzled in squiggly lines over the top.

It had been a long day, and I was ready for some sleep. Tomorrow, I would see the doctor for my physical first thing in the morning so I could play football. I remembered part of the exam was to drop my pants to check for a hernia. I told myself I would never drop my pants for a man ever again. The thought made me anxious, but I stuffed down the haunt of Weston and knew those days were over forever. I would also meet the team and practice some football tomorrow—so I definitely needed to recharge. The first day of football two-a-days would start—the morning practices were usually more physical, then we had an evening practice filled with summer heat that naturally slowed players down. Hopefully, my new teammates would be worth going to war for and with.

I was back on the football field and getting my old competitive vibe back with my new teammates at Horseshoe High. It was grueling and intense, just as I remembered Hell-Week at Academy High School in K-sea. Morning and evening practice, we called two-a-days, where the inevitable pecking order had to play out—seniors to freshmen, and the loyalty nut-rolls of former teammates deciphered what the face of the new team would look like. Talent and the hunt of victory, its only trump.

    I would not be leading the team as a quarterback, as I hoped. Politics—being the greatest force on earth—had some blond, floppy-haired attorney's kid, Peyton, getting the nod. It didn't take long for my new teammates to inform me that Peyton's dad, Barron Saxxy's, picture was plastered on the back of phonebooks, billboards, and was on every other local TV commercial. The kid did have a pretty good throwing arm with a tight spiral on his long ball, though.

    I knew the playbook, but sitting on the sideline as the second drummer was not an option. I talked with the coaches and switched back to my old hat: defensive free safety, which didn't make Tommy Hogan very happy. He was now benched as my backup. Nothing personal—I didn't know him or owe him. I did the work and trained like a madman. So, I got the job, that's how I looked at it, anyway.

    I missed the faces of my old teammates and the wars we waged together on the football field. My new life was flowing swiftly through my mind, rearranging my thought patterns. My brain was most likely beginning to resemble the Grand Canyon with deep dried-up fissures of no content. It was a simpler life here. An eerie hush consistently swept through the nights. There were few quiet nights back home, and I was immune to the constant sounds of police cars, ambulances, firetrucks, and train horns shredding the silence.

    It was unlike the shrill nights when Mom disappeared for days in a row. I never knew the hour the chaos would return—maybe three o'clock on Tuesday morning escorted by loud, drunken men and women, or maybe tiptoeing to her bed at noon on Sunday. It was always random and unpredictable.

    In my mind, I knew Father Time had been generous. I now had a roof with Mike and Melissa. Each had a job and seemed to have good friends. It was a stable environment. I made the football team and had new shoes with replaceable cleats to play in. I also had a new public library card with a handful of books in my room.

    Even though I was a junior, I felt like I belonged to the freshmen class—easily lost in the maze of hallways and elusive classroom numbers. Initially, the feeling was like large crows trying to fly as fast as possible through miles of thick blackberry bushes—kids bumping into each other and rushing to beat Horseshoe High's tardy bell. Everything seemed like a treasure hunt, weaving through the halls and stairs like deranged, smoked-out honeybees trying to find our classes. After the third day, I was golden, meeting a handful of cool kids, but no Toozoolee yet. My best friend would most likely be unearthed from the football team.

    I was leaning toward Rusty, our middle linebacker, but he chewed tobacco. It was a habit that disgusted me as much as smoking, alcohol or popping pills. I didn't know if I had it in me to tell the *Field of Snow* story to another soul. It never seemed to help my mom much. I thought it should be so clear to everyone that we were a sack of chemicals contained by skin, and when you added a habitual toxin to the mix, life would just become more difficult. People who were not altered and controlled by such would always have the advantage in life.

    Rusty was short with sawed-off tree trunks for legs and arms nearly as big. He hit like a tank on jet fuel and went full speed on every play. On the field, there was the meanness of a bully when it came to the football play of Rusty. If he were able, Rusty would send our entire opponent's offensive team to the emergency room. He was a rogue headhunter who loved contact as much as I did. We seemed to click when talking in the weight-room.

    Rusty could actually hold an intelligent conversation and seemed to be dealing with similar single parent issues as most kids did these days. The lack of loyalty, the lies, the control, the hate was all balled up into one giant childhood issue the universe would have to settle out later. Parents doubled as egoic mountain goats who pushed their kids off the cliff first with a fiery sea of hellish rock to catch them.

Our first game was coming up on Friday. We would be underdogs as the seniors that graduated last year took most of the team off the field. The quarterback, running back, two-star receivers, and seven of the eleven defensive players graduated and were gone. From what I could see, I doubted we would win many games this year. We were good, but the passion and talent I remembered in Academy Highschool just weren't there.

I had noticed Anglaia and her swimming pool friends on the sideline practicing their cheer routines, while intently sizing up the mounds of new meat tackling each other on the football field. Funny how we tried to look tough wearing what looked like ballerina tights. I had mentioned I had already met Anglaia to a few teammates, and it wasn't long before chatter echoed up and down the sideline. I think most thought I was full of "cow crap," a term foreign to me until I arrived here in Queenfield. It seemed they thought I was looking for attention, living in a fantasyland or something.

I knew for most teenagers our age, words like love and acceptance could be stretched into funky meanings. Although Anglaia outwardly expressed great dislike for me, facts were facts. We knew each other. I sat with her and her family in church. I rode in her car. I spent hours with her and her friends in our swimsuits. And I knew her immediate family by name. The boys at school didn't need to know all that, though. I'd let it ride, let the cards of fate reveal themselves naturally.

Just as the smile formed across my face at the notion, Anglaia and a trio of cheerleaders were coming in like a jumbo jet for an emergency landing. Anglaia's body language needed no words. She was not happy, pointing her cellphone in my direction as she came. Most of the team had no problem having Horseshoe High cheerleaders invading our sidelines. They were all beautiful, fresh-picked hotties in bloom.

"Listen, foster boy! I'm not your damn answering service. You need to get a phone. I'm not your cab either. Tell *Melissa* to get you a car, too, while she's at it. My mother told me to give you a ride home because *Melissa* forgot about a dental appointment. I am not giving you a ride, foster boy. Last time I'm telling you," Anglaia said. She was pulled away before I could respond.

Some of the guys were laughing as if they had never laughed before. For the lack of a better idea, I laughed, too. The girls were lined up like a band of wild west renegades ready for a shootout. It was said Anglaia was still angry at her ex, Danielle. Anglaia noticed we were looking her way and sent the middle finger. Beau Panderson, Danielle's now boyfriend, sent Aglaia the middle finger back. Without pause, she doubled down and flipped Beau off with both hands.

She huddled her squad together and was in coaching mode. They, all together, said, "Beau and VeeLee suck!" Pointed their butts our direction, and in some absurd rhythm, shook them at us. It was the weirdest damn thing I think I had ever seen. Then they flipped us off again and giggled as if they had taught us a great lesson and had put us in our place. The cheer squad pulled Anglaia toward the stands to résumé their practice. There was no doubt we were acquainted with each other now.

The "foster boy" comment was sharp, but Lara London had taught me how to tie the hands of time together with silence and space in these awkward situations. Damn, I really do miss my librarian right about now. Beau had his own reasons, but I sent him a silent thank you by nodding my helmet at him, which he returned. Beau played right defensive end.

I could already imagine the improvisation to come at Horseshoe high—unruly rumors that would breed into a swamp of lies. Lies that would continue to give birth to more rock-star offspring: Anglaia Clintin verses the K-sea Kid, VeeLee VonVouge. Which would most likely grow into a huge distraction I could live without. Funny how I didn't even have to say a single word. Not to mention, I was informed she had ties to the Glue Crew and thought it might be in my best interest to have some fingernail polish remover on hand at all times. This could be a sticky and frustrating beginning to my junior year if I weren't careful.

Chapter 10

Anglaia roars

"CAN YOU BELIEVE MY MOTHER? SHE wants me to give the new kid a ride home after football practice," I said to Jennifer.

"Right. We should do your Boogie-Woogie-Shake-n-Bake-Duck-Butt dance. Give him a Horseshoe High welcome," she said.

"You girls with me—it's Beau and VeeLee," I said. We then performed my grandfather's dance—turned around and all together and cheered, "Beau sucks," another dance, turned around, "VeeLee sucks," followed by another dance and a flock of middle fingers.

It did make me feel much better, but we were loud-mouth busted. Coach Brock, our coach, came through the gate at that very moment, escorted by the head football coach, coach Duke Donetea. She was very disappointed and ripped us a new one, followed by twenty minutes of running bleachers. Of course, I really didn't care about one thing she had to say, although many of the girls rolled their eyes at me.

I was half-done with high school. Horseshoe High knew my name without question, and I was now on the front line, cheering—basically for myself. There were many girls in surrounding high schools who wanted passage into my tribe. This visibility was priceless.

Seeing Beau on the football field reminded me of Danielle and that she would be giving birth to a child soon. She would soon have baby lips on her nipples instead of mine. I had a feeling she had to be missing me. Hell, Beau and Danielle were both cheaters, and I hoped they ended up hating each other as much as I hated them. Sometimes being a positive role model, being cheerful, and cheering was hard to do.

Practice was soon over, and a couple of girls hopped in my car to go for a burger. Of course, we passed VeeLee walking, and I laid on the horn and waved my finger as we passed. He tipped his ballcap when a horn from a truck blared behind me. It was Beau and Ray who had cut across traffic, jumped the curb in his monster truck, then stopped and picked VonVouge up.

"Losers," I said. I turned the bass up on my radio and vibrated down Dazzlefield Street. We all laughed without a care in the world, until I pulled into my driveway a few hours later.

All I could do was scream... so I did. I could not believe my eyes. There he was. Foster boy was sitting on my damned porch. I stomped the brakes making the tires squeal and parked my car.

"You are really starting to piss me off, VonVouge. What the hell are you doing at my home?" I said. He didn't reply, so I stormed through the front door and noticed Melissa sitting with my mother. "Melissa, do you have to bring the foster boy here when you come," I said.

"Now is not the time Anglaia," Mother said.

"Of course, you always say, 'Be quite!' And I say, 'Bite me.' Look. I don't want that kid in my home. Church and school is bad enough."

"It's okay, Sarah. Anglaia, Mike's mother has died," Melissa said.

"Oh no, Melissa. I'm sorry to hear that," I said and began to walk out of the room, leaving them to their glasses of wine.

"VeeLee will be staying with us for a couple of weeks until Melissa and Mike return from Basston," Mother said.

I stopped dead in my tracks and spun around to face them, "Hell-no-he's-not," I said
assured without hesitation.

"You'll be taking VeeLee to school with you and bringing him home from school as well," Mother continued unfazed.

"Hell-no-I'm-not," I said and yelled obscenities all the way to my room. I wanted and needed a solution to this gigantic problem fast. I couldn't think of one of my friends who wouldn't want to be the first to bring this crazy-ass life of mine to the masses at school. I cranked my stereo up in my room and tried to clear my thoughts. After the football episode just hours ago, VeeLee riding in my car for two weeks was more than I could take. I had to call my grandmother. I turned down the music and placed the call.

"This is Adamina-Rose. Sorry I missed your call. Please leave a message," her recording said.

Beep. "Grandmother, call immediately. I'm in *hell*," I said. I threw my phone like a lump of hot charcoal at the window and cranked the music back up. I could just imagine the looks and comments I'd be receiving at school when the foster boy hopped in and out of my car twice a day. Maybe I could convince Father to pay for a cab for two weeks, and he could take it out of my inheritance.

"*Not even playing,*" I said to myself over and over again. The longer I thought about it, the more traumatized I became. I had to talk to Father about this before I required a prescription of valium. This must be how day one of insanity begins. My normal life might just be over. Father usually had a good answer when Grandmother was unavailable.

"Well, Bruce, I think you should know that Anglaia seemed upset with me today at football practice," VeeLee said as I rounded the corner. I stood there waiting for the foster boy to go ahead and cash-in and take my father away, too, like some low budget, twilight-zone Hollywood flop. I glared hate as intensely as I ever had in my entire life. Father was getting too cozy with the son he and Mother could never have. It wasn't long before I squeezed my face so tight that the blood left my lips altogether, no doubt projecting a bluish-gray distortion of pure ugliness—a zombie cheerleader.

Apparently, the doctor had to remove half of Mother's innards after I was born due to endometriosis—a topic she and Melissa had a million conversations about over wine. I lost my phone privilege for a week after telling them they could shove my toy dolls up their butt and give birth all they wanted. Neither could see the humor. Don't think my parents liked the fact that Mother's baby-making days were over.

"VonVouge..." I growled deeply while grinding my teeth.

"Hey, honey," Father said.

"I need to seriously talk to you about all this. *In private,*" I said sharply to my father. I had to figure out a way to chase foster boy off my planet. Earth was not big enough for us both. He needed to get on the space shuttle and go back to Mars or at least back to K-sea and get far, far away from me. I grabbed my father's hand and dragged him through the house, leaving VeeLee in the kitchen with nothing better to do than look stupid.

We passed through the living room. Mike had arrived and was teared-up, huddled with wine and sobbing women. Mother and Melissa loved crying together, anyway. In the past, I would just leave the nonsense the moment the boohooing sparked the first tear. Most often, the topic they cried over was utterly ridiculous. I skipped the jury and went straight to the judge, my father.

"Father, I beg you to help me!"

"Anglaia, VeeLee does not mean you any harm, honey. It's your thoughts. You are safe," Father said.

"What about my reputation at Horseshoe High. Does that matter?" I said with, of course, a little loving daughter spin and dramatics.

The solution my father proposed was not much better. I didn't know which was worse, VeeLee riding with me or with one of my parents. Each scenario would surely initiate scandal at Horseshoe High. The cab idea was flushed down the toilet immediately.

If I took VeeLee, we would be deemed a couple. If my parents took him, my peers would definitely start sniffing around. If it got out that he was staying at my house for two weeks, I would be tortured by everyone forever. Yeah, not good. It was a huge matter. Perhaps the universe would send me a great answer through the radio. Music had been helpful in the past. I told my father I had to think on the matter more and headed to my room and slammed the door.

I really needed a Catholic saint to sequester, the Big Guy in the Sky was giving me the silent treatment again. My life was making my hormones run full speed down a jacked-up trail in the woods and sending every species of insect to sting, bite, and torment me. My emotions were on high alert. I could really use any available human to share some of this pain with.

Soon my grandmother's ringtone began playing on my phone. I hurried to answer it and said, "Grandmother..." I could say nothing more and began crying. She tried to convince me that VeeLee had no choice in the matter, and I was being very insensitive, which bothered her to the point she was considering sending my grandfather to have a talk with me. She said I should adopt a kinder heart and not refer to VeeLee as foster boy again.

She also informed me that she and Grandfather also needed me to house-sit next weekend. They were headed to Key-la-fornee to sell her business, while a construction project was underway on their mansion. There were just too many valuables that could not be left unattended. Yay for me, another hidden cost for a Mustdang. It was a talk that pretty much summed up the worst day of my life. I was exhausted and so ready for sleep to carry me away to a perfect kingdom where I was treated like a true queen and in charge of *everything*!

Scream one woke me, and I was doing the countdown when my door frame was highlighted by light too soon. Before scream two came from my parents' room, there was knocking at my door, and VeeLee's voice rattled into my room.

"Anglaia…" VeeLee said.

"Effing go to bed. Mother is having her nightmares," I said. My father's voice soon filled the air in the background, and like a snuffed-out candle, the home went dark, quiet, and sleep-ready again. *Mr. Rocky Wino* had whispered to me, but I didn't listen and bring him his bottle of wine. VeeLee now had *more* personal information. I clenched my fists tight, gritted my teeth as hard as I could, and grumbled, "VonVouge…"

Morning sun washed across my eyelids, bringing me back to life. Father and VeeLee picked at their breakfast plates of ham and egg, looking at me with wanting eyes. I had slept on the matter and thought it best to become a foreign exchange student, which made Father snicker. I sat down to eat and told VeeLee he could ride with me. It was the most sickening thing I had uttered since the day I told Danielle to get out of my bed and my life. Breakfast left a rusty taste in my mouth as if I had sucked on old water pipes. "Come on, foster boy. Let's go!" I tossed in a piece of gum, and we hopped into my car.

I turned the key, and the Mustdang grumbled into a purr. VeeLee buckled up, and I put the car in gear to drive myself to my very own execution. High school kids could be ruthless when it came to such matters. I should know. I would have been one of them. My heart and thoughts were racing like a cheetah being chased by sounds of gunfire. Every second seemed to have the power to kill me. The closer we got to the school, the more nervous and anxious I was getting.

"I have an idea," VeeLee said.

"Bite me, VonVouge… I do not care about you or your ideas, foster boy," I said. It was an instinctive response before I had a second to think about what I was saying. I could almost feel Grandfather waiting at school to have the talk Grandmother threatened me with last night on the phone.

We drove another three minutes or so—VeeLee sitting like an expressionless statue. The look of him snuck into the corner of my eye and danced around a bit in my mind. The morning light defined his masculine and raw shape. I shook off the boy thoughts, which made my brain feel like cubes of jelly inside my skull. "Okay… I'm listening. What's your idea?"

"I don't mind walking from that gas station to Horseshoe High. You could drop and pick me up there. No big deal," VeeLee said and hooked a thumb at the gas station that was coming into view.

"Seriously?"

"Seriously," he said.

"Yep, that'll work, foster boy," I said.

"Is Rebubblelick's football team very good?" VeeLee said as we neared the gas station.

"We beat them last year. Who knows about you boys?"

I pushed down on the brakes and said, "get out." *No time for small talk*, I thought to myself. A calmness came over me, and I was now relaxed for the first time all morning.

The entire school was getting pumped up for Friday's football game. No one was asking questions about VeeLee riding with me. For a change, not starting the week off in high drama was making me happy.

The simplest solution dissolved what I had made into a huge nightmare of a problem. I had seen him in passing twice in the hallway and couldn't help but notice how in control and mature he carried himself. Everyone was critically judging everyone. A prerequisite to high school life in general. Winners and losers, success or failure.

We all had to learn to manage each other's teenage immaturity. There were nearly two thousand students in Horseshoe High. VeeLee was fitting in, and he seemed to be assembling his new tribe effortlessly. His personality had a strong magnetism to it, attracting and connecting to all forms of folk up and down the economic ladder. Mine was locked in and most likely would never change. I would not be wallowing around in pigpens for anyone. Not my style.

Sharing classes and the hallways of school was one thing, but seeing him at my home on a daily basis was very annoying. Bumping into him on a bathroom run, dinner, or seeing him chumming it up with my parents really ticked me off. I had never spent this amount of time with any dude before. Not to mention, I didn't even like this foster dude in the first place. It was Thursday evening, and Father had forgotten his cellphone in his office at Top Chops.

Foster boy was all giddy to go with Father to get it, which I was sure he would get the grand tour and the full, from the ground up, story of our family business. Two hours later, they returned. I was pissed and made it known. "Flat-tire, out-of-gas, fishing trip… it doesn't take two hours to get a cellphone! What the hell? VonVouge, I'm about to get physical with your ass," I said.

"You know you're always welcome to come with us," Father said.

"I'm with that kid more than I am with anyone else in the world. What makes you think I want to spend one more minute with him than I have to, Father?" I flounced to my room and slammed the door.

It was Friday, and us cheerleaders were center stage. I was on the front line in the gymnasium where we stirred our classmates into a frenzy during the pep rally. The football team was introduced, and for the sake of losing my voice or straining every muscle I possessed for nothing, I hoped we would defeat Rebubblelick Highschool. Luckily, it was a home-opener, and half of Queenfield would fill the stands. We did have great school spirit and tons of community support in most of our extracurricular activities.

And so, it was a victory with the final score twenty-eight to thirteen. VeeLee blocked an extra point and made some great tackles, but the star of the game was definitely Peyton Saxxy, our quarterback. Three touchdowns in his first game as our team captain. Ray scooped up a fumble and ran it in for a touchdown at the end of the third quarter. It was what we cheerleader's practiced our butts off to do—inspire boys to play like men. Good job, and you're welcome!

Chapter 11

VeeLee eyes murder

SUNDAY AT THE ASSEMBLAGE, PASTOR DOM imparted a message out of the book of Job about how mankind really had no way to understand the intelligence of God, no matter how much wisdom they had acquired. It was very interesting as he lay out the debate. Of course, I had never gone to a real church before. I had only renderings of shade-tree well-wishers, usually drunk, to go on when it came to religion. I listened intently to his message and thought I might even read the book of Job someday.

Anglaia was quiet today. We rode with Bruce and Sarah to her grandparents'. She didn't feel like driving. After church, we made our way through Bronson and down the curvy country roads like sober civilized people. Bruce pulled us into Jacob and Adamina-Rose's driveway, where a construction crew had equipment strewn haphazardly all over the property.

I could not imagine doing a facelift on what I felt was a flawless and beautiful entrance. We stayed outside where I posed as one of the guys, and Jacob explained to Bruce, his son, the details of the remodeling effort. The renovation goal was to create a sweeping view of the lake and make it easier to witness more of nature. The natural sunlight would support more indoor plant life and make the home a healthier space to live according to Adamina-Rose, meaning it was her idea. The sooner the project was completed, the better off everyone involved would be.

There was a convoy of trucks and trailers hauling every form of machinery. On every work truck door was a cartoon of a smiling hammer that was winking its big cartoon eye, snapping its fingers, with a caption that said, "Let's get Crackin'."

The construction contractor Harry McCrackin of McCrackin's Construction, Inc. and two of his hired hands were making their way toward us. Harry had essentially built the town of Bronson and every notable home on Table Lock Lake. He was the best and semiretired. It took a pretty good payday to pique his attention, something Adamina-Rose could do in a whisper. From the stories I had overheard so far, she loved to spend money.

Two huge forty-foot-long, ten-foot-high, and three-foot-thick crates packed in foam guarded the curved glass walls imported from Europe. Each was being unloaded from their own semi-truck flatbed trailer. They were expensive, fancy glass Adamina-Rose had read about in a magazine—apparently, a giant computer corporation headquarters was built using the exact glass.

The mansion updates would be as statuesque as the Shangri La and would undoubtedly taunt the neighbors into spending some renovation money as well. Especially true when it came to Lonnie and Meryl Nitzenslobber. I had heard various stories about this couple who lived next door. All were horrible and almost unbelievable that people in million dollar homes could give the ghetto folks of my old neighborhood a good name.

Jacob had stated he would need Anglaia to house-sit over the weekend. They had a trusted family friend there during the week, but the couple was not available over the weekend. The whole situation was totally unexpected and time sensitive. They had received an offer on Adamina-Rose's financial business and thought it best to sell—right now!

They had to go to Key-la-fornee to tie up loose ends and officially retire. Sarah was asked to pick them up on Tuesday and drive them from Bronson to the Queenfield airport. They would be back Monday evening sometime depending on flight delays and that sort of thing. Her grandparents would require a ride back home as they rued leaving their luxury vehicles stored in airport parking. Jacob had had horrible luck in doing so over the years.

We lost our second football game on Friday versus hometown rival Jendale High School. They most likely had the best quarterback, receiving-core tandem in the state of Mizzeree. They were receiving tons of publicity, spotlighting their talent and potential of making professional teams someday. College scouts were everywhere. I knew they were the same scouts who would be watching my boys in K-sea. We still had another year to get redemption. The studs of Jendale were seniors and ready for the next level for sure.

We were coached up and had the game in our hands. Everyone in attendance could sense the upset. All we had to do was make one more play, and we would win. They were on their eighteen-yard line with three seconds on the clock. Ray tipped the ball, and I dove for the interception. Number eighty-two had the better angle and caught the ball right in front of me. I quickly collected myself off the ground. Ray and I gave chase but could not catch number eighty-two before he dove into Jendale's end-zone. Eighty-two stood back up and raised the ball high into the air. We lost the game.

The locker room was somber and funeral like, as was every loss. Tonight, we were on the wrong side of today's daydreams. Number eighty-two's dreams had come true. He had won the game for his team.

I had been involved in some explosive collisions. My right butt cheek was deeply bruised. I landed on someone's helmet going full speed during a tackle, and it felt like a cannonball had been transplanted there. I was sore, and it hurt to walk.

The bed here at Bruce's was the most comfortable I had ever slept in. All I wanted to do was stay here in bed and stare at the ceiling fan—block out every thought.

The rumble of Anglaia's engine fired up, and the Mustdang backed out of the garage. She was most likely on her way to her grandparents' to house-sit. Soon the noise transitioned back into the hum of the ceiling fan. My thoughts morphed to the curvy Oatzark Mountain roads the Mustdang would be soon roaring around. It was pointless to remain in bed now, no matter how comfortable. I took a shower and met up with the smell of bacon and Bruce in the kitchen.

Bruce said he had a skeleton-crew working a half-day this Saturday. There was a large expedited order that had to be delivered to an uppity wedding reception. I could feel where the tug was taking the conversation, and I volunteered to help. I doubted he really wanted to leave me idle in his home. Sarah had yet to show herself. I noted her absence and left it at that. She may have ridden off with Anglaia for all I knew. Most of the morning, we waited in Bruce's office at *Top Chops,* where we shared life stories.

We imparted a great deal more of ourselves than I imagined possible. We clicked. We could laugh and be open. I told him of my dad and his military service, and the internal war in his mind that he lost shortly after returning from the wars in Iraq and Afghanistan. He told me of his uncle, who died in Vietnam, and how he and his father, Jacob, loved and supported the military men and women who served our country.

Somewhat kindred spirits emerged. He was a good, honest man. I had intended to address him as Mr. Clintin but was stopped the first time I did. He asked to be called by his first name. Bruce was one of the rare men, like a few teachers and football coaches I had found respect for. The only difference was I didn't owe him an academic or athletic effort. Very refreshing, but nowhere close to Lara.

I asked him about his wife, Sarah's, screaming, and at first blush might have crossed the question and answer line. A deliberate pause and then the explanation I could hardly believe. It was a childhood memory that she did everything humanly possible to suppress and forget. Even the best mental health providers had yet to rid her of the nightmares. Every conceivable psychological approach to allow her to accept and move on with her life had failed.

Sarah's childhood seemed to paint outside the lines of normal. A blurred identity shrouded in secrets and shadows that were shared by her daughter, Anglaia. These narratives always made me want to deliver my *Field of Snow* story, to take a new path of thinking and change their life experience. I'd always be reluctant to think about changing people into the version I imagined would be better. They'd hopefully get there someday—or not.

Bruce would drive the box truck filled with Top Chops's choice cuts of meat to the wedding reception. After we loaded the truck, he released the two workers to enjoy the rest of their weekend with a little extra pay. He thanked them repeatedly as if they had saved his life or something. We arrived at the twenty-five-year-old wedding castle thirty minutes ahead of schedule. It was a lovely structure dreamed up to make money.

Once on the castle property, we followed the plastic signs with "Catering" in block letters above a red arrow that pointed us the way we needed to go. Bruce backed the box truck up to the double door, and we unloaded the iced-down meat stored in huge white coolers. They were heavy, and my bruised butt cheek had me limping as if one leg was a foot longer than the other. After the delivery, we switched vehicles at Top Chops, where Bruce handed me fifty dollars and thanked me.

He asked if I might be interested in working part-time for him and maybe do some odd jobs on weekends so I might earn my own vehicle. I had to look out my window for a moment before I could steady my voice enough to say it sounded good to me. Like a foreign language translator, he made sense of the words I was thinking when he went on to say there would be more hours when the football season was over, which had me looking out my window again.

We pulled into Bruce's home at the same time as Sarah, who pulled in behind us, answering the question of her going to Bronson with Anglaia. She must have had other things going on.

The evening was winding down, and I had it in my mind to go to my room and try to finish reading a very interesting book on cellular respiration and the role of the mitochondria when Bruce's cellphone blared with the sound of a tornado siren. Oddly enough, it was Anglaia's ringtone. "Anglaia," he said and then answered.

"Hey, Daughter," Bruce said. He sat down and entered into conversation with Anglaia. I sat down and quietly tried not to listen.

She was freaking out. The entire front of the home had been removed to emplace the rolled glass walls. It wasn't the safe place she remembered. All the beautiful shrubs and bushes had been removed. The ugly, deep, muddy ruts left by the tires of the heavy equipment seemed to have hurt the ground. The entire place seemed to be crying and in pain.

She felt like something might get her in the night. The wind was blowing directly into the home, making the tarps sound like someone constantly crinkling up empty soda cans. She said she felt like she was sitting outside in a two-thousand-dollar leather lawn-chair with no door to close. The darkness made the stars shine brighter than she remembered stars could shine, especially when viewed from the inside of a mansion. It was the first time she felt alone and scared at her grandparent's home.

Bruce somehow knew that if he said yes to her request to allow a couple of girlfriends to come over to keep her company, he'd be back at three in the morning with a handful of freaked-out teenagers telling ghost stories. He summoned Sarah from the study, where they determined we'd *all* go to Bronson and camp-out with Anglaia. Sarah needed twenty minutes to wrap up a few more sentences on her thesis paper, and we would navigate her way.

"Thanks, Father. Love you," I overheard Anglaia say. It wasn't long before we pulled into what looked like a condemned disaster zone.

Every manner of nylon tarp whipped in the wind, and Anglaia had every light turned on. The huge castle doors were on four-by-fours and laid flat on the east side lawn, doubling as tombstones in the artificial moonlight. With the face of the home cut off, it appeared the McCrackin Construction crew was in a hurry to get home and neglected to clean up before they left. Bruce made it known to me there'd be a conversation with Harry in the morning concerning the matter.

Anglaia visibly relaxed the moment we arrived. She smiled a sweet smile at her father and flipped me off with her middle finger. It made Bruce and I grin. She was serious about both greetings. All became right in her world for the moment. We settled in various rooms for the night. It did feel sort of weird not having a front door to lock. That was one of my primary concerns in K-sea—a survival pattern fixed in my mind that I doubted would ever change.

In the K-sea projects, we had door and window checkers—crackheads and other crazy opportunists who would dart into someone's unlocked door or window, grab anything that could be pawned for drug money and dash off. Most often, the residents were home during the intrusion. The perpetrator was usually highly stoned and didn't plan on getting caught.

The law was harsh on home invasions, but they got away with it more often than not in low-rent areas of the city. It was my practice to always check the doors and windows when we returned home. I looked under beds for a body and closets for feet. I wouldn't be able to relax or sleep until I did. Here in the country, the feeling was not the same. It could have been that Bruce was here. Having a real man near was oddly comforting.

It was an abrupt Sunday morning wakeup. The construction crew shattered the silence by cranking on the generator and moving heavy machinery around. After being rudely awakened, we all staggered in an aggravated one-legged march to the kitchen to collect ourselves. Sarah wanted to go to *The Assemblage* and hear a divine message. It was an easy choice for me to volunteer to stay behind and watch over the place. When Sarah said, "It's not your responsibility, VeeLee. You don't have to go to church, but a Clintin will be staying behind, too. Anglaia, do you want to go to church or stay here? Otherwise, your father can stay; it really doesn't matter to me," Sarah said.

Anglaia seemed to weigh the advantages and disadvantages and elected not to get dressed or leave her father alone with me. She rarely had a choice in the matter. "I'll stay here," she said as if making a huge family sacrifice. "But that Harry guy creeps me out, Mother! Maybe it's his name?"

Bruce had just walked back through the hole in the house, midstream of our conversation, and thought it better if I stayed with Anglaia. It felt good gaining the Clintins' confidence. "Me and ol' foster boy! Yay…" Anglaia said.

"*Anglaia* Clintin! Maybe you *should* go to church with me. Geez, child!" Sarah instantaneously said.

Harry was giving his crew a *good* morning meltdown type of butt chewing for leaving the place in shambles. Bruce told us that Harry looked like he had been smoking some seriously strong marijuana, as his eyes were bloodshot and swollen. For some reason, he felt Bruce should know that his fiancée Sofia had broken off their engagement and had left him with only two months to go before the wedding. Harry wasn't doing well with the thought of being single or about losing the woman he loved. Harry would not have time to collect himself, as the contract stated no days off until completion, which was to be a fourteen-day project.

Bruce and Sarah showered, dressed, and hopped into the Hummer headed to church. The taillights soon blinked out of sight, the occupants not to be seen again for a couple of hours. Anglaia and I had gone to our respective space in the mansion for approximately twenty-five minutes or so when we found the need to reunite. We could hear Harry yelling at someone. We looked at each other, and Anglaia put her index finger over her lips, shushing me, then curled her other index finger, directing me to follow her toward Harry's voice.

"I killed her! I killed Sofie," he blared to the listener on his phone. Our eyes flung open wide, and I read Anglaia's exaggerated lips silently say, "*What the eff?*" I just shook my braced face to the poisonous words booming around in my ears. We listened to the confession for a little longer. When Harry said he had never seen something so utterly mangled, we quickly tiptoed to Anglaia's room to let out the air we held tightly in our stomachs.

It was if we had seen Sofie die in person, giving us the feeling we could be next. There was panic in our blood. Christopher's heart was drumming wildly inside my chest. I closed the door quietly so that we might make soft sounds with one another. I did not intend to alert a killer, noting to myself that his preferred method of killing was death-by-mangling. We had to exercise great caution.

"My parents' cellphones will be turned off at church, so I think we should call the police," Anglaia said. It was the second time she opted for my opinion in the same week. On this occasion, I had her absolute full attention.

"I need to think a minute," I said. We made our way to the window and watched Harry's mannerisms and nonverbal communications. He was visibly not acting normal. He still had his phone pressed to the side of his head, throwing his free arm around in the air as if scolding the sun for being too bright. He would take a few steps one direction, stop, turn in an unpredictable direction, take a few more steps, pause, talk some more, and then do it all over again.

For reasons I could not understand, his workers did not seem phased and kept working. They had to be hearing all this, as well. It was as if Anglaia and I were watching the dance of a mad spirit—something only we were able to see. His workers had most likely become immune to his antics and were more interested in their paycheck.

I, on the other hand, had heard enough. I snatched my cellphone off the nightstand and looked at Harry one last time. VeeLee cocked his eyes up into the left limit of their sockets and nodded his head in agreement.

"911, what is your emergency." the operator said.

"Yes, it is," I answered through the noise of tractors rumbling in the background.

I told the 911 operator the confession we had witnessed Harry share on the phone. She took down my name, phone number, and asked if we felt we were in danger. "Not at the moment! Should I call when we're being mangled?" I said sarcastically and looked at VeeLee, who focused his gaze outside, his muscles on high alert. She said she would notify the sheriff's office and to stay by the phone. "Yes, ma'am. We will," I said.

Deputy Sheriff Travis Hartley, stuck on weekend duty, soon called back and listened to my account. He sounded reluctant but said he was on his way out and would get to the bottom of it. I called both of my parents' cellphones and left a high drama message. It would be at least an hour before the church service would be over, and their cellphones turned back on.

VeeLee and I would most likely have to put this criminal away ourselves. Deputy Hartley's police car soon crept into the driveway. I was surprised to see no lights, siren, squealing tires, nor backup. *Thank God we weren't being tortured. Don't they know my grandparents are super-wealthy and that their precious granddaughter might be in harm's way? What the eff!*

"Should we go out?" I said.

Harry was now contorting his entire body as if possessed by every soul hell had to offer. The deputy was not backing down nor intimidated in the least bit. We watched the argument from the safety of my bedroom window, and thought it better to stay put just in case Harry went crazy, pulled out a gun and shot everyone.

"He will come and get us when it's time," VeeLee said.

I was completely freaking out. VeeLee, on the other hand, remained calm and collected. I don't know exactly why, but I slapped foster boy in the back of the head, a bit harder than I expected to—this had to be his fault somehow. He needed to know I still harbored animosity toward his intrusion into my life. He just wrinkled his forehead, squinted his eyes in confusion, and hastily reverted back to focusing on what was unfolding outside.

The color of Deputy Hartley's face turned a robust red, and his voice soon soared above Harry's. He physically turned Harry around, flipped out his handcuffs to secure his captive, and placed Harry in the back of the police car. The engine of the patrol car started, and soon they drifted down the road.

It could have been Clintin politics or that my story was quickly validated upon questioning Harry. It was strange, though, not to be asked one question. Even weirder, the workers simply went back to work as if no big deal.

"What just happened, foster boy?" I said.

"Uhm… Good question. Maybe he confessed?"

Mother soon called, and I told her that the sheriff's department just hauled Harry off for murdering his ex-fiancée. She said Father was hurrying. They were twenty minutes out and would be here as soon as possible.

Thank God she wasn't in her college closet this time. It was nice to have a little motherly support for a change.

It was a wonder the wheels had not come off the car. Father was driving like I expected the sheriff's office too. I ran out the door and raced into his open arms as if he had just returned from a foreign war or something.

Chapter 12

Lara London whistles away

I HAD KEPT CLOSE TABS ON VEELEE, AND HE seemed to be adjusting to his environment in Queenfield rather well. Mike and Melissa had been in our program for three years. Due to their ages—late thirties—they were not eligible for infant placement, which disqualified them from being able to adopt but were qualified to become foster parents.

The couple had been scrutinized in every possible way. Inception into the FBI or DELTA Force would have been easier as it tested the individual. When you had to pass as a married couple, the above candidate courses would be considered a practice exercise. There was a great celebration of black suits and white ballroom dresses when they earned their Nonagon parenthood accreditation. The Matches had no idea who any of the people in the room were, but they danced like bigshots anyway, as they should.

The inception ceremony was held in Washaton-D-sea. From there, they would be flown to the mock Nonagon to meet the Nine Kings' representatives. Mike and Melissa's induction was not taken lightly. It was the most classified program in the world. If successful, they would retire in two years with essentially anything money could buy—a seven-figure payoff, zero taxes for the rest of their lives, and a phone call away from the solution to any imaginable problem life could throw their way.

The Matches would be on board for maintenance roles throughout VeeLee's college years as needed—mostly for holiday mental and emotional support. If they failed, the ramifications would be a low-key vacation where the Swiss Alps might gobble them up.

I was watching the Matches from a distance, a condition of my employment. The Nine Kings of the Nonagon were my life's purpose. I had figuratively been promoted to "watcher" in the chain of command, cloaked in librarian attire. Watchers were placed at every level of government all around the world and had their own structure and hands in everything. The shadow deep state government always trumped the puppets we had placed into elected office positions. My loftier goal was to become the first female Nonagon queen ever. The ancient model established over a thousand ago was not intended for a woman. Times had changed. I wanted my name to be written down into the most ultimate directory on earth. There was no such thing as good enough at this level—you had to be great enough.

I had informed the purple cloud of my full intent from day one. I wanted to change the world's consciousness into a noble domain of fair play and joyful existence. Not a fairytale utopia, but to lessen all peoples' continuous stress from birth to death. The taxation system would be first on my list. The only true way to make sweeping changes was to be on the inside of the Deep State. It had gotten back to me—mostly through retiring librarians looking for a bold exit—that I might tone down the badass persona as it made me come off as bitchy. They'd usually receive a "whatever" wink as I knew my confidence was intimidating. Courage never caters to wishy-washy wonders—such thoughts gave me the heebie-jeebies.

If nothing else, my second dream goal would be to meet or see an actual king—to see and go inside the Nonagon. It was said to be the size of nine Pentagon's stacked one atop the other, being nine-sided, of course.

A visit to the Nonagon would be the "x" spot on a treasure map for me. Its location would always remain secret, but to step foot inside would be worth all the hard, cranial work. I was always digging for answers to this great mystery of mine. Some accounts stated the structure was built above ground in such eloquence and splendor that only heaven itself could rival it. I had arranged some snippets in my mind and would dare not put most to paper, or a hard drive for that matter.

If I were to tell people that the Holy Grail was located in the Nonagon, they would think I was ten kinds of crazy. That the power source that once provided energy throughout the pyramids of Egypt was now essentially powering the world, thanks to Moses and Tesla's sneaky selves.

There were only two ways to gain entrance into the Nonagon in person. First was to be a sitting king, his wife, and one child, or his replacement when dead. The second was to be on the king's staff. Each selected one hundred of the top people in the world, and once incepted, it was a lifelong commitment—a lifestyle where everything you desired was brought to you according to the records I unearthed. Every century or so, a few leaks did occur, mostly from family members who managed to leave the Nonagon before the policy of vacations was changed. Some found ways to tell tales of what they had experienced. Most all information had been captured and destroyed to include the information I had managed to find.

Just before World War II, the biggest recorded leak occurred, where the K-9 code talk used by the Nine Kings of the Nonagon was uncovered. K-9 was then introduced into the military to classify war dogs. The media never put the leak together. The homophone of canine took off and was spread into the civilian police force. The Nine Kings of the Nonagon had been cloaked till the end of time. In the last thirty years, technology was so good that it was an effortless task to track down and destroy nearly all records.

Tracking genealogy bloodlines was one of my specialties. Once I had a person's surname, I could run it through my database and selected search engines and tell someone all the famous logs in their woodpile. On occasion, it did provide medical significance. Most of the accounts of the Nonagon were like reading unbelievable fiction. The structure seemed too far-fetched—something the brain couldn't comprehend. Mine, on occasion, would bog down trying to imagine such a place, turning the stories into an alien ant farm on Mars.

You really had to know what you were looking for and understand that the author was telling a huge secret. No information came out until the guardian of the information was dead. Most accounts went into landfills as most benefactors had no idea what they were looking at. I was addicted to this intellectual property and the foreboding challenge so much so that I received a rather harsh reprimand for some of my diggings. I was told if I liked using my fingers to type that I might be careful. So, I became extremely careful. I was on a low rung. A watcher. A powerful librarian.

Every choice I had ever made was dredged from the depth of my knowledge gleaned from educators, libraries of books, papers, and computer search engines. I intended to outsmart and outwit every person on the planet. The love of power consumed me more than my drive for money, success, and possessions. In truth, life is one hundred percent about *position*.

Comments like, "If he wasn't the owner's son, he couldn't get a job." Or, "I've got a four-year degree, and that dumbass without one is my boss." *No kidding*. I'd laugh to myself. The irony of "I'm in the *position* to help you," or "the higher the one's *position,* the more power he or she had" was the bottom line. Money, after a while, is simply a bonus, pampering the ego. There comes a point where the lifetime hunting trip for more clutter comes to a joyous end. Power, after all, takes up very little space. Being the top librarian in the world at my age was something I took great pride in.

Seeing the sparkles in VeeLee's eyes when I explained the distance of infinity is incomprehensible, so it was meaningless. Such ideas would swell into his synaptic reasoning and vanish into a billow of logic. He reminded me of myself when it came to soaking up information.

I flew into Basston's Lonesome International Airport and made my way to Harbor-Down Funeral Home to pay condolences to Mike for the passing of his mother.

At the funeral, I curtly hugged the couple. Mike's tears rained down onto my neck, soaking the collar of my dress. It was a busy day of travel and communications. I was informed I'd be in Basston for the remainder of the week to assist in wrapping up his mother's estate.

Mike gave the majority of the household goods to charity and shipped a couple of boxes of heirlooms, photo albums, hairbrushes, jewelry, knickknacks, and the like to Queenfield. His mother's home went at quick auction for one hundred and seventy thousand dollars. It would have been worth much more if he had gotten a realtor. I wrote a footnote and put an asterisk by this fact. Perhaps a little compensation bonus might be in order down the road when they retired from the foster care.

I was back in my college stomping grounds. Crumbbridge was just around the corner. I had several friends who never left the Basston area after graduating from M-ITZZ. I had made friends with some Barvard and Basston University students, as well. They were people, too, my friends and I joked back in the day.

If there were ever a time to see my old friends, I deemed now as good a time as any. As I crossed the Beonard P. Makim Dunker Hill Bridge, my thoughts soared back to working at the Presidential Library. The place where everything in my mind and career developed and matured. Academics were simply a time factor. I took sixteen to twenty semester hours of classes every semester, finishing my Ph.D. in a little over six years. A doctor at twenty-five years of age was fun to say out loud. My family was impressed, but the expectations had always been high. Never would I have dreamed I would land a top librarian designation.

My sister, Lacie London-Bridges, was very motivated, as well. Her passion was in the fine arts. She was an accomplished pianist, painter, and freelance writer. We enjoyed spending time together when we could, but it was not very often. They were quaint sister dinners that required a reservation, a dressy-dress, and high heels.

We loved to fill the air with the family biz and buzz, followed by contemporary issues. Add a little wine, and we would take all guests hostage with our flamboyant prater. We would play our childhood game of seeing who could crisscross their legs the most while leaning in close to each other with our mouths open like Marilyn Monroe and pressing our hands down on our dinner table with wild laughter. Wine times with my sister always makes me smile.

Lacie was more outgoing and enjoyed the outdoors up close and personal with hiking and photography. I, on the other hand, liked solitude with my stack of books and a computer—

what you'd call a city girl. I enjoyed star watching while holding hands, as long as the street was well lit.

We did differ greatly in our taste in men, as well, which was night and day different. Her husband annoyed me to no end, and I had thought of sleeping with him to break them up. I did threaten to skip her wedding and told her that I hated the man outright and that she could do much better. She held her ground, and now Lacie's happiness was all that was important to me. I had fallen in love twice and had sex with nine different gentlemen, each for different reasons. My sister had only been with three different men. The first two never happened, we did after all have our little sister secrets. I even told Bobby so, "She's untouched and pure as snow!" And the genius believed me...

Lacie's husband, Bobby Bridges, always poked at me for becoming a librarian and thought I had waisted an Ivy League education. He, a Barvard Lawyer, was as arrogant a soul as you would find roaming the free world. He frequented the boxing gyms of Basston North to spar for fun, and from my sister's account, he was exceedingly good at making love. His family and friends were judges and attorneys, which always led to conversations of statutes and fees—very mind-numbing to me.

I suffered the agony of listening to his egotistical snobbery for no other reason than to be a part of my sister's life. I was glad she enjoyed a great existence, though. Dear Bobby would never know I had the connections and power to shut down his entire law firm. If I truly had a serious grievance, his LLP established in 1899, filled with tenure and stature, would simply become a raindrop falling into the ocean and disappear—gone. I could shut it down if I so desired.

One call and I could rewrite his existence. It's why I love being a librarian and aspired to be the first Nonagon queen for the rest of my life. True power. I think my sister liked having this ace up her sleeve. We confided in laughter on most days, but I could only scratch the surface of my contemporary reality, even with my twin sister. Her safety was very important to me. Lacie was my greatest love, and I would do almost anything for her except have her baby.

Lacie and Bobby were trying to have children. She had flushed the contraceptive down the toilet a year ago and was beginning to wonder the state of their reproductive organs. They had an appointment with the nation's premier fertility specialist in three weeks. Lacie was nervous, and we impersonated what our parents would have said, had they known. I suggested adoption or foster care, being a subject-matter expert.

She laughed at me with the howl of insanity, knowing neither would be interested in anything less than extending their bloodlines. Lacie reminded me we were twins, and it could be hereditary. I howled back, knowing I had no interest in extending our bloodline. I was mothering a prospect who may rule the world with no labor paroxysms. My figure, nor my schedule, would allow such. A pregnancy would be death to my career and was why I most often avoided having casual sex with men these days. On occasion, I liked the physicality and emotional exchange, but in my heart, it was simply exercise. Right now, I needed to exercise my brain and fingers.

I needed to set up appointments with fellow librarians and friends across the city of Basston. It was time to reminisce and revisit our old haunts that included coffee shops, theaters, and of course, the awesome libraries in the area. We would share our mental gallery of galactic news spanning all areas of prevailing human knowledge in person, rather than on the phone or computer screen. I had to be very careful in what I said and guided most conversations as I knew everything I said would be reviewed by exceptionally well-educated minds. I had to avoid the Nonagon getting nasty with me at all costs.

Knowledge was the primary draw into this career field, and I soaked up any new information I could find. Most ideas and thoughts were recycled and regurgitated novelties a friend had stumbled across that I already knew. Sometimes I would act surprised and fascinated when a colleague made the presentation, timeworn or not. My interest was to stimulate others for the sake of positive relations, keeping the channels of information flowing. It was through this philosophy that I was introduced to the Nine Kings of the Nonagon in the first place, and I kept an open mind. From that one conversation, that one moment in time, my life had irreversibly changed—for the best, in my opinion.

The London family had driven its roots deep in Vergina soil. My twin and I grew up in Washaton-D-sea, with politicians prancing in and out of our home for as long as I could remember. Politically, our family was Demoncrats when all was said and done. I tried to hover around the middle-left but would lean right with the Rebubaicans when it came to limiting the government's gross taxation of its citizens. I had heard many of the raw conversations before they became law, most of which would make voters cringe. Some still leave a bad taste in my mouth.

My bosses ran Washaton-D-sea, and the world, for that matter. It gave me such an adrenalin rush to be a woman in such a powerful position. I could have the head of any senator, congressman, governor, or judge anytime I documented the need. Several had gone down without a clue as to what bad luck had befallen them. "You pissed off the wrong librarian," I'd say with a laugh when telling Lacie of my general endeavors.

Of all my accomplishments, VeeLee VonVouge had the potential of being my top achievement. If he earned entry into the purple cloud, he would make my ninth non-king accepted. If he made king, we would both be set to harness great power for the rest of our lives. We would be tethered together like an umbilical cord until he graduated college, screwed up, or died.

My priority was to deal with his living situation. And yes, his mother's arrest was no fluke accident of bad luck. Jillie Jo was brought in on warrants for bad checks and two failure-to-appear charges while having no idea about the new charge. When I was done, Jillie Jo would be doing her full sentence of ten years on a class-A felony—assault of a pregnant woman resulting in termination of pregnancy. The video evidence could be refuted by a good attorney, but for now, I had her and two other strippers being charged for beating up a mouthy store clerk who said, "I'm not selling you nasty hoes cigarettes and Jägermeister." Lilly, from what I could see on the video, was watching the fight, but I knew a free public defender would not be digging hard to find the whole truth.

VeeLee had returned some books to the library and had told me of the incident the day after. I took the liberty to have the gas station camera footage copied when I learned the unfortunate outcome. It was like winning the lottery for me, and most likely VeeLee, as well. I stashed the video and my notes of who was involved, knowing the perfect time to use it to my advantage would present itself. The truth of my actions would never be fully disclosed, but the information was now in the right hands.

VeeLee was a vibrant young man, and I knew he was attracted to me in obvious ways. I had to be very bland and matter-of-fact with his youthful energy. I could ill afford an emotional teenager falling in love and going wacko on me. I shut down any notion of excited hormones as soon as they arose. It was natural and understood, and simply something I was required to manage—part of the job description, literally. He already had an enormously negative environment to squeeze an existence from. Survival in the K-sea projects was not easy for anyone who lived there. I felt bad for him when I had time to think about it.

VeeLee was my prized pup, the exceptional soul from a litter of several billion. He constantly managed to amaze me with his acuity and intelligence. The two most important things in the world to me is power and exceptional brilliance!

Chapter 13

Anglaia juiced

NEEDLESS TO SAY, MY GRANDPARENTS booked the first available flight back to Queenfield. They would be picked up by my parents around midnight, who would drive them to their wounded house in Bronson. It would be in the wee hours of the morning before Father would find his pillow. Foster boy and I would be sound asleep by the time they returned. The official house sitter had been contacted, and we gladly passed the responsibility torch.

Morning came with the surprise of a pounding heart and eyes that darted in every direction of my room, searching for Harry. When I finally realized that it wasn't real—nothing more than a crazy-ass dream—my mind settled down. I was watching Harry McCrackin load giant trash bags filled with his fiancée's heavy, stiff body parts. His facial expressions were terrifying. Thankfully my dreams were not printed in the Queenfield Daily Report section of *The News Peeper.*

Somewhat relieved, I made my way to the kitchen to find no fresh breakfast waiting for me—just a note that said, "Expecting you'll put on your big-girl pants today and find some food. You and VeeLee have a great day at school. Love you, Mother."

Bite me, Mother! I said to myself and grabbed a granola bar as the scent of soap from foster boy's fresh shower wafted into my nose. I pitched a breakfast bar in his direction, which was intentionally uncatchable as it rattled onto the floor somewhere under the kitchen table. He had no right to be in my effing kitchen in the first place. He just looked at me with that, *"Really?"* expression. I had never felt so ill toward anyone in my entire life.

I could not find an escape from this boy. He was everywhere and in every part of my effing life. My parents did not seem to be interested in slaying this dragon for me. They were actually giving him a cozy bed and feeding the monster my food. If I find the time, I might just have to elicit action from the *glue-crew*. VonVouge was treading on the thinnest of ice.

I dashed to my room to grab my backpack and barked, "Let's go!" VeeLee hopped into my Mustdang and off to school we went. Mike and Melissa would be back at the end of the week. Surely this week would be much easier and go much faster.

Before I could bat my eyes, the school day and cheer practice were over. I picked VeeLee up at the gas station. He was standing there propped up against the brick wall waiting. It was nearly five, and I was running late.

He wasn't contributing gas money, one of my extra income sources, so I didn't care if he got annoyed. Thus far, he seemed to be well composed no matter how I treated him—eerily similar to my father. It seemed he wanted to have a conversation or watch me chew my gum, but didn't. It wouldn't take much for me to go off on him. I was considering making him sit in the backseat as it was.

We soon pulled into the drive and let ourselves into my home. With a toss, my wad of keys bunched together with my parents' on the kitchen counter. It was one way of knowing who was in the home. Cars in the garage didn't mean one of us wasn't out with a friend, which was often the case. It was more notable when I was younger and without a Mustdang.

I walked into the sitting room, where father was flailing his arms through the air as if trying to convince his circulation to be more enthusiastic about its function. "I love you, too, Mother. I have another call coming in," and immediately began talking to someone else on his phone. It was a cancellation for the Texas Hold 'Em card game to be played this weekend, "I'll let the boys know," Father said, scanning my face as he talked on the phone.

VeeLee was soon busy at his plate of food. Football practice must have drained him.

Mother was also on the phone, talking with Melissa. She abruptly passed the phone to VeeLee. He swallowed his mouthful. "Yes, ma'am. Everything is going well. Yes, ma'am. Thank you! Goodbye," VeeLee said and passed the phone back to Mother.

Soon the phones went silent, and Father's voice filled our ears with details of Harry McCrackin. Initially, Grandfather was embarrassed and intended to circumcise the personalities of the two Clintin generations below him. Grandmother Adamina-Rose had just explained the details of the murder.

"What did the Sherriff say?" Mother asked.

Initially, I was excited, thinking I may have nabbed one of America's Top Ten Most Wanted. Maybe VeeLee and I would split a reward. The more Father talked, the more I realized there would be no heroic bantering in the community, and if anything, me and foster boy would make for good coffee-shop talk. Semantics, phonetics, and stupidity rolled into an eavesdropping cheese-log of rash judgment. Apparently, there is a huge difference between Sofia and Sofie when it comes to the death of a living soul.

    Grandmother was able to use the family emergency to lay out a final business bluff and tied up the final sale of her beloved business, and it did get her and Grandfather home nearly a week early. And now I didn't have to worry about housesitting under the stars anymore or seeing my weekend time massacred with responsibility. Seeing my slice of heaven turned into a trashy junkpile of Grandmother's home makeover ideas had been a painful experience.

    There was a true and deep sadness I felt seeing my second home cut up and hammered on, almost matching the depression of losing Danielle to a dude. Danielle knew all my secrets. She knew the *me* that even my grandmother didn't know. Grandmother knew everything—except how I *really* liked to be tickled.

    VeeLee managed to piss me off again on our way to school Tuesday morning when he brought up the notion of working at Top Chops with my dad after football season. He was hoping to buy himself a car, going on and on about it. "Something simple and affordable," he said. Hopefully, a vehicle that would last him through college. He was serious as he could be. I thought it dumb for someone to want to own a car for almost six years

    I do not care, kid. Shut up! Shut up! Shut up!

    "Bite me, VonVouge. I DO NOT CARE," I finally said out loud, cutting my eyes at him, which ended his dreamy twaddle. This time it was me who looked out the side window. I felt like my mother was morphing through my thought stream, and I wanted to hide this boy in her closet, but knowing him, he would volunteer to go grocery shopping with her. My family had done enough for the K-sea kid. He needed to find other options—fast like.

I really wasn't interested in having a conversation with this kid at all. I didn't want him to be a part of or know me at all. He was seeing me naked with my clothes on, like a thief sneaking around parts of my soul that were locked, private, out-of-bounds, and off-limits to everyone.

Melissa would be back Friday, and that would be the last ride to school I planned to ever give VonVouge. Mother had gotten on to me twice this week for calling him, *"Foster boy."* I absolutely could not stand saying or hearing his weird-ass name. But I didn't need her to come out of her homemade confinement closet and be an oppressive teenage whisperer with ridiculous punishments that molded my free time into a ten-year-old's existence.

Why she felt the need to confine her only daughter to her bedroom, making it a personal prison and agonizing torture chamber, I'll never know. It doubled as a private church, where she made me listen to unsolicited advice and preaching until my heart fell numb and my brain died a million deaths. All because I did not want to share my life with a strange stranger.

On occasion, when I couldn't bite my tongue long enough, I'd simply scream as loud as I could for as long as I could, hoping she would poke her fingers into her ears and leave me alone. Sometimes I'd run off, slam and lock my door. I chose to bow out of the foster boy conflict for now and decided to just chill out for the time being. Being separated from my car was too high a price to pay at the moment. VeeLee was getting close to pushing me over my conscience limit, though. Surely, I could survive this last week.

I did alert the Glue Crew to issue a reminder to VeeLee. I had to make use of my membership and put a hit out on him and Beau. I was not over the football field faceoff. Beau was still my mortal enemy for taking my love away. Oceans of glue could not stick my heart back together the way it once was. He had shot eleven holes in my heart, and no matter how I tried to plug the holes with all my fingers and thumbs, the hurt and pain would gush out the eleventh.

Driving home from school, I smiled at him, knowing the two of them were going to learn not to jack with me. Foster boy may have thought I was being nice to him, but he would be wrong. The details were never discussed, but I hoped they glued their helmets together—with them in it. Or maybe even mummified them with Kevlar cloth and hang them like a piñata from the football field goal post just before the Friday night game started. Yeah, that would be perfect.

Anglaia was late again. After she picked me up at the gas station, we made our way over to the Matches to check on the home and grab the mail. I opened the door and placed more letters and junk mail onto the growing pile. Everything seemed in order. I locked the front door and then hopped back inside her car.

There was no doubt her insatiable ego would allow one good chill day to pass. Her personality was starving for attention and constantly needed feeding. She sat in her driver's seat with her left leg cocked against the door. Her miniskirt was nearly rolled up completely. It looked more like a headband she'd doubled as a butt wrap.

Anglaia knew the hint of her panties was bare to my eye. I caught her looking down between her legs to make sure she was in the correct pose. I knew this sort of bait-and-switch stratagem. My mom wrote the book. I did not intend to dote over Anglaia's toned and tanned legs. She had literally hundreds of guys cooing in the halls of Horseshoe High every single day as it was. I knew she was hunting for one misguided comment—sexual in nature—to set me up. Just one and I'd be banished off the face of the earth. She could literally drive nude, and I would not give her a single syllable to use against me. In fact, I'd most likely ask to be let out so I could walk, which I was considering right now.

I had much greater thoughts to focus on than her teenage games. I had to remain vigilant and visualize the future I wanted to create. I noticed a forbidden smile on Anglaia's face, no telling what she was thinking, but I was not going to fall for her wet lips and bright teeth. I trained my gaze out my door window and watched the buildings, cars, and people zip from left to right across my eyes. I needed to be able to engage and communicate with Anglaia in a positive and productive manner. But not while she was in a temptress mood. My financial future depended on this fact. Surely, there was a neutral—and maybe even a good—mutual co-existence to be found. I don't know that a friendship could be obtained, but that was what I hoped we could somehow find.

I thought we had come close at her grandparent's mansion, but since we were wrong about Harry, that special bond was not created, just a memory that made us look silly. I am glad it was Sofie and not Sofia who died, but still felt a little bad for Harry, who was having the week from hell made worse by two teenagers trying to do the right thing.

Sheriff Hartley hauled Harry to jail for intimidating an officer of the law while under the influence of alcohol. Apparently, Harry confessed he had lost the love of his life, his fiancée, Sofia. Harry was in the process of returning her cat, Sofie. Sofie hated traveling in cars and was one pissed off pussycat, her back hair raised, hissing, and bawling from the time they had left his home.

Sofia always complained about Sofie's behavior on trips to the vet. Harry agonized over the thought of seeing Sofia again so soon after their breakup. His feelings were still raw, and the lump in his throat seemed to grow with each passing mile. Insane thoughts like, "What if her new man came out to claim her pussycat. What would I do? And on and on..." Bruce explained.

He went on to say Harry was forced to slam on his brakes. The kennel slammed into the dashboard, and Sofie managed her way out of the carrier, scatted across his lap and out of the open car window. Do-it-yourself movers had lost a dresser and some boxes on the road ahead of him. Several cars ran off into the ditch. Sofie's bolt for freedom sent her body directly into the mayhem of the dismayed drivers on the highway. She was hit by the car traveling behind. Harry pulled onto the shoulder and watched helplessly through his rearview mirror.

Sofie's back was broke. Her front legs and back legs no longer worked together. She jumped in unnatural directions in the air like a trapeze act in a circus and clawed at the highway pavement. Harry said he had gripped the steering wheel so hard that he bent it. Sofie used her last bit of energy to complete a few more circles on the double yellow line. A faint meow captured her last heartbeat. Sofia didn't buy his story when he brought Sofie's remains to her in the kennel. She filed animal cruelty charges against Harry.

His work crew had known about the accident details, and that was the reason they just continued working. Anglaia and I were shocked when we learned Harry had been released. Jacob was initially upset with the interruption of their very important business meeting, although the family emergency ended up benefiting him and Adamina-Rose. They were officially retired.

I had attempted to mend fences and patch things up with Anglaia, but my words always fell clumsily into her ears. She was not receptive to my small talk, nor did she seem in the slightest way interested in getting to know me. I knew the pattern she was building in her mind and knew every time we were put together, the more resentful she became. Her hormones would be roller skating downhill on the ice soon if I didn't start taking making a new path through the deep snow.

I had to find something she needed on a deeper level. Anglaia had all the things that money could buy. She was extremely attractive. She had long, sun-bleached blond hair, a sexy, tanned barbie doll body, and her large artic blue irises were surrounded by the clearest, whitest sclera genetics could provide. She was a social diva, her tribe rather large—all the while being very selective when it came to those who stood close to her. She had family support and love. It seemed that I was merely a mosquito who was pestering her peace.

Life had thrust us together, nearly like a downed airplane in a barren desert. There was nothing to shade or shelter her perception of me. It was a personal grievance, a conflict that urged a war. Anglaia was on her home turf, and her rules were in play. She was accustomed to getting her way. The circumstances were uncomfortable for us both, but I knew her family held many keys I needed.

My options were very limited—the doors had to be opened. There would never be a better opportunity to create my successful world than right now. It was personal in every way. I wanted a good life. I would be back with Mike and Melissa Matches tomorrow night after our football game, and hopefully, the tension between us would simmer down a bit when I left her home. I was not afraid of her—she had no belt—but I would need to maintain some softness and silence.

Sarah must have had wine again. Her screams pierced the bubble of my dream, and I sat up stiff-legged in my bed and watched the light come on and then off again. In the two weeks I had stayed here, she averaged four episodes a week. I was becoming conditioned now, and my heart wasn't racing when the screams shattered the quiet of the night.

It was just an annoyance now. Sarah was a very determined woman, yet lacked confidence for some reason. It seemed she was always out to prove something to the world. I dared not tell her the world was mostly filled with careless souls. The vast majority of people would have laughed at the pressure she put on herself if they were in her financial position. Everything was done in a hurry, and life seemed to be a panic attack for her.

I was in my away-game football jersey and at the breakfast table with Bruce. We lightly talked about the Oatzark football team, located in the same town as the Assemblage church. They were average with a few scholarship-caliber players. They were primarily a something-to-do football team who enjoyed a great hometown buzz. I knew not to underestimate them, though. Bruce's tone lent confidence that we should be able to out-play them as he rattled *The News Peeper* newspaper around and forked at his vegetables.

There were four plates of breakfast on the table. Sarah had gotten around early and cooked. The two eggs had the yokes plucked out of them, sitting beside some lightly sautéed spinach and onion, and cold sliced chicken breast, with a large glass of water. Way healthier than a breakfast bar, the pickin's of processed cafeteria food at school, or what I was accustomed to back home—microwaved imitation noodles with welfare cheese melted on top.

"Great. Mom has been talking to Grandmother again. I'm *not* eating that! Come on, VonVouge, I need to get to school early this morning," Anglaia said.

"Let VeeLee finish his breakfast," Bruce said.

Sarah came into the kitchen, seeing Anglaia standing with her arms crossed, staring at me while I tried to gobble down my food. "Sit down and eat," Sarah said.

"I'm not hungry! Let's go, foster boy," Anglaia said, slinging her backpack around, intentionally hitting me in the head as she huffed out the kitchen on her way to the Mustdang GT. "*Let's go-wa!*" She pouted and slammed the door behind her.

"Thank you for breakfast, Mrs. Clintin," I said, scarfing down the last bite.

The garage erupted into a thunderous noise. Anglaia revved up the engine repeatedly, an echo that made me think she might just blow the motor any second. I opened the car door, and the music was so loud that I had to remind myself I was looking at the keys to my future life. I hopped in and decided to simply smile. Probably should not have winked at her, though. I truly wanted to reach over and turn the music down and tell her to grow up, but I didn't.

It was a fifteen-minute ride to school. Anglaia was enjoying yet another power trip I'd simply add to the growing list. I knew better than to react to any of them. None were going to mean life or death for me, just very annoying. She glared at me as if she wanted to smack the winking eye right out of its orbital socket and launch it into outer space. "Seems like your mom struggles with her childhood. Her dreams really seem to plague her nights," I said loudly, trying to rise above the music.

Anglaia reached for the radio knob, turning it down, "What are you blabbing about my mother," she said sharply. Her glare then seemed to want to sew my lips together so she might never hear another word come from my mouth.

"Your dad told me what your mom's nightmares were about. It seems like she disowned her side of the family. Her brother and his cousins really messed her head up," I said.

"I have no idea what you're talking about, foster boy. Wait… are you telling me my parents knew what created the nightmares and have failed to share this little tidbit of ginormous information with their *daughter*?" Anglaia said, slamming on the brakes when we reached the parking lot of the gas station, "Get… *out*!"

The tires would need to be changed soon. She left twenty-five thousand miles worth of tire tread on the street, leaving black marks for a hundred yards behind her as she left. It must have been some sort of magic act. I couldn't even make out the shape of the Mustdang for all the white smoke that boiled into the air. With all the talk of my intelligence, I was struggling to crack Anglaia's code enough to get on her good side. One damn thing after another seemed to inevitably arise, creating an even greater rift between us than before.

Thank God it's the last day of dealing with the foster boy, I thought to myself. The feeling was almost like visiting Danielle's home back in the day. She and her brother fought like cats and dogs. I personally could not stand her bratty brother, either, and made him cry on more than one occasion—actually as often as I could. For some reason, he didn't like bloody noses or when we joined forces against him. All the dumbass had to do was leave us alone. We were busy talking, trying to cuddle and kiss, or watch videos. He refused to just go away.

My stomach was already grumbling at me for skipping breakfast. Mom's yokeless eggs freaked me out. I was making good time and would be early enough to grab something from the Horseshoe High cafeteria. My parents were going to get an earful about discussing Mother's dream thing with foster boy the next time I saw them. The faster and farther away I tried to get from him, the more personal things seemed to get. He had learned way too much about me while he stayed with my family. If he decided to become popular by running his mouth, he would pay dearly.

I parked my Mustdang GT and made my way into Horseshoe High, ordered my usual, sat down with my girls, and started munching on a cheese omelet and tater-tots smothered in ketchup.

"Guess you've heard?" Cortney said.

"I guess I just sat down, so duh," I said, rolling my eyes at her like she was the queen ignoramus of our table. Which she pretty much was, twenty-four-seven.

"Your girl lost the baby last night. She and Beau were in a car accident. They swerved to miss a car and went into the ditch and hit a tree. It was all over the news," Cortney said and winked. "Sorry 'bout your ex's luck, Anglaia."

"What…" was all I could come up with. My thoughts rolled up like a giraffe's tongue, and every drop of blood in my brain drained into my lungs, making it hard to breathe. I had bashed Danielle at this very table with my girls every week since our breakup. My puckered lips hung on my face like a freak of nature, as if I had weighted them down with too much tender rose lip gloss. I so wanted to gush a sarcastic retort back to Cortney, but couldn't.

My heart was beating hard and fast, pushing pain into every capillary cell that my skin offered. I felt my bones for the first time, and they throbbed a dull ache independent of all the other hurts that spontaneously erupted like the big bang inside my body. My universe was expanding past my grasp to control. My soul might just perform an exodus and leave this human form altogether.

A light rain fell from my eyes and onto my omelet. I had succumbed to the defeat of tears. Danielle had once again made me cry. I began to cry so deeply that I had no control of my body and felt like I was a nightcrawler being put on a fishhook. Horseshoe High students had no business seeing me wounded like this. My girls were trying to hold and support me, but I had to get out of there.

"I've got to go," I told them. I stood up and was on my way to my Mustdang GT. VeeLee had just made it to school and walked through the cafeteria door. For some inexplicable reason, I didn't punch him in the face. Instead, like a lost puppy, I whimpered close to him, my shoulders slouched, and arms limp—eyes floating in tears.

He, for some reason, did not struggle with the personal space I violated. We were nose-to-chest. He gracefully danced me around in his arms, and, in a split second, we disappeared from the view of five-hundred wild-eyed students. "Will you drive me to the hospital? Danielle has been in a car accident," I said.

"Of course, I will," VeeLee said. His voice steady, similar to when we were in the midst of the cat murderer.

"She lost her baby, VonVonge..."

He was now behind the wheel of my Mustdang—something I told myself a million times I would not allow—ever! My father was the only one who had ever driven my car. I was sure twenty pictures would pop up on social media tomorrow. *Eff my life.*

A childhood memory of Danielle clawed in my mind. The one of when we got her kitten, Wowie, into heaven. When Danielle was ten years old, her mother and father agreed that she could have a pet. They would go to the animal shelter and rescue something. I happened to be spending the night and went with them. She looked at the dogs first and then the cats.

Danielle fell for a rambunctious kitten that was a little fireball darting all over the cage, making the rest of the kittens look lame. "Wowie, look at that one!" she said, which became its name forever after. Wowie, a white-gray haired, blue-eyed Siamese, was as spunky as they came. Meowed a lot and purred a lot. Wowie was always getting into everything, basically a brat like Danielle's little brother. She slept with us, and I usually awoke to her big eyes staring directly into mine, purring and dancing her claws into my arm or chest like an oil well pump. One time I pushed her away, and she dug in her claws into my hair. I sat up, and she was hanging from my braid. Danielle laughed. Honestly, the cat always got on my nerves.

Danielle said she wished Wowie could go to heaven with us. I told her that I didn't see a reason why she wouldn't go to heaven. She said that no one gets into heaven unless you are baptized. So we convinced her mom to let us take Wowie to Pastor Dom to see if he would help us get Wowie into heaven. She agreed. Pastor Dom smiled at us and sprinkled Holy Water over Wowie, said some words, and Wowie was now heaven bound.

Of course, our story was shared during the Sunday Morning sermon for laughs. Danielle and I got the last laugh, though when all the other kids in the church wanted their pets to go to heaven, too. Pastor Dom's days got a lot little busier. The parking lot looked like Noah's Arc for several Sundays after. Now heaven had animals thanks to us. You're welcome. Every time the story was brought up by our families, we laughed. After the continuous clawing over the years, I should have just let the fur-ball and its needle claws go straight to hell. Bite me, Wowie. No wait, she had bitten me a million times. Not nice. Eff-off, Wowie.

I called Mother to inform her that I was heading to the hospital. VeeLee was driving me. She needed to call the school and have my absence excused and have Melissa do the same for foster boy. In between gulps of air, I knuckled at my irritated eyes. Mother kept asking me a hundred basic questions that I had no answers to. I didn't even know which hospital to go to. I was directing VonVouge to Socks Hospital, one of the main hospitals a couple of miles from Horseshoe High, just down Assemblage Freeway.

We entered the lobby and saw Danielle's parents talking with family and a husband and wife couple who were family friends. I knew them all since I was a kid. They seemed shocked to see me coming. Danielle's mother, Linda, just opened her arms, and I fell into them. David, her dad, patted my back like a puppy.

There was nothing to explain. They had always accepted me as a second daughter. They were clueless we were sexually inspired until Father overheard us and Mother busted us out the night I asked Danielle to tickle me in the hallway. It seemed like a lifetime ago. I didn't want any details. I just wanted to see her. It was too early, though. Visiting hours did not start for another hour. I would have to agonize in the company of people I had dismissed. I didn't really have a game plan or know how to act with my old bestie, Danielle.

I introduced VonVouge to them. We then listened to the details of the accident. I could care less about Beau's broken shoulder and four ribs or the fact his football season was over.

Within thirty minutes, Mother and Father brought more hugs to me. We all floated around in a circle like a community of floating turds swirling around in a giant toilet bowl, waiting on the effing clock to hurry the eff up.

Mother let VeeLee know that Melissa had contacted the school for him. He promptly stated he would like a ride back to Horseshoe High after visiting Beau and Danielle, if possible. Father said he would take him. The mood then drifted back to anonymous toilet bowl floaters. The loss of baby Victor Angelino crept back into our moralities. It was sad. The little guy only had a few weeks to go.

I had to wait my turn and have Danielle's permission before I could visit her. In her current state of mourning, I would understand if she chose not to see me. VonVouge was escorted back to visit Beau. Linda came to the waiting room and wagged her head side to side, nonverbally expressing painful disbelief of life's game plan.

"She will see you, Anglaia," Linda said. My heart pounded the tingles into a rash of thick goosebumps on my arms, so large they resembled marbles planted underneath my skin.

I entered Danielle's room on my tiptoes for some reason, as if not to wake her. Her eyes were half-closed, and she was morgue pale, resembling none of the beautiful images my brain had collected. We had been sick as dogs over the years. Yet she had never looked so deathly. The hospital room was somewhat cold and smelled of alcohol and medicine. The air was heavy with an unseen cloud of sorrow.

I started to cry again, which instantly evoked our out-of-tune duet—a serenade of fractured souls that soon developed into a love song of heartache. We sounded terrible, though. We were a pair of hound dogs snared in a barbed-wire fence. It was the deepest pain I had ever felt. Life simply was not fair.

I crawled through the handrails at the bottom corner of her hospital bed. Danielle flipped the blanket onto her lax body, a pre-spooning routine we had performed hundreds of times in the past. I scooched and pulled on her until our forms matched, and we melted together as one female blob.

My hand rested on her belly momentarily—it felt like I had put my hand into a restaurant size jar of mayonnaise. It was squishy and gross. My first thought was, "*yuck*" and I almost jerked my hand off in disgust. I managed my fingers atop her ribcage, and we started to breathe in unison.

"Thanks for being here, Anglaia. I cannot believe I was driving! I never drive," Danielle said. I squeezed her in response. No sooner did we settle into a comfy position, her parents, Linda and David, came in with a hospice nurse. My parents and a gaggle of others trailed into the room. Danielle was like a museum exhibit.

The grief counselor injected his voice and instantly assumed command of the room. He asked no questions. Instead, he went straight into his spiel. He introduced himself as Dan. He was very average looking and was not glowing, nor did he look like Jesus or tote a Holy Bible. He asked us to relax and listen to him for one minute-nine seconds. He said we could close our eyes if we liked. His voice soon had the vibration of a Stradivarius cello—beautifully deep, full, and healing. Dan began,

"The Storm of Death…

"It sneaks up on everyone. It grabs your attention with a crack of thunder that booms loudly into your ears. Fear raises its head. We are to deal with this attack of death in our own way. Rain falls from the sky so fast and hard that it takes away all light at first. It is hard to see. It is hard to understand. Suddenly you feel the cold water inching up your leg. A current begins to flow around your legs until it becomes so swift you are swept off your feet.

"Into the darkness, you are carried. It's a struggle to survive. You feel you will surely drown. You quickly hang onto pictures, a necklace, a million memories that are floating around you. Everything you dearly loved is now hurting you as it swirls around in the floodwaters of your mind, stabbing your heart as it passes by.

"You keep getting pulled under the water every ten seconds, twenty-five seconds, thirty minutes, then every hour or so. You will eventually swim yourself out of energy. The emotional currents will wear you down, and the only option is to float for a while. Occasionally you're able to hang onto a calm memory and tame grief's tide of tears. It's a challenge to live on.

"The storm will rage on for weeks and months or maybe years, but there will come a time you will be able to catch your breath. The pain and hurt will lessen as the days pass by. You will never be able to predict what will trigger the storm of death.

"The attack may revisit you when you smell a flower. It could be a song or dates on the calendar. Holidays could pull you back into the deep, cold, swift stormwater again and again. Sporadically your feet will touch solid ground again, and there will be spaces in between the thunderstorms. They will slow or stop for a while.

"It is in the pause that you remember you still have in your heart the one who has left you. The more you loved them, the larger the scar will be. The more scars your heart holds, the bigger it becomes. So, may we all have a million storms of death and greet each of them with smiles of remembrance, celebrating the enormous hearts of loved ones that left their mark, their scar on our life.

"For there will come a day that you will become a scar on the heart of all who have known you—hopefully their largest. A long life lived well will have a heart filled with scars of love. All souls are eternal and cannot be destroyed.

"Danielle, you mothered a soul that lives on for millions and millions of years. Heaven holds little Victor Angelino for you now, but you and the rest of us will see him again one day. Let not little Victor Angelino's life become a mood of darkness, rather a brilliant light of remembrance that floods your heart with love. A beautiful storm, a beautiful scar."

By the time Dan had finished, there was not a dry eye in the place. The energy in the room was the strongest I had ever known. Grandfather Jacob and Grandmother Adamina-Rose had made it just in time to hear Dan's message, and I think Grandmother was crying the hardest for some reason.

Beau, who was hobbling around in the doorway, was dabbing at his eye, foster boy by his side.

Beau made his way bedside. "Do you mind," he said, gesturing with his head for me to get off the bed and most likely for me to leave. I squeezed Danielle tightly as if stating she was mine again and was ready to give him a good beatdown.

Harry McCrackin was visiting Socks Hospital to pay his respects. He was there at the accident and had seen Beau's truck stuck to the oak tree in the ditch. He had seen the ambulance leaving while he was scraping Sofie off the road.

"It's fine," Danielle said. She looked at him with eyes that had just turned the page. The room emptied in slow motion. Father took foster boy back to Horseshoe High. Reluctantly, Beau left with his parents as he no longer had a monster truck to come and go as he pleased.

Beau's mother had commented that they needed to make funeral arrangements, and Linda and David, Danielle's parents, agreed and followed them out to do so.

Danielle and I talked and talked like we did in the good old days. She had told me everything. She was not in love with Beau, but with me. I listened but didn't feel I could go back to her. She was a cheater. I told her that we could work on our friendship, but I was getting nauseous at the idea.

I stayed with her until I was forced out by the visiting hour guard dog patrol—an old, cranky leather-faced sea hag in nursing scrubs. She escorted me directly out of the hospital wing without using a single word. I cranked up the Mustdang GT, looked at the time displayed on the radio, and thought it was about half-time at the football game and decided I would to go cheer for a while. It had been such a depressing day. Maybe a football game would help? The Oatzark High School football field was only twenty minutes away.

We had won our football game, but I felt much better about the freedom of walking in my panties and bra again. I had my home back. Hopefully, foster boy would never be allowed to stay another night here for as long as I lived.

Morning came, and Father was yapping on the phone, and I could tell it was a Texas Hold 'Em poker day. Frankie was helping get the card table organized, and Mother was stirring salsa into the cheese dip that was cooking in the crockpot.

And then I heard it—that voice. He was here again. Mike Matches had brought him along, not to mention his own annoying voice. VonVouge would be here for the poker game. Apparently, he was playing for someone who had called off. I felt like reporting the game to the police just to make this constant brain-ache go away and disappear out of my life.

I cannot get rid of this kid for anything! Gawd.

VeeLee sat with wide eyes of excitement as man after man took up a chair at the card table. He spewed the look of an eager attorney ready to take his first case in court. I could tell he was sizing up the competition as they were of him.

Chapter 14

Lara London—on patrol

I THOUGHT, BEING IN MY COLLEGE HAUNTS of Basston, I would be able to hit reset—a catch-my-breath kind of break. The truth was, I felt my energy level being sucked out of me like the last swallow of strawberry daiquiri from the cocktail glass. I had just wrapped up the paperwork for Mike's mother's death and assisted in some of the final funeral details when I received a message that VeeLee VonVouge was in the hospital.

My mind reeled in and out of various scenarios. Was he sick? Hurt or maimed? Would he need to be dismissed from K-9 contention altogether? It was all news a parent always hated to hear, but in my case, it was a potential world leader, a king. I was on my highest alert possible.

I quickly diverted my plans and set course to the library, the computer system there would morph into a makeshift headquarters where I could elicit a combat scenario, a war room with similar intensity. The finest doctors in the world would be summoned if needed. I went down the protocol checklist in my mind, when my phone buzzed.

Sarah dutifully had contacted Melissa with the news of Danielle's accident. VeeLee was visiting the two friends in the hospital and needed her to contact the school that he would be late. Melissa informed me before I had to activate my resources. Thankfully. No sooner did my mind settle back to thoughts of who I'd have dinner with tonight than my phone buzzed again. Disturbing news from K-sea flashed across the screen in purple. I would, in fact, need to continue to the library. Jillie Jo, VeeLee's biological mother, was being released from jail.

I parked and quickly walked the halls of the library, sat down, kicked my shoes off, fired up the computer, and logged in. I immediately activated the purple cloud and proceeded to assimilate networks. I needed information and needed it fast. Within a few minutes, I had the top brass in the country digging. These were the moments I loved so much about my job. The power rush I craved, my version of winning a presidential election.

This new surge of adrenaline quickly zapped my energy, and I realized I needed food. My energy level could not be derived from positive thinking alone. I reached out to a friend to bring me some takeout and asked for a raincheck to hang out another time. She understood and had my back. Jillie Jo was a singularity now, my only priority. Initially, I was to take Mike and Melissa to the airport tonight, but they would be put in a cab instead.

Details began to trickle in. Aarontino Jackkson was, for some reason, working for her release. How would he recoup the fees of the best attorney in K-sea from Jillie Jo waiting tables? It would never happen. One thing I knew for certain, his attorney had extraordinary clout to have already gone through the court and gotten Jillie Jo released on bail.

I had to wrap things up here in Basston. My friends and mini-vacation were now over. It took two seconds to book the next flight out. The funeral had been respectful. Mike now knew he had the support of Nonagon, and that was all that really mattered. I had intended to vacation an extra week, visit some friends and perhaps read some papers from the latest crop of minds at my alma mater.
Not to be, though. It would have to be another time.

The next flight to K-sea took off in two hours, which meant I'd be in a state of go-hurry-go. I sent a message to my friend who was bringing dinner. We would meet in the parking lot. Time for a hug, grab the food, and go-hurry-go. I would most likely eat in the airport concourse somewhere. Flying in first class would alleviate hearing the rattling of Mike Matches' voice on the way home. I had peeked at the manifest and noted we were, in fact, on the same flight.

I checked out of my hotel and dropped off the rental car at the airport. The wheels of my luggage clanked behind me in one hand and a plastic to-go box with a dragon, rainbow, and shrimp tempura sushi rolls in the other. I checked my suitcase, printed my plane ticket, and then sat on the first bench I came across so that I could scarf down my meal.

I entered the gate, and Melissa eyed me in surprise as if I had deliberately set them up with the stinky, ill-mannered cab driver. I approached them and explained the new development concerning Jillie Jo. My phone buzzed, and the screen turned purple, which meant it was a message from the Nonagon. I excused myself and walked to a vacant corner of the gatehouse.

The message simply said to prepare to relocate to Queenfield. Meaning I would be handing off my K-sea office to someone in the watch. Hopefully, it would be another librarian and not a stuffy retired politician type. I would need to organize a move, establish contacts, set up a dwelling—electric, mailing address change, internet, trash, and the like. I did see the move coming once I had Lilly locked up. Now I had to corral her again, and it had to be accomplished very quickly. I could not allow her to potentially derail her son's amazing progress.

The four-hour flight in first class allowed me to get a better understanding of what was transpiring in Jillie Jo's case. I was able to get a great deal accomplished and managed a twenty-minute power nap. Aarontino had apparently contacted his father, Geovanni Jackkson, who was well known up and down the west coast as a highly educated and successful businessman. He was a high-end entertainment guru who owned a chain of twenty fine-dining restaurants named *A-Rose*. They were scattered across the country.

A-Rose specialized in international cuisine, Italian and seafood, making up the majority of the menu. Geovanni expanded to the Midwest intending to take his west coast vibe east, creating a national brand. After graduation from college, Aarontino, his youngest son, managed two restaurants in Mizzeree—one in K-sea, the other in Saint L's.

It was one-thirty in the morning before I snagged my luggage and made it to my K-sea home. I needed more sleep in the worst way. My books of knowledge were blurring together in my mind. I could not cast the net inside my brain to catch the correct answers I searched for. Mike and Melissa Matches had three additional hours of car travel to go before they would arrive in Queenfield, I imagined they would pick VeeLee up in the morning.

Since I didn't have to deal with Geovanni or Aarontino directly, there was not much to be concerned about personally. But this father and son duet was not to be taken lightly. Everything that came across the screen—blocked bank account balances, clean records, and Ivy League educations—meant I needed to be more aware of my actions. I wasn't a fan of co-opted offensives as it leaves a darker trail of evidence. My eye was on Aarontino, my target, Jillie Jo. But I might need to find a badass librarian to watch my six on the west coast, employ a campaign divisive in nature if I was to defeat Jillie Jo's newfound freedom.

There were exotic peculiarities blooming like pink roses across the fire-burned field of my electronics. I could not allow intrigue to be a distraction. This Jillie Jo incident needed to be diffused. The quicker, the better. The manifestation of malefic misfortune had winked at me. My job now was to ensure the Nonagon was not drawn into the radius of this probe. It was settling to have the best resources in the world. Anything I could dream up was about to happen.

When I digitally caught up with Jillie Jo, she was back at the Tanner apartments. I assumed she'd go back to work at the *A-Rose's* restaurant or dance. She had linked up with her sister, Janie, and niece, Kaylee. It would take some coordination, but I had a plan. Soon I would cast a sticky net over Jillie Jo that she wouldn't be able to slip out of this time.

I first had to send a songbird to Aarontino Jackkson with a song of understanding, one that would calm the urge of confrontation. A message that men of his stature understood well. The loss of personal finance usually did the trick. It would end up costing him and his father a great amount of money to chaperone Jillie Jo any further.

There was a commingling miasma of riotous thoughts that swept over my call to action. This occasion had, by far, reached beyond the scope of my typical job description. A general pause was in order. The thoughts in my mind needed to be sifted through cheesecloth and put into a logical order. They were swimming around in the soup of neurons and becoming a sludge of darkened deliberations. Attorney-like—they needed to be more judge-like.

When the plane landed in K-sea, I hurried for my parked car. I didn't bother with parting words and left the

Matches to fend for themselves. I was on a mission to unlock the door of my home and hop in a comfortable bed for a change.

Before the cock could crow, I snapped awake and jumped from my bed reinvigorated. It was time to change into my workout attire and head to the gym. An hour of hot yoga would release most of the cortisol building up in the muscles of my body.

The shower water was as cold as it would get and was the finishing touch that cycled into a refreshed feeling. I gnawed at an apple on the way to the library. Traffic on the interstate was heavy for a Saturday. Must have a big-name baseball team in town to take on the Crowns—most likely the Saint L's Red Beards. I pounded on the keypads of my electronic devices for a couple of hours and waited for the purple notifications to cascade across the screens, giving me the proceed endorsement. If not, I might need two hot yoga sessions and two ice-cold showers today.

No sooner did the thought cross my mind than my plan was set into motion.

A bright, shiny, banana yellow Whorvette pulled into the gas station. The vibration of the radio music was drowned out by the raucous base pouring out from the trunk—far from music at all, nothing more than loud noise. The car whipped around Janie's car and parked in front of them to get gas. Inside the Whorvette were two casually but well-dressed men. The passenger exited the car and went into the station. The trunk opened, and the driver exited the vehicle, pulled out a small black bag, and then a cooler setting them on the ground, one beside the other, and began pumping gas into the yellow sports car.

At the pump in the next lane was an office lady with long legs in high heels, her dress tight and short. She began a conversation with the driver, and it appeared they might have known each other. The passenger of the yellow Whorvette had returned with a bag of ice and twelve-pack of beer. He filled the cooler and put it in the trunk and then closed it, then hopped into the car to join his friend in conversation with the woman. She finished fueling, slid into her Lexxsis, tamped the gas pedal a couple of times, which made very little sound—then sped off. The driver of the Whorvette quickly put on the gas cap and squealed the tires out of the gas station, leaving the receipt dancing in the wind on the pump, the black bag forgotten in plain sight.

The black bag looked like an abandoned baby left on the front porch of a stranger. I was watching the video stream live from the security camera of the gas station, which I had already preselected based on all the compiled data collected for my sting operation. There was no sound. My view was strictly an optical interpretation. Janie froze at the pump and looked like she was shooting sign language to a blind lady. Janie was frantically pointing at the bag.

My team had successfully baited our prey. Being the opportunist, Janie instructed Kaylee to get out of the car and grab the bag. Kaylee refused her mom's instruction and slumped out of sight in the back seat of the car, showing signs of embarrassment. With wide eyes, she glared at Jillie Jo and pointed absurdly at the bag. Jillie Jo exited the vehicle and grabbed it, playing it off as if a lost puppy had been found. Janie placed the gas cap on and intentionally chose a contrary direction of the Whorvette.

They were now being trailed by law enforcement. The plan was to let some time pass before apprehension. All human emotions needed to be triggered. Inside the bag were smaller bags of redbud marijuana, a bottle of crystal meth, some white horse heroin cheese, two bottles of ecstasy, and large bottles of Vicodin and Oxycodone. Underneath the pills were stacks of cash, conveniently divided into three stacks of ten thousand one hundred dollars—a virtual gold mine in the projects. This sort of find could get someone killed very quickly in K-sea.

Six hours of dream identity was allowed to elapse. There were odd numbers of pills that they would divide three ways, an inheritance of give-and-take would make the bonds stronger. As far as I was concerned, I could care less if any of the garbage was recovered, to include the money. I just needed a successful conviction this time.

The three of them had gone to 432 Ohm Street and had been inside the dwelling for three hours. It was a renthouse of a fellow dancer, located close to A-Rose. Lilly, Janie, and Kaylee wasted no time trying to move the drugs to dealers. It would be way too easy to make the jackpot of money grow. They knew the hard men of the streets. I was made aware of most of the drug pushers. For those who danced to my music, a few pending charges would be dropped, a pre-plea bargain agreement sort of arrangement had already been made for helpful participants in advance, like twenty minutes ago.

Melissa had called to inform me that VeeLee was now back in their care and that children's services had left a message to inform them that Jillie Jo had been freed from prison and wanted her son back. She wanted to talk to and see him as soon as possible. I assured Melissa not to worry. I was currently dealing with the matter.

The tapped phone showed Jillie Jo had contacted her boss, and she needed some help. Aarontino Jackkson's SUV pulled into 432 Ohm Street, parked, and went directly into the dwelling. A random bonus, I thought, as the net of black and blue uniforms descended over the inhabitants like thick, unbreathable, toxic smoke.

The video I was watching was beyond top secret, taken from a private drone the size of a golf ball. The FBI nor the federal courts would be allowed to request a subpoena to view it. I wasn't interested in typical formality. However, I, too, would be filing a report of facts to the Nonagon, which was an entirely independent and more critical legal system. If someone goofed up along the way, *they* would be held accountable or disappear, not me. I wasn't taking any unnecessary chances and intended to utilize all available technologies at my disposal.

Aarontino had never been in trouble before, let alone in handcuffs. He had always been in complete control of his surroundings until now. Yet he said nothing during the interrogation and exercised his right to one phone call. The one phone call reached the west coast, contacting Geovanni Jackkson, his father. Aarontino did not utter a single word after that. I was told he remained in a serious state of pissed-off and paced nonstop in his cell. It was exactly the suffering I needed him to feel. Hopefully, he would stay out of my way going forward, and Jillie Jo would remain locked up this time.

Within twenty-four hours, the big guns filed off the private jet in K-sea, all in three-thousand-dollar suits looking like a Hollywood cast—six in total. The purple cloud on my computer identified three of the passengers as attorneys, two males, one female, very successful, and impressively attractive. He had two other females who were unknown at the moment, perhaps an accountant and a bedmate, or both were both.

I was trying to find out who they were from my fellow librarian watcher on the west coast. Typically, face recognition was fairly easy information to attain. Simply go through the passengers' manifest, and you could profile them down to a match. Private planes, however, were private for that very reason—influential passengers liked privacy. When that freedom was challenged, it could morph into a complicated matter very quickly. When entities of money, ego, and power collided at my level, it was nothing more than cashing in an insurance policy—casualties be damned.

Geovanni's first stop was not to set bail for Aarontino, but he instead went directly to Aarontino's luxurious home to set up shop. Within two hours, Geovanni relocated to the *A-Rose* restaurant and checked the computers for a couple of hours. A team of three soon left K-sea and flew to Saint L's to most likely perform the same investigation there. Searching and sorting through the financials to discern if his son's management of the two satellite restaurants were being managed correctly.

He obviously knew his son was in jail for a reason and saw fit to close any loopholes before they could be exploited. Meanwhile, his attorneys were at the courthouse making motions and filing arguments with grandeur in the likes that had not been seen by the Mizzeree court in years.

Motions would be heard on two fronts in two courts—the three attorneys would rotate from the two cities. In K-sea, the lawyers would focus on clearing Aarontino of all erroneous charges dealing with the drug bust. Lawyers in Saint L's would be suing the court of K-sea for defamation of character, financial losses, and police brutality as Aarontino suffered deep bruises around both wrists from the handcuffs being wrenched down so tightly that his hands went numb.

I never thought a pair of food guys could be so challenging. Geovanni brought his A-game. I quite frankly didn't care about his son whatsoever. He could be set free, land a decent settlement, and disappear back into his culinary world. Jillie Jo, Janie, and Kaylee would be going down—supported by a millionaire or not. I'm a librarian for God's sake.

Chapter 15

Anglaia's war campaign on Mother

IT WAS SATURDAY MORNING, AND HIS body was not occupying the chair in the corner of the kitchen. That chair had never been sat in regularly by anyone before. *VeeLee's chair is empty*. I kicked myself for the thought. He will never have a chair here—ever! It was quiet in a good way. Father said Mike had come to pick VeeLee up in the wee hours of the morning, and my response was simple and to the point, "Yijaaa!" I paused. "Good riddance, foster boy!"

Father smiled at me.

My mind was still reeling around thoughts of Victor Angelino losing his life so tragically. Not even one lungful of air. His eyes would not leave one tear nor capture one vision. His brain would not create one memory of the outside world—ever. Danielle's milk-filled boobs would not be sucked dry one time by her sweet son. I had to go with Dan the hospice nurse's *storm of death* story and focus on sunshine thoughts of today. Hopefully, Danielle's heart could find some peaceful spaces in the storm soon.

Motorcycles and cars began to snake around the curbs outside our home, and noise began to echo around in the poker room like old times. I couldn't help but make an appearance. It was a duty of mine. I liked getting massive amounts of attention.

I always liked to see Frankie's tight shirts showing off his soldier-boy, badass muscles. I wasn't physically attracted to him, but he was a beautiful man-form and a friend who would back my family and me up no matter what. It drove all the other players nuts when he treated me like his little girlfriend, calling me cute-stuff and such. In return, I always cheered loudly for him when he won a hand, which even annoyed my father. Occasionally, a player would get ticked-off and huff out of the room to smoke a cigarette outside.

Frankie had only one response, "Don't hate the player, hate the game," and would laugh out loud in a cocky manner. He could most likely whoop everyone in the room at the same time in five minutes. Every now and again, I'd sit on his meaty thigh, trying to bring him good luck. Sometimes he would tickle me until I laughed so loud father asked me to go play in my room. William, the police officer, did not seem impressed by Frankie. He usually had a pistol hanging off to his side, on duty or not.

No sooner did I dismiss Frankie's baggy shirt for the skin-tight ones he usually wore, I noticed in great disbelief foster boy had managed his way back into my home in less than eight hours. He sat smugly as Mike introduced him to the players. Just the occasion Mike relished: open air to rattle his voice.

Most stumbled over VeeLee's name. Some would try to assert the abridged "Vee," which he quickly countered. I had heard him correct a hundred people in just a few months of knowing him. It was so annoying to me. I couldn't figure out why he even bothered correcting the pronunciation of his name. People screwed mine up all the time. The only reason I had to correct them was that I was a princess—*he* is not.

My first thought was to hop in my Mustdang GT and get out of here. Just as I grabbed my keys from the kitchen counter, I overheard someone crack a joke aimed at VeeLee's age. A little pregame gamesmanship, yet he seemed unaffected by the intimidation tactic. I thought, "What the hell?" It couldn't hurt to see if he was any good. I actually knew how the card game was played and had sat down to fill in for absent players before. I didn't have a poker face and didn't care about the game one bit. I would just toss the cards down. If they won, they won. When the poker chips were gone, I was done. Pretty simple.

VeeLee held his own for a while. He outlasted half the players. In a shocking hand, he was defeated by what was known as a bad beat on an "*All-in*" bet, which meant he had bet all his poker chips on his hand. His full house of aces and eights was beaten by two pairs of kings.

Everyone went into a tizzy and called for a cigarette, beer, and bathroom break. VeeLee smiled at me—so I flipped him off and said, "You suck," performed three pirouettes and left the poker room laughing at him.

"Thanks, Anglaia," he said.

VeeLee had managed to stay on the playing table longer than Mike, which might make for some annoying conversations for him later in the evening. The thought rang in my ears for a hot minute. I then smiled to myself at how perfect that now sounded to me.

Give him hell, Mike…

While they sat around the table playing cards, Father described the facelift being applied to Grandmother's home in Bronson. We would see the work effort first-hand tomorrow after the church service was delivered at the Assemblage. The boys could talk about construction all they pleased. My focus bounced from that topic to my mother. It was time she was cornered about her dreams again.

My mind kept going back to the conversation I had with foster boy Friday morning on our way to Horseshoe High. Mom and Melissa were visiting over a glass of wine. Melissa promptly grabbed the bottle and put it between her legs. Mr. Rocky Wino might be out of luck again.

"Mother. How is it foster boy knows about your nightmares, a*nd I don't?*"

Melissa's attention roused, and Mother rolled her eyes at me as if I had poured ice water onto the spirit of her wine.

"Not now, Anglaia," Mother said

"You should just tell her, Sarah. The world will not come to an end," Melissa said.

"Not now, Melissa. We have a house full of people," Mother said with a tone that ended the subject. No doubt the nightmares would be back tonight as they had uncorked bottle number two already. So damned annoying. Mother picked up on their previous conversation and asked, "So, have you told VeeLee that his mom is out of prison?"

"There has not been time for a sit-down, yet. It was three-thirty in the morning by the time we made it home with him this morning. We haven't been able to contact social services, either. I want to know the facts better before I become stressed or freak him out with bad information. It will have to wait until Monday," Melissa said.

"Wow! I hope he does go back to his mom in K-sea," I said helpfully.

Melissa looked through me and my comment as if neither made much sense. Her attachment to the mothering gig was beginning to materialize. Melissa liked the kid and the idea of having a sort-of-a-son dialog to preserve.

"Melissa, not to change the subject, but are you going with Anglaia and I Wednesday to Victor Angelino's funeral services? Danielle's baby?" Mom asked.

"I would like to be supportive, Sarah, but I have been away from work for two weeks, and I'm sure my supervisor would not be understanding. I could come over after work and be with you and Anglaia if you like," Melissa said.

We were in the middle of a chick-flick conversation, so I had to press Mother again. "Mother..." She filled her eyes with my moving lips, "There are just us girls in this room. I want to know about the nightmares. Everyone else knows but me. *Please*." I glowered.

"Not now," she snapped.

I moseyed back out to the poker room, where they were wrapping things up. Mike was chumming it up with Father and Frankie. Others had left, and there were only three guys left at the poker table.

"Nice to hear your mom is out of prison, VonVouge," I said. Everyone in earshot became perplexed and put on murky masks of confused facial gestures. I skipped away outside, fired up the Mustdang GT, and took off. My point was to let him know that I knew things about his mom that he didn't know, too. Next time he wanted to bring up something about my mom's nightmares, I would bring up something about his mom being in prison. Sounded fair to me. I felt better as I drove off but was sure I would hear about my comment later.

Anglaia had managed to make me as mad as I'd ever been. I had absolutely no idea what she was talking about or trying to prove by throwing my mom under the proverbial bus. Mention of my mom and her prison stay was something I realized was out of my control. But for her to casually blab it out to strangers in an insulting manner pained me and the heart of Christopher, which seemed to twist into a hard knot. Her goal was simply to disrespect me.

The last forty-eight hours were a blur. I was extremely worn out. Bruce had come to my room and shook me out of my sleep at three in the morning to go home with Mike. It seemed no sooner was I back to sleep, Mike was shaking my bed again at eight to eat breakfast, and I would be heading back to the Clintins' home at noon. I really wasn't interested in playing Texas Hold 'Em, but I felt obligated to say yes. We were there for seven hours.

I couldn't see any life situation that could bring Anglaia and me closer together. We had been through more than most married couples in the last three months. Anglaia's mind was spinning in the opposite direction as mine. I was the heat that made her feel uncomfortable—a fire she had to put out as soon as she could. Her soul was heavy, her heart hollowed by the clutter of conceptual things. She was ruled by thoughts and more thoughts. I was trying not to identify with her as such, but anger was seeping into my mindstream.

I missed K-sea, Lara London, my old friends, Toozoolee, Berry Alpha and Berry Omega. Darwin would tell me to adapt to my environment or die. I knew my situation was getting better by the day here in Queenfield, but if my mom was truly out of prison, I would need to un-evolve to my former style of existence. A very stressful proposition. If I were put in the position where I had to choose—God help me, but Mom would get the nod every time.

I looked at Mike, ballooning the whites of my eyes as big as I could. I raised both empty palms of my hands upward, nonverbally asking, "What's up, daddy-dude?" He pointed to go outside, where he had fumbled around with various "not sure" answers. I tried not to be dramatic, knowing he had just suffered the loss of *his* mom, and I think we were all still shaken by Victor Angelino's death. I could tell Mike was upset with Anglaia, too. We left it as an open matter. Children's services should provide better answers on Monday.

A tipsy Melissa snickered when she missed a step and nearly fell to the ground. Mike opened her car door and poured her into the front seat, buckled her seatbelt, and drove us home. We parted ways the moment we walked through the door of their home. My bedroom smelled new again as if day one had returned. I put my shoes under the bed and stretched out spread-eagle on the mattress. My eyelids slammed shut as if spring-loaded.

Early morning birds were calling to the worms, and squirrels ran up and down the gutters, performing great acrobatic feats in well-rehearsed raids on the bird feeder mounted next to my window. I rolled from the bed and stood at the window, sipping on the morning sun. Inspired, I pulled on my running shorts and shoes and decided to go for a run. The outside air was crisp and felt good as I gulped it down. The trot around the neighborhood was exacting a chemical chain reaction in my muscles, a suffering that would release all forms of dead things stored deep in my cells, toxins that would be flushed out sometime during the day.

The longer I ran, the more my mind sorted through every dialog and event that had recently occurred. I was laboring through the heavy thoughts that surrounded my current situation. It was near impossible to humanly rationalize into a favorable context. Thoughts of every manner flashed like lightning in my mind. My football performance was replayed in a loop for a time, followed by the manner I played my hands in the poker game and processing my classes and homework assignments due at Horseshoe High. For once, I had no overdue books that needed to be raced to the Library.

The hottest topic right now was my feelings of being returned to my mom and my hostile relationship with Anglaia. I might need to run the circumference of the earth a couple of times to get it all lined out. I was trying to set free all ideas that did not serve my greater good. Most were out of my control, anyway, and I had to remind myself not to give most issues any attention at all, as they were simply exaggerations of the voice inside my head.

I would rather focus on my theories and formulas for capturing the sun. I discovered in recent readings on thermonuclear fusion that photons from the sun delivered over one thousand benefits to the human body other than vitamin D, which most know is a powerhouse in metabolism and so much more. I ended my run on these thoughts and smiled to myself.

I rounded the corner and back onto the street I now lived. I slowed to a walk and pressed footprints into the dew-soaked grass. A red squirrel raced up the oak tree and settled on a limb long enough to bark at me. It sneaked around the tree as I moved to the front door of the Matches home, watching my every move.

During breakfast, Mike and I were informed by Melissa that we would be going to Jacob and Adamina-Rose's for the home make-over pool party.

I had not been there since we had Harry McCrackin arrested for the murder of Sofia and had no idea how the home with a new face underwent the knife. One thing for sure, there would be subject matter galore to converse over. I was asked to bring out my laundry for Melissa to wash. I would also need to roll my swimming garb into a beach-towel and bring it along, as we were going to Anglaia's grandparents' in Bronson straightaway after our church meeting at the Assemblage.

Once showered, the mirror reflected a fake person in foreign attire. The church clothing made me feel dorky. The fabric, colors, and design were way off from my personality and stung my eye like onion juice. Melissa's voice reached out from the kitchen, calling me to come to breakfast.

"Coming!" I said.

I grabbed my rolled towel of pool garb and made my way to the table. The teabags under Mike's eyes told a tired tale of their own. There didn't seem to be any downtime in the foreseeable future. We loaded up and headed to Oatzark to listen to Pastor Dom at the Assemblage. We would leave kinder kindred souls. Amen.

Mike parked, and we loafed to the front door and made our way into the sanctuary. Melissa scanned the pews of the congregation in search of Sarah, who was waving to us. She, Bruce, and Anglaia were about thirty rows down and to the left.

We shuffled over knees and shoes and shifted sideways past people unknown to us until we reached the seats Sarah had reserved. I think Anglaia received the exact same "you're unbelievable girl" look from all three of us as we passed her to get to our seats. Church or not, I still got flipped off and read her lips that said, "Bite me."

All I could do was smile and consider it part of my job interview. Bruce was watching my every move. There were only a few more football games left, and there was no way our team was good enough to make it to any postseason playoffs. We were average. My focus would now shift to going to work at Top Chops and earning my independence in the form of four wheels—my first car.

My mom could potentially change my plans, but I would not allow Anglaia to pinch the life out of my goals with her miss-priss, I'm-better-than-everybody, me-me-me attitude. No matter how challenging that may become.

The Assemblage had a guest speaker on the stage, a preacher named Larry Luck out of Palace, Texus. He went over Jewish roots a bit and then transitioned into his main topic, *Take no Offense.* He told of his mistakes, a prison stay, and that basically, all the suffering in the world took place on a wooden cross. No one needed to suffer anymore. Everyone's heart and mind could be healed. He was a wise man and motivated the crap out of everybody. Christopher's heart was open, strumming to a happier beat than the okey-doke thoughts waffling inside my mind—we didn't always agree. Be that as it may, if I had a dollar, I would have most likely put it on the offering plate. When the service had ended, we bunched into a bouquet of people. After the adults rendered a thousand yesses and okays, we exited the Assemblage.

"Do you want to ride with me," Anglaia asked. Everything in my being became confused, and I wanted to say no thanks immediately. I felt as though I had just walked in front of a firing squad without a blindfold. The invitation caught me off guard. She was showing her unpredictable side. Everyone else seemed shocked, too. I thought she might have dug a deep hole on her way to church and wanted to toss me in and bury me—most likely alive.

I didn't say a word. I just followed her to the car and watched everyone shrug it off in their own way. We sat in the car without a word. All the cars going to Jacob and Adamina-Rose's place were driving off. Yet, Anglaia did not start the Mustdang GT. She seemed to be enjoying a power trip. I took off my tie and loosed the first two buttons of my shirt. I took a deep breath and blew it out as if trying to blow out the candles of Mother Nature's birthday cake. A very long breath.

"I want to know, VeeLee."

"I've been wanting to get to know the good side of you, too, Anglaia. I'm really not a dragon you must slay. We could be friends," I said.

"I'm not talking about *you*! I want to know what you were told about my mother's nightmares. That is all," Anglaia said and started the engine.

"Sure. I will tell you what *I* was told, anyway." She turned off her radio and cocked an ear as she pulled out of the parking lot. "Can I have a friendship truce first?" I asked. She brought the Mustdang GT to a stop at the red-lit traffic light. She flipped her lighted sun-visor down, rumbled through her purse, grabbing for lip gloss, quickly applied, and clanked it back into her purse.

She tightened her shiny, sparkling, wet lips together and rolled them against one another like mating anacondas. Her eyes rolled up as she gesticulated with her right hand for me to tell the story.

"Truce?" I repeated. Her head bobbed mostly up and down. So, I began to give as descriptive a narrative as my mind owned. No frills nor fluff. A version that might connect the dots to the current relationship with her mother, or lack thereof. I started by saying, "On a rainy day when your mother was a young girl, she was chased in the woods by her brothers and cousins—" That's when she promptly stopped me.

"Stop. Nope. Never mind," Anglaia said.

Not a story she could handle coming from me, in this venue I supposed. She cranked the radio up, and I gripped the door tight as she recklessly drove the white-knuckled curvy roads of the Oatzark Mountains again. I hoped we would survive her heavy, go-fast foot. The Mustdang came to a purr, and we pulled up to her grandparents' home, our lips puckered tight into areolas of wow.

It was grandeur with a capital G. It seemed that an artist had repainted the blush of beautiful tulips, saffron crocus, parrot's beak, and yellow-purple lady slippers exactly where they had previously been, even the rare, blue-green jade vine that mustached across the top of the late bloom of rhododendron had been put back as it was. The giant castle doors and big wood were back in place.

The new facelift of the mansion was spectacular. It simply amazed my imagination. The effort and tons of cash did create a priceless view. It was magical and beautiful—everything a mansion was supposed to be. It was doubtful that any neighbor would attempt to top the ultimate one-up.

"Wow," came from my mouth, without effort.

"Nice," Anglaia said with a smile and parked the Mustdang.

Her mood shifted, and she swooped from the car and bounced on her tiptoes to her Grandfather Jacob and latched on. Adamina-Rose was explaining their undertaking and all the challenges they faced during the project. To include coming back from Key-la-fornee early, due mainly to our fabulous detective work of Harry. I doubted we would be allowed to forget that story anytime soon. We shuffled inside and viewed from the inside out perspective and were awe-inspired once again. The view of Table Lock Lake through walls of glass was spectacular.

After the niceties, the group fanned out to vacant rooms to change clothes and relax the flattered look plastered on our congratulatory faces. It was now time to enjoy the pool for a few hours. Anglaia summoned her cheerleading friends over who produced girly squeals and laughs. Happiness splashed on the light breeze and danced in ears like a bear feasting on fat salmon. The pool water felt amazing, and I was back in the purple swimming shorts that featured a gold silly sun situated right over my package, shorts the Clintin's had instructed me to keep. Anglaia thought it hilarious, yet it mattered not to me.

I straddled a pool chair and took off my shirt. Where conversation over Christopher's heart followed. I explained that all I knew, which was a very little. It was a genetic deviation that would degenerate over time and quit working. Only that mom said it was a miracle that her baby boy found a match. The doctors expected it to take many years to get a heart, if I could live long enough to find a match. The match came shortly after my dad shot himself, I explained.

Bruce said, "So, did they tell you anything about Christopher?"

His expression curious—his voice upbeat.

"Not really sure his name is even Christopher… I just know in some of my dreams boys are playing and the one that feels like I'm seeing through his eyes calls out to his big brother Johnny—who always replies back to Christopher."

"I think I actually remember reading about a similar story. Where a girl was murdered, and her organs were donated. The girl who got her heart ended up catching the murderer by the vivid dreams that followed. True story not kidding." Mike said.

Bruce and Jacob looked at him. Mike shrugged his shoulders and showed his top teeth.

"That's all I know. It's a strong heart and I'm grateful." Christopher's heart fluttered a patch of goosebumps down my side.

"Yes, happy you received it VeeLee," Bruce said.

"Thanks. Me too." I said and the conversation turned to the meat on the grill.

I was distracted with other thoughts and pressed to consider other matters—the main one being that this might be my last visit here. Monday was blackening my spirit. I shook my head to the log jam of thoughts pouring into my brain about the potential reality of being reunited with my mom and rebooting my life in K-sea.

Up until this point, I had not walked the banks of the Table Lock lake nor ventured away from the Bronson home and out into the wilderness, a stretch only footsteps away. The benefits of my morning run had fizzled out. The blood in my veins seemed to thicken into a sludge—a sputtered flow that created a stagnant, yucky feeling in my gut.

I approached Jacob Clintin, who was flipping every sort of meat around in the flames of the grill and asked if it would be okay to take a walk around the lake and woodland.

"Why sure! just let Mike know," Jacob said.

"Yes, sir. Thank you, Mr. Clintin," I said.

I approached Mike with the question, who said, "That's fine. Just stay close by. Don't think we need to organize a search party today. Now, do we?" he said and laughed obnoxiously while he nodded yes with all his top teeth showing again.

"No, sir, Mr. Matches," I said and left the pool area.

I trekked out of the yard and down the dirt road. Sounds of the get together became muffled and distant with every step I took. Soon the silence was broken by the occasional outboard motor of a boat, then returned to silence. I sat at water's edge for a bit, listened to the waves crash onto the shore leaving invisible wounds in the chunks of limestone littering the bank of the Lake. I watched a few fish break the surface of the water in random places only to return to their indiscernible struggles of the underwater world.

A pronounced game trail came into view and opened up into the womb of nature. *Perhaps this ancient gal would lend me a few drops of wisdom*, I thought to myself. I traveled the mountain's backbone for a time, focusing on various landmarks to guide me out later. I came to a creek and spent some time chucking rocks into a bridge for a dry crossing. The ancient gal motioned me to a stop with a challenge, which I soon scaled—a nine-ton boulder that I fashioned into a seat for a king. Streams I could now see trickled around me like blood veins and arteries, supplying life throughout the land.

Darwin, Mark Twain, and philosophers galore might have been on to something when it came to nature, I thought as I listened to the wind carrying sounds and frequencies on the air. The wind transformed into a music conductor of the classical variety, utilizing the spilling water over rocks, trees' limbs and leaves, birds, and insects, composing every manner of sounds into a symphony—a classical crossover.

Earth was singing a song of love into my soul. She had practiced this one for millions of years. Her music was aged and ripe and perfect. Not one word—yet I understood and felt every note. It was a masterpiece to be played only once, just for me. I wondered what Mother Nature's prescription would be to heal the hurt of my human heart and my messy mind. I was feeling better just by being silent. Perhaps I had found my new physician, one who had no fee. She made me feel so free. I would have to see her in the future for a follow-up as I liked the way she composed her magical lilt, and could gulp down her medicine by the gallons.

"Thank you, Mother Nature," I said out loud and slid down the rock face, giving leave to the next passerby. In my mind, this was a sacred place. I named it: *Curevibesea*. The vibration I felt was incredible, and the space was so alive and beautiful. I would have guessed I had been gone two hours or so when I made it back to the pool scene.

Little had changed other than a few people had left. The contrast did make an impression. There were a million things going on in nature just a short distance away, and no human would ever be the wiser. Man might one day reform her here, too, which would be upsetting to know that I had felt her love here in this place. But, in the end, Mother Nature will outlive men's silly piles of Egyptian pyramid stones and iron skyscraper shadow projects, which I have deemed nothing more than a provisional period of caveman ding-a-lings, no matter what year it is.

Chapter 16

Lara London, courting Queenfield, caging questions and colliding conclusions

I WAS UP ATE SUNDAY NIGHT DETAILING MY next wave of orders. The only difference between my war room and some military joint task force was I had no physical people, per se. Members of my staff were all virtual, computer-generated, and managed. They were all librarians like me, for all

intents and purposes. We could end or resolve most any war without a bloodbath if the kings so allowed. War, however, is a moneymaker, and the kings of the Nonagon did like to boast their bank account balance to the entire world every single day.

The Nine Kings' total worth was, in fact, the national debt of every country in the world. The North American continent was twenty trillion, add that to every other country's debt in the world, and you have *nine* massively, beyond-wealthy egos. It was completely mind-boggling that not one of them, in the last thousand years, had had an emotional meltdown or was discovered by some past whistleblower entity.

The Nonagon's shadow tide of power ran all governments, politicians, taxes, billionaires, and sometimes they felt the need to control the weather on the planet, too. The trickle-down, in turn, ran every living soul.

Each king in the Nonagon was a multi-trillionaire and would scoff at the Forbies top one hundred richest people in the world. Those mentioned in a magazine were billionaire baby fish in the grand scheme of things. Most suspected for centuries that there were wealthy people in the shadows managing politicians in government. The Deep State. Luminaries—powerful vampiric puppeteers taking whatever they wanted. And they were right.

The billionaires who controlled Washaton-D-sea were merely puppets for the kings of the Nonagon, also known as K-9. Representatives were planted through general elections in Washaton-D-sea, and at all times. Nine watchers representing the Nine Kings roamed freely in the chamber of the house, and nine watchers roamed the senate floor, making for a pretty good-sized power projection platform of persuasion.

It was early Monday morning, and the purple screen on the computer had a dozen menu bars awaiting the tip of my acrylic fingernail. It was showtime, and the execution orders were sent downstream. I noticed my smile reflecting in my coffee cup, took a satisfying sip, and thought this could get rather interesting, and quick.

The purple cloud was an all-information system, the highest level in existence. Completely separate from the world wide web, both systems were the property of the Nonagon. Occasionally, in the best interest of cashing in on the chaos, computer hackers were allowed to publish digital viruses and create general mayhem. The purple cloud monitored all governments, in all languages, at all times. The internet was as successful as law, war, religion, tax, the stock market, farming, medicine, and insurance. The Nonagon knew how to make money, and what power of the people really was.

Generic computer-based versions were created for folks in the CIA, FBI, the theatrical stars of Washaton-D-sea, and other mainstream countries. Again, the purple cloud mandated and monitored all intellectual property. Organizational use was not optional. The public version, the world wide web, was released free of charge, and the goldmine made the kings unstoppably unstoppable.

In a nutshell, anything that put out a signal, I had access to instantly. It was time to get to work. After viewing the court motions and law enforcement data, to include the latest videos the purple cloud provided, a picture morphed in front of my eyes. So curious, these puzzle pieces, yet they fitted together like flames and heat. The picture I was looking at was making me gulp down my swallows. A picture where the painter used florescent, eye-popping paint that made my eyes itch. The purple cloud information added exquisite attention to detail, and the true Jackkson family story began to tattle on itself.

The filters of the purple cloud were astounding. It could focus in on any person of interest and project, prevent, predict, and protect the interests of the Nonagon. Everything and everyone in the world was fair game. Unbeknownst to the outer world, the center of gravity was the Nonagon. Its echo and vibration were many bandwidths ahead of comprehension. A knowledge pool of thousands of geniuses in the caliber of Leonardo da Vinci, Isaac Newton, Galileo, Tesla, and Einstein had been handpicked over the centuries—they had engineered the most sophisticated organization in the history of mankind.

The information I was collecting was getting very spicy. The universe was playing a movie titled, "It's a very small world," produced and directed by God. Everything was beginning to connect in unpredictable ways. Geovanni was much more than a restaurant owner, and the former bad boy I had characterized him as in my initial judgment.

His son, Aarontino, was indeed a profiteer, but not engaged in the dark underworld where most activities were frowned upon by the law. His father had thrust him into a place where mental toughness was key. His father, Geovanni, knew the hidden way, the great things—he owned untraceable bullets that could erase the blackboard of Nonagon problems. He knew how to wipe someone out. You had to be extremely intelligent to collect the hefty profits and last as long as the Jackksons had in culinary cuisines. Geovanni's dream of making A-Rose the Micky D's of fine dining had been underway for twenty years now. The Jackkson family had earned respect, money, and *influence*. They were better connected than I could have imagined.

Aarontino had been bailed out and was now stowed away inside *A-Rose* with his father. From the purple cloud, I was watching them through the cameras on their computers, phones, security cameras, and smart TV. The devices were giving me real-time footage and critical communiqué. There were some bizarre incongruencies zapping my computer I had not seen before—some form of interference that resembled a lost signal or something. I couldn't put my finger on the glitch.

Jillie Jo was the main topic, and VeeLee their main concern. This knowledge blew my mind. Two Ivy-educated and highly successful men concerned about a poor inner-city white kid piqued my curiosity. So much so, an electrical fire was set ablaze by the neurons in my brain. Soon a synaptic dance of chemical signals merged into a hot soup of hormones and emotions, creating a synergy of conceptual formations in my mind. It seemed we all had a thing for VeeLee VonVouge.

VeeLee was my sole purpose for the past few years, and I was prepared to fight for him. Fortunately for me, Geovanni could not see what I was now seeing on the purple cloud. If we were on the same informational playing field, I would have the fight of a lifetime on my hands. They were getting along pretty damn well, without the advantages I enjoyed.

Geovanni's lawyers were now determined to set Jillie Jo, her sister Janie, and Janie's daughter, Kaylee, free by getting the entire case dismissed before it even had a chance to sprout legs in the minds of the DA's consciousness.

I had the prosecutors notified that this was a high priority case, and there would be no deals for the ladies. I buzzed Melissa and told her that Jillie Jo was locked up again and to gently let VeeLee know that his mom was in trouble again, back in jail, and most likely headed to prison.

I now knew Geovanni wasn't going to go quietly. He was a strong, wealthy man and used to getting his way. He and Aarontino had a personal interest in Jillie Jo, and I now knew it was a great deal more than a chemically challenged, chump-change, stripper-slash-waitress. There were a thousand Jillie Jos in the K-sea area they could hire. Just about anyone would have been a much better choice to hire, especially for part-time help. The puzzle pieces kept heating the fire.

Jillie Jo had been connected to Geovanni years ago, all the way back to when she and her husband Robert were in the military, stationed on the west coast in Key-la-fornee. It was possibly the motive Robert ended his life over. Robert had gotten involved with some bad actors, drugs, and gambling. His wife, Jillie Jo, was hired by Geovanni to wait tables according to court documents filed against Robert by Geovanni. Initially, Robert met his wife's boss, Geovanni, at A-Rose, and had pleaded for help. Geovanni tried to help save Robert's military career and made some calls and paid off the debts owed to the bad actors. When Robert did not honor the payment agreement, Geovanni's long-forgotten personality raged.

Late at night in the back office of A-Rose', Jillie Jo tried to ease Geovanni's growing anger and made an interest payment on the debt, taking off her clothes. Robert, tired of waiting in the car for his wife to get off from work, walked into the restaurant, opened the door to see his wife's feet saying hello to the ceiling fan. Robert steadied himself in the doorway and glared with vomit in his throat. The pressure built up into a drunken verbal volley and then Robert exploded physically on the two. Once his suit pants were pulled up, Geovanni easily dispatched Robert and escorted him out of A-Rose. It was a significant night Jillie Jo would never forget—Geovanni was unforgettable.

Robert, wholly defeated, packed Jillie Jo up and vanished from the military and Key-la-fornee, the six thousand-dollar debt never repaid.

Geovanni had ruffled quite a few feathers over the years regarding his ideas of business payments. When it came time to pay for your food, you better have the money you owed him. Back in his college days, where he managed a strip club, he was not as well mannered. From what I was learning, he enjoyed the power and the constant flow of sexy dancers, bouncers, and mounds of money that were under his control. He liked being out from under his father's "always do good" control and the pressure to be Superman or a super athlete.

Geovanni was impressionable in his early twenties. The raw street life was alluring and more attractive than becoming a professional ballplayer like his father. He wanted no part of the harsh ridicule of fans and announcers, morons he had watched criticize his father on television for how he played the game. Power was the first thing he set out to achieve. He, on occasion, accepted trade or an interest payment on unpaid tabs and small amounts of drug money owed. If a man had a gold watch, necklace, attractive wife, or girlfriend who was interested in a quick sexual rendering, it would be considered an interest payment and buy some time. Geovanni did not forgive money debts and kept track of every dime. Every penny was worth giving someone a black eye and sore ribs over— immediately and repeatedly if need be.

Fear equaled respect, which went hand in hand with loyalty. Geovanni demanded respect and loyalty over all else. Life was not a game. It was serious business—insurance against returning to the nightmares of childhood poverty Geovanni's father railed against. Every minute of every day, reminders were sent out to all who did business under the same sky. Anyone who knew Geovanni knew if he had to open his mouth and say something, somebody was most likely about to have a bad day. A basic meal at A-Rose was a hundred-dollar bill. Politely pay the bill—it's the deal.

A scumbag on the take could only hope to be gifted with common sense enough to avoid contact and take wide routes around him. If he caught the perpetrator, the violence of his voice would come first. Methods of doing business changed to hot hands if roaring failed. He simply hated thieves. Pain was the punctuation when the message needed to be clear, especially for repeat nonpayment offenders. As his success and bank account grew, his temperament aged into a classier man. Lawyers would come out from the wild blue yonder and attack his offenders and thieves. Any person who thought of getting out of paying for a chef-prepared meal had another thing coming when it came to balking at A-Rose.

He was now mild-mannered and projected a sweet smile to the men and women who visited his world. They were always met with his cavalier personality. In the olden days, Geovanni made patrons at the strip club feel lucky and that they would soon get lucky with whatever fix they were looking for. Now, laughter was his prized ingredient. Many a stuffy staff member was fired for frowning on the job.

Geovanni had learned he had to work a person within the first two steps of entering his establishment. The seductive bewitchment began when breath mixed. It was when the money spell was cast. The art of talking was the trick, the magic. In the strip club, dirty-minded money generated by nakedness, drugs, and the naughty world Geovanni created made its way into his home safe by the truckloads of untraceable cash. Crackheads and horny drunks with money needed this venue. Geovanni delighted in entertaining their desires and ape chest-pounding needs up to a point. It was a venue where access to drugs, drinks, and his dancers could be had, but there were the *rules*. Geovanni's. Period. All the deals were to finance his dream and the eventual bloom of A-Rose, his five-star fine-dining diamond.

I had to leave the interesting court documents and put my focus back on VeeLee.

Information was coming across my screen, one cargo ship after another. Melissa messaged that she had informed VeeLee of his mom's situation. In her opinion, he seemed a little disappointed but stated it was simply a dropped pickle kind of deal, and he would just have to enjoy the rest of the cheeseburger—enjoy the rest of the day—the rest of his life. I recognized this analogy and could see his face and his sincere eyes. It was the kid I had molded, a knowing that made me smile. It was clear he was making an impression on Melissa, too.

I was collecting information for my move to Queenfield, as well. I had narrowed my realtors down to a bright young lady who was willing to do virtual tours of potential homes. I would be paying cash and needed a physical address so that I could begin making arrangements for new things to be delivered.

It would most likely be a very temporary home. When VeeLee graduated high school and went off to college, I'd move back to K-sea and take back the helm of the library I loved. For now, it looked like a two-year tour of duty in Queenfield, Mizzeree. Ready or not, I'll be southbound soon.

I informed Melissa of my impending transfer. I was mater-fact when I told her I was not a foster parent and was not going to do her job. VeeLee, on the other hand, would be welcome at the Queenfield library any time, and we could continue our informational journey of books and thoughts and visit more king prerequisites. He was heavy on my mind today. Time was pocketing seasons since we last spoke, since our lips made sound together.

I was closing the loop on the whirlwind of friends I stirred up in Basston. Most calls went unanswered. I would return them when things were more manageable. It was likely I would be requesting some legal expertise from Bobby, my sister's husband, a jerk, and genius. He would need to brush up on some Mizzeree law for me. Seldom would I consider using him for my personal gain. If ever there was a time to let bygones be bygones, it was now. I consciously accepted option A—to win.

Bobby's ego was like licking a porcupine—sooner or later you'd be pulling out a quill, nothing made him happier than to take money from me. Working with him would be like dumping a tablespoon of salt into my mouth, but worth it. Contending with Geovanni and Aarontino's lawyers would take a mastermind counselor. Bobby would get a kick out of the challenge. The Jackksons were making some waves on the purple cloud, and it was becoming clear my involvement would need to be heightened.

I spent the next forty-five minutes recruiting my brother-in-law over the phone. He adamantly declined and said *no* in every possible manner. It was only when I offered information that would guarantee victory in three of his current lawsuits that he agreed. He would basically be a court cop in the case of Jillie Jo, Janie, and Kaylee anyway.

He would be a chef directing a buffet line—feeding the prosecuting attorney all the right morsels for a satisfied tummy. I needed guaranteed convictions. I was good with a shameful victory. I notified my twin sister of the business matter involving her husband. And told her if Bobby did, in fact, need to come to K-sea for court, he could stay at my place. I would likely be living in Queenfield full-time very soon. I would be keeping my home in K-sea. It had taken a great deal of effort to adorn this home with all the nuances that made me comfortable and happy. I identified with and loved the "thing."

Bobby would legally break the key off in the door of the prison cell. VeeLee's mom, Jillie Jo, must remain locked up this time. It was crucial.

I was learning that Aarontino would likely vote for a Jillie Jo's lock-up if he could. She had always been a thorn in his shoe. Showing up late, making dramatic scenes in front of influential guests, and her attire most often looked as if she had pulled it from a duffle bag. Geovanni, his father, on the other hand, was fully attuned to her state of affairs. In watching their live conversations, Aarontino was disgusted and more concerned about public opinion and damage control. The media loop needed to be addressed, and the Jackkson family's good name returned to highfalutin, upper-class status.

The private jet had made another round-robin from Key-la-fornee to K-sea, to Saint L's, and back to K-sea. At Aarontino's home, rental cars spotted the driveway like ink stains on a wedding dress. I was getting access inside through the purple cloud. The information was becoming increasingly fuzzy, though. My peeping-tom footage was being turned off device by device. It was obvious they had brought in tech support and would soon be off the grid in all locations in Mizzeree. Aarontino's homes and the *A-Rose* Restaurants in both locations would not be transparent for much longer. The Nonagon's purple cloud would need to step up its high-tech game.

It would be increasingly difficult to maintain any semblance of control of this situation alone. I now needed to officially anoint half a dozen fellow librarians. Over-kill, perhaps, but if I had a knockout punch, I would have already thrown it. I initially thought it best to simply contact Geovanni and Aarontino personally, asking them to stand down and let fate have its way with one of their employees.

My overseer axed that notion promptly and was becoming more involved in this matter. Typically, I had two or three monitoring my electronic movements on a daily basis, which would be displayed in a box on my computer or phone, something I was completely comfortable with. Now the display had twelve viewers to include a king's crown, denoting one of the most powerful people in the world was interested in my actions. Even the Government had no access to my system, so this situation was getting really important, really fast.

Each of the surveillance connections I had lost began popping back to life on my computer monitor. I smiled as the camera feeds dotted down the right margin of my screen to include my helpers who would assist me in viewing the goings-on in all locations simultaneously. There would be no way of missing anything. My confidence had initially taken a hit but was now somewhat rebounding. Each device signal was back online, but the cameras were not working, only audio. We could listen but not watch. Then just as that realization came, the audio was mixed with a high pitch frequency, and we were back to square one and plugging our ears.

The flow of information did not stop, however. It was a heavy downpour of data coming in at a furious tempo. The knowing it produced clogged my mind like ten pounds of bentonite clay being pushed through the course of my intestines. There was a secret yet loud scenario being birthed on the negative film of my brain. The information was creating a different picture altogether. There was much more to this story. VeeLee and the people connected to him were not average everyday citizens. It looked as if the only average person in his life was his mother.

There were tons of connections and history tying everything to the Nonagon, my precious top-secret world. The more I learned, the more I understood the wisdom of the Nonagon. It was getting more difficult to contemplate how they knew exactly how I would react to various situations without their guidance. My Ivy League education and what I assumed was genius-level intelligence was hacked like an infant's shitty diaper.

It was a humbling feeling that I, Lara London, could ever be predicted or that I was fed the precise amount of words to guide my ship in the direction K-9 wanted it to go. VeeLee's situation I was to attend was simply a skin cell at the bottom of one's little toe when it came to the worldwide footprint of the overall Nonagon operation. Even so, at the moment, it had the attention of the world's largest nuclear bomb, and I was in charge of guarding the red button. How this dark shadow, deep-state world government could exist cloaked for centuries still utterly astonished me.

VeeLee would one day learn these very intricate relationships and his complicated family tree. I was extremely challenged to understand it all myself. For now, he needed some space and time to focus on the next two years of high school at Horseshoe High. My job was made clear. I had to stabilize his surroundings.

My internal chances of earning an invitation into the upper folds of the organization became evident. In the grand plan, my elevated stature of librarian had its limits. I was a role-player on the chessboard of the Nonagon. A pawn with the moves of the queen. We, the selected librarians, could go in any direction we liked but to the source. We would never be allowed to experience the true essence of the game. We could not claim victory or achieve a crown. We were watchers.

The life I was living was extraordinary and surpassed all expectations. One filled with intrigue and power beyond the scope of what the vast majority could conceive. It took some time to accept that I would not be made a queen. Don't know how or why the revelation had just dawned on me, yet it felt as if I was told in person. A youthful ambition that I now deemed myself overqualified for. It was better to leave the matter to the gods throwing lightning bolts at each other on the playground of my mind.

One thing I did know, was every king had a staff. If I managed VeeLee correctly and he was crowned, I would not need a résumé. Otherwise, I would meekly oversee watchers in the waning years of my career and get to know eight VeeLee VonVouges along the way. Time would tell my story and the story of VeeLee VonVouge. We had enormous potential. I had to get the pieces of the puzzle put together right. Put the heat and flames together. The puzzle's theme did not have to be beautiful or perfect. The pieces just had to go together.

There was more than a college connection between Geovanni and Adamina-Rose. His interest in Jillie Jo was greater than the pocket-change she brought in as a server. Geovanni was much more than a successful business owner, too. If the current government had not gone after him and shut him down by now, there was a damn good reason—they couldn't.

He had first been protected and allowed to succeed in the world of questionable entertainment. He was making enough money to open a chain of A-Rose fine-dining restaurants. His son, Aarontino, had a similar micro-level role like mine. He could move around the chessboard of Mizzeree as he wished. He was playing at both locations, K-sea and Saint L's, with built-in trips to Key-la-fornee, Peareese, Fronze, and various other shorelines across the globe.

Until I became involved, that is. I had intentionally interrupted the flow of the Jackkson family. They would now be trying to flush me out into the open sunlight. Like me, they knew nothing in a successful world happened by accident. I was sure they realized someone was pulling some strings in a derogatory manner. They would not be on defense for long.

My team was going through all unknowable records the Nonagon kept on people of interest, individual notes, phone records, college transcripts, bank account transactions, medical history, tax filings, and similar child's play data. VeeLee's entire family's DNA was being dissected down to the chromosome and seconds of conception. Files on Adamina-Rose and Geovanni kept popping up.

Adamina-Rose seemed to know her father's mysterious death and disappearance all those years before had a better explanation than she and her mother were given at the time. Her suspicion was her father, Cleo, had discovered her college pregnancy and most likely was over-matched by Geovanni, who may have made her father disappear without a trace. It was clear to me now that Adamina-Rose must have had a great fear of Geovanni. That fear was most likely a perpetrator of much more than a bad choice of getting naked in her twenties.

I had the complete version of everything the modern world could connect to VeeLee. I would require many hours to delve into the condensed versions my fellow librarian watchers were compiling for me. It was recorded in HD for all practical intents and purposes. Typically, within hours, I could ascertain the entire scoop on anyone I needed to learn about—that person's historical information, family members, friends, and finances. I requested emergency access to Geovanni, Aarontino, and Adamina-Rose, respectively.

From the day VeeLee was identified as a candidate, the purple cloud stamped his profile with a bold capital G on his profile screen picture, which meant golden. K-9 wanted to pursue him, and I felt like a new parent when he was stamped. He was unsuspectingly living inside the Nonagon bubble very shortly after I had met him at a book fair when he was in middle school K-9 was showing even more interest now. His case file was very detailed and was captured in the likes of a personal journal written in a technical and scientific manner.

All the while, K-9 was allowing VeeLee to experience all the pain and suffering associated with being raised by his dysfunctional mother and her dramatical existence. It was necessary for him to draw his own conclusions about one's life pursuits. He had endured many harsh and negative years, and I had concluded that his life now needed a positive change. Jillie Jo and her stripper lifestyle with various addictions had reached its pinnacle. If she had cleaned up and worked at A-Rose like a good little girl, my involvement would not have been necessary.

Change had been snatched from the hands of time. The narrative of the Nonagon was depicting the desired result, much like the course of a gutter-ball at the bowling alley. VeeLee's life needed a very direct and more predictable outcome. He would soon have a contrast of life experiences to measure—a stable family life he had never known. Robert, his dad, was profoundly jacked up and was Jillie Jo's alter ego. They were psychotic parents. I don't feel any child could have survived those parents with their sanity. Against all odds, VeeLee somehow managed heartache like Rocky Balboa and Rocketman.

There was an emotional void and imbalance in VeeLee's soul, a shaky foundation that needed to be dug up and remade solid. He had aimed some of our conversations at healthy families and how life might feel being part of a normal one. Family topics were always in question form, almost like talking of outer space and the awkward magnetic currents of the sun. Balance would be vital down the road.

Chapter 17

Aarontino and a bag of peu importe (whatever)

IN ALL MY LIFE, NOTHING COULD PREPARE me for life in K-sea. My father had insisted on many things I disagreed with through the years, mostly his ideas of how best to raise me. My birth mother was unknown to me. I had never met her, nor did I even know her name. I suspected she was a traveler, a forgotten bed dancer who had either overdosed or was dead. She was dead as far as my father and I were concerned.

I really didn't have a need or desire to meet her. My father had known many women over the years. When Father connected romantically with a woman for any period of time, a baby usually materialized. The mother would mysteriously vanish soon after, not to be seen or heard from again. I'm sure it was my father's doing. Most likely, an inequitable agreement between the two had been reached. When Father put his foot down, he would not be moved. He was always in control of every conversation, and most who knew him found it easier to avoid general conversation altogether.

Oddly enough, my siblings and I did not struggle with not having our biological moms around. It left the job open to many women our father surrounded us with. We felt that we were blessed the way things were. There was no conflict, no mamma drama whatsoever. We all were raised in Peareese, Fronze during our primary education and returned home to Father in the summer every year until college. My siblings and I were armed with Ivy League college degrees and spoke fluent Fronzsay.

Our Nanny, Brigitte, was a foreign exchange student back in the day. She had completely fallen in love with Father from the time they met in college. She basically raised us. She would do anything for him and us. She liked it when we called her Maman. Brigitte spoke English with a heavy accent—it was about the only thing cute about her. Time and the aging process was at a double time. She looked like she should be our grandmother. Her heart, though, was platinum adorned with gold. We were loved unconditionally. Every word that crossed her lips was dipped in love, even when the honest truth was hard on the ear.

When we were young and walking on the streets of Peareese, Fronze, she would be called bad names for having mixed the colors of the rainbow. Granted, we were not white and not even her children. She, in a polite manner, fussed back at them to leave us alone. As we grew bigger, the comments stopped when we snapped back and challenged the bigots to do something, which they never did. Brigitte seemed proud of the pride of lions she had raised and smiled nonstop when we walked in front of her on the sidewalks downtown. Some of my fondest memories were those of us all walking together.

She knew we would not accept someone disrespecting our family. Father would whip our asses if we did. The only drawback in Peareese was living the meager lifestyle. There were not many perks in Fronze. That is why we all preferred life on the west coast at Father's home in Key-la-fornee. He loved to show us off and show out.

College was not a give-me by any means. Should any of us become distracted and fail a class, we immediately had to get a job and pay the college directly. In an Ivy League environment, that meant you would be washing a lot of dishes. We all had Father's rules to thank for the great lives we now had.

Due to the pecking order, I had no choice but to head up the Midwest A-Rose restaurants. I certainly wanted to be on the east or west coast, but Father had spoken, and I would manage the heartland of the country. His mandates were fixed as wet to water—not going to change anytime soon. Father also required me to keep an eye on a former employee and her son, as well. Apparently, I had too much extra time managing two fine-dining restaurants located on either side of the state of Mizzeree.

I had three other brothers—Maxx, Redding, and Dominique. They lived in the different hot spots located around the country running Father's other A-Rose restaurants. We had one sister, Goseeia, who was Father's pride and joy. She made it to the Olympics in the hundred-meter dash. She was also the second runner in the four-forty relay, the fastest on the team, just not fast enough on the world stage. The team did not medal. She gained uncommon confidence in the process, but it still seems to trouble her to this day.

She did manage to win Father's favor. She was always on an airplane or driving the roads to keep up with us all. She had the key and access to every A-Rose restaurant Father owned. Goseeia kept up with the business side of the empire and a team of lawyers ensuring the liquor license, insurance, light bills, taxes, and the like were all up to date. She was a brilliant manager who ran a tight ship.

Goseeia liked to accessorize, wielding wigs of the latest styles to include dreadlocks, long and short straight hair, some highlighted in every blush of the rainbow. Most wigs did not bring out her beauty whatsoever. I thought them unnecessary and a fake, childish, narcissistic fantasy.

Occasionally I would see her bald, shaved head, and would screech loudly as if I had encountered the devil. All I could do was laugh when she came at me, slapping and punching. If any of us boys wanted to draw Father's hand, all we had to do was hurt Goseeia or her feelings. At the end of the day, I loved my sister to the moon and back. We had loyalty, which trumped all other human acts—according to our father, anyway.

She loved the world of glitter, sexy clothes, high heels, and long, fake eyelashes. She was curvy with bronze, tight, smooth skin with toned muscles underneath. Her smile was tempting as a drink of cold water to a destitute in the desert. Her extraordinary white teeth would reel a person in, and then her matter fact personality would have most folks slowly backing toward the nearest exit. In her mind, I think she felt she was a famous actress or singing diva or something.

Most people did get out of her way. She carried a heavy, confident spirit and spoke loud and boldly most of the time. She was the spotlight Father enjoyed watching. Goseeia had a knack of raking in money through lawsuits. She would file on anyone in a heartbeat. She was a taker and had no problem with that position. She joked death would steal all her money anyway. Her mind was always churning, always engaged with her surroundings. Music seemed to reenergize and light her way, reading novels calmed her.

Maxx, the eldest, was as chilled a soul as there ever was, almost as if possessed by Buddha. His spirit likened to an expensive bottle of aged wine and could make anyone feel good about being alive. He was the virtuoso of the first class. A showman, he didn't need to say anything to anyone to make a point or his position known. He had mastered body language like no other I had ever seen. Complete strangers would seem to give way and acknowledge what Maxx wanted simply by his gestures. I think he had studied our father more than the rest of us. He had a confidence that was rare, but most similar to Goseeia. Loyalty and family filled his heart, deep as space. You could see it simply by looking at his own family. His wife, Joanna, was picturesque. His three children were prissy and proper in the most respectful way.

Maxx's children were taught manners and addressed us as uncle or sir without any parent coaching involved. We all enjoyed speaking Fronzsay with Maxx. He would go so fast that he would screw up sentences and pronunciations. Dominique would mock and impersonate his jacked-up Fronzsay. It was the funniest damn thing in the world. You didn't even have to know the language. If you were in the room, you would laugh your ass off.

Redding was the most intimidating, always out to prove something. He had a dislike of most people and trusted no one outside the family. He tolerated us and respected our father. We knew to stay out of his way or get beat up. Growing up, Maxx and I usually had to gang up on him to get him to settle down. Growing up, the police had been called on him over his temper and fighting. How exactly he made it on his own without us was a great mystery.

I think he was more confident having us around to back him up. Otherwise, I truly believe he would have landed in prison. Redding had a mean streak. I don't know the truth about how he now behaved in private, but he had somehow figured out a form of adulting. Redding's main story was the little voice that played inside his head. The reality was years of negative thought streams that he constantly fed. He was a saint and a profit to the dreadlocks, do-rags, and skullcap-wearing friends he surrounded himself with. There was a hunger in his heart, anger that he fed by inflicting hate onto those he felt were to blame. One's race was to be construed as a judge-able offense. Maybe just a phase similar to our father's college days?

Dominique, Father's third son, loved to eat and was extremely overweight. Father said he cleaned his plate so well that he licked the shine off them. He was the life of our gatherings, the comedian with the jolly, loud, contagious laugh. It was his special way of loving us deeply.

Quite frankly, Dominique was our family medicine-man. He could talk to any of us in such a way that we had to let our problems and the craziness of dumbass people go. When we laughed, we were healed. Don't get it twisted. He could rumble and was in charge of four hopping A-Rose restaurants. He could and would battle for any of us, anytime. He was straight-up good people.

Most years, we would all meet up at Father's place in Key-la-fornee over the holidays and catch up with each other in person. Goseeia would go over financials and give one of us bragging rights on the top A-Rose restaurant of the year. It was a good feeling to see all the numbers from everyone's efforts as a family and our successful franchise. There was much respect and love and laughs during those get-togethers.

No outsider could really fit into our family completely. Girlfriends, wives, or boyfriends would always remain an odd piece that would never fit into the family puzzle no matter how hard they tried. We considered it the exclusive Jackkson privilege—blood first. We took it very seriously. During our talks, it was clear the A-Rose restaurants we managed would become ours on the day Father passed. It, therefore, provided the motivation to make them as successful as we possibly could. Goseeia would have the gems in Key-la-fornee. I would sell out immediately, as I truly had other callings.

Food, pushing dessert, alcohol happy hours that created drunken dumbasses, catering to snobby fake people, and one hundred and fifty thousand a year was not fulfilling on any level to me. Obviously, it was a fact I knew I had to keep guarded and secret for now.

Running a restaurant sucked out loud to me. It was sixteen-hour days of life-draining energy I would never get back. I hated all of it, even the smell and sight of twenty dozen fresh roses that were delivered daily made me nauseous. Most single men would have given their firstborn, a kidney, and a bag of chips to have the opportunity I was afforded—beautiful women swooning and looking for a ring, judges, lawyers, and upper-ranked law enforcement, business owners of every sort offering quid pro quos up the yin-yang.

It was all so fake and pretty much predictable. Anyone you hired and paid money to had the potential of setting you up and taking all they could. I liked money, too, and was careful. The Jackkson family understood the longer you kept an employee around, the more likely they would figure out your weaknesses and exploit them for some form of financial gain. Being a sober, educated man helped to hold the line. No friends nor family members would be working for me. Honestly, I didn't want their business either. It always boiled down to a complimentary hook-up with a waitress, a free drink, free meal, or free something or other.

The A-Rose restaurants had been streamlined into an exact blueprint over the years. I remember coming home from Fronze during the summer and would try to note all of the renovations Father had made to the Key-la-fornee A-Rose restaurant while we were in school in Fronze. Now all Father had to do was send the specifications to his contractor, and a new A-Rose restaurant could be built in nine weeks— everything down to the kind of doorknobs. The building itself was unique, a split-level, light tan sand adobe structure adorned with a large red rose neon light that mirrored the minora and majora labia. It was very artfully done. Unbeknownst to most at first glance, you had to look closely or be told. "Sex sells," Father said. A lesson brought along from his college days of managing the strip club.

If there were a thorn in my side, it would have to be Father's mandate to keep Jillie Jo and the kid around. If it were not for the fact that I was instructed to take it easy on VeeLee and we had met randomly elsewhere, I'd most likely have completely ignored him. Though our paths crossed many times over the past few years, I intentionally did not know much about him. I considered him a helper, but he was mostly in the way and annoyed Chef Beerbabe to no end. I did feel he had a difficult life due to his mother's choices. It was not my intent to save the world. I knew plenty of heartache souls who reached out for charity every single day. Goseeia knew the value of charities and sent large contributions that ultimately benefited our family.

 I drew the professional line in the sand with a backhoe regarding Jillie Jo. When I think of all the shit she was putting me through lately, handcuffed and jailed was enough for me to deliver an ancestral rage on her. I was not in the mood for her son VeeLee and his annoying teenaged friends either.

 VeeLee was taken away from K-sea the week my ass got set up at Jillie Jo's house. Drugs, money, and police had never been something I ever had to deal with at the felony level, until now. All of my contacts in the K-sea area would be called on. The Jackkson's were also swarming in the state of Mizzeree. K-sea and Saint L's were getting the full measure of my family and our friends' influence. We now had to fight and would not soon be forgotten. VeeLee would have to fend for himself, just like me. I really wished his mom would not have paid the interest on her husband's debts. Father's fault for not staying oral, but now the association is costing me.

 It was the first time I felt handcuffs zipped tight around my wrists. The cold helplessness rolled up into a thunderstorm in my mind. I remember the police car floated atop the road like it belonged to someone's grandparents, yet the criminal cargo back seat was not meant to provide a comfortable experience. The police ride still pisses me off.

 Jail was the awakening of how much I detested Jillie Jo. She had talked me into coming over to pay me the nine hundred dollars she owed me. I took the bait, hook, line, and sinker. A Jackkson did not get caught up in the world of stupidity often, nor made ridiculous uneducated choices—well, maybe Redding did occasionally. Yet I was the only one in our family who had ever been locked up. The morons who surrounded me in the jail made me want to fight. They yelled and made noise all night long—my first experience of pure hell. Freedom was gone, and boy did I ever learn a valuable lesson through this round of suffering.

 My attorneys were the best and completely confident I would beat the charges. It was, however, becoming later rather than sooner. Every time my attorneys felt I was about to be cleared or released, something crazy would happen. None of it made any logical sense. The whole damn fiasco kept churning on and on as if some alien life support system was keeping the case alive. Father had stated that someone was pulling some bigtime strings somewhere, and we needed to find out who it was and deal with their ass.

 Father was getting outraged the longer he was kept from his life in Key-la-fornee. For me, he needed to do a little suffering, too. He was the sole reason I was dealing with her crazy ass in the first place. Nothing more than straight-up bullshit!

 It was a period of death. Many things had died inside me, and from the ashes, a new me began to bloom. Freedom would never be taken for granted again. My cellmate nattered on and on about his brother, a soldier who made the world beautiful, that he was so proud of his many combat tours overseas, "giving us our freedom just so I could screw it up," as he put it. He wished he would have been a better person in life, which I didn't give two shits about or needed to have one single conversation with the guy. All I knew for sure, was I am a tax-paying, law-abiding citizen, good person, and had been jailed wrongly.

 In the past, I had spotlighted military folks with comps—a free this or that, but mostly recognition, which seemed to make warriors smile. It was our family's practice to do so. But as for my cellmate, well, he could go to the hottest hole in hell. He was a loser, with a capital L. He was in for murder and robbery. A scheme he and his girlfriend had gotten away with for years, apparently. They would watch the obituaries, key in on elderly deaths, find the addresses online, break into their home, and raid the place.

It was a very quick process—if there were no cars in the driveway or lights on in the home, they broke in and filled their bags. The last home went completely wrong. The deceased's sister flew into town, was dropped off by taxi, and was asleep. The rest was in the morning paper. In listening to this punk, I realized how lucky I was. I wanted, more than anything, to be back at work inside A-Rose. I needed the smell of roses and Chef Beerbabe's bacon-wrapped filet mignon with béarnaise sauce generously drizzled atop the most tender meat in the world.

My attorneys had, at last, argued me out of lock-up, but the trouble hovered overhead like a heavy raincloud filled with battery acid. I felt it could burst at any time and melt the skin from my bones. Father and the family were here at the jail to scoop me up. Smiles were stuck on their faces as if I had redeemed Goseeia's Olympic run and captured the Gold Medal.

There were no judgments projected onto me. They knew me and knew I was being set up. We piled into the oversized black SUV and were headed back to my place. When the wheels started rolling, I released a pent-up deep breath of air and acknowledged to myself that I was, at last, out of jail.

"I took the liberty of calling Chef Beerbabe to cater our dinner. He should have it ready and delivered when we get to your home Aarontino," Goseeia said.

"Now that this fiasco is half-assed under control," Geovanni interrupted, "slow this ride down and pull into the next parking lot to the right, Maxx. We need to tribe this shit. Thank you, Goseeia," Father said.

Maxx guided the SUV into the parking lot, and Father went on to break down the latest information and added that the FBI or likewise entities were watching us, and that's why it had been so challenging to get this mess cleared up. My home was bugged to the hilt, and it appeared Jillie Jo was the focal point. He wanted us to keep all conversations to a minimum and to speak Fronzsay as a diversion. Father's Fronzsay was not the best, but he could limp through a decent conversation if need be. Should an important conversation crop up, we were to get into the SUV, which had been scanned and cleared for any listening devices. Maybe we'd just go for a ride if something important came up.

He had tracked down VeeLee and stated we needed to, once and for all, find out if he was blood, regardless of his ghostly skin tone—there was not even the hint of a sandy, ecru, café au lait about the boy. His appearance was derived solely from his mother's European descent. I knew him better than the rest of the family, but I had been pretty rough on the kid and his mom. I was her boss, and I worked her as hard as I could, just like I worked everyone else who made my money. They, after all, lived off A-Rose, too. If Jillie Jo had been a good employee, things would have been much different, but she was always late, and customers frequently complained about her. Maybe karma did not like my father charging a married man's wife interest in the form of in-your-face sex and was going through me to punish him back?

I really didn't need to know her or her son any more than I needed to know my own mother—how she looked or lived. Apparently, Father had found out that VeeLee was living south a few hours away in Queenfield. He was being cared for by foster parents. Again, I didn't give two shits. I was fresh out of the hell his mom had created for me.

I didn't want to be responsible for watching him or his mom's ass any longer. I was happy they both were out of my life. But for some strange reason, Father was reaching out to him like never before, asking all kinds of damned questions. My siblings seemed to hang on every question and answer like their inheritance was in jeopardy and weighed in the balance of my responses.

To my chagrin, Father had planned a morning trip for us all. Our destination was Queenfield. He wanted a blood sample from VeeLee. Father's lawyers advised him to go the paternity route through children's services. Father didn't want to raise any more red flags or attention to the matter than necessary. VeeLee knew me, so he might listen to me for a minute, a notion that made my head involuntarily wag from side to side.

I was not sure how he would react when it came time to ask him to get stuck with a needle—that we came for a blood sample. It was a pretty extreme proposition for anyone to accept. Let alone me popping up randomly, wanting to see him in the first place. I already knew in the back of his mind he would remember me running him and his friends off and my hot temper directed at his crazy-ass mom. As far as VeeLee VonVouge knew, his dad committed suicide. End of story. So, the truth, or a version we might suggest, would come across like a bad episode of crackheads live.

"Why the hell do we even need to get involved with the kid?" Maxx asked calmly.

"Yeah, later for him. I'm starving, and our food is getting cold. My fat ass is ready to get out of the damn vehicle, out of the damn state of Mizzeree, and out of these stretchy underwear that's crawlin' up my ass!" Dominique said.

Everyone but Father laughed. Sitting next to me, I could see the laugh was short lived by Redding, who was filling with anger. The helium balloon exploded when Redding cutting Father off mid-word of Listen, "Lis—"

"Fuck it. I'm out this bullshit! My ass is on a plane tomorrow. I have restaurants to run. I came to support my brother *right* here. Not some damn 'hunting Casper-the-ghost' cartoon story!" Redding said.

Goseeia, seeing the logistical nightmare of rescheduling everyone's flights, messaging all involved, and another day of zero visibility of the entire empire, sweetly said, "There is a lot at stake, Father."

"You damn right there is. All of you know, I know *this*! Don't cut my ass off again, Redding. You don't want me to snap on your little badass. You all will be having your asses right here tomorrow, going exactly where I tell your asses to go. Period. I would never deliberately endanger the A-Rose empire. We have all worked too damned hard to create it. I know the most powerful people on earth. When they speak, I listen.

"They have an interest in VeeLee more than *me*! We are all headed to Queenfield in the morning. End of conversation. It's very important we get the blood sample, Aarontino. It could be of great benefit if he is ours," Father said.

"How?" Goseeia asked.

"We will have hours to talk about this on *our* trip. *Tomorrow*. Let's now get to Aarontino's home, eat, speak a little Fronzsay, have some drink, rest our heads, and hit the road in the morning. Children… open your eyes wide. You 'bout to see some real-life shit—for real," Father said.

Maxx parked, and we swaggered into my home. I felt so grateful to be back inside my home. Familiar food smells filled the air, and I noticed everyone's personal items haphazardly strewn about the living room. We took up a plate and sat with food held up to our faces. I turned on the giant TV to kill the silence in between our creative conversations to come.

The food Goseeia had called in was delicious and filling. K-sea, hands down, had *the* world's best BBQ, but could never compete with a Chef Beerbabe prepared dinner. We were having our fill of giant racks of ribs and blackened tenderloin and two buckets of fried chicken. The sides were huge, hot pans filled with grilled corn on the cob, twice baked potatoes, mac-n-cheddar-cheese, a pan of okra, pan of collard greens with thick strips of bacon littered throughout, and two giant, artfully colored bowls of tossed salad and peeled fruit of every manner that most likely wouldn't be touched but the gallon of banana pudding would be devoured.

Mostly braggadocios, the Fronzsay conversation leaped from our lips like lighting coming from a sky tormented with severe thunderstorms.

"Dominique, do you remember when you were a kid, and Maman caught you raiding the refrigerator? She cooked a great meal the next day, sat us all down at the kitchen table, and each of us had to bring you our plate and watch you eat it. I wanted to take your chubby ass outside and beat on you for a minute," Maxx said.

"Yes, I remember. Luckily, Maman sent us to our room where a plate of food was waiting. She wanted to teach all of us the lesson of consideration and not to be self-centered and selfish," I said.

"We need to fly Brigitte down for the holidays, Father," Goseeia purred in Fronzsay.

"Make it happen, Daughter. It's fine with me!" Father said.

"Least you didn't turn out selfish, Dominique. Your love of food will never be fixed by anyone, though," Redding said. He laughed and smacked Dominique's butt cheek as he walked by with his second helping.

"I'm 'bout to replace yo teeth with damn rib bones sticking out your face. Put yo hand on my ass again, bitch," Dominique said in Fronzsay.

We all damn-near died laughing. That shit in Fronzsay was too much. Maxx spewed his drink in the air, and Father laughed an honest, loud laugh for the first time since he had been in K-sea.

"Dominique, clean that shit up. We not going to trash my house," I said.

"Little brother, don't make me take yo silly little criminal ass back to jail. You clean yo own damn house, bitch-ass," Dominique said.

Again, in Fronzsay, it was funny as hell, provoking another round of laughs. We amused ourselves until the weight of the food settled on our stomachs. One by one, the family drifted off to bedrooms to sleep. Morning came, and Goseeia was hard at it in the kitchen, putting her hands to cooking breakfast. Huge ham steaks along with two dozen eggs scrambled with onions, bell peppers, cheese, salt, and black pepper. It always hit the spot. A couple more fake Fronzsay phrases for those who might be listening, and then we loaded up in the SUV and headed to Queenfield.

It wasn't long before Father had our complete attention with conversations none of us had ever heard before.

"Aarontino, our empire is named after your mother, Adamina-Rose—'A-Rose,'" Father said. He explained that he had run her off as soon as he got his hands on me as an infant. One of his dancers had just had a baby a few weeks before and helped nurse me. It was my mother's intent to put me up for adoption. She didn't want children.

Adamina-Rose had told only her father, Cleo, about the pregnancy. He was a powerful man in his own right. Cleo was a successful banker on the west coast and had come to see my father concerning the baby—me. Father threatened them both to back off and go away. He was not going to deal with her changing her mind, or having any say in how Father decided to raise me.

Father stated that Cleo grabbed his daughter's arm, huffed out of the college dorm, and said, "We will see about this, tough guy!"

My father said he responded by threating to take his entire family out if he had to. It was his best gangsta-thug talk he had ever delivered. They both left the argument red-faced and very upset. My father didn't know Cleo's intentions—whether he was just getting his daughter, Adamina-Rose, away from the altercation and coming back later with a gun, cops, or what. But Father didn't care what they did—they would not be leaving with me, ever. Before anything transpired, Cleo was sent on an urgent business trip overseas and never came back.

My father's lawyers handled the matter soon after. Adamina-Rose was left to her own thoughts and thinks to this day that my father killed her father. The icing on the cake, Father said, was when I was nine and received my heart transplant and literally died on the operating table with no heart in my body, he sent a death certificate created for me when, telling Adamina-Rose that I had died on the operating table from a heart disease in Peareeze. Failing to state my new heart from Johnny brought me back to life. Something Father now says was the wrong way to have handled it, "But what's done is done," he said. Every girlfriend I ever had always enjoyed rubbing the lightning bolt scar on my chest after sex. I caught myself rubbing it in the morning when I first awoke. For some reason I could actually feel my heart like it was a metal engine contained by my ribs. And always seemed to hum, "Go Johnny Go!" to myself when I was nervous.

They never talked again.

She thinks I'm dead.

Wow.

The information blew my mind, and I was thinking all manner of crazy shit. But for some strange reason, I had been so numb to her my entire life that I still couldn't feel anything. We had traveled for forty-five more minutes to close the loop on her and then abridged mommy stories were relayed to each of my siblings. We learned that Goseeia's mom was the love of Father's life and he would have married only her. She died of brain cancer that hit quickly and killed her within six months of diagnosis.

Next came the story of VeeLee and his mother, Jillie Jo. Brigette had tapped out on raising any more of Father's children and simply wanted to come and live her last days with her love in America—my Father. It wasn't going to happen. Father only shared his bed with forty-year-olds or younger. Women sixty-plus had no chance in hell. So, he just left the kid with his mother this time. Everything pointed to a crackhead's lie, anyway. The man VeeLee had grown up believing was his dad was, in fact, another little secret his mother, Jillie Jo, had known but kept from him. Secrets, debt, debt interest, cigarettes, drugs, and alcohol most likely culminated in Mr. VonVouge's suicide.

The man suffered from a blood disease, and the natural donor option would be his son. However, when the blood tests came back, it was determined he was not the biological father. Jillie Jo stated to my father that he was the only other man it could have been. She showed that the date of the insurance payment and the birth all matched. Father didn't argue. He didn't do anything at all but keep track of her after they left the military and settled back in their hometown of K-sea. Thus, my lot in life.

All five of us were wondering what the hell was going on. Why did it take our father all these years to clean up some of the dirt floating around in his mind? There were all sorts of unsightly, almost possessed looking gestures dancing on our faces throughout the SUV. Awkward hands and arms flailed through the air, the back of heads crashing against the headrest, and of course, our sermon in response, "Right-right…"

"Damn…"

"What?"

"Hold up. Whaaat?"

"Hell, naw."

"Whaaat?"

We fed off each other and echoed continuously as Father broke the past down. And then from out of nowhere, he slammed us with some future.

"I visited with my doctor the other day. He says I'll need another heart," Father said.

"The hell you talkin' bout? You just had it replaced a few years ago," Maxx said.

"I see you every single day, Father. Why in God's name haven't I heard anything about this?" Goseeia said. Sister was pissed. We were all drowning in a thick soup of change, heavy thoughts pushing us all together like baitfish under attack. Life was pressing down hard on our family at the moment, and there was much to do.

The first priority was to get VeeLee into the vehicle and get his blood for testing. Father's plan was crude and had every reason to fail. I think he, more than anything, wanted to at least meet this soul in person, if only for a minute or two. We were on a DNA recon. The spotlight would be placed in my hands. My relationship with VeeLee would be front row, center stage. The audience was my entire world, all five of them. I hoped not to let my entire world down! My nerves swelled and throbbed as we passed the road sign: Queenfield, fifteen miles.

We determined to let VeeLee know we had hired an attorney to represent his mom. Hopefully, she would beat the charges and be set free soon, like me. I would tell him she was having medical issues with her liver and needed stem cells. Maybe he would be a match and could help her. It would be much easier if he cooperated and helped us help her.

We would get what we came for one way or another. He would know this as soon as we asked to prick his finger and collect a blood sample into the plastic straw tube that came in a packet Father passed to me on the ride down. I had put it inside the seat pocket in front of me. It went without saying, he would know it was a serious matter and not to play games or we would just hold him down and take his blood.

We drew into a collective silence, feeling flogged from Father's information dump. Much was shocking and a little hurtful. What if VeeLee was my actual brother? I was ashamed of how I had treated him in his time of need and great suffering. I had sometimes felt I didn't matter much growing up with a foreign nanny in a foreign country. I had my brothers and sister to get through hard times with. VeeLee was basically on his own to deal with life's struggles. I would never forget the smell of them when they were homeless for the days it took Jillie Jo to find a place for them. Wow. It now makes me so sad to think he might be blood. My brother. Jillie Jo makes me madder the more I think about her. Sorry, VeeLee VonVouge. *Goddammit!*

Chapter 18

Lara's Queenfield Showdown

THEY THOUGHT THEY WERE BEING SLICK with the fronzsay gibber- jabber, but I knew it was a distraction. Normal morning conversations over a cup of coffee wouldn't include using a secondary language. I simply downloaded a Fronzsay translator and laughed along with the silliness. I was watching their phone pings moving on the purple cloud. Within ten minutes, they had crossed the K-sea city limits, then the county line. The Jackkson family was on the move, driving in the direction of Queenfield. I knew they wanted to make contact with VeeLee. The purple cloud looked like a pissed-off beehive, blips of activity flooded the entire computer screen.

It was go-hurry-go time! I hopped in my car and gave chase. My supervisor contacted law enforcement to provide an unmarked escort. They were given stand-down orders and would only get involved if the Jackkson's tried to leave Queenfield with VeeLee.

It wasn't long before the unmarked car flashed its lights at me from behind. I tapped my brakes three times in acknowledgment and was more confident knowing I had real ammo backing me up. Really, I wasn't awfully concerned, other than five against one never looked good on paper. Two if you counted VeeLee, who would, without a doubt, take on anyone for me. I had no intention of putting the kid through any unnecessary risks.

I was pumped, though!

My heart was pushing blood through my veins so fast and hard that any goosebumps I may have had were corralled into one location beneath my bra. My nipples could have doubled as lug-nuts that I might be able to twist off and put a knot on someone's head with. I was trying to focus on driving safely at this high rate of speed while maintaining communications with the Mizzeree state trooper and my support team on the purple cloud.

We had closed the gap within an hour and backed off. It seemed the trip took no time at all. We entered the Queenfield city limits and closed in on the parked SUV. They were parked at Horseshoe High School, which would be letting out in twenty minutes or so. I had suggested we call ahead to the school and have VeeLee held in the office. We could simply have law enforcement run the Jackksons off, but that idea was shot down promptly. The purple cloud wanted to know Geovanni's intentions. My marching orders were clear: no. Wait and watch!

When the end-of-school bell rang, the ants were released back into the forest of the world. Aarontino boldly walked toward the front door of Horseshoe High, wading through the waves of jutting juveniles who were making their way into their cars, school buses, or a parent's vehicle. The trooper had come around and hopped into my vehicle. I pointed out Aarontino to her for the record. She was a no-nonsense personality, somewhat distracted by the whole convoy arrangement in the first place. She would get little information from me. She must have believed I was a federal agent or the like. I did not care about her assumptions.

Once I identified Aarontino, she returned to her unmarked patrol car and sat like a tiger ready to pounce if directed. Within five minutes, contact was made. VeeLee was walking voluntarily with Aarontino.

My attention shifted to high alert as the doors of the SUV closed. I could feel the padding of my bra once again. I had one hand on the ignition key. The other held my phone. I didn't know exactly what I would do if they took off right this second. A high-speed car chase was greatly outside the scope of my librarian job description.

Thank God, within a few minutes, VeeLee exited the SUV. He was stopped a short distance away by an older woman with red hair. They were having a conversation on the sidewalk. It appeared she was there to pick him up from school, making me wonder where Melissa was. I believed it to be Adamina-Rose. She looked somewhat nervous as if she was about to singlehandedly stop a child abduction.

Adamina-Rose had been watching just as we were. She had almost made her way to the SUV to save him when he exited the vehicle. Upon VeeLee and Adamina-Rose connecting on the sidewalk, Geovanni and Aarontino exited the SUV and, with a fast pace, made a concerted effort to make contact with them. I signaled to Officer Blazer, and we, too, briskly walked to the rendezvous. Officer Blazer and I parted the pairings just as they came together.

Blazer impressively took charge by introducing herself as a Mizzeree state trooper and asked if there was a problem. VeeLee was staring at me, Geovanni was staring at VeeLee, Aarontino was staring at Adamina-Rose, Adamina-Rose was staring at Geovanni, and I was staring at everyone. Not a typical day at the bookshelves.

"Hi, VeeLee," I said.

"What in the world are you doing here?" he asked.

"Well, I was coming to check in with Horseshoe High. I am moving here to Queenfield soon, so I thought I would start connecting with the local schools. I will be working at the library just down the road on Dazzlefield Street. You looked a little off when I noticed you heading toward that SUV, so I grabbed the school security, which happened to be Officer Blazer here.

"It is so crazy seeing you again. Especially here in Queenfield. Wow!" VeeLee said. Excitement hummed across his forehead. He must have been somewhat dazed from the last five minutes of life in the SUV—a chance encounter with the Jackksons—now starstruck with me. It was the first time my eyes collected Adamina-Rose's face in person. Intel pictures did not do her justice—she was beautiful, even when she seemed to be in a state of shock.

"I know. It's such a small world. Huh. You'll have to visit me at the library sometime.

"So, is everything okay here?" I asked and removed the hair from my right eye.

"Yes, I'm good. This is Adamina-Rose. She is picking me up today for Melissa. And this is Aarontino, my mom's boss in K-sea. He came down to check on me and let me know what was going on with Mom," VeeLee said.

He smiled a crooked smile, as did everyone else, nervous facial expressions meant to mimic one another in some awkward human agreement. Eyes zipped left and right, attempting to capture as much information as possible from unspoken words. Layers of lies, pain, and misgivings surfed on a volatile wave of toxic emotions—so many secrets, questions, and answers in close proximity to each other. Yet, no one seemed to want to ask pickpocketing questions in the grouping.

The faces remained in anonymity—painters, painting a masterpiece with a white grease pencil upon white paper, rendering nothing more than raised white marks. I sensed that there was a knowing we all shared—truths we each held close, possible realities that might transcend into an awakening.

For now, it seemed we all would be better served to be forthcoming another time, in a more private environment—not on a public high school sidewalk. In this collision of many worlds, everyone had the potential of quickly losing the game or giving up their advantage in a one-second babbling. There was too much at stake. The best play at the moment was noble silence, and it seemed everyone knew the rules.

"Sorry, guys. Better safe than sorry," I said, looking at the pair of Jackksons, who nodded at me and seemed to want to make a heritage squelch.

"Hello, Adamina-Rose. It has been many years. This is my son Aarontino," Geovanni said in the pause of conversation.

"Hello," Aarontino quickly followed, staring directly at her all the while.

Go Johnny Go...

"Hello," Adamina-Rose said. Her voice grasped for volume, but the word fell flat and faint. Something of a soul recognition had resurrected decades of doubt. A dull, powerful ache flayed through each layer of her heart. She visibly fought off becoming emotional and gave her voice another go. "Let's go, VeeLee. We have people waiting on us," she said as sweetly as she could and turned her back on us, leaving nothing else to discuss.

She walked away on wobbly knees and with both hands clutched at what must have been a queasy stomach. VeeLee strolled alongside her, rubbernecking back at me a few times on the way to the car.

Inexplicably, a suggestion we all accepted for some reason—cloaked by the students of Horseshoe High—we broke in different directions to our respective vehicles. Any dams we had holding the river of thoughts at bay were suddenly removed. Surely as we breathed oxygen, we each experienced swift mind streams of thoughts gushing through our brains, questions engulfed in the fire of emotion.

Everyone involved in this meeting would have a smorgasbord of legitimate questions ten minutes from now. The purple cloud gave me most of the answers already. Confirmations did make my mind comfy. Yet a great question never has an answer—just as time is the ultimate criminal in the universe, leaving evidence of its passing, knowing it cannot be caught.

I had just buckled my seatbelt and noticed that Adamina-Rose had doubled back in the direction of the SUV. My adrenalin spiked again as I exited my vehicle and trained my eyes on her white, flower-print summer dress that mixed in and out of the clothes of the mobile student body.

She was moving quickly, wringing out her eye sockets with her boney knuckles. Out of nowhere, Adamina-Rose doubled back, intent on engaging the Jackksons a bit further, it seemed. She motioned for more conversation, but the driver of SUV romped on the gas, whipped around a minivan in front of him, and soon drove the SUV out of sight.

The excitement dissolved in the thin summer air. I sent the trooper a goodbye hand salute, then called and met up with my realtor in hopes of utilizing my time here as best I could. Seeing potential homes in person made a huge difference. The buy vibe I needed to feel was one a picture and video could not provide. Within a couple of hours, the house hunting had ended, and I was on my way back to K-sea. I don't know why, but I was feeling anxious. Like someone was watching me or was going to get me.

On the drive back to K-sea, I felt as if I was traveling slowly in reverse. No state trooper escort and a slight paranoia that at any moment the Jackkson SUV would sneak up on me, run me off the road, and murder the crap out of me. Trooper support was just a call away, and I knew Officer Blazer's co-workers couldn't be far away.

I was listening to messages and doing my best to assimilate the latest information. Hopefully, this was not going to escalate into a state of emergency.

All I needed was for this day to settle down. I was pretty sure I had found a temporary home in Queenfield. It was an upscale loft that would be perfect for my requirements. The move-in date was next weekend. I had so many loose ends to tie up in K-sea that it was starting to drive me nuts. But great progress had been made.

Chapter 19

Adamina-Rose unfolds

"VEELEE, THIS IS TOO MUCH!" SHE SAID WITH a sniffle and whipped the car onto Dazzlefield road. She was again knuckling at the hollows of her eye sockets, faucets she could not shut off. Sorrowful tears flowed down her face and bled softly into the top of her summer dress. I sat silently, not knowing if this was an adult venting or if she planned to have a conversation. When my mom was upset and crying, my job was to listen. If I said a word, she would scream and start throwing whatever her paws latched onto. Adamina-Rose paused briefly to round up the next cluster of speech, "I need to have a private conversation with someone. Can I trust you never to tell a soul?"

"Yes, ma'am. I'll not tell a soul."

Christopher's heart squeezed ten doses of oxygenated blood into my brain.

"I cannot think and drive. We'll go to the park and find a bench," her nose sucked in air involuntarily, sounding like a hog snorting in the mud. Her cry deepened into a broken, sad song. I felt I might need to have a cry myself. Her pain somehow was making me hurt, too.

"Yes, ma'am." We pulled into the Chinese Botanical Garden, and I eyed an open bench by the pond. We exited her car, and I pointed at it. Adamina-Rose nodded, and we soon sat together wrapped in the stillness of the moment, looking at the glinting sun reflecting off the ripples of the water. Sounds of songbirds and a distant dog barking crept through the thickness of thoughts. Adamina-Rose's lips loosened, her face heavy with seriousness.

"I don't know why it's you that I'm telling this to. I don't want people to judge me and think I'm a horrible person, VeeLee."

"I won't judge you, Adamina-Rose. It's going to be okay."

"Okay? Nothing is okay right now. Everything is a screwed-up mess. My entire life is boiling down to an ugly mistake and secrets that will make everyone hate me."

"Are you a good person now?"

"What?" she stretched out in a long draw—more of a confused question. Her eyes squeezed more tears out onto the chest of her dress. Her legs crossed with her hands stacked on her lap.

"It's thoughts, ma'am. If you forgive yourself, it doesn't matter what the world thinks. Everyone deals with the past differently, but it doesn't exist anymore. It's an illusion—

thoughts need not be imprisoning if you're not actually in a prison cell like my mom."

"Alright, young man. We'll see if you feel the same after you know the truth."

Her great college secret had a powerful sting to it, one of power and great pain. It, too, had mourning attached, and at random points of the recounting, she bewailed inconsolably the death and loss and rebirth of her firstborn, Aarontino. I was completely speechless. I knew her son. Better than I wanted to, but had no idea of any of this.

She said initially, late at night, she coddled a pistol named *Fart Dragon*. The name came from what it smelled like after target practice. That she hated the smell of gunpowder. It was as if a dragon was too lazy to breathe fire and had farted all over her. It stank.

I chuckled at the images it created in my mind. When asked, *Fart Dragon* was for self-defense, yet Adamina-Rose's suicidal confession took form as a sad silk sheet and was gently draped over my heart. Her truth was, every time she held, pointed, or pressed *Fart Dragon* to the temple of her head or heart, she turned coward. A pile of pills would not have been as forgiving. She would be dead now. The conversation was raw and would no doubt torture my imagination in the days to follow. It was heavy, too much for anyone to try and carry alone.

Adamina-Rose believed she had successfully cremated the thoughts of her first baby. She felt the memory had been reduced to a tiny speck of dirt. She had hidden the speck deep beneath the earth's surface, a random place in her mind, never to be found or remembered again, or so she thought.

What I had witnessed there on the sidewalk of Horseshoe High dug up what was buried years ago—he was very much alive. Aarontino's heart did beat freely, and he roamed the planet in human form. Her finger had raised on the sidewalk of Horseshoe High to touch the lie of death she had believed. Timidly, it curled back into her hand to form a fist, then fell limp along her side.

"With a quick sprint, I could have taken him into my arms. It might have been worth the dysfunctional response he may have given me. Courage failed me, VeeLee."

"It's okay," I uttered like a spell-struck buffoon, my bottom lip sagging limply on my face.

"Again, nothing is okay right now, VeeLee."

She explained that her youthful ignorance had been a corrupt, selfish veil of ideas where her destiny and the life her parents and friends expected her to have was not attractive at all. Her parents would not have participated in a college misstep of this magnitude, and she knew it. She truly did not know her father's intention, but he disappeared or died shortly after standing up for her. Adamina-Rose's mother was way too judgmental and would have disowned her altogether, just as she did when she fell in love and married the wrong Mizzeree farm boy.

"I tried to cowgirl-up, hide the matter, give life, and go on, VeeLee."

"You were young. It seems like you had tons of pressure on you."

"That would be an understatement. Geovanni unequivocally was my taunt-monster, and for some reason, he woke up today and decided to put our families through a torture chamber mankind had yet to devise. I did not name him Aarontino. But I do know, deep down inside, that the young man standing beside Geovanni was the child I gave birth to."

I nodded at her, letting her know I was listening to her story. No words had strength enough to sample the tense air.

"Aarontino may not want a relationship with me, and I can respect that. I did give up all rights to his father. I didn't fight the fight. I wasn't there for his birthdays, school days, good days, bad days, fun, sick, or sad days. Aarontino has every right to hate me to hell and back. My choice made me an ugly human, and now I'm being punished with guilt and shame on the inside, no matter how deep I hid the matter. How in the world did this happen, VeeLee?"

"Life is unpredictable, for sure. I don't know why things happen the way they do."

"And who was the woman with the trooper?"

"Her name is Lara London! She is a friend of mine from K-sea. She has taught me so much over the past few years. She is a librarian and practically knows everything."

"She just shows up here in Queenfield at the exact same time as Geovanni. That doesn't make a damn bit a sense to me. We don't have to figure everything out right now. But we will! Or I should say, *I will*. Well, we better be getting along. Please do not share our conversation with anyone. Promise me again, VeeLee!"

"I promise." We stood, and she pushed the wrinkles of her dress downward. We walked to her car and eased inside. She flipped down the lighted sun-visor and pawed at her eyes. Her face was a make-up mess. Blacks and browns smeared into an ugliness that I was having a hard time looking at. It reminded me of how my mom looked most mornings after partying the night away.

"So, how do you know the men in the SUV?" Adamina-Rose asked.

"I only know Aarontino, the younger one. Your son."

"For gods sakes... this is *crazy*!" she interrupted.

"He is my mom's boss in K-sea. He's not my favorite person in the world. He treated me like crap from the first day we met. The older one I'm guessing was his dad. I just met him today. Surprisingly, they just gave me a cellphone, too. Do you need me to drive?"

Her eyes ricocheting off the Lexxus symbol of the hood was answer enough. A light smirk blinked from her face. "Thanks for your thoughtfulness. Not many people have ever seen me in this fragile, delicate state, VeeLee. I'm embarrassed you had to deal with this. Aarontino... my son. Wow!" Adamina-Rose said aloud, shaking her head in disbelief.

I knew without her saying so that she had always attempted to project a strong, educated, successful woman—a redheaded fireball no one would ever want to challenge. On this day, her fingers trembled atop the steering wheel. It was clear she could not contain this day with a beautiful ribbon tied into a bow. Her successful reputation and millions left her walking on the moon alone. Her emotions seemed to be breeding like Ebola, the bloody virus where blood cannot clot and oozes out from the body anywhere. It seemed the storm was gaining momentum in her stomach. It was as if she had eaten a rotten sandwich made of fear and pain and pinched off half of it for me to eat.

"So, what was your mom's job?"

"Her main job is a dancer, a stripper. I think she did most anything for money, though. She waited tables for Aarontino at the A-Rose restaurant part-time but didn't like to work with Chef Beerbabe or Aarontino. They were both very arrogant and cranky. She made much more money stripping.

"Mom and Aarontino were both arrested not long ago. He just told me his charges are being dropped, and they're trying to clear Mom. The day they were charged was the day I was placed into foster care. I had to spend six hours in the hallway of the jail waiting for Connie, my caseworker, to come pick me up.

"Now, Aarontino says Mom is having medical issues and took a blood sample back to his law office to have it medically tested. Maybe our cells will be compatible. I might be able to help her with my blood." I raised my pricked left ring finger, showing her the small harpoon wound jutting out from the swirl of my fingerprint.

"Dear God in heaven," was all she said. I think it was there that we entered a conversation truce. For the rest of the drive, we swam in our own interpretations of the fortuitous information.

I pulled into Bruce's driveway. Sarah met me at the door, and I walked in. Melissa would soon join us. She was attending a mandatory happy hour celebration of a supervisor's promotion. VeeLee stayed on the front porch fiddling around with his new cellphone.

My thoughts seemed to be attached to the end of a rubber-band and kept pulling me toward all that I had suppressed for so long. How exactly my father, Cleo, had found out I was pregnant in college was still unclear. I did not plan to tell anyone and had it in my mind that an adoption service would be the best option for the child who grew in my selfish college-girl womb. Father and Geovanni had words, and I expected Father would be looking out for our family's financial interest and take matters into his own hands. It's what he and Mother were all about—a banker thing.

Father would most likely hire something done. I knew other than some wild sex, Geovanni and I had no matrimony future ahead of us. He was much older and had already told me he had three other children. I knew my father would never allow such. Why Father had kept the pregnancy from Mother may have been his means of damage control. It certainly made my life easier over the years that followed, before I moved away, while she was alive anyway. No questions or judgments Mother would have certainly imposed. Perhaps my father had a futuristic intelligence that was not ingrained in my learning genes. Finding peace in the dance of life had always been a challenge.

I had not made the pregnancy a big deal. Unless someone was taking pictures, all photos that captured my belly were seized and destroyed. My sorority sisters thought I had lost my mind when I went crazy on them for taking pictures of me. I did not even plan to tell Geovanni, but on a lonely night, my clothes came off, and the truth bulged before him.

I did not expect Geovanni to step up to the plate and told him so—but he did! Two weeks later, I gave birth to my baby, and my father disappeared. Geovanni only had to threaten me once. He was a serious man, and I knew it. I took him

Freddy-Krueger serious. I did not want to be the next to disappear, so I handed over the baby. On the birth certificate, I had named the child Tommy Clintin, but that obviously changed to Aarontino Jackkson.

    Early on, I would ease my mind with the story I told myself—that my son was being loved better than I could possibly love him. That I was too busy to raise a child right now, and it was simply God's plan. All this changed when the sword of guilt was run through me a million times after I was told he was dead. There would be no do-over, no make-up day in the future that would numb *the* dumbest choice of my life.

    That choice of naughty and naked did not sit well with my old bones at the moment, and I was trying to remember where exactly I placed *Fart Dragon*. My hands had not gripped the second dumbest idea in years—a pistol and a prayer. Even God knew I was a fool's joke.

    How in the hell was I going to tell Bruce he might have a brother? That potential conversation took on characteristics of zero gravity my mind could not make sense of. It resided in the phenomenal realm of the universe. I had no idea how I would even approach the subject with him, let alone Jacob, my husband of thirty-five years. He had no idea or knowledge of my dead dark-skinned child who had come back to life.

    It had been hard to find a cup of sunshine in my life until I met Jacob. And now our entire marriage was teetering on a rocky ledge that overlooked the deepest hole in the ocean. May as well put on some concrete boots.

    I felt I was wrapped in heavy chains and had no choice but to throw myself over that ledge. Maybe death needed a bride. The guilt was back. My brain was torturing my heart for that choice all over again. Whoever said drowning was a painless death had no idea what they were talking about. I was drowning in all these emotions. It was the most painful thing a human being could ever feel. I didn't need water.

    It had not been stated that Aarontino was mine during that sidewalk masquerade party. It was only my assumption. Thoughts of Geovanni had also factored into my choice to leave the west coast. To envision never running into him again made me smile at the time.

Here in the Midwest of all places, in the eye of a needle that no one can ever seem to find, here he is, blown in on a rabid western wind wrapped in a nightmare. My bank account could fix millions of problems, but could not buy a single second of my past back. Geovanni was a businessman and would most likely take every penny offered. I knew that was not what this was all about for some reason. He could have come for money long ago.

He was not the sort to back down from a fight. I had seen his savageness up close and personal back in our college days. Fighting each other in court may be where this was heading. It pained me to put so much power into the hands of law firms who would dredge our past up for the world to have a say. Money nor a victory in court would ever put me in good graces with my family when they learned of my secret. For some reason, he didn't start a fight on the sidewalk of Horseshoe High. The conspiracy of a million "what ifs" and "why nows" piled into messy outcrops of sharp, angry philosophies in my mind.

I was too old to be banished. I was already shrinking like an apple on a summertime windowsill. *What am I to do with this today?* I thought to myself. So impressive was the speed I was sliding down this slippery slope of depression. It was making me angry, annoyed, and irritated, almost instantaneously. This morning I had the greatest life a person could have built, overflowing with all the love the universe had to give. I had the best of everything.

Today... Why was today unfolding as if it were on serious drugs? Today is the most challenging today ever! And then I thought, babies... Today is going to have *baby todays*. I will be dealing with dysfunctional *baby todays* until hell has me.

I gathered myself in the sitting room, took a seat, and shook my head. What the hell am I telling myself? "*Sarah*... I need a glass of *wine*. No. I want whiskey. I need a shot of whiskey and a glass of wine, pronto," I said. Sarah looked at me as she always did. Timid. That deer in the head lights look.

That dirty word, *change,* was now at hurricane strength breathing sewer breath into my face.

Chapter 20

VeeLee's junkpile of thoughts

   I PREOCCUPIED MYSELF WITH THE features of my new phone, yet my mind was scrambling to make sense out of this wild-ass day. During third block, I received a note from the school office letting me know Adamina-Rose would be picking me up after school. *I could have gotten a ride*, was my first thought. Bronson was a bit far to travel to pick me up from Horseshoe High. I'm sure she had picked Anglaia up many times over the years—but Anglaia was family.

Adamina-Rose was extremely upset with the meeting on the sidewalk. The old adage, "It's a small world," made my eyes do figure-eights inside my head. How she could possibly know my mom's boss's dad blew me away. Never good to see a woman cry, though. Little chance I would ever be good at consoling an adult female. Anglaia would most likely have a fit when she found out her grandmother had picked me up and transported me back to her lovely home.

Yet I, too, was wrenched tight seeing Aarontino again. He provoked traumatic thought streams. At the moment, these thoughts were storming around in my guts. If asked yesterday, "Do you think you would ever see Aarontino again during the course of your natural life?" my answer would have been one hundred percent: *Not a chance*. I was doing all the reasoning I could to make heads or tails out of his random visit and at Horseshoe High, of all places. None of it made a damned bit of sense. Pretty sure this was not part of the parenting plan Melissa and children's services would have checked off on.

Taking a blood sample for my mom in an SUV right after school in the parking lot—all the while getting a stare-down by what looked to be half of K-sea crammed into the vehicle Aarontino came in—was as weird as sucking your thumb while hanging upside down in your underwear on a flagpole at the police station in the wintertime. The icing on top was Lara London in the flesh, here in Queenfield, as well, and on the exact same day. And she just happened to have a state trooper by her side. Not to mention hundreds of classmates gawking as if they were seeing a falling star. Wow!

Yeah, life had brought me a giant trash bag of tangled Christmas tree lights. I got started by throwing the entire bag into a virtual pool of quicksand, way back in the farthest corner of my mind—a place where I tossed all the crap and trash life threw my way—and slowly watched it sink from sight. I let each thought dissolve into the blackest tapestry of darkness and replaced it with a quiet sun-scape of calmness and silence, the place where all the great answers had come in the past.

It was a knowing Lara had taught me. I knew everything in the universe renews itself—all the way down to the tiniest particles of existence, which are constantly being reborn, unfolding from one form into another, always changing. This bizarre unraveling would settle itself in psychological time. It did not need a drop of my energy. It was atomic already.

Within the hour, Melissa and Anglaia joined Sarah and Adamina-Rose in the recollection of the Jackkson encounter at Horseshoe High. I was not invited to hear the telling in person. Nor could I corral my curiosity, which led me to invent an occasion to enter the home. Once to use the bathroom—where I just hovered over the toilet like a moron trying to hear the conversation—and then again for a drink of water. Each time I found a good enough reason to go into the home, they muffled their voices, and I could not pick up the true essence of the story. When I entered what they called the sitting room, I was met with half-baked smiles and the bird from Anglaia's right hand.

Bruce must have been called by his wife, Sarah. I wasn't outside longer than five minutes working on another ridiculous home invasion idea, when he drove into the driveway, honked his horn, motioned with his hands for me to come to him. He drove us back to Top Chops. "We have two trucks to get loaded before we can leave tonight," he said.

"Not a problem!" We walked into the meat plant, and the workers were busy as bees. There was excitement in the air, much different than that of the ladies in Bruce's home. It was alcohol-free and positive. I nodded for approval to join the collective, and once my job description was established, I was mushing along. A dog in an Alaskan sled team comprised of mixed breeds—Alaskan Huskies and Siberian Malamutes—getting the job done as quickly as possible. I could tell it really mattered to the team. Everyone seemed to project their own version of a winning-the-race sort of smile.

On the way back home, Bruce brought up my need for a vehicle. We discussed how I could earn it there at Top Chops after school. I tried to contain my excitement over the thought of having a job and my own transportation, but couldn't. I smiled at him. Bruce was going to help me for some reason. It was just as healing as Lara London's mentoring me. Perhaps I could take an occasional weekend trip to visit Mom in jail and see my homeboys in K-sea. This talk was the exact distraction I needed from the chaotic day I experience earlier.

Now that football season was nearing its end, it was time to shift. Bruce would loan me twenty-five hundred dollars. The money would be taken from my check until the loan was repaid. I wanted an older pick-up. One I could use to move things for people over the weekends. There were plenty of old-timers at the Assemblage church who may need some help, and there was no shortage of single parents who frequently moved. Hopefully, I could wear the wheels off and pay it off sooner.

I wanted the truck right now but knew Bruce was right. I did not want to get in a hurry and end up with a clunker that sat in the driveway leaking oil everywhere. I needed to find a sound and well-kept truck. It may take a little more time, but in the end, it would be time well spent. Mike and Melissa agreeing to this was the next natural step in evolution, a checkmark in their parenthood, and my progression into adulthood. They had experienced some hardships trying to get me to and from events already. I was sure Bruce could make a better pitch and sell our idea, "Could you talk to Mike and Melissa about this?" I said.

"It will be a done-deal in five minutes," Bruce said. He winked with the sureness of a slam-dunk, and we smiled at one another.

The first truck that came to mind was one like Beau's—jacked-up eye-candy that might put a head with a ponytail sitting next to me. The little ego posturing came and went. The reality of fuel prices settled over an empty wallet—my pathetic wallet that held a couple of class pictures of friends from K-sea, my Horseshoe High identification card, and my driver's license.

Some cash would help keep them from falling out every time I had to scan my ID for a school lunch.

The whole horrible hue that surrounded Beau's monster truck still left a bad taste in my mouth, anyway. I would never forget baby Victor Angelino. Beau had let me know that his family had decided they were moving to the southeast coastline in favor of an ocean view and a better paying job. He asked if I would visit Victor's grave once in a while to check on his son—I agreed. He and Danielle were officially over.

I turned the light of reality back on. I needed to buy a small, fuel-efficient form of transportation. I would be looking for a four-cylinder, my mind replied, ending my daydream and said, "I probably need to find a *Nice-on* pick-up truck or something similar."

"Probably a good choice, VeeLee," Bruce said.

Bruce parked, and we entered the home to Mike's chatterbox in full vibrato talking to himself. The ladies, sozzled by the spirits of bottled wine, easily ignored him. They were completely enthralled with Adamina-Rose's sidewalk tale of strangers and a state trooper. We entered through the garage. Bruce introduced our arrival by tossing his pile of keys clankingly onto the kitchen countertop.

Mike seemed to catch lightning in a bottle when Bruce willingly engaged him in conversation. The topic being my potential job and vehicle. My foster parents perked up, and the matter overtook the torments of Adamina-Rose's abridged tale and Mike's emotions. I was invited to listen as Bruce assured them of a four-hour per day work schedule, from four to eight o'clock in the evening. It was agreed upon fairly quickly, just as Bruce had predicted.

For the first time, the conclusion of adults actually felt like it was in my best interest. I was stoked and excited beyond belief. Melissa stated they needed to have a heart-to-heart with me—that there would be boundaries and responsibilities. "Of course!" Bruce said. He winked at me again. I smiled again. I could start work tomorrow after school.

"Well, don't look at me! Furthermore, I'm not the foster boy's taxi," Anglaia said.

"Manners," Sarah said.

"Bite me!" Anglaia said.

"Anglaia," her Grandmother, Adamina-Rose mumbled.

"Well," Anglaia said, "I have my own effing life!" She had things going on after school and was not dropping me off anywhere, anymore. It was over. She was done. Period. "If anyone is going to be riding in my Mustdang, it will be my friends. End of story!" she said.

Now that she had an audience, she seemed to raise the pitch and volume of her rant. She raced from the sitting room and with her greatest effort, slammed her bedroom door, rattling the upside-down hanging wine glasses in the kitchen. It was astonishing how the door-hinges could possibly hold up to her constant temper-tantrums.

"That young lady might need her bottom heated up, or grounded, or something. Holy moly. Yikes. Wow! Kids these days," Mike said. He waited for what he thought would be adult support. He was, after all, a parent for ninety days now and had it all figured out.

"Anglaia is fine," Bruce said. There was a calmness in the tone of his voice that took the sting out of the air. "We'll get you a ride to work until we find you a good *Nice-on* truck. I may send one of my workers over for you. They would love a paid get-away break," Bruce said. We smiled again.

Mike, blind and clueless as to how the world actually received him, stood smugly as if anointed the new chief of the tribe. His entire presence was a protrusive invasion of common sense. Time had failed to wring out the superhero ten-year-old streaming from his personality. Surely many a person had tried before to convince or otherwise encourage him to lasso noble dignity—to change him for the betterment of mankind. All obviously failed. His mannerisms and personality traits were set deep into the foundation of his soul—unmovable. I would use my energy elsewhere. My experience with my mom was enough for me to know I had much better things to accomplish with time.

    The evening was quickly wrapping around the clock, and the beautiful sun had crawled into bed over the horizon to sleep. Jacob had come to take his wife, Adamina-Rose, home. She had had her hands full of whiskey shots and wine all evening. She walked with her right hand resting on her right hip, which was half-cocked in the air as she talked and made her liquored-up loops around the sitting room. Jacob, not as frail as I presumed, had cornered her, tossed her bones over his left shoulder, and waved goodbye with his right hand. I hurried and opened the front door for him. We watched as he and Bruce loaded her up in his vehicle and were Bronson bound after. It was the signal everyone used to call it a night.

    The new semester had begun, and I had switched last block football to debate. It was initially a blow-off class in K-sea until I found I was good at it. Now it was a serious passion. In the beginning, I suffered great angst. It was not easy for me to talk in a public setting. Lara London taught me techniques to capture the wind in my sails. It wasn't long before it became another game like football that I wanted to win. Fear was, in fact, an illusion. It did not exist. Fear was nothing more than a thought and easily defeated by understanding the concepts of the mind.

    There was magic I found in words and the articulation of words when groaned across my vocal cords. In competition, words were irrevocable and permanent, even when retracted. I was learning word choice applied in real everyday life, too. Words were little pointers that could paint a picture of understanding. We gathered words together to form a language of communication, thus the meaning of life. WORDS.

    Arguing with idiots was not the point of a serious debate. Lara had once said I did not need to become an experienced idiot by babbling nonsense with morons. Furthermore, the practice was toxic and unproductive. Some debaters thought this was the way to practice and would easily be defeated when they encountered an actual mind.

It did take a few weeks, but Mike found me a decent six-year-old white *Nice-on* pick-up truck. A man at the *Assemblage* had it for sale. Bruce honored his word and flipped out twenty-five one-hundred-dollar bills to the seller. Bruce and Mike helped me get it inspected, insured, registered, and tagged.

Having my truck and job was transforming. The only drawback was that weeks could pass by before my busy body would register the date on the calendar. I was waking to the new sound of the next month rolling over the tongue and out my mouth. October, now November, was pushing my first holiday season away from K-sea into view. I had little free time to hang out much with my new classmates, nor go for a visit to see my mom and old friends back home. It was just as well. I had a great productive routine that was satisfying. Especially like right now, pulling up to the library in my truck to visit Lara London. She was expecting me today, and I was beyond excited as usual.

I checked in with my library card and was going to use the computer lab after our visit. I wanted to go through some of my science chat groups and see if anything new had been learned and posted on the sun. I saw her assisting a man in a suit. No telling what he needed to know, but I knew Lara would not let him down. She spotted me and smiled. My heart sent out a wave of inner joy from head to toe. She looked amazing. "Hi, VeeLee. I'll be with you shortly," she said. The man in the suit looked over his shoulder with a wrinkled expression. As if I had interrupted him asking her to marry him? *I know she's amazing, but you don't have a chance, dude.*

"Okay, Ms. London," I said and tried not to bite my tongue off. I had to look away from her gorgeous face. When I turned back, her index finger was wagging for me to follow her. I looked over my shoulder to the man in the suit, sent him a wink and smile, and strutted like Conor McGregor, the Irish MMA fighter. Cocky as I could. Lara turned and caught me acting out. She just shook her head with a smile. Puppy love was better than no love at all. We went into her glass office and took up chairs. "I have a truck now."

"Really? How nice. You've been busy, huh?"

"Yes, Ms. London. I'm working at Top Chops, too."

"Goodness. You are doing so well. How is school?"

"Typical. I'm really excited about debating here in Queenfield, though. It might be easier than in K-sea."

"Well, you are no rookie. I foresee a great effort from you, VeeLee. I have some mind ammunition to give you today, as well. No matter what, just have fun and enjoy the memory."

"I will, Ms. London, and thank you. I can use all the help I can get. It's so crazy having you here in the same city. I cannot believe how happy it makes me, now that you're here."

"I know, VeeLee. It makes me happy to have a friend here, too."

"So, do you like your new place?"

"Yes, my place is comfortable. I kept my other home, as well. Don't know how long they need me here."

"Hopefully you'll be here for a while. If you need help with moving your things, let me know. I can round up some buddies and do whatever needs doing."

"I know you would, VeeLee. My place came fully furnished, and the movers placed the items where they needed to go. Thank you so much, though. Very thoughtful."

"No problem. Can you get your phone? I was going to give you my phone number. I have a phone now, too."

"Sure, VeeLee."

We exchanged numbers and chatted until the library closed. We went over debate strategy and what I thought about the Matches. We compared versions of the Horseshoe High meeting between Geovanni, Aarontino, and Adamina-Rose, all the while honoring my promise to Adamina-Rose to keep quiet about our private conversation. Lara was shocked at the new details and seemed to file it away with her own remembrance. I told her about Adamina-Rose's house and how wealthy she and Jacob were. That I loved going on their property and visiting my special place I had named *Curevibesea*.

It was so inconceivable the odds of Lara being here that I just thanked my lucky stars and accepted the amazing coincidence. I made my way to the library most often on Saturday mornings when the doors opened. This morning timing also meant I'd see Lara in her stretchy yoga pants. It was the closest thing I had to sexual pleasure. I never expressed that I wanted to kiss or hold her in a private setting. Lara would seriously embarrass the crap out of me if I did. I knew better than to even hint at such a thing openly.

She was helping me prepare for my upcoming debate competitions. I loved being tutored by her boundless resource of knowledge. It almost seemed I would have an unfair advantage. The process of exchange did nothing but strengthen my attraction for Lara London. I was bedazzled by everything about her. It could have been my hormone glands running amuck with testosterone again, although I was leaning toward the conversation my heart wanted to have.

There, too, was the mystery of her ways, as well. Lara was not forthcoming on most matters. Even if I asked her point-blank questions, she managed to guide our time together somewhere else. She had offered little—actually nothing—on the Jackkson sidewalk meeting. I was not going to bring it up. Maybe she would be more curious and engage me on the matter another time.

For now, it was enough to see Lara decked out in her professional librarian attire, usually some irresistible ensemble that most men would have no choice but to guzzle into their eyes. Every time I saw her, my entire body seemed to shut down and go into slow motion. She had caught me on many an occasion, staring at the sparkling gold chain with dancing charms, ever so gently draped around her petite ankle. The pattern of habit then took the journey up her toned legs and quickly crossed over her bubble butt and her perky boobs where my focus would intensify as I zeroed in on the outline of her angelic face.

There my eyes would stay, focused on every detail of her flawless skin melted on soft female bones. Contemplations of form. Art. Her one of a kind lovely face. It made no sense that it was not being touched and kissed every single night—selfishly, things are better the way they are. Lara was my supreme interpretation of what the perfect essence of a woman should be. Even her breathing was put through the lens of my judgments, olfactory recognition of the smell of her breath, so, so sweet. I intended to capture every nuance of her beauty and commit it to memory. I dissected her ways as completely as my presence would allow, or until she caught me staring and moved me along in my thoughts. She was very patient with me. And I tried my best not to be annoying.

Time had moved me to my first debate at Horseshoe High. At the end of our last practice, Ms. London gave me a high-five and assured me that she would come and support me Friday night. She emphasized that learning to philosophize or debate well would be very important in the political arenas of life. I had fully expected her to bring up her deep state, K-9 Nonagon jargon, but she did not. In turn, I did not bring up some of my new findings on capturing the sun, new modified calculations of my silly sun pill formula.

I would face off against Holly Hammerbuns, an honor student from ten lifetimes ago. In class, she spewed the spelling of logorrhea and its meaning of excessive and often incoherent talkativeness or wordiness.

Most thought she had a mental condition that proceeded from the time she squirted from her mother's DNA tummy tank. Holly's mannerisms magnetized my notion that she could, perhaps, be a family descendant of Marie Curie. She winked cuteness, yet her personality resembled a stuffy, snotty math teacher. The vast majority, however, simply considered her a crazy bitch. I would not be the one to argue the sentiment.

Well known. Not liked. Holly walked the halls of Horseshoe High as a loner. It seemed she had no story to tell and intentionally pushed people away with sharp, attacking statements. She may have been mirroring some dysfunctional home life. There was no way of knowing, and no one really cared, as there was no shortage of drama queens at Horseshoe High.

I had known intimidation in the streets of K-sea, and she did not have the potential to strike an ounce of fear in me. She would need to bring her A-game. I knew our war of words would not leave me literally dead, in pain, or in the hospital. So, I planned to break her down into a limp noodle and swallow her whole.

It was six o'clock sharp. The hands of time were straight up and down. Friday evening, and we two and our judges were introduced. It was time for our critical thinking and public speaking skills to be displayed, our rubric scored. My palms and butt-crack filled with sweat, and I felt like a mop that was pulled from a hot, steamy bucket. Yet I had goosebumps from the frigid air-conditioning in the Horseshoe High drama theater.

To Holly's chagrin, the moderator, Mrs. Kimberly Polyoski, had been brought in from Saint L's and was a judge in real life. The other two moderators were bored retired college professors trying to stay relevant. I had already determined Mrs. Polyoski was the key to victory. In my opinion, she could rattle one of the others to pick the winner of the debate.

Honestly, it was grueling—a very arduous debate. My confidence was high. I made it clear that of the one thousand sounds a human ear could hear, I had to project poise in my voice, a voice that would linger and echo defeat in Holly's ears. She needed to hear and believe she lost before she actually did. I had to change my speech patterns, rhythms, inflections, and the cadence of my voice she was familiar with in class. It would catch her off guard and stump her for a bit.

I capitalized on the ten million shades of color the human eye could see. I chose a blue suit with a violet button-up shirt and bowtie for its stunning effect on the brain. I would not omit any of the human body's senses. Each of them could make for a slight advantage if one focused on them.

Of the one hundred thousand tastes of the tongue and one trillion scents of the nose—I wore a generous amount of cinnamon essential oil tamped into my suit jacket and a mixture of rosemary and peppermint oils that I applied inside both nostrils of my nose—little tricks Lara London had suggested. I was grateful to the Matches for hooking me up. Essential oils were little gold mines to me, and I did my best to keep some on hand. When visiting Lara, I would dab a few drops of Egyptian musk on my neck. I think she liked it.

I can still see Melissa's shocked face. I think she thought I was cuckoo when I asked for nearly two hundred dollars worth of stuff for a single day event. I assured her that I would pay her back, which she shrugged off. She thought my preparation was extremely odd but agreed to my suit and oil requests. The spotlight had been flipped on, the battle of Holly versus VeeLee now commenced. The countdown was over—no turning back. No prisoners. My flag would fly high. I would win this war. "Victory O' Victory," sang my mind, sang my soul.

Most would cringe or rue the onslaught of presidential caliber topics—for those of us in the debate, it was simply the sugar that made ice cream good—the harder and stranger the better. Our responses would be dissected by the moderators and the three hundred people in attendance. For a high school debate, it was an exceptional turnout. I tried to absorb as much of the electric vibe in the air as possible. It was time to open a can of gotcha-girl. So, I did. I enjoyed the applause at the debate's end and the small talk with Lara and the Matches.

Bright and early Monday morning came my first interview ever. A senior, Kelly Mosier, conducted it. She was being graded. The interview was her assignment in broadcasting class. Kelly and Holly had an old childhood beef, which stoked the fire of karma and poetic justice. The PA system began to echo loudly through the hallways and classrooms of Horseshoe High.

"Coming to you live, I'm Kelly Mosier with your debate champ Vee…Lee…Von…Vouge," Kelly said.

Emphasizing my name as would a professional announcer introducing a heavy-weight boxing champion of the world.

Christopher's heart blasted blood through my veins like a river.

"First VeeLee, congratulations on your debate victory."

"Thank you, Kelly."

"People felt your political views on social security, insurance, and tax laws made a lot of sense," Kelly said.

Kelly stuck the microphone to my lips, "I know it's not as easy as I made it sound, but the Government should find a greater love for its citizens that matched its love for money."

"For sure, VeeLee. The idea of repealing daylight-saving time seemed to be a crowd-pleaser, and government reform seemed to be where the scales started to tilt in your favor. Could you talk to our listeners on your ideas of reforming social security?" Kelly said.

"Sure. Social security is a retirement fund! It should be taken out of government control and given back to the people who earned it. Citizens should not be forced to participate in a government retirement system that makes no financial sense. People pay into this fund their entire lives. Most never live long enough to use their savings. The government keeps what you don't use."

"It makes the most sense to roll social security into the working classes 401K and made available to use at age sixty. The 401k should not be controlled by the corporations a person works for or the government, but by independent investment firms of the workers' choice and monitored by the government. A retirement fund created by working people that benefits the working person until death.

"At the end of the day, there needs to be an option that a person could give the money they work their entire life for, to gift the money to their loved ones or a person, church, college, or charity of their choice, not stuffed in D-sea lawmakers' pockets, earmarks that end up in the bank accounts of their family and friends.

"All insurance—home, auto, life, flood, and health care—should be combined into a bracketed reasonable tax, which is what all these insurances are when they become law—an additional tax. All federal, state, local, personal property taxes need to be rolled up into the great tax bundle and paid to the state a person lives in. That state would then be responsible for paying the Federal government a tax payment based on its collection of tax from corporations and citizens. The better a state—for example, Mizzeree—treated its citizens, the more citizens would move there, the more revenue it could generate to make its state more attractive to live in. Let state and federal politicians fight each other and not the people. Nothing wrong with making life good for people. So, *one tax*."

"Right. And very boring! Can you quickly touch on daylight savings time?"

"It's the simplest thing the government could do for its citizens. The practice is outdated and serves no purpose. The country repealed it in 1919. They should do it again. All publicly traded companies should pay 10% profit sharing to its workers, all worker getting an equal share from the CEO to the cleaning crew—the Government would benefit the most at the end of the day collecting more taxes. We just need a leader to get it done."

"The next great shift came when your religious views were highlighted. Do you believe there is a God in heaven or not, VeeLee... Von... Vouge?" Kelly said.

"It is true that I don't believe in a religious heaven, per se—a mansion in the sky. It's my opinion that souls have no need for a home, a bed for a bodyless body to sleep in, and have no need for food or water, as the stomach and rest of the organs decompose eight to ten days after death. I, too, question a place where streets are adorned with gold. I cannot envision souls have feet or the need to walk, and I assert the presumption there would be zero cars in this heaven, either. I would have challenged horses in the Roman days if I would have been alive then and was in a debate during those times.

Christians might have killed me for my ideas of the soul or spirit back then."

"Hmm..." Kelly said.

"You don't get to keep your current spouse or be given a soulmate when you get there, so to speak, not according to Jesus, anyway. So, love in terms of emotions will be different as there is no heart to pump the blood that pumps hormones that emotions attach to and circulate thoughts around in the brain. It's impossible in a spirit form. I couldn't even tell you how the brain could possibly work as a spirit. There are a lot of delusions and illusions of the afterworld that I approach differently than others.

"The spiritual world is, of course, something no living human will know until they die and enter into the spirit form. I plead guilty as charged, I am a spiritual idiot, as I feel we all are. But there will come a day when the soul will separate from human form and return to the source—to God!"

"So, you do believe in God? You're confusing me..." Kelly said.

"Yes, of course. I one hundred percent believe there is a Divine God—the great "I am," and we are His and Her children, His and Her plants and animals, His and Her universe. The beauty of love is found in the knowledge that life is both masculine and feminine, a balance. I do believe our mind and consciousness evolves and adapts. But I'm not a fan of the evolution theory that everything started as creatures of the salty sea, nor Darwin's natural selection, survival of the fittest, either. Basically, its survival of one's genes first and foremost, yet all life on earth share practically identical DNA. It all boils down to having sex."

"Sex?" Kelly said.

"I would lean more toward Sigmund Freud, haha. No, but seriously, a gendered male could not have sex with its male self and give birth to a baby girl to start a specific species that could have sex together to create the millions of uniquely diverse animals such a fish, lizards, birds, lions, elephants and humans that breed unto themselves. Nor could a female have sex with itself to create a male to have sex with to create offspring. Our Divine Father created every form on purpose to serve a purpose. Period. Sex should solve most of the mystery.

"In death, we will shake off our bones and set our spirit—the essences of our soul—free. We will then learn the truth regarding the fabric of heaven and our creator. Everything is perfectly designed and has a perfect purpose. I imagine thoughts of God and heaven are simply limited by one's culture, language, and words. Ultimately limited. One must find in their own heart and mind their own truth. Everything is God, wrapped in skin or tree bark. It really doesn't matter the form it is packaged in."

"Hum... interesting... Thank you, VeeLee, for the interview. I can see why you won,"

Kelly said.

"My pleasure."

The entire interview lasted three minutes, thirty-nine seconds. For the rest of the day, kids were giving me thumbs-up and wanting to shake my hand. After school, during dinner, I told Mike and Melissa that it seemed I had gotten far more attention out of the debate than I thought possible. "I think I made some new friends today."

"We can never have too many friends in life, now can we?" Mike said.

"No, we cannot, my honey. We enjoyed it live Friday night as well, VeeLee. You did a fine job!" Melissa said.

"Thank you, Melissa," I said.

"There were some areas in your political and religious notions that were juvenile, but you'll learn. You'll learn eventually, VeeLee," Mike said in a somewhat condescending manner.

"I'm sure he will, my honey. We had to learn life as we went along, too," Melissa agreed.

"I'm sure by the time I reach your age, I will know much more, Mike," I said appreciatively, all the while knowing Mike had nothing to do with my debate win.

"Yes, you will. I'll try to share my knowledge with you as best I can," Mike said.

"Yes, I know you will, my honey," Melissa agreed.

"Thank you, Mike," I said and scraped the last bite of dinner onto my fork. "Thanks for the nice meal, Melissa. I need to take a shower and get my homework done."

"Dear boy, you are so welcome," Melissa said.

"We'll need to come to the cross on some of your thinking. Being a Christian can be a difficult transition. I know you never went to church before. But you'll get there. You'll catch up," Mike said and chuckled.

"He sure will, my honey," Melissa said and placed her hand over his and laughed along.

I smiled, grabbed my plate, took it to the sink, rinsed it off, and placed it in the dishwasher. I took a shower and thought of the debate, my Mom, my conversation with Adamina-Rose, and wondered if I should reach out to Aarontino and tell him the whole truth about his actual mother and what she had told me. Then I remembered I had promised her I wouldn't tell anyone. So, I called Toozoolee and caught up on K-sea news. Our conversation, my friend's voice, made me feel much better—centered. I then transitioned to my homework and barely finished the math equation before I succumbed to sleep.

My jog brought clarity to my morning, and I looked as closely at the sun as possible. I knew it held many answers I needed to know—information that was in the area of plant photosynthesis of spinach and spirulina, magnetic fields, light, and heat. I reviewed long-known facts of our super star, its atmosphere hotter than its surface, it's two seasons—solar minimum and solar maximum—that occurs every eleven years. It's mostly made of hydrogen, the most common element in the universe. My main interest is the energy and how to store it in the likes of solar panels. I need to recreate the positive and negative magnetic field lines crossing them and capture the explosions of photons and electrons at the speed of light on a micro, edible level. I needed to capture a piece of the sun's intelligence to fuel the masses with the encapsulation of my ingredients in gelcap form. Perhaps a time-released gelcap within a gelcap construction. The sun sings through vibrations. I will record her song and market her melody of magic and hopefully heal a ton of sickness in the world.

When I arrived at school, it was evident something had gone wide of the mark—the air was saturated with tension and anger. Of the four hundred police officers in Queenfield, I was guessing many were now on alert. There were a dozen police cars with lights flashing across the parking lots of Horseshoe High.

Melissa was giving me a ride as my *Nice-on* pick-up truck was in the shop for repairs. We didn't know whether we should just drive off and go back home, or what. Maybe something awful like a shooting had happened. Melissa asked the police officer next to her car what was going on, and if the school was closed.

"Several church leaders were here for some sort of protest. The news crews and radio stations decided to make it a big deal. Now we have quite a few upset parents here, demanding answers," the policeman said.

"What is the protest about?" Melissa asked.

"There was an interview broadcasted over the announcement system yesterday with religious undertones. That's what I'm hearing anyway. Some parents are apparently outraged," the policeman said.

I knew he was talking about my interview. Suddenly, I didn't feel like I had just scored the winning touchdown for our football team. The jagged lump in my throat seemed to swell to where I couldn't swallow. My stomach knotted up tight like nylon rope wrapped around the blade of a lawnmower stuck on full throttle.

"That was my interview," I said. Melissa looked at me and gulped down a breath of air.

"Well, guess we better head to the office and straighten this out, dear boy," she said. Melissa parked the car, and I noticed Anglaia and Danielle headed in our direction. Before we could close our car doors, they were in our face. She must have cued the yearbook photographer who then tipped the photographer for the *News Peeper*, Queenfield's newspaper.

"Good job, genius," Anglaia said. Just as she flipped me the bird, ten flashbulbs blew up like fireworks in my eye.

"You really should grow up, Anglaia!" Melissa said, and we dodged them and the rest of the paparazzi. We made our way into Horseshoe High and went directly to the office where there was a much-to-do going on. My debate teacher was up in arms, rattling on about the constitution and the first amendment and the right to free speech, being as animated as she possibly could. Horseshoe High's superintendent and the regional board of directors had their own ideas of what being a spectacle looked like. They both were hopping around like headless grasshoppers. It was determined an assembly would be held in the gymnasium during first block, immediately after attendance was taken.

Apparently, all we, the student body, needed was some Ph.D. adulting. Hopefully, the same lame preachy speech would relax the Queenfield community. A buzz swirled in the air over comments made in the morning paper. Bible-thumping religious squires and pontiffs were in a tiff over the pew-crew's second-hand version of my opinions of the human soul and heaven. It was most likely religious leaders seizing the opportunity to fill the seats and coffers.

Anglaia and I made the front page of the *News Peeper,* and for some reason, she was credited for standing up for religion by flipping me off—go figure. I was surprised how good we both looked in the picture, though. Astonished that the photo-bomb did not make me look like a blurred Frankenstein, eyes closed and mouth half-open—a paparazzi smear sort of deal was not used, instead. Queenfield's concerned were back at the school in full force for day two of another round of complaints Tuesday morning.

My after-school co-workers razzed me jokingly. I could tell they really didn't care about any of it. They had a cut-out of the *News Peeper's* article pinned on the breakroom's corkboard. The owner's daughter and me having a public spat. They seemed to think it was hilarious.

I dreaded going home to hear Mike's afterthoughts. I knew it would be mind-numbing, and I would not see my room again before ten o'clock in the evening. It would not be the first time I would turn in hurried homework. Mom usually kept me up until one-thirty in the morning most nights. The lack of sleep would be the cross I could contentedly bear. A perchance preparation for the college days ahead, perhaps?

As our Horseshoe High fame grew, more stories circulated throughout the school. Insinuations that we would make great looking babies, that we were secretly already a couple, and we were simply attention whores. I thought it was funny as hell. Anglaia, on the other hand, became extremely pissed. Most knew she was testing the waters with Danielle. There had been too many sightings of playful petting and them riding everywhere together in the Mustdang.

I was grateful for my phone and had over fifty phone numbers saved in it. I was getting many social media requests from kids I couldn't imagine getting to know personally. My short answer was a silent *nope*. Being connected to some of my old buddies, to include my best friend Toozoolee in K-sea, did give me some peace mind.

Toozoolee and I talked at least once a week, and I was planning a road trip to go see him and Mom in the near future. It sucked to have to get everything I wanted to do cleared twice, once through my foster parents, who then had to have it cleared through the state of Mizzeree's children's services. I had almost forgotten where my phone had come from until an unknown number flashed across the screen, and my phone vibrated. It was a phone call I was nervous to answer.

But I did. It took a second for me to recognize Aarontino's voice over the phone. It sounded much different than in person. I was tense and guarded. I wouldn't put it past him to drive to Queenfield, crash the door in, and rough me up as he did in the good old days of last year. Nothing like Reggie or Weston Wickit, but his voice still made me jittery.

    He seemed rushed and pressed for time. Aarontino stated he was checking on me and that my mom was getting sicker. There was still no word from the doctors regarding my blood matching my mom's. The court was moving slow. His voice was a little more chill than I had remembered it in the past. He even seemed to be acting nice to me. It was a very foreign vibe.

    I told him about making the paper, and I made him laugh for the first time, ever. He ended the call soon after and told me to call whenever I felt like it. It was a very strange and random interaction that made very little sense. For some reason, I felt I was getting dumber by the day. I was struggling to understand why all these people who should not have a care in the world about a kid like me were extending themselves and participating in my life.

    I was dreading church at the *Assemblage* Sunday and figured Pastor Dom and or his disciples might wad me up in his office, bring in a dunking booth filled with holy water, have me tossed in, and hold me beneath the water until *all* the demons had left me altogether. Hopefully, if I survived the exorcism, I would be allowed to recuperate in my sacred place of silence. These awake mares could be very annoying at times. Like now.

    What I felt would be most therapeutic would be a trip to Anglaia's grandparents' home in Bronson and visit *Curevibesea*. My wonderland tucked deep into the woods, hidden from all the world. I needed to sit atop my king's throne, the giant bolder and squelch all thought or even lay on the negatively charged floor of the earth and dump all the positive charges building up inside of me. I needed to release the heaviness building up in the trillion cells of my body and lighten my mindful soul. Maybe if I harkened seriously enough, Mother Nature might order up some stardust wisdom from the universe for me.

    To simply stomp through the creek bed and enjoy the season of fall in full form. To relive the beauty of death a million times as I watched the short lifespan of the leaf fall and float on the wind. Leaves in a transformation like a caterpillar—wonderful designs that died to create others. Eventually, tiny particles carried on the wind, water, or air, breathed in or excreted out into forms of reforming forms, the old renewing into something new. I delighted in thoughts that I might be comprised of pieces of a flying pterodactyl dinosaur, a tulip, a drop of the Amazon river, dust from the endless plains of the Serengeti, and maybe even a piece of Marcus Aurelius and Beethoven's carbon floating around inside me.

It may take a thousand years, but to be broken down enough to change into something beautiful again was a spectacle that played like a movie in my mind. Maybe the composition of leaves becomes a microscopic building block of a human or a horse or dolphin or a hawk someday. Anything God decided to use the elements for, some form of love that needed to be created, I guess. These thoughts of being with Mother Nature seemed to spark wonder into my psyche. Everything was interconnected and always would be.

Chapter 21

Anglaia plugs her ears

YES, I HAVE HAD ALL THE EFFING VEELEE VonVough I can stand. HE is a little foster boy maggot, who is ruining my glorious life. Everything was perfect before he came into my wonderful life. If I could, I would have he and Victor Angelino trade places in a heartbeat. Well, maybe, as long as it didn't screw up my relationship with Danielle again.

I had never seen my grandmother so utterly bamboozled and panicky as she was the day she had picked foster boy up from school. The four of us, Grandmother, Mother, Melissa, and I were chatting it up in the sitting room. We were trying to organize what the hell she was trying to tell us. A boogeyman tale of sorts that, at first, I considered shrugging the story off and going to my room. There were productive things I could be doing, like catching up with social media.

Eccentrically continued by saying something along the lines of, "then these two black men came right up to VeeLee and me." She mentioned the name Geovanni, and I realized I had actually heard the name before. That got me. Stopped me dead in my tracks. Now, Grandmother's story had me. I was not going anywhere. I remembered her college day stories of Geovanni. I was down for the count. I wondered if the wine and whiskey shots would loosen all the stories. Mother and Melissa just might get freaked out.

There was not a strong enough rope ever created that could pull me from the sitting room or her story now. I don't know how many shots of my father's top-shelf whiskey and wine she had taken before I arrived, but the alcohol was having hella effects. I had never seen this stately woman behave like this. She was acting just like me, although I didn't need alcohol to guide a rememberable performance.

She kept going on that VeeLee got into the SUV with them, and she thought he was in big trouble. That VeeLee's mother, Jillie Jo, worked for Aarontino, who was Geovanni's son. That she had met Geovanni in college but felt he was bad news back then, which was the opposite of the private Geovanni stories she shared with me.

She had told me things in the past that she wouldn't share with Mother or, most likely, anyone else. So, maybe the alcohol and having all of us in the room together threw her story narrative into a delusion of warped reality.

I could keep my mouth shut about certain things if I wanted to. The story itself hardly compared to the circus show she was putting on. I literally laughed-out-loud ten times. She,

Mother, and Melissa whipped me with their eyes when I did. After a short pause, Grandmother would retell the loop of insanity again. Never the same way, it changed every time.

It was a night of wine. Grandmother was making for a great diversion. Yet Mother managed to remind me that her turn would be coming next. Her dreams would be, without a doubt, waking me later on tonight. There were a couple of empty wine bottles and a freshly uncorked bottle sitting on the table before me. Mr. Rocky Wino crossed my mind.

I was way outnumbered tonight, and the odds of me losing my Mustdang were too high. The good news came when I flipped the script from Grandmother to my mother. If VeeLee knew, I should know about the details of Mother's nightmares. I have had to deal with them for seventeen years now.

"So, Mother… are you ready to scream your ass off yet?" I said.

"What in the world, Anglaia?" she said, Melissa and Grandmother gawking like neutered hoochies.

"You're slamming your wine, Mother, which means you're going to keep me up all night, screaming your ass off," I said.

"Anglaia," Grandmother and Melissa said together as if my mouth could be corralled by the two of them.

"Manners, Anglaia," Mother said.

"Mother, it seems everyone but me knows what happened to you as a child. I would like to know what your nightmares are all about," I said.

"Now is not the time. We are supporting your grandmother tonight. She has had a terrible day," Mother said.

"There is never a good time. I demand to know! Right now," I said sharply. I set my wildness free on the wine-soaked air of the sitting room. Silence sorted our souls, and my seriousness broke through the snore of Grandmother's tenth evolution of her story.

It was hard to give my grandmother a pity-party for having one bad day with VonVouge—poor thing. I had over one hundred bad days attached to the foster boy. Yet I could not get any support from them whatsoever. Instead, my father gave him a damn job, a damned *Nice-on* pick-up truck, and allowed him to play in the damned poker tournament. The asshole goes to my damned church, has driven my damned Mustdang, goes to my damned school, stayed overnight at my damned house for weeks, and my grandparent's house, too. Yeah, the jackass is standing right there with my father, in the damned doorway of my damned sitting room at this very damned moment, and had already heard about the damn dreams! I wonder if Grandmother would be impressed with my story if I drank a gallon of wine, too. I may not be as funny as her, but I know my rants had more "pissed off" in them.

    I needed to know something real. I was chasing the meaning of my wacky life. Each new day only confused and annoyed me further. A little family insight might help me crack the code on why everything seemed to be in such a dismal disarray. Mother crossed her legs, and we hushed for her blab-about. Hopefully, her account would not become a hereditary sleep default bug in my brain, creating a scream-fest duet every night.

    "Okay, Anglaia. You want to know? I'll tell you what happened to me," she said. I didn't know if I would ever be ready for this, but the story started just as VeeLee had started it in the Mustdang.

    "It was a rainy day. I was your age. My brothers, sisters, and cousins were outside on the screened-in covered porch visiting when my brother looked at me with deviousness in his eyes—eyes that told me he and my cousins were up to no good. Instead of running into the house where the adults were, I lit off the porch, and they chased after me through the woods.

    "I knew these woods like the back of my hand and could usually get away. There were too many of them to elude this time. They cut off all my paths of escape. The ground was wet. I could not get traction, and my long dress was pinched by the forks of a limb jerking me to the ground. They surrounded me and then tackled me to the ground and held me down."

Mother's voice sped up, and she uncrossed her legs, squeezing them tightly together side by side.

"I was not strong enough to keep my dress down. My brother pried my knees apart and spread my wet legs apart. He then shoved his snake beneath my underwear." Mother gripped the arm of the chair, and Melissa reached out and cupped her hand over the top.

"What? Are you kidding me? No way," I said in great curiosity.

"It was his black pet snake he called, 'BoBoy.' That is when your father, who had heard my screams from the neighboring farm, ran to my rescue. He tracked down my screams and the pile of boys holding me down. He jerked them off one by one, punching, kicking, and hollering at them."

"You did, Father?" I said, turning to him.

"I did," he said, and I smiled a sad smile.

"Your father was too much for them. I was still terrified. I was terrified of snakes, and it was still moving around in my panties and had bitten me twice on my private part. I made it to my feet and held my dress up, and your father grabbed the black snake by the tail and smacked it against a white oak tree numerous times until it was dead. Bruce remembered to kill it for identification. At the time, he didn't know what kind it was. Snakes, poisonous or not, need to be tested for disease or identify which antidote was needed for the venom."

"Bruce offered me his boots, which I declined. He held my hand and walked me all the way back home. I cried the entire way. My father came out the door with my uncles and was about to take after your father until I assured them, he had helped me. Bruce had come back later, don't know when, and put my shoes on the porch—no telling how long it took him to find them. The boys, all four, were lined up at the woodshed and switched for more than an hour.

"In the days to come, my privates became infected. I came from an Amish family who believed in horse and buggy, no electricity, and who absolutely detested modern everything, including medical doctors. My mother and father had every

Amish herbal specialist coming into our home with a salve or balm that would most certainly heal my swelling, infected, and painful vagina.

"My father would chaperone them, men and women alike, into the back room where I was instructed to raise my dress, take down my panties, and lay on the bed so they could all have a look-see. I could not just go to town and get some antibiotics and be done like normal people. Weeks later, your father came back out to the farm to check on me. I didn't know he had always had a thing for me, but he did. I liked him, too, but he wasn't an Amish boy, and that meant he already had three strikes against him as far as my family would be concerned."

"He made you show everyone your bagingo, Mother?"

"Anglaia, a lady would never use that word. Never. Ever. Use that word again," Grandmother said sharply.

"Sorry, Grandmother!"

"Yes, he did, Anglaia."

"Wow," I said.

"Your father later said he could just feel something terrible was going on by the way I hobbled stiff-legged on the porch to visit with him. He asked if I was okay, which I shook my head no. He asked if I wanted him to help or do something. I told him that the snake bit me, and I needed medicine for the infection. He came back in two days' time and brought me seven antibiotic pills stating it should clear matters up. I felt God had heard my prayers. Goosebumps followed my smile as I raised the glass of water to push the magic down my throat.

"At precisely that moment, my father walked into the kitchen and caught me attempting to swallow the cure. He made me spit the pill into his hand and clawed the rest from my fist. He yelled at me, spanked me with a belt, and forbid me any further contact with Bruce. That is when I knew the Amish, bonnet and dress wearing, strict religious lifestyle was not for me, and I ran away," Mother said.

"You ran away?" I said. I was learning what I always wanted to know—the details of Mother's side of the family and the explanation of what tormented our family late at night for all these years. Mother's story was far more exciting than Grandmother's Horseshoe High sidewalk regurgitation of the foster kid. "Wait, Mother. The snake bit your vajayjay? Seriously?" I said.

"Yes. Now let me finish," Mother said. Grandmother was still boomeranging around the room, not paying one bit of attention. "I ran to Bruce. I told him I had to leave my parents' farm. I needed help. I sat on his porch and waited while he explained to his parents. Adamina-Rose was not going to allow me to stay with them. She made a call, and someone showed up with some more pills and told me to take one right then, and Bruce would bring one each day. She was very nervous about how much trouble there would be if anyone found out she had supplied prescription drugs to someone and told me to go home," Mother said.

"It was my friend Karen from the *Assemblage*," Grandmother said.

"How rude, Grandmother! You made Mother go back to that crazy-ass place?" I said.

"Anglaia," Grandmother said, her lips tight. Mother's story was doing nothing to ease Grandmother's wrinkled forehead.

"Anyway, Bruce and I started meeting in the woods in the evenings for seven days in a row where he gave me the pill. Sure enough, my infection in my privates was cured. My family said God is good, and I didn't have to expose myself to others any longer. The pill came with a couple of hours of genital conversation and after a week, ended with a kiss. We had fallen madly in love and continued to meet in the woods nearly every evening. Neither of our families would ever allow us to be together, let alone get married.

"So, the next day after Bruce graduated high school, we eloped to Arkinpaw and became husband and wife. I followed him to college, played catch up regarding getting my formal education, and now you can see why I try so hard. I don't think Adamina-Rose will ever accept me anyway it goes. Just like I was banned from my Amish family, which I wouldn't go back to for all the money in the world. They all make very ugly jokes about me and what happened. So. There it is, Anglaia. That's my nightmare," Mother said.

"I accept you, Sarah. Christ Almighty," Grandmother scoffed. Grandfather abruptly moved in with the stealth of a lion and took hold of her arm. Keeping her still.

"So, the bottom line is… we come from an Amish family! Horse and buggy, rhubarb pies, Bible believers. You are Amish, Anglaia!"

"No-the-hell-I'm-not!"

"Yes, my dear, you are," mother said.

"Grandfather says were from Eagleland and that's good enough for me."

"Half your blood is Amish my child," mother said.

"Why the hell are you doing this to me for?"

"You demanded me too, dear daughter of mine," mother said.

"I now demand you, too… STOP!" I screamed.

"You'll have to forgive me some day Anglia," mother said softly.

"Why you haven't forgave anyone. I don't even know those Amish people I'm supposed to be family with?"

"Forgiveness… maybe we need to examine what forgiveness actually means Anglia. When you truly forgive someone, you're actually forgiving yourself. Once you know it's only your thoughts about a bad day or someone who caused us pain, you simply give it no more attention and let it flow away out of your mind. When the thoughts come back to visit, make it sit like a dog, literally say, 'sit memory!' then walk away to a beautiful beach somewhere. To say it's not okay, is okay and we need not hug and kiss ugly souls. Just walk away in your mind."

"Bite me, mother!" It was information overload and I had to get the heck out of here. I left the sitting room and raced to my bedroom, slammed the door behind me. *I'm not Amish either, "Sit Amish thought—where the hell is that beach Mother?"*

The day was done. All the nightmares and screams I knew would come chimed like a rigged clock. It was much different, though. I understood now. BoBoy was in her panties, chomping at her vajayjay. Doubt I could be pissed at her anymore.

It seemed if you were a woman in my family, the rules of life were set on advanced difficulty. We had to play by these effing rules whether we wanted to or not. I had my hands full trying to work things out with Danielle. She was still a train-wreck from losing Victor Angelino. I understood completely but had my issues of how she got there in the first place. I nearly went off on her a couple of times when she was working through the pain and loss. The temptation was to let her know I felt the same hurt and loss when she cheated on me. It was just as extreme to me, even though no one would ever agree with me.

Now she has to deal with the control freak she created in me. I do hate the playa. Game-on, babe. Karma works for me. But so help me God, if Danielle cheats again, I will demolish her prissy little soul. I'm still waiting for her to come around and tickle my titties, though. She knows how I love that. Laughing together always relieved tons of stress. We needed to have fun again. Matter of fact, it's Friday.

I told her I would swing by around seven o'clock and pick her up and to put on something sexy, a boobie-blouse, short skirt, and to wear the lace-up high heels I gave her for her birthday. There was going to be a private sorority party downtown that would be made up of couples like us. My plan was not to be there long.

I had gone there a couple of times when we had our breakup and had lots of laughs there. Mostly an older college crowd of twenty-somethings and a few cougars on the prowl. I remember a couple of drunk girls tried to come on to me, but I didn't go there. The chemistry just wasn't right, especially with the fat-ass girl named Pam. Not happening, chickie-poo. I knew I was way too hot for the majority of them. Of course, all the really interesting girls were taken.

I picked up Danielle, and we made our appearance at the party. Danielle seemed to be having fun and laughed a lot, as we all did. We stayed for a couple of hours then left when we had filled with fun. We hopped into the Mustdang, and I drove us down Dazzlefield Street for a bit, listening to some thumping music. I pulled into an upscale apartment complex, and we walked the asphalt path around the lake. We took a seat on a park bench, where she challenged me to see who could look the deepest into the night sky filled with stars. The giant, silvery new moon was huge, inspiring, and bright.

I rubbed on the leg she had thrown over mine and talked about nothing in particular, mostly Horseshoe High gossip intermixed with a few kisses here and there. She got tickled when I talked about punching fat-ass Pam in the face if she would have kept flirting with her. Danielle straddled me, and I filled both hands with a butt cheek. "Anglaia," she said softly. We kissed deeply for the first time in over a year. It felt good.

The white teeth shining through Danielle's beautiful smile were worth way more than any star or moon. The time had come—time to take her back to the hotel room a friend had rented for me and hold her all night long. That's when her phone starting ringing. Danielle's mom was calling her to find me. My phone was in the Mustdang charging. I needed to call home. It was a family emergency. I was pissed. Our high heels clanked like hurried Clydesdales trotting through a ghastly alley on the bad side of town.

If this had anything to do with VeeLee VonVouge, I swear he was going to be sorry.

Chapter 22

VeeLee's Phone Bomb

IT WAS THANKSGIVING DAY. JACOB AND Adamina-Rose threw a massive three-turkey feast together for dinner. The pool was covered, and a nip in the air called for warm clothing. The meal was scrumptious, and everyone sat, belly full, waiting for the fat to form under the skin. Light music played in the background along with continued table-talk I had tuned out. I was approached by Adamina-Rose, who asked if I would show her the place I had come from earlier. The place I always tried to visit when I was here. *Curevibesea.* She wanted me to take her to my special place, the one she actually owned. Selfishly, I wanted to keep *Curevibesea* a secret but agreed with a smile.

    I cocked my neck until the tendons and vertebrae released a series of pops that sounded like fingernails running across the frets of a guitar. I said sure at first, thinking to take her in the opposite direction to a random place she would never want to see again. Then I thought of how much this family had done for me. It would be the least I could do. *Curevibesea* would receive my first guest.

    Adamina-Rose announced we were taking a walk to everyone. We abruptly left the gathering, closing the massive castle door behind us. Nearly all the beautiful flowers and leaves had shown all the love they were meant to show and were dissolving into the earth with other dead things, an evolving matter that someday would create an entirely new form. Only the universe would know what the next bloom was going to be. Maybe the rolled-up tongue of a toad?

    At first, I felt she was simply curious about where I always went when I came to visit. But before we even hit the shoreline of Table Lock Lake, questions concerning the sidewalk of Horseshoe High dribbled into sound. "Could you please tell me more about your mother's boss?" she said.

    "Aarontino?" I said. Her face pooched a haunting sadness when hearing his name.

    "Yes, VeeLee, Aarontino!" Adamina-Rose said. Our pace slowed to navigate the stairsteps of uneven rocks, and I was keeping my eye on our exit point. She was wearing a pair of rainbow-colored *Likee* running shoes that did not fit her persona nor the five-hundred-dollar black, waffle-collar pantsuit, adorned with huge gold buttons lined down its middle. When you're as rich as her and her husband, Jacob, I guess you can make up your own rules.

    "Well, what exactly would you like to know?" I said. We started our trip into the woods, swimming through the tree limbs. I didn't realize Adamina-Rose was following so close behind and released a limb that smacked her directly in the face.

"Damn it, that hurt," she said and rubbed it like she was wiping at the spot of a spilled ink bottle.

"Sorry, Adamina-Rose." I felt bad, and my face sneaked from her view and kept our advance steady.

"Well, I want to know what Aarontino is like—if he talked about his family, his mother—things like that," she said.

"I could do even better than that." I pulled my phone from my pocket. "I have his phone number. I could call him and let you talk to him," I said. Her eyes flung wide open, shocked as if she had fallen through thin pond ice. The limb that smacked her just a minute ago on the right cheek gave rise to a sizable white welt—a thick, wiggly lump highlighted by a thin ribbon of blood leaked out to be warmed by the sun. Likely the most pain her pampered face had known.

"Have you lost your mind? No, I do not want to talk to Aarontino. I just want to know about him," she said.

"Oh, okay," I said. I looked back every now and again to check on her. I was glad I couldn't read her mind. Her facial expressions said enough. Thankfully the trees were beginning to spread out, making it easier to navigate.

"How much further?"

"Another ten or so minutes. We'll have to cross a spring pretty soon, though," I said.

"Great..." Surprisingly, she wasn't out of breath yet and did a good job of keeping up. I was almost walking on top of my own footprints from my earlier trip to *Curevibesea*. We wet the bottoms of our shoes in the spring water, hopping across flat rocks I had planted many trips before. We rounded the ridge where I was interrupted by my king's throne. I didn't mention we had arrived, just began climbing the boulder. I looked down to see Adamina-Rose's hands on her hips. "You're kidding, right? I'm a grandmother, VeeLee."

"Go slow. You can make it. There is good footing all the way up."

"It's one damn thing after another these days." She grunted most of the way of her climb but managed to get to the top of the bolder. My hand tingled from the final tug. She spun her butt under her to sit and ripped the fine fabric of her suit pants on a sharp shard of rock. The hole exposed most of her upper thigh. "Damn it." She blew out an angry breath and flopped her hands on her tummy. When she had calmed her mind and caught her breath, her eyes began to process the view. It was the reason I came back every chance I got. The scenery was one of Mother Nature prancing in the nude. "Wow!" she said.

"I know, right?"

"Let me catch my breath a minute." We sat in silence as she scanned in every direction, taking it all in. I had done so a million times and had all the basic features memorized. I knew where the trees, rocks, and the folds of the terrain were. The only thing I could not memorize was the vibe Mother Nature would give me during each visit. It was different every time. "I really like your spot, VeeLee."

"Thank you. I love it, too, but you own it," I said. We smiled at one another. "I was thinking Adamina-Rose… I could call Aarontino and ask how my mom is doing, have him on speaker so you could at least hear him? I could ask him some questions for you if you like?"

"You know, VeeLee, that might be interesting. I do not want him to know I'm listening or that this ever took place. Do you understand me? If you screw this up, I will have my son, Bruce, fire you and maybe even have your head painfully removed. And I'm not kidding," Adamina-Rose said.

"I got this. No worries! Hope he answers, though." It sounded good as I scrolled down my list of phone contacts until I saw the name "Aarontino" highlighted on my phone. For some reason, Christopher's heart began to beat faster. I had never actually called him on my own phone before. It was as if I was plugging in my own electric chair. Every cell in my body was now resisting. I remembered Mom having me call him to skip work in K-sea. I would tell Aarontino she was sick or had a court date or whatever she told me to say. He then cursed me as if I was a thirteen-year-old adult. He always asked to talk to her. I always hung up.

Adamina-Rose was waiting for me to push call. She rubbed at her welt, smearing the blood into a war paint pattern.

"Did I mention I'm ready? Let's go," she said, rolling her eyes to the top of the trees and spiraling her right hand up into the air like a smoke signal.

I was getting a sense where Anglaia might have picked up some of her personality. Adamina-Rose could be arrogantly pushy. "Okay. Here we go…" His phone was ringing, and I touched the "speaker on" button. It rang nine times, and I felt a hint of relief coming over me, thinking I was going to be sent to his voicemail. Then he answered.

"Hello, VeeLee," Aarontino said. Adamina-Rose sat in full attention. Posing as a kid pretending, they weren't hearing adults talking naughty. It felt as if we were both blindfolded, and she was holding onto me riding a motorcycle in the Grand Canyon. My mouth and mind were going to blindly lead us down this invisibly dangerous trail. There was no map or directions. I leaned on my debate experience and felt I could carve a conversation into something positive. Something that would not snowball into a giant regret.

"Happy Thanksgiving, Aarontino. I thought I'd call and check in on Mom."

"Happy Thanksgiving, VeeLee. Where are you?" he replied. I wasn't exactly expecting a question for a question. Adamina-Rose could not even blink. She was staring at me as if we were already busted. It was Thanksgiving Day, he may have been quieting his family, and had me on speakerphone, too.

"I'm in Bronson, visiting Mike and Melissa's friends. We just finished Thanksgiving dinner. How 'bout you? Are you in K-sea?"

"No. I'm with my family in Key-la-fornee."

"That's cool! So, have you heard anything on my mom?"

"Funny, you bring mothers up. You know the woman you were with at your school?"

"Yeah!"

"My father said she's my mom," Aarontino said.

"*What?*" I said in utter surprise, looking at Adamina-Rose. Her face transitioned from an opaque, clear fight or flight white into a dull, deep, somber red of surrender. She gave up instantly, waving her hand across her throat and wanted to silence the conversation. With her index finger pressed against her lips, she shushed the air. I could not just hang up him, but I did have to look away from her. She was making me even more nervous.

"That was the first time I had ever seen her. What is she like?" he asked.

"Yo, this is craziness! Wow! Don't know her that well. She has always been nice to me. I like her." I turned to Adamina-Rose and winked at her, hoping she would validate my conversation. She looked away, still fanning at her throat to kill the conversation and dabbing her finger over her lips to shush me more sternly.

Christopher's heart stumbling—like a toy building block tumbling down a flight of stairs in slow motion.

Adamina-Rose was overwhelmed. She most likely wanted me to roll the boulder we sat on back enough so that she might crawl beneath and hide forevermore. "I'm sure Keyla-fornee is nice this time of year. So, how is my mom?" I said again.

"A-Rose..." he said in a drawn-out pronunciation.

"I'm confused," I said.

"My father named all of our restaurant's A-Rose, after Adamina-Rose. Wow! He never told any of us where it came from until our trip down to Queenfield to see you," Aarontino said.

"Good deal," I said. I was grasping at straws, trying to stay with the flow of our conversation. It seemed a great revelation to him, similar to meeting Jesus in the flesh.

"When you get a chance, tell her I want to meet up with her sometime. Give her my phone number, VeeLee! I think it's time…"

Adamina-Rose had reached the apex of what her heart could hold. The boulder became a pot that was boiling her alive. She had to escape the private emotions. There was not supposed to be any witnesses of her secret. I could almost feel her heart pounding so hard that it seemed to send vibrations through the boulder where we sat—vibrating the entire world, for that matter. She haphazardly whirled herself down to the ground and ran. She slipped at the bank of the spring and fell into a bunch. She collected her wet, muddy body from the ground, stood up, and ran like a deer on a frozen pond falling to her hands and knees several times. She was headed in the general direction of her home.

"I will, Aarontino. Is my mom doing okay?" I nearly demanded. Watching Adamina-Rose was making it hard to focus on our conversation.

"Last I heard she was feeling a little better. Her court case—not so much! It looks like your blood is a match, but the doctor is trying a new medicine that may be working. Father says hello," Aarontino said.

"Thank God! I was hoping I could help her. Glad my blood was a match. If they need it, please let me know! Hello back to your dad," I said. A random hello from his dad was a little weird. Confirming the possibility I may be on speakerphone.

"You have no idea the odds of blood matching! If anything new comes up, I'll be sure to let you know. We will talk more about Adamina-Rose in the future. Try to find out what you can for me."

"Okay, sounds good! We'll talk soon."

"And one more thing, VeeLee."

"Yes?"

"I want to tell you that I'm sorry for being so hard on you in the past."

"Umm… okay."

"Well, better be going. Happy Thanksgiving, VeeLee."

"Happy Thanksgiving, Aarontino," I said, and we hung up. I did have an idea—it was called DNA. Matching blood could be nearly impossible sometimes. I was relieved knowing I might be able to help my mom if she needed it. I knew I needed to get with Mike and Melissa and make arrangements to go for a visit to K-sea soon. It was one of the most bizarre phone conversations I had ever had.

I could not imagine how Adamina-Rose would be received. There would be no hiding the mud, blood, and ripped clothes. It would not be another hidden secret. At the moment she had left my throne at *Curevibesea*, many years of stress showed up all at once and settled in her puffy red eyes. She had the look of a wounded warrior leaving a rain-soaked battlefield—a mindless, numb zombie. I did not have to be told I should keep my mouth shut on this one.

I'm sure when I returned to the Clintin mansion, I would be looked over thoroughly as well, due mostly to the fact I did not have a hair out of place. The more I thought of what had just happened, the more I realized how small this world really was. And that it was getting crazier every day.

The odds of meeting Aarontino's real mom, who was a redheaded white woman, was mind-blowing. Wow! I personally did not like Aarontino. I had always considered him a dumb schmuck. It was the nickname my friends and I fondly referred to him as in our general conversations. "Seen dumb-schmuck lately?" my friends would say or, "yeah, dumb-schmuck is at it again. He harassed Mom again last night and made her stay until three in the morning sweeping and mopping A-Rose," I'd say. Even though he was now the nicest I had ever known him to be.

My thoughts were scattered, as were the points of light in a clear night's sky. I could not grasp the universe in its whole completeness. It was too massive to set my gaze. There were too many parts to consider as simply one form that was so impossibly huge. I did understand the universe in general. It was simple. It was a thought.

It was an environment just like earth, a place where God played—exactly as I played on earth, only the scale was proportionate and perfect to our being. To complicate it would be to account each of the trillions of cells that gelled together making one human body. The ridiculous audacity of scientists to make sense of it all with the use of words cracked Lara and me up when we engaged the topic.

Adamina-Rose and Aarontino's story was a dynamic one, and I had no idea how it would unfold. The sound of a gunshot snapped me back to reality. The sound carried on, echoing three more times through the neighboring cannons. At first, I thought it was maybe a deer hunter, but it was way too close to the house. After what had just happened here at *Curevibesea*, I sickened with dreadful theories of what had just occurred.

I panicked, and without a thought, jumped from my king's throne with every intention of running faster than I ever had in any football game. I would get to Adamina-Rose with lightning speed and save her, or whoever else might need saving. I didn't know, but from what sounded like a wooden spoon being snapped, I knew I had just broken my leg.

Lara London and I had gone over anatomy pretty well. I knew, without doubt, it was the tibia poking out of my skin, the larger of the two bones connecting the knee to the ankle. I took a series of quick short breaths and felt I was about to give birth to an agonizing pain-baby. Then I yelled as loud as my voice ever had. The khaki jeans showed my deformed leg and soaked up the blood like a cotton ball. I held pressure on my leg as best I could to stop the bleeding. It occurred to me then that I needed saving, myself.

Chapter 23

Lunge of Lara

THERE WAS A SHOOTING. THE PURPLE

cloud confirmed VeeLee was admitted into Socks Hospital. I read he was headed to the operating room. The purple cloud was on full alert again. All my information systems were buzzing like Super Tuesday following the first Monday in November of an election year. The virtual reality realm of my home doubled as a makeshift election headquarters. The Nonagon wanted answers before the questions were even asked. I almost felt that if VeeLee's life did not make a heavenly shift, one of the Nine Kings would be metaphorically moving into my home soon.

Medical reports were being siphoned by the purple cloud and made available to me, much like the court documents of Jillie Jo. Reliable information poured in. My core librarian staff was back on the hot seat. I could see their faces. It was seven twenty-one on Thanksgiving evening with bellies full of turkey, eyes heavy with sleepiness. I'm sure coffee pots were gurgling, reading glasses wiped clear, and pushed up the ridge of their noses. The three librarians monitoring Jillie Jo would now split time on the breaking news.

They had shadowed everything regarding Jillie Jo and would do so indefinitely. Oddly, her incarceration seemed to make monitoring her more complicated rather than easier for them. Her case was a runaway train of egos that came by way of lawyers—attorneys filing red tape motions one after another in court, cashing in. There was too much energy and resistance in her court case not to. Piranhas filtered every drop of blood they could find through their gills. The frenzy was alerting sharks and fishermen in every direction. My fellow librarians were adept at multitasking and would shift to the priority at hand. They were sharp, intelligent, and experienced in the organization of each day. No class or training required.

My team at the purple cloud had managed our victory in court. Jillie Jo, Janie, and Kaylee had been found guilty and would be institutionalized for three-to-five years with a three-year minimum. There would be appeals and the like filed, a natural progression that did not concern me much. Jillie Jo was out of the way, and that was the endgame. Aarontino's case was dismissed.

VeeLee would have a Horseshoe High diploma and two years of college completed at age eighteen. His mother, Jillie Jo's scheduled release, would not come until he would have his bachelor's degree. By then, his path would be clearly understood without being constantly compromised by his mother. The fruition of his courtship by the Nonagon would also be reaching its maturity. Deep-state king or commoner—decided. Jillie Jo would be transferred to Merryme County Woman's Reception Center in Flow-duh. Hopefully, the east coast would keep her out of my hair. Jillie Jo would be gone in a few weeks.

My primary focus now was VeeLee's medical condition. I pulled the handle on my recliner and stretched it out. It was new and stiff, but I liked it. Steam tornadoes whirled up from my hot cup of chai tea. I breathed it in and relaxed a moment. I was now established in Queenfield, except for a few nonessential boxes stacked in the garage—boxes I could care less about right now. I needed a moment—a genuine break.

The streets of Queenfield were becoming familiar. They ran east and west of the eighty-two square miles of city limits. Very small when considering the three hundred and nineteen square miles of K-sea. There was a softer essence here, with a hint of nightlife, but not much.

I found myself bored quite often in the evenings and made the commute to Bronson to take in some shows and have a nice dinner a few times a week. I needed to make a few friends. Going places solo was not ideal. Fingers crossed, my hot yoga membership should connect me with a dinner-and-a-show, fun-friend kind of person.

The medical reports were coming in on VeeLee and Adamina-Rose. VeeLee had intramedullary titanium rods hammered into his bone. He would also have a three-inch titanium plate zipped in with screws to secure the bones of his broken leg. I would not need to race down to see him at the moment. A broken left leg was not a game-changer.

Playing football in his senior year may not be an option, though. We would work through the thoughts together during his healing and rehabilitation. I would make an appearance when notified through normal channels. I'm sure he or Melissa would contact me soon. There was little support I could provide until the pain meds wore thin, anyway.

Just as I was about to disconnect from my electronics, a short message concerning Jillie Jo appeared. She would be granted a medical extension and not moved until her health improved—she was too sick to travel. The tainted mozzarella string cheese sticks we planted through her cellmate had become more symptomatic than expected. She was being taken over by the invading bacteria we introduced into her gut system. It had moved into her blood and tissue.

Her lifestyle of heavy drinking and drugs had weakened her immune system more than we had expected. It looked like her liver was shutting down, and she might die. It was not the intent of the Nonagon, but collateral damage was sometimes inevitable and unavoidable when the stakes were so high. Her parenting was substandard. VeeLee had to be cared for properly. He was destined for a world post that included a king's crown. A position seven and one-half billion people knew nothing about or could qualify for.

I was beginning to understand Geovanni and Aarontino's involvement in the big picture, as well. Geovanni was a purple cloud cardholder and the reason I was having so much difficulty dealing with him. He had been responsible for setting up Cleo Ray's disappearance forty years ago. Cleo Ray had been crowned.

Cleo had made a king. King Cleo opted not to take his family with him to the promised land—he kept it a secret. Banking had lined his soul with a green, greedy stripe that he could not overcome. He thought he would be able to outmuscle and maneuver the other eight kings once he learned the inside workings. His big hurry to have it all led to his final disappearance act instead.

The Nonagon used Geovanni's relationship with Adamina-Rose, her abandonment of Aarontino, and the accidental drowning of the college classmate to hush her and keep both of them out of the picture. Geovanni threatened to sue her mother, Charlotte, for every dime she had. Geovanni made bolder threats in person, of which were all used in the great cover-up in court.

Unbeknownst to the Clintins, Geovanni was under protection the entire time. He had been out of the country at the same time, which I secretly found out for myself. He most likely shoveled the dirt onto Cleo Ray's body. Charlotte, Cleo Ray's wife, did put up a good fight and millions of dollars of financial effort trying to find her husband or the truth. To be perfectly clear, Geovanni was no librarian. He was an enforcer.

Now, Adamina-Rose lay in Socks Hospital with a gunshot wound. Fiber optics told me the Jackkson's had already learned of the shooting and were on a flight to K-sea. It would not be long before they were loaded into the SUV and traveling for Queenfield again. This time I would not need a state trooper escort but would be making my way to Socks sooner than I intended.

The purple cloud informed me that VeeLee had a conversation with Aarontino via cellphone. I was very curious as to what they may have talked about. At the same time, I wondered if the purple cloud was keeping Geovanni informed, too. It was making my life a hellish bowl of stress soup. I asked them flat out in an email message. No answer came.

The battlefield was being set. I unleashed my woman war-cry, which sounded like Tarzan but prettier. I dawned my superhero cape and was ready to plunge my sword into the first message that came across the purple cloud. Then it occurred to me that I really might need to listen to my instincts a bit more.

What the hell was really going on here? I had peeled back many layers of the Geovanni onion. Yet, I did not have access to what he was looking at on his electronics. He may have a camera focused on me and listening to my every conversation... perhaps at this very moment. Did the purple cloud have something completely counter in store for my life?

The Nonagon knew, without a doubt, exactly how I thought and how I would react in almost every scenario imaginable. They had observed my dealings with other prospects that never materialized. I thought of all the craziness the Nonagon watched me go through—setting up my sting operation to nab Jillie Jo in K-sea and many others. The kings knew I was aggressive and did what needed to be done. My way seemed to work with them.

Had Geovanni gone rogue after his son, Aarontino, had been implicated? Why and how exactly was it that I could consider babysitting a successful career, anyway? If I would have been informed upfront that Geovanni was *purple* and Aarontino was his son, I could have approached things differently, especially after learning his job description.

I knew he would be trying to track down the individual who was pulling strings to keep his son locked up. If he had the same access to information as me, it would not be long before he had my address. I knew he wouldn't forget my face or where I worked from our introduction on the Horseshoe High sidewalk. I really didn't want to disappear.

I rewound my memory as far back as I could. I needed to know if there was an obvious reason the Nonagon had selected me and trusted me with the greatest source of informational power in the world—the purple cloud. Was the Nonagon even in the business of recruiting? Was VeeLee a legitimate prospect? Why in the hell were the Jackkson's immediately flying from Key-la-fornee to K-sea if they knew it was a broken leg? Was I being set up?

I was worth millions of dollars and could throw my hands up in the air anytime I wanted—take a two-year all-inclusive holiday complete with a cabana bath boy toting frozen margaritas. That was my plan at some point in the distant future, but right now was not the time. I typically took two-week vacations during winter, spring, summer, and fall each year. It was important to reset and relax. The constant involvement with VeeLee had put me eight months behind on my me-time. Rejuvenation would have to keep waiting. Yoga would have to suffice.

Many sacrifices came with working for the Nonagon. Mainly the thought of having a family. I wanted a long-term man. The whole wedding dress and rings and children proposition was occupying my thought stream, and I had no reason why. To have my own little family to be fascinated by was not something I had ever desired.

Here lately, it may have hinged on the fact Geovanni had the power to snuff my light out. The Nonagon would not have kept him around all these years if he was half-assed at his job. I knew he was a professional at everything he did. He and I were about to lock horns again. I would not be backing down from anyone. Fear was not etched in my DNA. "Victory-O'Victory," I hummed to myself. The moon whistled at me, and it was time for bed and to try on a random dream-man.

Morning came, and I showered, did some naked stretches, and checked out the state of my backside in the mirror. I made myself some eggs with chopped onion and spinach and then fired up my laptop. I put a marker map up on my computer and zoomed in on Highway 13. The Jackkson family was up-and-at-'em. The SUV was two hours removed from K-sea. I tagged it with a red light that moved in unison with the SUV. Now marked, I had the exact time and distance to their arrival at Socks Hospital. I had approximately an hour to put myself together.

The skirt I put on was short. My V-neck blouse lightly fell across my breasts, hinting to their perfect proportion. I had no problem exposing bare flesh. It alleviated guesswork for one, but also kept whoever was looking at my body engaged in multitasking, managing more thoughts. Every advantage was exactly that, an advantage. I was better able to focus on the environmental situation. My high heels showed the arch of my foot and was topped by my favorite gold ankle bracelet with its random charms. Today the charms were cherubs, baby angels—some singing, some sleeping.

A sexy, educated woman could usually work a crowd or law enforcement with a calm voice. I even decided to accentuate my face with some highlights of make-up and shiny lip gloss. My teeth check came back as thirty-two trophies to show off, bright white—no egg or spinach to floss out. I sprayed a tease of my favorite perfume called Nightingale into the air and danced under the misty rain. Nightingales were birds with a beautiful song. Hopefully, the scent would sing melodically to those I encountered today. It was mysteriously sweet, a mellow love and inviting. I felt I was ready for the showdown.

I sat at my computer chair and scanned the purple cloud. It was a manageable amount of information, nothing like the Jillie Jo/Aarontino bust—by far the most insane week of my life. I ordered the antidote prescription for Jillie Jo and the illness I had slipped into her string cheese. I had to get her healthy so she could be transferred to Flow-duh and out of the way. It would be a trial medicine she would have to agree to take through the prison infirmary, a series of three inoculations.

The red light had moved a few inches along Highway 13. It moved on the screen like a fly on fire. I had one hour and nine minutes until contact. I was getting that adrenalin rush no cabana bath boy would ever be able to generate. I was getting stoked. I turned my fingernails toward me. They looked perfect. It was go-time.

I wanted to get there a little early and talk to VeeLee before the Jackksons invaded. I needed to know what their previous conversation was about, the one on the phone just before he was hurt. I wanted to know what the hell happened to Adamina-Rose. No details were coming in from the hospital reports, which I found a bit odd. I sent word to my librarian squad to leak to the *News Peeper* that the K-sea kid was stirring up the public again. This time he was involved in a shooting.

Hopefully, the media would slow the Jackkson's down a bit. The police department would be asked to put a guard on his door due to a bogus death threat. I shut down the purple cloud on my home computer, grabbed my laptop, phone, and purse, went to my car, and made the commute to Socks Hospital.

I pushed the number nine inside the elevator of Socks Hospital, closed my eyes tightly for a second, took a very deep, mind-clearing breath through my nose, and released. I exited, went through a series of double doors, and made my way to room number nine-sixty-three. I spotted Melissa and Mike standing with the charge nurse huddled together at the nurses' station. Perhaps being delivered the prognosis of VeeLee's state of repair. I eased into the group and lip-synced, "Hello," which was greeted with nodding heads from everyone.

We waited for what must have been twenty minutes in his room. The police officer had arrived, came into the room, and verified who we were. I was deemed a friend of the family. "Mr. Mike Matches," the officer said, his voice low and teasing.

"Hey, William Huttson," Mike said.

"How's he doing?" William said.

"He'll be laid up for a few weeks, but the doctor says he'll be fine. Hey bub, may not make the poker night this weekend. If you have someone who wants to play for me, let me know!" Mike said.

"You may not make it out of here. The news media is on their way up, I heard. Just so you know, there is only so much I can do when it comes to the media, friend or not. We need to keep it professional. I'm Officer Huttson!" William said.

"It's all good. What are you doing here, anyway, *Officer*?" Mike sarcastically said.

"Heard VeeLee's name over a dispatch. Headquarters was notified that there was a threat placed on him. So, I told dispatch I would respond."

"Oh, thank you, dear William," Melissa said.

"Yes. Thank you, friend. Officer," Mike said.

"It's my duty to uphold law and order now, so don't bring up our private life again. The hospital most likely agreed to have a police officer on the floor. They have a ton of pull at the department."

"Yes, Mike, my honey, we cannot stir the media up and get people riled up again. I know from experience it can be terrifying," Melissa said and draped her hand on his shoulder.

"There is no shortage of weirdos in the world," I said and was quickly acknowledged by the charge nurse. We made our way into VeeLee's room. I sat down in a visitor's chair, crossed my legs in a flirtatious manner. William smiled as if we had made a monumental secret connection. There would be no more eye contact. He was scanning my body, which I kept moving in subtle ways, suggesting I was getting comfortable in my chair, intent on giving this good-looking, seasoned officer an eyeful. Men in uniform—*yummy*.

"Oh, yeah," he laughed, "you have to be careful these days. With all due respect, your perfume smells wonderful, ma'am," William said, shooting a smile at me.

"It's called Nightingale. Thanks for your service, Officer Huttson. Nice of you to be here," I said. We now had our private protector. Mike seemed to like the privilege of having a police officer for a friend but also seemed offended he couldn't flaunt it to today. William was right, though. He could find himself in quite a predicament if Mike went on a mouth-a-thon.

The hospital bed rolled into the room, VeeLee in a fog, half-dazed from the anesthesia. He had rods sticking out of his left leg, which was stabilized by a wire cage contraption and elevated by a cable system. He smiled at me and then sent another to Melissa. "Mike or Melissa Matches, the media would like to speak with you," a nurse said, poking her head in the room.

"No, thank you. We have no comment," Mike said.

I conducted a time-check on my phone and knew the Jackksons were here at Sock's Hospital. There had been no outpouring of information—zero regarding Adamina-Rose's condition or what had actually happened. VeeLee would be in traction for a week and then put into a hard cast for six more. Now that he was out of surgery and coming around, he might be able to fill in some blanks.

I had to figure out how to get the Matches out of the room so that I could have a private conversation. The bed behind the curtain was empty for now, but I knew someone would be filling it at some point. My chances of an honest talk would then be over. I intended to guide our conversation with VeeLee as best I could to glean nonessential information. Some things no one in this room needed to know, but me.

I contacted Toozoolee and let him know the situation and asked him to contact the Berry brothers. I felt his K-sea friends should know there had been an accident. Word was getting out through the grapevine in Queenfield, as well. VeeLee already had a couple of Horseshoe High football buddies in the waiting room here for a visit.

"Oh, there's Jacob, Bruce, and Sarah!" Mike said. We could see and hear them through the open door of the hospital room. They were at the nurses' station getting cleared to come in.

As I looked out the entrance to acknowledge them, shadows of the Jackkson family shuttered by the door like stripes of a zebra blurring in an African heatwave. They looked intently into VeeLee's room, which was filled with people, and kept walking. The Jackkson wave poured over my mind. I became anxious in my gut.

They did not stop, disappearing down the hall, which summoned a massive cortisol dump being released into my human tube. The presence of inflammation would set in and cause pain if not removed by yoga exercise later.

It could get messy with all the secrets and lies of crisscrossing bloodlines. Never had they been in such close proximity. Geovanni would first have to get past Officer Huttson posted at the door if he was here to get to me. I aborted that story in my mind fairly soon after I birthed it. He was not alone, which I'm sure was one of his professional protocols of erasing someone. He would not jeopardize his entire family to off me in public. Nothing pointed that he was coming after me, anyway. It was the fact that he was here in

Queenfield that triggered all the red flags. I zipped a message to the purple cloud, letting them know contact was imminent.

The Clintins filed into the room and circled VeeLee's bed. "How are you, VeeLee?" Bruce said. The chatter fell numb, giving Bruce the floor. Hopefully, he would get many of the basic answers we all wanted to know out of the way and into the open.

"I'm okay, a little foggy right now. I am still confused about what happened. I remember hearing a gunshot, and I jumped from the boulder to go see what was going on, then I realized I hurt myself," VeeLee said.

"Uh-huh, yes..." Bruce urged.

"Well, it reminded me of when my dad shot himself in front of me on Thanksgiving. I was scared to death again! The Thanksgiving holiday really sucks for me, for some reason."

"Sorry about your dad, VeeLee."

"It's okay. It was my dad's choice," VeeLee said.

Bruce put his hand on his good leg, and continued with his train of thought, "You and my mother went on a walk together. Did she seem out of the ordinary or acting differently? We're trying to understand what happened, as well. Why did you two decide to separate during your walk?" Bruce said.

"So, the gunshot did have something to do with Adamina-Rose?" VeeLee said.

"Yes, VeeLee. She was in surgery most of the night. She is resting and responsive. We don't know the extent of damage, but it looks like she'll live—she's a fighter. Anglaia is with her," Bruce said.

Jacob's face seemed poised with a serious slant—an executioner standing at the ready with careful aim. His brow sagged heavy over the ache of tired eyes. He had aged overnight—the comforts of his mansion far removed, every cell stiff and stressed. As I watched the facial gestures of all in the room, Jacob projected a gritty demeanor toward VeeLee—not quite blaming, but close. Everyone wanted to understand what happened on Thanksgiving Day.

Chapter 24

Aarontino takes notes

UNLIKE VEELEE'S ROOM, THERE WAS NO one guarding Adamina- Rose's door, and for the most part, this hospital wing was free of noise and was too quiet. My family just walked in. She looked at us in narcotic recognition. Her eyes danced in deep reflection as I boldly approached her bedside.

"Check the other bed," Father said.

Redding peaked around the privacy curtain that divided the hospital room. "Empty," he said and pulled it all together against the wall, opening up the room. The sun and fluorescent light mixed expelling all shadows in the room. Adamina-Rose lay helpless as a lamb floating in the middle of the ocean.

"All right, Aarontino, make it quick," Father said.

How on earth one was to make his first conversation with a mother he had never known quick made no sense at the moment. I did manage to lose my train of thought, and I stooped into a dumbfounded-speechless state of being as I looked at this hurt woman. My prepared script vanished.

We didn't know if Adamina-Rose would be dead when we arrived or not. How exactly Father learned of the shooting all the way in Key-la-fornee so fast would be as mysterious as many other instances in the past. He had a way of finding things out. He never shared with us the "how" part. Goseeia might have an idea, but we boys knew she'd never tell us half of what she knew about Father, either. Maxx was in the doorway, watching.

We were not breaking any law, but it felt so wrong. It was hard to believe we had lucked into a perfect space in time. The Jackksons were primed to go to battle if need be. We had game-planned the last ten minutes of the trip down from K-sea. It was my time to at least be heard by this woman, "Are you okay?" I said. Adamina-Rose did not move other than batting her eyelashes. I put my hand on her arm and expected her to pull it away or say something, but she didn't.

I didn't know if she was paralyzed by the bullet or from our intrusion. She looked sad and numb. The medical monitors beeped and showed her vitals. The squiggly heartbeat patterns and numbers were a foreign language unknown to me, but I looked at them for answers anyway. I had a one-way conversation with the egg and womb donor who I really had no feelings for. We had two memories, one on a sidewalk, and the other was her being absent all my life.

They were thoughts my brothers and I shared in one way or another regarding our mothers. When Goseeia's mother died, we all felt she was somehow the lucky one to have at least known her. I looked at my father for strength, hustled my vocal cords into an immortal conversation. I could not see the hurt child that I had seen a million times in the mirror. The words flowed from my being, into her soul. It was as if her chest had been pulled apart by the doctor, and I could see and feel her heart for the first time.

Go Johnny Go... "I know you're hurt and cannot talk, so you'll have to listen then I'll be on my way. I will tell you what I know and then I'll tell you my hopes, Adamina-Rose... I know many things, but I do not know you. I hope you heal soon and that you are a happy person with a wonderful family like mine. I hope you know I am a strong educated man," and as gently as my voice would allow, I said, "I hope you know I forgive you, Mother." My heart—now, a giant caged elephant—swelled five times its normal size, taking up the entirety of my chest, for a moment I thought it might break free and beat so hard that it would exit my body through my mouth. *Go Johnny Go—Go Johnny Go...*

Goseeia and Dominique stretched their faces into iron displays of support and I instantly felt changed. Adamina-rose's lips quivered, and tears flowed down either side of the pillow where she lay.

"So sweet, Aarontino," Goseeia said. Dominique flicked at his nose with his thumb and sniffed.

I poured honesty and truth into this strange woman like a warm, soft waterfall. Some of my thoughts shook my family up a bit. Redding and Maxx listened as if they were not listening. It was obvious this was supposed to be a private conversation. Their heads contorted like dogs to high pitch whistling when I dropped my message like it was boiling hot. There was no time for the way she and Father had dealt with this all these years. It was time to go Aarontino on this shit.

We might be able to create a relationship. We might not. It was not all that important to get to know her. I was fine with the way things were, but I was open. I had said my piece and felt better for it.

"Man, I got to go," Dominique said, and quickly came back in Fronsay, "Oh, Merde!" after he opened the bathroom door to see a girl perched on the toilet seat, petrified. She had heard the entire interaction.

Father looked into the bathroom and said, "I'm Geovanni."

"I know who you are," she said and clumsily unfolded her legs off the toilet to stand upright and waded through the Jackkson family members. "Why is that man screwing with my grandmother," Anglaia said sharply, looking at me while going directly to Grandmother's side. "You people need to leave. *Now!* Before I effing *scream*," she said. She pointed toward the door, red-faced. I had to admit my niece had some heart.

I was done. I said what I felt I needed to say. There would be nothing gained by making a scene now. I nodded to my family, and we walked out of my mother's room and closed the door of the high-end deluxe hospital room. Now, Father wanted to talk to the son he had never known. We might soon be going to war—a ginormous family feud. His room was guarded and full of people. We were the Jackksons, and we feared no one, especially when together. VeeLee's room was two wings over in the non-private section of Sock's general patient population.

We marched straight to the police officer, and I told him I needed to talk to VeeLee about his mother. I was her employer, and it was critical I spoke with him immediately. The police officer asked my name, interrupted the Clintin conversation, and asked, "Mike, do you know a man named… excuse me, sir, what was it again," he paused, "a man named Aarontino?" Officer Huttson said.

"Yes, I know him…" VeeLee said.

We walked in like we owned the place, and I said, "Hello, folks. Very important! We need just a moment with

VeeLee, and you can come right back in and visit with him. Thank you for your consideration." I said, pointing at the door in a similar manner as did Anglaia. It seemed to work for both of us. I did not need to put on a red face. My raised voice sufficed, as it did when I asked drunks to leave A-Rose. The five-minute hostile takeover was in effect—they were leaving the room without confrontation.

I noticed the woman we encountered on the high school sidewalk. She was wrapped up in the finest fashion and drew my eye quickly. She sat on an armless chair, legs crossed, dangling her shoe on her toes, and flashed a smile full of white teeth at me. She didn't seem to take the emergence of my request seriously. She stood, gave her short skirt a couple of tugs downward.

"Typically, there are introductions… *I'm Lara London*! There is a waiting room for a reason. You folks can wait your turn. We were having a conversation," Lara said.

"Look, lady. So—not, interested in who the hell you are. We'll only be a minute," I said. I felt my temper rising. I could very well lose my mind and go off on this Lara chick, whether she was sexy as hell or not.

The migration of their group stopped dead in their tracks. Lara had everyone's attention and looked as if she had no intention of backing down. I didn't know if she was a drama queen or what, but she certainly had witnesses now. It felt like she was attempting to set me up, make a giant scene that she could use later.

She might have been intimidated by the strength and size of the Jackkson family, thinking we might hurt someone. Lara seemed to need to create some form of evidence of an argument that occurred on this day, something she could point to down the road.

"It's okay, Lara," VeeLee said, trying to keep the peace.

"Well, no, it is not, VeeLee. This man is being disrespectful to this group and me. I will not be bullied by… what's your name, sir?" Lara said.

Go Johnny Go... "I'm not here to bully anyone, Lara. We have already met on the sidewalk of Horseshoe Hello— again—my name is Aarontino Jackkson—so if you would— please give us just a moment, *ma'am*." *Go-Go, Go Johnny Go.*

"Lara, we do not have time for this nonsense, get your ass out. Now!" Father said. His voice was purposely loud to incite a touch of fear. The vibration pulverized every soul in the room—hooking his thumb towards the door.

"Not playing girl," Goseeia powered up and pointed to the door.

I, too, gave her that "now, then" look... as Officer Huttson walked into the middle of VeeLee's room. Lara always seemed to have law enforcement around every time our paths crossed. Perhaps that's why she was always so bold. If the day came where she had to deal one-on-one with a Jackkson unrestrained, she might have nightmares indefinitely. Lara only knew what the purple cloud shared and was clueless about the true nature of the people she was pissing off.

"The information is private. It concerns the medical condition of VeeLee's mom. Five minutes folks," Officer Huttson said.

"Well... I'll say you men, and you, young lady," pointing at Goseeia, "might get away with pushing some people around. I personally am not intimidated. I think you owe Lara an apology before any of us go anywhere," Jacob Clintin said.

"Let's give them a minute, Father," Bruce said, putting his hand on his father's shoulder in solidarity.

"Welp, you Jackksons are a rude bunch, if you ask me—" Jacob said in a volume similar to the one my father had used moments before. Two old rams about to lock horns. My brothers, for some reason, had refrained from their typical tendencies of rising up. The man was lucky he was walking out of the room without his ass beat. None of us needed assault charges, but we all perked up when Jacob raised his voice towards our father. We all stood in front of our father and stared directly at Jacob, Bruce, Mike, and the police officer with the utmost confidence and dare in our hearts.

"Hey, everyone, relax, relax. We are the foster parents," Mike said, searching the air behind him for Melissa's hand. "Say, Aarontino, why don't you go ahead and give VeeLee the information. Surely we can all handle the news of his mom. Don't know why we need to leave. We're all friends here," Mike said, looking at Jacob as if to say, "I got your back!" His ego was trying to project a chest-pounding ape and the new King-Kong of the room.

"This mug is 'bout dumb-as-hell," Redding said.

"The policeman there just asked you folks to give us a private moment," Maxx snarled. We all put our arms out, shooed them to the door like wild chickens. Lara, the last out the door, had her lips held tight in its smirk of "whatever."

"Lawfully, the Matches have the authority here," Officer Huttson interrupted.

"A few minutes, please. VeeLee has been here less than a year. I have known him and his mother for years," I said, looking as humble as I possibly could in the direction of Mike and Melissa Matches. I'm sure VeeLee had thought to chime in about our relationship over the years but had not.

"Let's give them a couple of minutes! Mercy me. Okay, Mike, my honey, please," Melissa said with her hand holding his forearm. The grouping left thereafter.

"Close that damn door," Maxx said. Goseeia, light of foot, clicked on the tips of her toes over to the door and gently brought the tension to a close. We settled into comfortable postures, scattered about the room unintentionally. Father approached VeeLee's bedside and looked intently at the rods pushed through his flesh, "Damn kid, looks terrible. How are you feeling?"

"Not sure, sir. I just woke up from surgery an hour or so ago."

"Understood. I am Geovanni. Let me introduce my children. You know Aarontino, that's Maxx, Redding over there, this is Dominique, and that's my lovely daughter,

Goseeia." Each came to the bed and bobbed their head. "We are here to let you know that your mother is not doing well and that, unfortunately, your blood will not help her as doctors initially thought. Her liver is struggling to get better," Father said.

VeeLee lay still and quiet. He seemed to be calculating some complex puzzle—his eyes scanning across the panoramic shadows that surrounded him.

"How bad is she? What exactly is her doctor saying is wrong with her, sir?"

"It seems the disease or bad bacteria in her liver is spreading to her kidneys, and they are afraid her entire system could shut down. The doctor thinks she may be going into renal failure, which is certain death. When you can, you need to go see her. I can have Aarontino come down for you if you need a ride," Father said.

"I have a truck, sir. I will go to her as soon as my leg is good enough to allow me to drive."

"I wanted to let you know that I knew your mother long before you were born. And that's why we have come to check on you. She has worked many hard years for us, and we will try to look out for you two. It wasn't a very happy Thanksgiving this year, but better ones will come.

"Okay, VeeLee, if you need us, get hold of Aarontino."

"One last thing. Do you know what happened to Adamina-Rose?" Father kept looking down at his phone that was vibrating and flashing a purple screen, with the words EXIT in capital letters appearing on it.

"No, sir."

"Okay, then! We better get down the road and let your friends back in before they have a fit," Father said. We all chuckled.

"Okay, sir. Thank you for looking out for my mom and for coming to visit me," VeeLee said.

"Are you going to tell him," I said.

"Someday. Now is not the time," Father said. He turned back to VeeLee. "You're welcome, young man. Get better,"

Father said. We all put our hands on him like some elephant remembrance, and each said goodbye, leaving the door open as we left.

The hallway was buzzing with energy. Camera crews and all manner of people clogged the hall. Father told us not to stop for any reason and make our way to the vehicle. We needed to get the hell out of Queenfield. It was getting crazy up in here.

Local reporters were sticking microphones in our face with bright lights glaring from their cameramen. "Do you know VeeLee? What happened? What are your names?" were some of the questions being hurled at us on our way down the hallway. Father signaled with his index finger over his mouth, instructing us to say nothing.

The elevator opened, and to my surprise, I recognized some of the occupants. It was some of VeeLee's K-sea crew, knuckleheads who I had made a habit of running off the sidewalk of A-Rose over the years. We locked eyes in acknowledgment. One of the Berry brothers must have been feeling cocky and bumped into me on his way out. His twin and the Polynesian kid smiled a smirk as they passed me. "Punk-ass," Redding said. We glared at them and their youthful ignorance.

"Baby clowns are funny. You will need a diaper change if we get serious, bitch," Dominique said in Fronzsay. We Jackksons laughed, and he finished with, "boys should not test grown-ass men." We shook our heads in agreement and laughed some more. It was hard to talk tough in Fronzsay.

"Right, right," Redding said seriously in English, glaring at them.

Goseeia got a kick out of the youthfulness of these young men and smiled at them. I had not seen this side from her in a very long time. The last time was when we were teenagers in Peareese, Fronze. Goseeia's only love was with a young man named Gabriel. They still talk to this day. Don't know if it was because their names sounded good together or what, but we all thought they might actually tie the knot someday.

Redding broke Gabriel's nose once and probably would do the same to all three of these punks if they didn't watch it. Berry O smiled back at Goseeia as if he had a chance to impress her… and made it clear he was undressing her with his eyes. He was a delusional youngster, but we all were once upon a time.

"Hey asshole," a voice called out in our direction. We turned not to see the three young men, but it was Jacob who was chugging down the hallway. The elevator door began to close when I pushed the ground floor button. "Stay the hell away from my wife," Jacob said. His voice rumbled into the elevator box.

We could hear the thumps from above. He was punching the elevator door. Anglaia must have freaked out on us and told him of my reunion with my mother. I cannot be certain how the truth may have been twisted, but I was sure Anglaia spiced the story up a bit. We just shook our heads, made our way to the vehicle, and were ready to get out of town.

We settled into our seats, buckled up, and Maxx drove us out of the parking lot. He pointed the vehicle toward K-sea, and off we went. Goseeia tried to change the subject and brought up her favorite topic, the A-Rose empire. I was excited to have a new building to conduct business from and knew my financial report was about to take off and reach new heights. The new A-Rose building and location was a hot-spot, easily accessible, and had great parking. The selling value had tripled, and praise be the day I'd be done with father's dream.

The focus then shifted back to what we all just experienced. The chatter in the vehicle was amped up, swirling around the cabin of the vehicle as if a jet engine had been mounted into every window and set on full-throttle-takeoff mode. Everyone had their own thoughts and feelings about what had just occurred. It was one of the most extreme memories we had ever shared as a family.

After an hour or so of listening to my people feast on the emotional salad being tossed around in their minds, I excused myself and put on my headphones to listen to some music. I needed to process the whole idea of seeing the woman who gave birth to me lying there in a hospital bed—my egg donor who had a bullet go through her body, and if it really mattered to me. I needed to reason with myself for a while. *Go Johnny Go...* whispered into silence as the R&B beats took charge of my mind.

Relaxing now, I could give no attention to the moving scenery outside the car window. Childhood hurts of not having my mother, surely had to have better meanings than the ones I had always clung to. When the answers did not come, I visited the topic of that female, Lara, looking sexy as hell. She was jumping around in the gymnasium of my mind even though Goseeia was 'bout to beat her down. I knew the rest of the family had grown suddenly sick of her sassiness. She had managed to get my attention in other ways, though.

VeeLee was gaining ground on great significance to me. His greatest value was potential answers to some important questions in my life. I would integrate VeeLee's knowing of the two women as soon as possible. There was much I wanted to know about Lara and my birth-giver. The future could not get here soon enough. I wished Father would have explained to VeeLee what we had learned about the blood results.

Chapter 25

Momma May I—VeeLee's Silver Cell-sit

  THE PAIN CAME AND WENT IN MY LEG. MY boys from K-Sea surprised me with their visit. They took the seriousness out of the room for a while. Berry O told me about bumping into Aarontino, and we laughed. They also shared in the confusion as to why he was down here in Queenfield. He had the hots for the beautiful lady in the group, how they had shared a smile. I told Berry O that her name was Goseeia, and he smiled like he was solving a love mystery. Now that he knew her name, she was his somehow.

As soon as they left my room, I had the Clintins, the Matches, and Lara London come back into my room wanting answers I wasn't sure I had. Not to mention, I had a ton of questions I would like answered as well. The main question being the one everyone kept asking me. What in the world befell Adamina-Rose? How was she doing? Could I see her?

Lara was much friendlier than normal. Every time I noticed her, she was smiling and sharing helpful information. The adults quickly fashioned an alliance and began consulting her on most conversations that needed a better solution. She was making new friends with my keepers. I was becoming happier, knowing she cared enough about me to infuse herself into my new environment. I felt she would look out for me, that Lara was the only one on the planet who knew my story and taught me everything I needed to know to change the ending. I believed I had inadvertently stumbled onto a very lucky life here in Queenfield, Mizzeree.

I could not get used to seeing holes and metal rods poking into my leg. It would throb, itch, and ache on and off throughout the night. Being immobile was what annoyed me the most.

I had connected with Adamina-Rose, making two trips to her room so far, which took a lot of persistence and persuasion when it came to my nurses. A couple of them seemed to have taken a liking to me. I think they considered me their temporary cute puppy or something. I must have made their shift pass by faster.

When I did get to visit Adamina-Rose, my entire bed was wheeled into her room. It was night and day different environments. Her room was more like going into someone's home. She had a hose poked into her throat, and she couldn't talk. Occasionally she would write a note, one of which sent goose pimples the length of my body. She wrote, "No storytelling." I just nodded okay. I knew she wanted me to keep quiet about my conversation with Aarontino, the one I allowed her to eavesdrop on at *Curevibesea*.

It seemed the universe was thinking the same, as well. Every time I was about to tell the whole truth about what happened that day, something or someone would interrupt the account. Explanation of my latest creepy Thanksgiving haunt would have to wait for the stillness of a calm, sunny day. Things were too hectic and going a million miles an hour right now.

Anglaia had her story, of course, and seemed to be blaming me, the foster boy, for her family's troubles. We were visiting Adamina-Rose when Melissa asked Anglaia if she would do her a favor. She wanted her to round up my homework at Horseshoe High and drop it off at the hospital. "It would be so helpful, Anglaia. We really don't want him to fall behind, sweet dear," Melissa said to her.

"All I want to do is help that foster boy right out that window over there, like right now," Anglaia said.

"Anglaia…" Sarah said, which sent Adamina-Rose to her writing tablet.

"This is not his fault. It's mine. Please bring his schoolwork to him. I love you. Thank you, Granddaughter," Adamina-Rose wrote.

"VonVouge…" Anglaia deeply groaned. The sound rumbled through her throat like an eerie foghorn. She always did this when she wanted me dead. Tapping on the door interrupted the mood.

"Hello everyone," Lara said and walked directly to my bed. "How's my mighty man this day," she said with great enthusiasm and delight. She squashed Anglaia's heavy vibe instantly. Lara had never lent a designation. I liked the title of "mighty man." It immediately imbued a sense of power, and I wanted to run with lions.

"Who *are* you," Anglaia sneered with her hands digging into her hips and her elbows cocked out.

"I brought you a couple of interesting books I think you will enjoy. One is about—"

"Excuse me," Anglaia interrupted, "this is my grandmother's friggen hospital room. I would like to know, who are you?"

"Anglaia, I—"

"How do you know my name?" Anglaia interrupted again. Lara turned and faced her with laughter and lightness. She was getting a kick out of the spunky confidence, perhaps a kindred spirit from long ago. Lara approached her for introductions, and it seemed Anglaia melted like ice in Lara's sun. Lara had mature-Danielle looks and was fashionably put together.

"I am VeeLee's friend, Lara."

"Ugh, sorry 'bout that. I'm not his friend, Anglaia." She smirked.

"You and I most likely have very little in common, then. I've known VeeLee for years. He is one of my favorite people," Lara said and watched the smile gape tight ear to ear on my face. Anglaia rolled her eyes.

"I really like your hair and appearance. I can tell you don't buy your clothes at garage sales." Anglaia giggled, her voice softening and deflecting the conversation in another direction.

"Well, thank you, Anglaia. I do not have time to garage-sale. I'm a busy woman."

"What do you do? An attorney or something?"

"An attorney? No. I'm a professional, though. I work at the library."

"Oh, gotcha. I'll come to check you out sometime. The one on Dazzlefield road?"

"Yes. Do that. What are your interests, Anglaia? I could prepare a booklist for you."

"I do not have time for a booklist. I'm a busy cheerleader." Anglaia giggled over the spoof. Everyone in the room snickered and enjoyed watching her relate to Lara.

"I see," haha, "I really must be going. Good to see you, VeeLee. Glad you will be leaving here soon," Lara said.

"Nice meeting you, Lara," Anglaia said.

"You as well, young lady."

Anglaia was leaving, too. She quickly kissed and said goodbye to everyone but me but did wave as she typically did. She then danced out of the room and Socks Hospital. I had a jealousy knot stiffening inside for some reason. I didn't want to share Lara with Anglaia. She had more than enough in life. Lara might be able to fix Anglaia's attitude and make the world a better place, but still, there was a chance Anglaia would try to turn Lara against me and take her friendship away just for the fun of it. I took a settling breath and realized I was creating a fictitious scenario in my mind and shook it off. Lara was a burst of sunshine that this negative hospital room needed.

The Clintin men, Jacob and Bruce, were watching my every move now and were suspect after Bruce intercepted the note Adamina-Rose wrote to me. It seemingly confused matters more. They were daunted by the Jackkson family and the stream of new personalities flowing into their lives.

Adamina-Rose explained that her written response was to settle me down, that she didn't want me making up stories. Reporters from the *News Peeper* had been requesting an interview from the time she had been admitted, and she wanted everything to settle down. It seemed the Clintin family was starting to lean toward Anglaia's way of thinking—that the foster boy was bad news. In looking at it realistically, a great deal of craziness had happened in a very short amount of time.

Thankfully, I was reassured in Sock's Hospital that the Clintin family still accepted me. Adamina-Rose demanded I be rolled into her hospital room to finish out my stay. Of course, the Matches didn't mind at all, but Anglaia, on the other hand, was furious. Jacob was none too tickled about the arrangement, either. He did not make a huge fuss about it, though. He simply pushed me next to the window where I required extra blankets to ward off the crisp, cool fall air that made its way through the large pane of glass and weak window seal.

When my homework made it to me in the evenings, it was usually scraped off the floor by the random nurse who succeeded Anglaia. The nurses usually wanted to know who was making the messes and complained mightily. Adamina-Rose's eyes smiled every time. I didn't know if my work was being turned in or not. I knew I could take any test on any of the subjects and pass with flying colors. I would be losing the hardware around my leg soon, be put into a full-leg cast and released on crutches.

I had been reading the books Lara had dropped off. Science was learning the sun's secrets found in vitamin D3. I found that the activation of gene expression was interesting. D3 influences a couple of hundred chemical reactions, communications, and was very important to the immunity and vitality of the endocrine system, one of the most powerful synergies for the absorption of all vitamins. It provided a great benefit for bones, brain, asthma, depression, and tons other things. Vitamin D will most certainly be a key factor in my sun formula. Positive vibes like the sun were usually snuffed out by Anglaia.

Adamina-Rose's tube had been removed from her throat, and she talked with Jacob and me a bit throughout the day. It was a croaking sound and seemed painful. I had, on a number of nights, thought of contacting the Matches and have them move me back to my old room. Jacob slept in the room, too, and snored very loudly, making it impossible for me to sleep. When I did sleep, it was mostly during the day. Adamina-Rose didn't want the television on, which was fine with me. She preferred classical music and therapeutic tones.

Thoughts of the Jackkson family and my mom crept in steadily every other minute. I wished I could have my mom's bed wheeled into this awesome medical environment where she could get the best treatment science had to offer. She would have no problem with the snoring as I did. Most of her drunken bedmates bellowed even worse. I was getting word that the Jackksons had come to visit Adamina-Rose the same day they visited me, which really pissed Jacob and Anglaia off.

I couldn't wrap my head around how our two-minute phone call on top of my boulder could have been so important.

She only listened and said nothing. There had to be things going on that I didn't know of.

Conversations did come and go throughout the week, and I did manage to learn that Geovanni went to Samfort University in Key-la-fornee with Adamina-Rose. She didn't want to talk about it. Jacob might lose his mind again and storm the hospital halls. I don't think they had ever talked about Geovanni before. She squirmed in her bed when I brought him up. It could have been her motive to have me close. She wanted to know exactly who I was talking to and what we were talking about.

I knew the subject of Geovanni and Aarontino was a tense and painful subject to talk about. The light of answers had been switched off. It was better I left the matter alone. I felt the same when discussing my mom and dad. Some monster memories needed their own habitat to dwell, thoughts tucked into the secret shadows of silence. If only the power of light could awaken them, the great fire of acceptance might take them away for good.

I was learning no sooner did life begin, it would be over just as soon. Of the billions of years before would come a billion more after. One hundred years was the greatest I could expect to share in my human form. The odds heavily stacked against longevity. One swing of the pendulum was all any of us received. Life started at its highest point of a baby, and hopefully, the momentum would carry us to the highest point on the other side, where we would be delivered back to the universe as a one-hundred-year-old baby once again.

Existence wowed me with wonder. It was like watching the universe dream—a real-life Hollywood production with a cast of seven billion. Everyone had an individual role and played a part, whether they wanted to or not. Mother Nature, with her birds, trees, and flowers, were living props that rarely received the ovations they deserved. It was a fascinating magical movie to me—a miracle, complex and simple at the same time.

It was my last day in Sock's Hospital at ten o'clock in the morning. I would have shed the immobilizing wire cage that allowed my bones to melt back together. For the next six weeks, I would torture my armpits with the job of becoming my legs. Hardly designed to do so, let alone lugging the cast around, an additional thirty pounds of nonflexible and awkward plaster.

It was a moment that could not have come soon enough. I would survive the snoring of Jacob. Melissa had my walking papers. I was being released. She was gathering up my things—get well cards and a few little gifts, most of which came from people I had never heard of at the Assemblage church. I was grateful for the love and kindness of those who had extended themselves to my debilitating act—my super-stupid sky leap. We were very fortunate to have Melissa there on the scene. Adamina-Rose most certainly would not be alive without Melissa's nursing skills being administered on the spot. We both may have bled to death without her initial triage before the helicopter showed up. I'm told it was a twenty-five-thousand-dollar ride.

From the conversations Adamina-Rose had with her doctor, she was healing nicely for her age. The gunpowder had caused some infection and scaring that her body and medical attention was restoring ahead of schedule. She could potentially get her walking papers in another week or so. Thankfully, today was my day.

I hobbled over to her bedside, and we said our goodbyes. I waved at some of the nurses and doctors as we made our way out of Sock's Hospital and awkwardly loaded my leg into the SUV. Melissa wadded her fingers into a fist and knocked on the cast full of my broken leg, it sounded hollow as a bongo drum, and for no reason at all, we smiled at each other. She started the vehicle, and off we went.

She turned onto Dazzlefield Street and stopped by Horseshoe High. I needed to know what the official status of my classes was. I would be out of school for the rest of the week, keeping my leg elevated and still as possible—I already dreaded the thought of taking my nightly shower. It would be quite the ordeal. My Horseshoe High counselor was prepared and had everything laid out for us.

I was behind on a few subjects but could lay to rest my fear of Anglaia trotting into her modern kitchen and feeding my homework into the industrial size food disposal. I might take my chances and tell her thanks the next time our paths crossed, most likely Sunday at the *Assemblage.*

Home at last, I wrestled my behemoth leg onto a stack of pillows. Melissa poked her head into the open door and sent my mind reeling in a completely different direction.

My heart sped up and started beating so fast and hard that I could feel it. Melissa shared we would be making the trip to the prison. I would be getting to see and visit with my mom this Saturday. It seemed like years had gone by. There had been so many changes from my old K-sea life. So much had happened. Most areas of my life were the best they had ever been. I thought, if nothing else, she would want a break from her cell and enjoy hearing about my broken leg.

Her constant hurry-hurry go-go was now walled in, and I was not exactly sure how she was adjusting. There had been two failed attempts at connecting on the phone. Most were shut down due to the ongoing investigations. Secretly, I almost wanted to stop the visit, maybe reschedule our visit sometime during my next lifetime. Then shook my noggin on the pillow, thinking of the noise I was creating inside my head.

I smiled at myself when I remembered how she looked at me when I told her my *Pickle* and *Field of Snow* stories. I did love looking into her lost eyes. They were beautiful—bloodshot or not. We managed to survive in a very toxic environment—most would not have fared as well. It was a life filled with horrifying, dangerous, and insane people weaved into what my mom considered normal.

In her prison cell, she could not see the skeleton trees holding their handful of fall leaves, and in the sun, these brown dead things transformed into golden bars of twinkling light. She could not see the silky silver spiderwebs dance on the cool breeze, flowing like seaweed on the currents of the ocean. It was mesmerizing to the mind. Magical. I could bring her some simple stories that might soothe her soul for a few seconds. I didn't know what I would find when I hopped over the fence of forgiveness but knew it would be better than staying on the exhausting side of judgment.

I had a few days to get my head right and would feel better after I looked into her eyes again. The stories of her health condition had me nervous. I surely did not want her to die without knowing the truth—that her son, VeeLee VonVouge, loved her with all his heart. And I'm sure she would be amazed to hear that the Jackkson family was unexpectedly going above and beyond to look out for us. There was much to tell her.

Mike made his way into my room a couple of times a night after work. If I heard him coming, sometimes I pretended to be asleep. I think he caught on, as he would come all the way over to my bed and shake me awake—he loved talking. I truly think he would shrivel up and die if his mouth malfunctioned and stopped vibrating constant sound. His quirkiness was growing on me, though, and I found him to be genuine. Melissa was taking my homework in on her lunch breaks and juggling a hundred other things without complaint. I really was beginning to have feelings for her. She was awesome. I felt indebted to the Matches more and more with every day that passed.

I awoke to amped-up nerves and really needed to go on one of my morning jogs, probably the only thing that could have settled my thoughts. Where the months had gone, I had no clue, but it was time to face the face of my creator. She most likely was being pestered by a similar junkpile of emotions and memories, which fed the very hormones that attacked the nervous system. Hers was simply an older, drug-dulled version.

We loaded up in the SUV and put on happy faces for our ride to the Chillakathy Women's Facility, located thirty minutes northeast of K-sea. The hours rolled along smoothly, keeping pace with the songs playing on the radio. Many songs I had never heard before. The last mile marker sign said twenty miles to K-sea when Mike said, "Oh, no… That's not good!"

"What is it, my honey," Melissa said. The SUV started jerking and bucking. Mike pulled over on the shoulder of the road. "Are we out of gas, Mike Matches," she warned softly. As a poof of steam spewed from the front grill and over the hood.

"I wish. The engine overheated, and I think it just locked up. We're screwed!" Mike said. He got out of the vehicle and lifted the hood, releasing a billow of white smoke. Mike then stormed up and down the ditch line absurdly in a raging motif. After a good tantrum, he came to the passenger window. Melissa instinctually pressed on the window button, but it wasn't going to work. He opened the door and squalled for his phone, "Give me my phone. My phone. My phone, please!"

Melissa was becoming irritated and was trying not to adopt her husband's state of panic. He was on the phone, flailing his arms like a marooned octopus. He had managed to contact Bruce at Sock's Hospital. He hopped back into the car, letting us know it would be a couple of hours before Bruce would be able to come with a car trailer to tow us home. "Sorry, VeeLee. Looks like you'll have to visit your mom another time," Mike said, hitting the steering wheel.

"Mike, my honey, calm down… please, my honey," Melissa said

"Okay, okay…" he said. "We might need to inform the prison, too," Mike said.

"Probably so, my honey. Right now, we just need to *calm* down," she said.

I agreed that he needed to calm down. We were close to my stomping grounds, and I felt one of my friends would come to my rescue. "Do you mind if I call some friends? They may be able to take us to my mom for a short visit and be back here before Bruce makes it here with the car trailer."

"I don't care," Mike said, looking at Melissa for her input.

"Thank you, VeeLee. Let's see what your friends say," Melissa said. She smiled briefly and looked out her window as if to examine the bare landscape for better answers.

I spent ten minutes trying to make contact. I repeatedly called Toozoolee, the Berry brothers, and their mom with no luck. It felt like the universe was jacking with me again. Then it dawned on me to try Aarontino's number. I think I was more nervous to talk to him than to my mom. He answered on the second ring.

"Hello," he said.

"Hey. It's VeeLee. I've got a problem and wondered if you could help."

"What's up, VeeLee?"

"Well, we were coming to visit Mom at Chillakathy prison, and my foster parents' vehicle has broken down. I was wondering if you would come and get us and take us there for a quick visit to see mom. Mike has Bruce coming with a car trailer to get us and their vehicle in a few hours," I said, which was followed by ten seconds of silence. "Hello?"

"Alright, VeeLee. Where you guys at?" Aarontino said. I told Aarontino our approximate location, and he said he was on his way. We assumed our waiting pattern that soon sped up when a state trooper pulled in behind us with his red and blue lights gyrating nervousness back into the cab of the vehicle. The officer verified Mike's information and then drove off as if he had received another call.

Aarontino whipped across the median, following the tire trails of most likely the state trooper we had just met. An illegal maneuver, but for some reason, I was relieved he had found us and was here. Mike stated he had better stay with the vehicle, so it didn't get towed away. He didn't want to deal with any bigger issues today. Melissa pointed for me to take the front seat, and she hopped in the back.

Aarontino's ride smelled fresh and new and was probably less than a year old. The music was mellow, and the climate was set at a perfect sixty-five degrees. Compared to the SUV, Aarontino's car floated like clouds on the highway. He was pushing the speed limit, but I knew we needed to. I just hoped that the state trooper didn't nab us.

Forty minutes later, I was getting cleared to enter the visiting room of Chillakathy's Women's Correctional Center.

I sat, listening to the gates of metal crashing together in the background, buzzers, and echoes of human chatter. I thought to myself that this literally sucks. I was looking through a plate glass window that had a dingy tint to it. There was an old-fashioned phone permeated with unknowable amounts of germs. I had hoped we could sit in a dayroom and have a hint of privacy and maybe even a contact hug.

We had one hour to catch up, according to the rules. I would have to wait four weeks before I could see her again. She did not like writing and didn't want letters. "So be it," was my response. One lady after another passed by my window, each getting the biggest smile meant for my mom I could conjure up. I was embarrassed to be in this setting as it was, but the false alarms drove the worse feeling, deeper.

Finally, at last, there she was—my sober momma. She had a light about her that threw me off. She carried her body differently—something nearer a butterfly. I could actually see myself in her clear white eyes. There was not a single red vessel to be found. She may have found some magic box and underwent a great transformation.

She smiled sweetly at me and put her hand on the glass, which I mirrored with mine. It was acceptance and love, the only form of hug we had. She picked up the phone, and her voice was calm, very different from what I remembered. She pronounced her words differently. They made a cheerful ringing sound when put together. Maybe the sound angels made when they sang to God. Not an ounce of stress, anger, nor pity did I detect.

There was so much I wanted to share with her. But she seemed to have much more she needed me to leave with. She told me she was feeling better now that the prison had found some medicine that was actually working. She said she was sorry she had put me through such a crazy life, that she had met some women here who had changed her life for the better. That she now had a great understanding of why and how she got trapped living such a dysfunctional lifestyle.

"We had to survive, VeeLee. It was the victim mentality, an empty drum that seemed to attract every narcissist and no-good around. Accepting jacked-up treatment by others was because my self-worth was absent. It was a void or a deep hole I tried to fill with someone else, or a thing, or a drug. I had to find someone to share the pain with. It was easy to find someone who could relate to my story in the rotten world I thrived in. Everyone was in pain there.

"They were pedestal people who could relate to what I was going through, those I believed truly understood the pain-monster that lived inside of me. Their pain-monster was only trying to survive, too—cruel people in a twisted world. I thought they would be my savior, carrying buckets of water that would put out the fire and extinguish the problems I continually created for us. Oh yeah, they were really there to save the day, weren't they? Not!

"I had no commitment to fulfill a sense of worthiness, a sense of importance. There was nothing authentic about me. I danced and partied a great life away. The victimhood mindset was repelling. It kept any good people from entering our lives," Mom said, placing her forearms together on the bench in front of her looking like a beached momma sea lion.

"I would hesitate to raise my standards because I never felt like I was winning the game of life. Something was always missing in life, an empty vessel I had to fill with the garbage that turned into tons of baggage I could not carry, way too heavy for a single mom. That's why all of my relationships with a good man ended very quickly.

"When I couldn't find a person, drug, or thing to fill the empty drum—to fill me up—I'd become more pissed and hurt. The pain-monster inside would take over, and I would go back to the only ways I knew to feel better. Which, as you know, was drinking, drugs, dancing, and sex. I was a taker and needed everyone I met to give me a better life. I was blind to see I already had it. It was crazy-ass thoughts that had tricked me my entire life," Mom said.

"I know, Mom," I said gently.

"I'm now learning when you are naturally full and satisfied with yourself and your life, you want to give. It's like an amazing river that completely fills you up and then flows through you. Your life will become like a fountain overflowing into the lives of those around you. A positive vibration and electric energy pouring out like soul juice, a cocktail of peace, joy, love, and happiness—all any person really needs. It's all inside. You don't need *people or things* to complete you. The hole or void will effortlessly be filled with good.

"Keeping negative people around is nothing more than self-sabotage. You know they will bring you down. If you're not fulfilled already or feel like you're winning, people will go hunting. When you find yourself beat down by poor choices, you'll be dragged down to the bottom, gobbling up any gross crumbs to keep the hunger at bay," Mom said and cleared her dry throat. She wiggled in her chair to find a better sitting position and continued sharing the lessons she had learned.

"When you can truly feel the powerful energy and vibration of love and abundance, you will feel internally wealthy, which replenishes itself forever—no darkness or negativity can fit or make its way into your life—in turn, making people great givers because they have more than enough.

Is this actually my mom talking? "Hey Mom…"

"Don't interrupt me, baby boy. You need to know this," she placed her hand to her heart, "so unfortunately, I dragged you along on my sick ride, and I am so sorry for that, my son. Hopefully, you'll be able to let go of the past, VeeLee. It was my excuse for years, and it became my badge and title. Every morning my *poor-me* mentality completely stole every new beautiful today I was given. We are the choices we make today. Yesterday is a waste of time and tomorrow, an illusion.

It's another mom day, just smile for her.

"I may be locked up, but I am, for the first time, free in my heart and mind. My life was a train-wreck, and I screwed everything up. You can choose my example and blame your mom for a crappy life, or you can choose to make a different life. You can have an awesome life, son," Mom said.

"Thanks mom, you're really getting better," was all I could come up with.

She had found people her ears wanted to understand. It seemed she had control of her mind. Time fed her a gourmet meal of delicious words that her emotions could reflect in her mind. She was scrubbing and cleaning up the plumbing in her thought processes. The corrosive funk that clogged her being was spiraling down the drain. The weight of her mistakes, decisions, horrible choices, and all the judgments of society had been released.

Mom would never become spotless, or a sacrificial lamb who would heal the world, but she was presentable, and a much better person. She had found a story of possibility, of change—her message might be helpful for a few. Maybe it would give her something to do. She would have years and plenty of broken hearts to tell these sobriety campfire stories to. These episodes had oozed from her lips in the past, and I knew if she had the opportunity to party, she would.

Nonetheless, I was amazed and happy for my mom. She nearly took the entire hour without pausing for a breath of my life, which was okay. Her message was medicine. She had elevated her existence to the highest level she could visualize and danced wildly on a positive cloud in the spacious sky above. Mom had never been bashful about nudity and the beauty of her sexy body. Now she showed me the nudity of her unclothed soul, and it was uplifting, magnificent, beautiful, and much preferred.

Her eyes wobbled childishly when she spoke, completing each sentence with a sweet smile. Her body posture was confident, relaxed, and self-assured. It appeared she had filled out a bit, or the pinstripes of her jumpsuit were toying with my vision. I had but five minutes to tell her some of my recent history.

I gained her attention by telling her my foster parent's vehicle had broken down thirty miles down the road and stood up to show her the cast on my leg for the first time.

"The car broke down? How in the world did you break your leg?" Mom said.

"Yes, Mike is going crazy!"

"Mike?"

"My foster dad."

"Sounds crazy hearing you say 'foster dad...'"

"I know, right? So, I could not get hold of Toozoolee or the Berry brothers, or anyone else from the neighborhood. So, guess who came to help us. Who brought me here?"

"I have no idea, VeeLee."

"Aarontino."

"My boss, Aarontino?"

"Yup, he and the Jackkson family have made a couple of trips to Queenfield. They have kept me posted on the court case, and your health problems."

"Okay, information overload. Slow down. My God!"

"Jillie Jo," the keeper announced through the phones, "your time is up."

"Wow. Next time I'll tell you about everything that's going on." Mom was stunned and most likely would give anything for ten more minutes. She was put in chains and escorted out of the visiting area. I walked back to join Aarontino and Melissa in the waiting room, and soon we were back with Mike at the broken-down SUV. Bruce had yet to make it. I thanked Aarontino as sincerely as I could. He winked and drove off.

It took longer than we thought to load and drop the car off at the mechanic's shop. After all was said and done, it was ten-thirty at night. My leg was throbbing, and I was one big hurt from head to toe. Mike had complained and rattled on and on the entire trip back to Queenfield. Comments like, "I knew it would break down. I knew better to buy that make and model." Next time this or that, obnoxious and annoying, giving us all a migraine.

"Aww, my honey, just calm down, won't you? It will be okay," Melissa consoled.

Sunday morning came quick, and I took a quick birdbath and wrestled into a giant pair of red basketball sweats that buttoned up on the sides. We loaded up into Mike's work truck and made our way to the *Assemblage*.

Chapter 26

Sore secrets, Anglaia knows

I DIDN'T WANT TO GO TO THE ASSEMBLAGE. I would have felt better going to Sock's Hospital to be with Grandmother. As usual, Mother threatened to start taking my stuff, which I think included the air that I breathed, and, in general, take my entire effing life away. I refused to do any make-up or comb my hair. A hint to all the saintly church people to stay far away from me. Nothing new, they had seen it many times in the past.

"Anglaia," Mom said. She looked at the sleep tucked into the corners of my eyes and my Halloween bed head.

"I *don't* care! Bite me, *Mother*."

Father locked up, and I hopped into my Mustdang, fired it up, and squealed off. A happy camper, I was not. And of course, the first thing I saw as I parked at the Assemblage was a vision my eyes wanted to vomit up. There he was, looking like a crackhead mechanical spider in his dumbass red sweatpants.

I had some creative ideas of what I would like to do with his crutches. I practically begged Mother to sit somewhere else to no avail. She was a creature of habit. She wanted to hear Melissa's K-sea story. And yeah, my father had to bail them out and basically dragged me along in mental agony. How I might not ever notice foster boy ever again, I did not know, but it would be a great medical cure for the insane.

The fact that my grandmother lay in the Sock's Hospital really upset me as well. It was not an accident. I blamed VeeLee VonVouge. If he had never come to Queenfield, we all would be just *fine*. She would have had no reason to be fumbling around with *Fart Dragon* and shoot her damned self.

I remembered shooting *Fart Dragon* with my grandparents in the past, and never really considered the damage that little ball of lead could do to us if we were not super careful. Firing it seemed more like a game that I bored with quickly—the noise was too much. I had no interest in guns whatsoever.

Grandmother's explanation was that she wanted to see foster boy's favorite place in her woods, that she had left him there and was coming back home when she saw feral dogs attacking a brown bear. She said she panicked and could only think of VeeLee getting attacked.

She raced to her car, got her Fart Dragon, and in her hurry to exit the car to get Grandfather and my father, it went off. The bullet traveled through her right side—taking out a portion of the right lobe of her liver and destroying one of her ribs that had to be fished out of the surrounding organs. Almost nine hours on the operating table. Before she went unconscious, she pointed to the woods and said, "VeeLee."

Melissa jumped on her doing CPR and told Mom to call for help. Father yelled for VeeLee, with no response. The last thing Father wanted to do was leave his mother's side, but he did on Grandfather's urging. He and Mike took off running and yelling. Fifteen minutes later, each had an arm of the foster boy over their shoulders, dragging him up the hill.

The helicopter had no problem landing in the massive yard. The two of them were loaded up and air-evacuated to Sock's Hospital. Blood had spilled everywhere. I could not imagine anyone living after losing so much. I was sure Grandmother would bleed to death. They each had blood pouring out of them. It was soaking into everyone's clothes, painted the helpful hands red, and the floor was tattooed with a crimson stain.

I didn't have a huge problem sitting with Melissa. She was old and boring like my mother. I know she saved my grandmother's life, and I would always think highly of her. I just had two major problems with her—drinking wine with my mother and bringing that foster boy into our lives. I had no problem setting Melissa straight on both issues. There was no timeframe. My message to her was get it right or deal with my flavorful attitude forever! Maybe I could smash VeeLee on Mr. Rocky Wino. There's a thought…

Things were coming at me so fast that I didn't have time to adjust my scream and wondered when exactly they would begin to come out at night like my mother's. Maybe my dreams would start waking *her* up at night. I owed her seventeen years' worth of interrupted sleep. I had every enticing prop for nightmares—my grandmother's bloody body, the aftermath of oozing yuck that came afterward—better known as the healing process—and VeeLee's dangling foot that dragged behind him when Father and Mike drug him up the hill.

The most terrifying would have been when I was cornered by the Jackksons in the bathroom of Sock's Hospital. It was one hell of a way to meet Grandmother's college studmuffin. It still makes me shake when I think about it—the absolute worst time to take a dump. At first, I thought the voices might have been doctors or nurses. Then, as I listened closer to the conversation, I thought she might have more visitors. One was clearly talking to Grandmother, while others mumbled in the background.

I almost barged right out into the room to make my presence known, maybe do a Horseshoe High cheerleading routine for them, until I heard the man say, "I'm sorry Adamina-Rose. I should never have lied to you about Aarontino being dead. Your *son* is alive." He went on to tell her that he never planned on bringing up the matter until VeeLee came into the picture. And of course, I knew foster boy had to be involved somehow.

"Then the shooting occurred," he explained. He wanted his son to have the chance to meet his mother, if still alive. So here they were. I pinched off my business and nearly flushed the toilet out of habit. My hand froze as if I about shook a rattlesnake's head. My heart sped up faster than driving my Mustdang a hundred and twenty miles per hour around the curvy roads of Bronson. I wasn't thrilled—I was really scared-scared!

Especially when one of the members of the group said he had to go. I knew I had nowhere else I could hide. I couldn't freeze in the shower because the curtain was clear, see-through plastic. I could hear each step bringing him closer and closer. For some unknown reason, I hopped up on the toilet seat, one foot on each side in a squat. I helplessly watched the door handle move down, click, and the door cracked open. My freaked-out eyes traced upward to meet his. With all I had, I screamed as hard as I could. But it was like some magic dragon cartoon, and only smoke came out. Not one sound could I make.

A huge man was looking at me. There I was straddled atop of the toilet seat, looking like a clown in a circus show. He called his father, who came and introduced himself. Finally, a face, it was Geovanni. Once the introductions were made, I settled down enough to take charge and flushed my poo. I went to my grandmother's side and ran them out of the room. I messaged Father and Grandfather to come to Grandmother's room at once. I know they thought for medical reasons, but I didn't have time to tell them what had just happened. I was still processing the whole thing, myself. They would be in a bigger hurry this way.

Grandmother, even more emotional, made me promise not to repeat what I had heard. Which was the worst thing to make a blabbermouth like me do. But I did promise her I wouldn't say anything about Geovanni and Aarontino.

The way my luck was going, there would soon be twenty-five horse and buggies pulling up, and a herd of Amish family misfits would storm the halls of Sock's Hospital. They would be armed with picnic baskets during the day and candle toting turds, singing Kumbaya by night. I would hate to see what my family tree actually looked like. I thought it had to look like some sort of deranged bush. In light of all the recent odd branches I was gluing on, it most likely resembled a sleazy, dysfunctional sitcom.

Without saying much, I managed to fire Grandfather up when he asked if that gaggle had been here. I just answered yes. He remembered passing the bunch passing VeeLee's room and then coming back—then he put the story of the sidewalk together. He and Father set out to confront them and let them know not to come back. Grandmother curled her finger at me to come near, when I was close enough, it seemed with whatever amount of energy she had in reserve, she used it to slap my arm.

I had only been caught off guard and slapped one other time in my life. When my mother slapped my leg for screaming at Beau with his arm around Danielle. She said that my mouth was going to start a war, and people would really get hurt. "It's time to calm down, Anglaia," she wrote boldly on her dry erase board, and then fish-lipped an apology for smacking me. I don't know how a normal girl was supposed to handle all of this. I guess I'm crazy! I didn't ever think it would be possible, but yeah, "Bite me, Grandmother!" Especially for insisting I take foster boy his homework back and forth to Horseshoe High. The school staff thought I was being so nice… It was a lie, "Sit VeeLee thought, SIT!" I don't think I'll ever get this forgiveness BS.

    I think I chose to be in denial of what I heard. It was slowly soaking in… sort of, but it still made no sense. How could a man lie about a child's death? The child should have been with its mother unless she gave it up for adoption or something. But Geovanni was the father, so he must have raised Aarontino. And my grandmother must have thought the mistake she made in her twenties would go to the grave with her.

    We did see her crying in her hospital bed from time to time and thought she must be reacting to incredible pain from the gunshot wound. I learned later it was severe pain coming from her heart. Now that I had stumbled onto her secret, she confided more details with me when we were alone in the hospital room. It was heartbreaking, but a good enough story to have me racing the Mustdang over every night to visit.

    Geovanni's apology was accepted, but Grandmother was so shell-shocked and overwhelmed by the unannounced intrusion that she failed to relay anything to Aarontino. Not even basic questions about his life. She felt terrible for any pain she may have caused him. Grandmother felt afraid and stuck because she had never mentioned it to anyone. The fake death news rocked her when she was young, but it set her free to move on at the same time.

    I would never be able to look at or be completely honest with my parents nor Grandfather again. I would have to guard and keep safe the secret of Adamina-Rose—my grandmother. It was a lot to ask of a teenager. It wasn't a fair request. I loved her more than my own mother, so I had no other option. If I did slip, I would just have to convince Father to buy me a newer Mustdang and go on with my life.

    Just before VeeLee was put into the same room as my grandmother at Sock's Hospital—which again, made me very mad—I delivered his homework, which I generously scattered all over the floor. He had stopped me for what must have been our only true five-minute conversation after the accident. I guess he felt the need to know why I preferred girls over boys—why I was gay. It wasn't a question I was ashamed of or hid from. So, I told him.

The reason was rather unorthodox as unthawing something, which is to freeze again, I suppose—none the less peculiar. I told VeeLee the truth for some reason. I assured him that if he told anyone, I'd surely kick him in the ball sac. He smiled. I was double mule-kick serious.

As it was, we were at a BBQ, I was around three years old, a baby, laying on my father's hairy chest when a wasp had landed in Father's wad of chest-hair and had stung me on the face, and him on the chest several times. Not only was I stung, but Father shook and ran with me, trying to get away from the wasp and fell, sending me flying in the air and crashing on the concrete. I developed a phobia after that. Anything dealing with hair—hairy arms, hairy legs, facial hair—body hair, in general, would make me very uncomfortable and cause me to freak out. There might be a wasp hiding somewhere in the hair, and it was going to sting me. Even the name Harry bugs me. So, I found refuge in the silky skin of a woman. No hair! No pain! That simple.

Inside the Assemblage, we maneuvered around the foster boy's cast that extended out into the aisle to take our seat for the Sunday sermon. I accidentally kicked his good leg and raised my hand at him. Surely he could figure out where my middle finger was. I took my seat next to Father and was somewhat rattled by the open space where my grandparents usually sat.

Chapter 27

Senior Year

SOME OF THE STORIES ADAMINA-ROSE TOLD did not make sense to me. She had not told them of the conversation with Aarontino. So, I could only assume she may have tried to commit suicide but failed. I envisioned her holding the gun to her head, changed her mind in disgust, slammed the gun down on the middle console where it went off into her right side, timed promptly after hearing Aarontino's voice on the phone. A secret she asked me to keep to myself along with his phone number. She didn't want it right now.

As much as Anglaia hated me, she had a bag of questions about my mom's boss, Aarontino, and his family. There was little useful information to give her. My opinion of them was constantly changing, however. It was like trying to explain what air or oxygen looked like. The good thing was that it opened the door to communication, allowing us to share a few normal moments of common conversation to include her hair phobia.

The passing weeks turned the page of the calendar. Christmas and New Year's Eve tapped us on the shoulder and disappeared like a dream. I won one of Bruce's card tournaments. I played for Frankie, who let me keep the money. My lucky hand also put Mike out of the money for the weekend and out of the point running for the big pot, which was won by William Huttson—ten thousand dollars. I had second thoughts later. Maybe I should have folded and let Mike catch a break. I would have given him ten thousand dollars if I had it. I did appreciate all he and his wife had done for me.

Other milestones passed, like the cast being removed from my leg, followed closely by my junior year at Horseshoe High coming to an end. I worked at Top Chop's all summer, added a few odd jobs of hauling stuff for older people who usually found me after the Sunday sermon at the *Assemblage.* My *Nice-on* truck had been a good investment. I rounded the summer out with a couple of summer classes that interested me, microbiology, and nutrition.

I still bumped into Anglaia around every corner. I had become her primary grievance in life, forgiveness becoming unimportant. The grievance was now a part of her identity. It had commandeered most of her thoughts. She had reserved a large portion of her brain to jail negative thoughts of me. I almost enjoyed it when my name rumbled from her tongue. It was now something special when she blubbered my last name in her deep, foghorn voice, "VonVouge…" It was Anglaia's calling card and permanently etched in my psyche. I could also pick her middle finger out of a line-up.

I had made another trip to Chillakathy prison to visit Mom for Christmas. This time she wanted to hear everything that was going on with me. She was still positive and smiling and ended our conversation by stating her transfer paperwork had caught up with her and that she was being moved to Flow-duh. Her sister Janie was dead, choked to death on a chicken bone was the story the prison told. Aunt Janie's daughter, Kaylee, was dead, too. She had made bail and died in a house fire two months after burying her mom. I couldn't attend either funeral service due to the delay in information. They were both scumbags that life didn't give a chance to evolve into good, loving souls. Some family blood does not belong in the heart.

I spent as much time with Adamina-Rose as I could, and now I had a clear path worn to the floor of her woods that would take anyone directly to *Curevibesea*. She lost some weight but was doing much better physically. Mentally she made tremendous effort to keep the little voice in her mind under control. Anglaia and I knew the Aarontino secret. It seemed to nibble at her sanity. She was holding onto a tight rope with greasy hands. The gravity of it all was powerful and heavy. She was petrified to enter the open door Geovanni and Aarontino presented her. She could not see explaining her mistake to Jacob or anyone else. She knew her family would never understand.

Jacob's noodles were overcooking beneath his skull, too. Things were sticking together like a blob of pasta. He was slipping into some form of dementia, Alzheimer's or Lou Gehrig's disease or something. For some inexplicable reason, his mind seemed to be crumbling alongside Adamina-Rose's. He seemed to be utterly confused all the time. It didn't stop the summer fun at the mansion, which hosted a number of pool parties and more great meals.

Occasionally, a phone call was made to the water patrol, asking them to find Jacob when his fishing trip on Table Lock Lake went long. He would usually just say he couldn't remember the way. Jacob went into Sock's Hospital for testing, and they found a tumor on his brain that was creating pressure and affecting function. He lay in Adamina-Rose's old hospital room for a week after its removal and was released. Jacob was soon back in the full grandeur of his former self.

Bruce's laid-back mannerism was shifting from hippy to more Sarah-like. He became much more serious after his mother shot herself. I think reality was knocking on the door, letting him know his parents were not going to be around forever. He had slipped their Last Will and Testament into a conversation at a pool party, where Adamina-Rose said that everything was in order and not to worry about such things as a will.

It was time again to select my classes for my senior year at Horseshoe High. I had completed nearly all the requirements to graduate, and if I wanted, I could drive down easy street the rest of the year. I could work at Top Chops half the day and chill until commencement in May. I made a conscious effort to project time conservation into my future and elected to work on more of my college requirements half of the day. The sooner I earned my credentials in formal education, the sooner I could pursue my true desires.

My doctor cleared me to play football, and our team had gelled together nicely. Peyton Saxxy, our quarterback, led the team to a winning record, but we lost our regional playoff game versus Flixa. I played four games before my previously broken leg was hurt again. It was torn ligaments and tendons this time in our game against Rebubblelick High School. It was evident it was not an accident when we reviewed the game film. Scouting must have led to my bad leg being targeted. Coach Duke Donetea was pissed. We won the game, but I was done for the season and was finished playing football altogether.

Holly Hammerbuns kicked my butt in our head-to-head rematch debate. The *News Peeper* had nothing to say. No foray of prickly parents or peacekeepers waiting for me on the grounds of Horseshoe High the next morning. There was some childish chatter like, "Dude, you got beat by a girl," sort of vibe dancing in the hallways, but that was about it. She was presidentially prepared, locked in, and seemed she was plugged into a Wi-Fi database somehow. Lara seemed a little disappointed.

I cannot be sure, but my theory and formula of the universe was most likely misunderstood.

Where:

(-neg charge of dark: Depth of Darkness x an Echo = infinity) -minus

(+pos charge of light: Real-Time divided by Frequency x speed of flow = Center of Gravity)

In my mind, it sounded great. It was clear I was not being received on any level the moment when I set the words free. Holly Hammerbuns gave an incredible debate and rightly won. She was best that night. Perhaps we would meet again at the college level some time.

There had been a few low-key conversations with Aarontino over the passing months. We were more so keeping a pulse of communication alive. I feel we were both discreet and generally guarded. I made a couple of trips to K-sea and stopped by to visit his new A-Rose restaurant with reservations one Friday night when it was hopping. I brought along my quarterback, Saxxy and Rusty from Queenfield, Toozoolee, and the Berry brothers. We were treated like bigshots and royalty. Our server was sweet and flirtatious. We all flirted back. Chef Beerbabe even smiled at me and made me and my friends the most delicious dishes. And we got all the virgin rum and coke's we wanted.

At the end of the meal, Aarontino and Chef Beerbabe came together with the bill, three-hundred nine dollars. I passed it around the table, and everyone scrambled through their wallets and pockets.

"Well fellas, what'd you think of the gourmet chicken souvlaki with tzatziki sauce and the gnocchi with sage-butter?" Chef Beerbabe asked.

"The goochee was really damn good," Berry A said.

"Boys, put your money away. VeeLee's got this," Aarontino said.

"What?" I said with a drawl, "I didn't bring three hundred dollars with me."

"Enjoy. Thanks for coming by A-Rose," Aarontino said grabbing the bill wading it up and tossing it into the air, Chef Beerbabe caught it in the top of his Chef hat. They both smiled and went back to work, visiting other tables together. We felt special, shocked, and happy. Truly one of my greatest memories.

"So, Berry O, have you found your lady yet?" I said.

"*Hell naw...*" I tried not to laugh, but we all did.

"You will, my friend," I said.

"You'll have to meet Hannah Morelight," Toozoolee chimed in.

"Yeah, you got lucky there. She's hot," Berry A said.

"We're new, but I think she'll be around awhile. She's different," Toozoolee said.

"Awesome, bro. I cannot wait to meet her." I said.

"I'm sending you guys a friend request. Your K-sea friends are cool, VeeLee," Saxxy said and fiddled with his phone.

"Thank you, Peyton—yes, they are," I said.

"I don't know you," Berry A said, meaning he would think on accepting a social media request.

"Alright, fellas, we better wrap it up here. Saxxy, Rusty, and I must drive back to Queenfield tonight. So good to see all of you," I said. We left A-Rose and moved outside to the sidewalk, and I gave them each a man-hug.

Toozoolee pulled his shirt off to show me that his tattoos were finished and could hold court in any Polynesian heritage tribal ceremony. His tattoos were amazing and impressive. Rork did him right. The people in formal suits and dresses stared as if they should be calling the police.

Toozoolee, Berry A, and Berry O had plans to take their football game to the college level, in which I felt they would be able to compete nicely. Reggie, the oldest of the Sandburg brothers, was now in prison for shooting a police officer. Thankfully the officer lived. Reggie was a dumbass and would likely be playing patty-cake with his dad.

Every high school and most colleges in the Queenfield area shared the Long Dew Salmons Center to conduct their commencement ceremony in. The students of Horseshoe High would walk the stage on Friday, May fifteenth, at six o'clock in the evening. We were herded like cattle back and forth, first was practice where Johnny Longsong jerked his best friend's underwear half-way up his back, giving him a wedgie. Mr. Lionlies threatened to pull Johnny's diploma out of the stack and send him home if he did one more dumb thing. We knew it was never a good idea to challenge Johnny to be dumber. Some snickered at the reprimand. We knew it was directed at us all. Fat-chance a grouchy history teacher would be able to take away the positive electric vibe and excitement away from us or the air of our accomplishments.

In between rehearsal and the real deal, I checked my phone, where I found I had a new message. It was Melissa asking me to have Anglaia call her mother. I waded through the sea of students until I had tracked her down. "Your mom wants you to call," I said.

"Mother! Not mom, foster boy! My mother wants me to call. You're about to graduate and still haven't learned how to talk." She pulled her phone from her purse. "Damn it. It's dead!" Anglaia said. I quickly offered her my phone. "VonVouge... *Go away*," she groaned and snatched Daniele's phone right out of her hands.

I moved over and leaned against the wall with some of my football teammates and watched the Anglaia show. She was throwing a hissy fit with her mom. It seemed Sarah had changed her plans, and Anglaia was none too pleased. She was also getting tons of interest in her great rising-up against authority. She ended the conversation with, "Bite me, Mother! Not going. I have plans," which shocked most of the listening ears. I was immune to her antics at this point.

"My effing mother and grandmother decided they would spend five thousand dollars on a lame surprise graduation party. Not happening! Danielle and I will be going to Peyton Saxxy's hotel party. Just saying," Anglaia said.

There were quite a few graduation parties going on all over Queenfield, to include the all-nighter sponsored by Horseshoe High—the alcohol and drug-free party. There were some great prizes donated by local businesses. I, too, would be attending Peyton's private graduation party at the Hillytin Hotel.

There would be security and the whole-nine-yards. He regularly bragged that his parents spent over twenty grand on it. It was probably why Anglaia had to throw a number out in front of everyone, as well. Along with a disk jockey playing all the cool songs. To include trips around town in a stretched limousine filled with inebriated girls in short dresses being courted by all the intoxicated boys trying to get lucky.

We were almost free birds leaving behind adolescence. Some would take longer to leave puberty and would resist adulthood with all their might. Some of our classmates would overcome the dysfunctional environments in which they were raised, while others cling to the poor survival options forever. Some would even pass the dysfunction along to future generations. The mélange of aptitude, fear, and responsibility did not often braid together into a strong rope that would pull them through a healthy, productive life. Most would learn through the school of hard knocks, failure, suffering, and heartache.

Chapter 28

Lara exposed

IT WAS TIME TO HAVE AN ENLIGHTENED conversation with my dearest VeeLee. The Purple Cloud was insistent that it be the day before graduation. I knew they had their reasons—I didn't need to know the details. I called Melissa Matches to set up our visit. VeeLee strolled into my office inside the Trueman Library, grinning as he had a million times before. Love in his eyes that I deflected away with a mature smile of acknowledgment.

"Hi, VeeLee. What do you say we take a ride? I need help moving some furniture I just had delivered today. Do you mind?" I knew I had completely disrupted our habit of sitting in my office for our chats, but we needed to get down to business. Somewhere more private.

"What? Of course, I will. I don't mind at all."

"I'll pay you."

"Are you kiddin' me. That's not happing. I would never charge you for anything, Ms. London."

"Aww. Thanks, VeeLee." He tailgated my car closely to the point it was making me nervous. There was no telling what was going through his head as this would be the first time he would be visiting my Condo. I had never allowed him to see my personal space in K-sea or here in Queenfield. We arrived, and we moved the mid-nineteenth century French fauteuil chairs through the garage entrance, flipping in odd directions until we had it through the door.

"I know this is a bit awkward. But I have asked you here for more than moving furniture," I said. He looked bewildered and confused. I quickly followed with, "No funny business. There are things you need to know."

"Oh. Okay, Ms. London."

He looked at me with catlike intent on prey. "Have a seat, VeeLee."

"Sure."

"We have been through a lot together over the years. Haven't we?"

"For sure, Ms. London."

"Well, as you know, I have with all that I know tried to impress upon you, philosophers and great leaders, and the power of politics. Haven't I?"

"Yes. I won a debate championship in my Junior year. Remember?"

"Yes, of course, I do. Now I know you want to be a scientist. You want to heal disease and do something great for the world. Right?"

"I really do, Ms. London."

"I know, VeeLee."

"A microbiologist who helps all of mankind."

"So, anything new on the horizon?"

"Well, the Ozone, or O3 trioxygen, is going to be key. You know, the unstable triatomic form of oxygen that kills everything. Ozone, the sun, and enzymes from assorted plants and animals should get it done. I'm confident I'll track down and destroy enough bad bacteria and virus bugs to actually cure disease using Mother Nature's medications—and heal some folks. I really wanted to be a respected doctor. What do you think?"

"I'd have to look at the specifics, but it sounds fascinating, VeeLee. You also know I have mentioned the Nonagon to you over the years. I knew you never quite believed me when I tried to explain it to you. But there is a real entity some refer to as the Deep State—a shadow government that runs the world. K-9 has been overrun with greed for the last two hundred years, and they are about to take out over half of the world's population when they put G5 Wi-Fi towers on every city block. There will be an epidemic of cancer the world has never seen before."

"WHAT?"

"It is in the works, and the people cannot stop it. Most have no idea what the government is planning for the people. They are being told it will make life so much easier. The G5 signals of phones, computers, televisions—even refrigerators and pill bottles—will send out harmful signals. These signals will painlessly enter the human body and start rotting it away from the inside out."

"Are you serious? Come on, Ms. London…"

"Seriously, VeeLee. Here's the truth. You know Adamina-Rose. Right?"

"Of course."

"Now this is between you and I. Never repeat this conversation with anyone. Agreed?"

"I won't tell a soul. I promise."

341

"I'm counting on your word to me. I do trust you, VeeLee. So, her father Cleo is a king! Adamina-Rose believes he's dead. He is in his nineties, though, and does not know how much longer he'll be around. He has had his eye on you from the time I found you in eighth grade. Maybe even before then."

"Why me? I'm nobody special."

This is getting really strange.

"You are incredibly special. Cleo and I both know it. I work directly for Cleo."

"So, wait a minute. So, if Cleo is Adamina-Rose's dad, why doesn't he want his son Bruce or—" I caught myself remembering my promise to Adamina-Rose, "or some military General in the Pentagon who loves politics?"

It took me some time to put it all together, myself. I was really confused about the whole Geovanni involvement early on. I learned he, too, worked for the Purple Cloud as an enforcer. He worked for one of the other Kings. Cleo wanted to make Geovanni disappear after he had gotten Adamina-Rose pregnant with Aarontino.

"Wait, so you know about Aarontino?"

"Yes, I have recently learned a great deal about the big picture."

"Okay, excuse me, Ms. London. Sorry. So, Cleo has two grandsons he can choose from. Why me? I don't get it!"

"VeeLee. YOU. ARE. THE. BEST. CHOICE. Trust me. Now please listen. Cleo wanted Geovanni dead, but a king with more tenure and authority would not allow it. Cleo was a rookie at the time but eventually used Geovanni to watch over his daughter without her ever knowing it. The thing is my boss, Cleo, holds his secrets for as long as he has to. He didn't want to ruin his daughter's life any more than he already had by abandoning her and her mom when he accepted the post."

I hope I'm being clear enough. He's looking thoroughly confused.

"Would you like something to drink?"

"I'm good. No, thank you."

"So, my main point is that when you go to college, please try to focus on some leadership classes. Philosophy and politics will come in very handy down the road if you are made king. You could tip the scale of the greedy kings who are in charge now. *And stop* G5, which will save hundreds of millions of lives. There is a turnover going on in the Nonagon right now. Several are very old and will be gone soon. Hopefully the new crop of kings will be morally good—the Nonagon is way overdue. The people of the world deserve to be looked after, not used. I know it sounds like science fiction, similar to explaining the FBI running around in black suits. We just know they exist but are never seen. We don't know the truth about them. Just like the world doesn't' know the Deep State."

"Lara, do you think that person is me?"

"I really do, VeeLee. Take your science classes, too. Do what makes you happy. Learn all you can. Create what you can create, cure what you can cure. Just know there is a chance you could be selected, and I wanted you to know now so you will be prepared."

"Thank you. Really crazy stuff, Lara. G5?"

"We will have an in-depth conversation about mass cancer-killing in the future. G5 is the evilest creation man has ever devised. Your Sun Silly pill will be so important as well."

"I do believe I have cracked to code already Lara. The answer is in the oils of the body, The Odes of Horace stated, 'poison loathes oil!' Oil is a fuel, solvent, lubricator and purifier —medication. Kalium, the tissue salts, the three types of potassium: phosphate, chloride, sulfate and iron may kick cancers butt?"

"Interesting…"

Chapter 29

Victory Vibrations

  THEY FILED INTO THE LONG TWO SALMONS arena in alphabetical order. I sat adjacent to the letter V, where I could better see VeeLee VonVouge. I noticed closer to the podium sat the Clintins in support and celebration of Anglaia. I scanned the faces in search of the Matches, yet to find them.

I had to do a double-take when my eyes locked onto the Jackksons who were in full-force attendance—dazzlingly dressed in bright-colored formal attire. They were a bouquet of purple, red, and blue flowers transplanted in the middle of some barren field in a faraway land. They looked beautiful from my distant viewpoint. They were sitting at my nine o'clock, a few rows higher up on the other side of the arena. If I'd be a lucky lady, they would not spot me in a crowd of ten thousand.

I jumped as I felt a hand squeeze on my shoulder.

"Hey, Lara," Melissa said as she and Mike sat down next to me. "Better let Sarah know we're here!" Melissa said and busied herself on the phone. My incognito cover was blown. I noticed the entire Jackkson family getting a kick out of waving at me. I waved back, and they all rose to their feet and disappeared in the concourse.

"Hey, Lara. Sarah and Adamina-Rose want us to join them. They saved seats for us," Melissa said.

"I think I spotted the Jackkson family, and I think they are coming over here."

"The Jackkson family?" Mike said.

"The family who wanted to visit with VeeLee privately in Sock's Hospital," I said.

"For heaven's sake, what in the world are they doing here," Melissa said as we stood up and made our way over to the Clintin troop. No sooner did we sit down, Mike's voice went into full vibrato, working everyone into a ball of stress over his new car payment. He had got the car at cost after mentioning his friendship with Bruce.

There had always been great perks by sucking on the Clintin silver spoon over the years. Mike's last conversation detailing his trip to the Chillakathy prison in K-sea damned near turned Bruce into Jesus. He lathered thick his appreciativeness and acknowledgments to Bruce for saving them from certain peril, as well as spinning Aarontino's comments to his wife in the waiting room. Most knew the story was simply exaggerated to the fullest of Mike's imagination, and nothing more.

The fact Aarontino would even sit in a prison waiting room, let alone hooking Jillie Jo up with a visit from her son, was remarkable. She had almost ruined his life.

Jacob entered into the conversation with an unintentional falsetto voice, "They better stay the hell away from us," clearly still angry over the hospital ordeal.

No sooner did his words stab our ears, the Jackkson family was standing in the area we had just left, their palms in the air, signaling in sign language, "What's up?" The Jackkson migration then moved in our direction, and the hot tension oozed like lava. Jacob and Bruce seemed to tense up with red faces at near the same time.

There were no seats in the nearby vicinity. The Jackksons hovered around for a short time, pointing and having a conversation. Soon a people defrag was conducted where they asked people to adjust their seating three sections over. In watching them, it was clear they made their requests kindly. Everyone in the area was smiling. They marked their seats with their suit jackets. Not dissuaded, the Jackksons—determined as ever for a meet-n-greet—headed our way again.

Jacob and Bruce aggressively stood up as the Jackkson family approached. Mike, somewhat erect, limply crouched on his feet. He was undoubtedly scared-to-death. I thought I would take point and try to defuse the building mayhem. I didn't know how successful I would be after the last exchange, where they clearly got what they wanted—getting us out of the hospital room so they could talk to VeeLee privately.

Adamina-Rose was visibly shaking alongside Mike. Sarah sat close with her, stroking her arm. Melissa sat staunch and collected. She seemed to be going through medical protocols, perhaps CPR, stop the bleeding measures, and the like. Her skill set might be called on again if fisticuffs broke out. Lip reading was not my forte. It was obvious the Jackkson's were communicating as they narrowed the gap. What they might be saying was anyone's guess, utterly indecipherable.

If I were to be completely honest, I was in my addictive element again. I was experiencing an extreme adrenalin rush.

My heart was pumping to some out-of-control foreign drumline—a downpour of fast-falling raindrops the size of bowling balls crashing on a tin roof. My inner Lara was having a blast.

My mind was processing that we were in a public setting, a high school graduation. VeeLee had turned eighteen in October—legally an adult. Even though the Nonagon was highly interested in the young man, there was no good reason to wage war in this setting. I made a plea to our faction, directed primarily at Bruce and Jacob, to allow me to handle this. I smiled my cutest smile and extended my hand to Geovanni, "And we meet again. Good evening, Geovanni," I said.

"It truly is. Good evening, Lara. Adamina-Rose," Geovanni said, contorting his head in such a way as to make eye contact with her. She politely nodded.

"Damn it, Geovanni. Why are you here? Trying to ruin my granddaughter's graduation?" Jacob said.

Well, so much for letting me handle things.

"Really don't care about your granddaughter, sir," Geovanni said. The tension suddenly ratcheted up. The Jackkson sons fanned out into a deimatic posture, shoulder-to-shoulder in force posture with their father. It was intimidating and was drawing the attention of everyone in Long Two Salmons Arena.

My personality did not own a submissive posture, but I did manage to conjure up a neutral dissuasion. We all were likely to be expelled from the ceremony if the conversation didn't shift soon. A uniformed policewoman must have been notified. I caught her out of the corner of my eye. She was making her way toward us at a quick gate.

"Look, Geovanni," I pointed at the officer coming our way, "I understand you are here in support of VeeLee and his mother. I know he will appreciate the Jackkson family being here for him," I said. Their faces remained emotionless.

Geovanni dug about the inside of his suit, pulling out a piece of paper, and handed it to me. The top of the medical form said DNA Paternity Test. The test results with ninety-nine percent certainty, established Geovanni Jackkson was VeeLee's father. "He is family," Geovanni said. He turned to Jacob and went on to say, "So, don't you ruin my son's graduation, Mr. Clintin. I have come to let him know the truth, tonight, directly after graduation."

The angry tension transitioned into an utterly flabbergasted pause. Aarontino followed with, "Hello, Mother," looking at Adamina-Rose.

"Dear God in heaven," Adamina-Rose said.

Jacob and Bruce looked at each other as if the young man was on drugs and shook their heads. There was no way to take the delusional young man's comment seriously. The policewoman parted the ill-willed water with her badge and asked if there was a problem.

"Have a good evening, folks," Goseeia said somewhat sarcastically. Maxx rendered a halfhearted military salute, and the Jackksons moved to three sections over and poured themselves into their seats. Our section fell silent. Pomp and Circumstance began playing over the sound system, and the graduates began to march in. We stood and seemed to continue watching each other.

The guest speaker stroked his accomplishment, and I could not make out the words over the ones screaming in my own head. I was shocked by the audacity of the Jackksons. The inference and information not up for debate. Name after name echoed throughout Long Two Salmons Arena, until our section at last applauded Anglaia. She received a general round of applause as she crossed the stage. Peyton Saxxy received much louder applause, most likely football fans who enjoyed his play.

I did not know how VeeLee would be received as he had stirred the community up with his debate and opinions regarding politics and religion. The *News Peeper* camera crew eased to the stage to take pictures of Peyton Saxxy and perked up again as VeeLee VonVouge penguin-shuffled closer toward his diploma. Camera flashes darted through the air when his name announced. An eerie silence swept across the audience.

Then the Jackkson family broke the quietness, signaling the greatest ovation of the night.

VeeLee looked sleek and dapper, a young man with great swag. He accepted the attention within a humble smile and wagged his right arm at the crowd. These "what if" thoughts had crossed my mind years before. He displayed uncommon character and class. I was so proud of how he overcame his adversity. I may have been right. I felt I had potentially resurrected a king from the ashes of K-sea's belly.

After final remarks were given, we filed out of Long Two Salmons Arena and gathered into two separate groups, close in proximity. Anglaia reunited with our group, beseeching her adulthood—her intent, to hop into the Mustdang and take Danielle to Peyton's party. As far as Anglaia was concerned, they should have already left five minutes ago. She had no way of knowing what had transpired in the stands earlier, but did recognize the Jackkson family grouped nearby and pointed them out to her father. His face crumpled and quickly reset for the pictures Melissa was snapping.

VeeLee made his way outside the arena and into our fold. The Matches posed alongside the young man they had raised for the past two years. The pictures framed the somewhat counterfeit showboat smiles and loving hugs reserved for men of war. We each congratulated him on his accomplishment and shared a handful of gifts. "VeeLee, some of your K-sea friends are here to see you," Melissa said and directed his attention to the Jackkson family waiting nearby.

"Wow, cool! Thank you, everyone. I'll go say hello," VeeLee said.

I walked to where the Jackkson family was standing. They congratulated me and let me know that they were staying at the Hillytin Hotel in Queenfield and wanted me to come back to their room with them. They had a gift and important news to share with me. I thought it was a wild coincidence that they were staying at the same place I intended to celebrate with my classmates later.

I told them I would have to clear it with the Matches first, but it sounded good to me as I was headed there anyway. I jogged over to the Matches and Lara who were standing together. They had been abandoned by the Clintins, who had already left. They told me to be careful and to call if I needed anything.

"Super proud of you, VeeLee. We'll have to get together soon for lunch and examine your college options," Lara said with the sweet smile that I loved.

"Sounds awesome, Ms. London!" I had to smile like a childish moron. No way around it. I made my way back to the Jackkson family and said, "We're good." We all walked slowly to their SUV like a pride of lions on a carefree hunt. Maxx drove us to the Hillytin Hotel, and we made our way up to the Jackkson luxury suite, one floor up from the Saxxy shindig. A few minutes more, and I would rejoin my classmates to add few more awesome memories to the best day of my life.

I opened my mental pelaj knife and split time right down the middle to examine it more closely. What was time offering me? I found it was an illusion that held nothing but ideas. An empty Santa Clause bag of nonsense handed down from generation to generation.

At the Jackkson family mass meeting, I was handed an exquisitely decorated royal blue envelope accented with gold letters and foil leaf. The University of Samfort was boldly embossed on its front. I opened the letter where I read "Full ride." I couldn't believe my eyes and said, "Are you serious?"

"We all attended there! Father's gift," Goseeia said.

"Wow! Thank you, Geovanni, and to all of you for coming. I will never forget this night. I cannot believe this. This is the greatest gift *ever!*" I said. I was shocked and could not even begin to put the big picture together.

They put on serious faces as they formed a semicircle around me. Geovanni handed me a piece of paper. I read it, and my mind offered no comprehensive tools to know what or how to respond to the news that dashed in front of my eyes. My bottom jaw unhinged and dropped in the direction of the floor. My eyes scanned the Jackkson faces.

Starting with the Goseeia who kissed my cheek—each hugged me, slapped my back with their hand, and said, "I'm down with you, my brother," and took a knee. Geovanni, my *father*, finished with, "I'm down with you, *my son*," completing the circle.

I looked down at them, seeing love in their eyes like I had never known—a dream.

My heart was beating a million miles an hour. Tears were running the course of my cheeks and falling hard to the floor. There was no mistaking six strong human beings. It was not a game. There was not another human being on earth the Jackkson family would kneel for, but they did for me. I was a Jackkson!

I reached my hand down and pulled each one of my family members up to their feet and went down to my knees. I took each one of their hands, kissed it and said,

"Thank you, Goseeia. I'm down with you, my sister." She smiled sweetly as I stood, taking her hand, kissed it, and then hugged her back. I then squared up to Aarontino and took a knee.

"Thank you, Aarontino, I'm down with you, my brother," I stood, taking his hand, kissed it, and then hugged him back. He manly cuffed my back three times. We looked at each other again, and he shook his head as if to say no, but was smiling and lip-synced the word, "Wow."

On down the line I repeated with Dominque, Redding, and Maxx until I reached Geovanni. I knelt and said, "I'm down with you, my father," which felt much different coming off my tongue. The word dad would need to be lost in my vocabulary. I stood, kissed his hand and then his cheek and hugged him. I finished by saying, "I love you all."

"All right. Bring it in," Father said. They pulled close around me and performed an abridged squat, each wrapping their arms around my legs, and then hoisted me effortlessly high into the air and where we all chanted, "Family... family... family!" I was let down where we the Jackkson family held one another's hands, and Father prayed in a thunderous voice, "To you, God, *we* will return."

"Amen," *we* replied.

"Family," *we* roared again, sending shockwaves through the Hillytin Hotel.

It was now time to change into my street clothes and join my classmates for our graduation party. I grabbed my duffle bag and headed for the bathroom, when Goseeia said, "Hey VeeLee, do you mind?"

"Not at all. Go ahead!" I smiled and propped myself against the wall.

When Aarontino called out, "Hey kid, come here a sec'." I went to the bedroom where he and Geovanni—dad—father had their shirts off. My attention went directly to the scars in the center of their chest. Now up close, I could tell it was just like mine. The shape of a lightning bolt. "Pull your shirt of VeeLee," father said, "Dr. Sigmund James, the top cardiovascular surgeon in the world, charged me an extra five thousand dollars each for theses perfect, *very small*, lightning bolt scars!" —five thousand dollars? "The three of us have the same degenerative heart condition and I currently need a new one..."—a new one? Does he want mine? Father put his hand over Aarontino's scar and then placed his hand over mine. *It gave me the chills.* Aarontino followed by placing his left hand over Father's scar and his right hand atop father's hand on my chest. *Go-Go Johnny Go.* I naturally followed their lead. "The hearts you now have were from brothers who both died in a car crash. *Christopher's beat quickened with deep thumps like confused conga war drums. Another round of chills coursed the length of my body.* You two never knew, but were in the same operating room at the same time receiving Johnny' and Christopher' heart's. *So that's why I hum that craze song all the time.* I have made extras."— extras? "Enough of this for now… Go have fun with your friends VeeLee." *It's done, now my sons know the hard truth."*—what the? Never, never mind… this is too much! We smiled a weird smile of understanding to one another—Aarontino looking just as confused as me. I took leave of their company and went to the bathroom to change my clothes.

My life was as complicated as the sun. My beloved's temperature twenty-seven million degrees—a hotty! No solid or liquid exists on its surface—angry, volatile, and very unpredictable—yet I found a commonality. The sun was nothing other than the sun—just as I was nothing more than VeeLee VonVouge. I know we will do great things together in the future.

"*Well,* Sister, what there was to do in Key-la-fornee?"

Goseeia placed her arm next to mine and said, "Well, my brother, someone needs to get *some* SUN—SILLY!" and we laughed.

. . .

Acknowledgements

What a strange and energetic relief to have Sun Silly released in book form. I could not have completed this work had it not been for the support of my sensational tribe – a collective of extraordinary and intelligent souls.

I could not be happier that my book found a home at Amazon Publishing. Their passion, diligence, and creativity have made the process of getting Sun Silly into the hands of readers an utter joy. My special thanks go out to:

YOU the reader. Thank you so much for giving Sun Silly a chance. Hopefully, the experience of reading this work of fiction was memorable. A huge virtual High-Five to all the Librarians and booksellers who have left fingerprints and footnotes – I thank my lucky stars for your help.

So grateful for Judith Henstra's Book Helpline at www.bookhelpline.com , where I met my developmental editor Jessica Montgomery/Devon Vesper (author) who forever taught me the craft of POV's, abrupt change of topic's, and how to pay better attention to details. My copy editor Ginny Glass (author) who put on a stethoscope and checked the heartbeat of the novel and chiseled away at the sludge of oops'. And then back to Jessica for the final edit.

My life is filled to the brim with loving people and I am for the lack of a better word: Blessed. The twilight of belief in my writing of poetry and prose came from Randy Evans and Aunt Doris Weber-cloud, "You should do something with your writing," they urged. I was ultimately inspired not to wait until I retired to begin this endeavor due to one of my bestie's little sister, Laura McHugh (author) who motivated the crap out of me with her amazing award winning novels www.weightofblood.com . Thus, a fiction writer was born –. A sincere thanks to my computer tech guys, Sean Feiler and Timothy Harrison, why the gods decided to plant such phenomenal aptitude into these two amazing guys I'll never know, quite ridiculous actually but nonetheless you two absolutely rock! My writing coach Diana Hughes was not only inspirational and tough she guided me with reading lists, amazing personal messages and priceless critiques. To my first readers, Kylie Harrison, Les Ford, Mary Hunt, Cassidy Carter (author), and Betty Rosenberg (whom read portions of Sun Silly aloud to me, which thrilled my soul)… the raw work was admittedly brutal and may have scarred your mind indefinitely – sorry, abracadabra, its readable now lol. I am forever grateful for the initial cover art by, Dustin White and Marina Kartseva www.marinart.land ; those images was passed along to Ginny Glass at www.wordsugardesigns.com , who got the ball rolling on my initial book cover idea, those ideas were then passed down to Billie Knipfer the greatest graphic design pro on earth, Billie crafted the most amazing book cover ever. The folks at Amazon then put it all together. Many thanks to Jordan White for the initial character divider vectors, the art was then fine-tuned and placed throughout the manuscript by Billie Knipfer. My suit tailor, Mina, stitched together my wild suit idea; which was then captured by my ultra-talented photographer, Erin Gamble @ Gambles Photography, she made the photo shoot for my author pic epic and so much fun; which was then sent back to Billie Knipfer www.designarticulate.com to do her amazing magic once again. I would like to thank my amazing Facebook Tribe for their support and comments through the two-year evolution of Sun Silly.

I dedicated this book to my Parents, Grandparents and great friend Bruce. I love, cherish and miss you all dearly and know you're are rocking the realms of the spiritual world, making heaven a wild and beautiful place. To my children and g'babes, family, friends and military patriots (active, reserve, retired and veterans), law enforcement and first responders. Know you are loved deeply.

I am so GRATEFUL.

Sun Silly is a work of fiction. Names, characters, places and incidents are products of my imagination and are used fictitiously. Any resemblance to actual events or locales or persons, living or dead, is entirely coincidental.

Love Life & Laugh

Aace AaBright

LOVE
by Aace AaBright

Wink as you tip-toe across the shallows of happiness
A heart of Love will hum harder in the void of emptiness
Emotions trapped in thought
Demons I soldiered and fought
Might the Angels stretch their smiles
To Memories of this awesome life I've filed
Alien God's teardrops of water
I dare not dissect or try harder
It cannot be corralled nor caught
Pain forms drip a constant rot
When a soul has healed
Simplicity and imagination will be revealed
Fall in love with everything as fast as you can
Every dream listens to an open hand
When poets are understood
Love is everything that is GOOD
Explanations of sorted words
Lick my lips - so absurd
Reflected and collected feeling of joy and light
Every GOOD answer is RIGHT

Sun Silly, is an inspirational story about VeeLee VonVouge, who has found the kind side of foster care and a somewhat normal life. Lara London, a Deep State facilitator has plucked VeeLee from the ghetto and his mom, Jillie Jo; she placed the teen in foster care with Mike and Melissa Matches – who also have Deep State ties. VeeLee immediately encounters High School (teenage) drama in Queenfield, the hometown of the antagonist, Anglaia, whose mother is best friends with Melissa Matches (VeeLee's now foster mom) the parents friendship continually puts the two teens together, which summons the devil in Anglaia's personality. All the while, VeeLee is being recruited by our Deep State shadow government, THE secret society – Luminaries. Lara London the attractive local Librarian who had found the beautiful mind of VeeLee early on, mentors and guides him with books and her own genius. Behind the scenes, Lara is also his very active guardian. Lara's main motivation is a higher post for herself within the Deep State and purposely hopes to use VeeLee to dismantle the 5G program and the powerful signals emitted from towers and satellites that could kill a billion people around the world if not stopped. The third braid that wraps the rope together is the Jackkson family and their secret blood line with Anglaia, VeeLee and the Deep State. VeeLee is sweet on the beautiful Librarian, Lara London, but not the nudge into politics – he wants to be a scientist and create a Silly pill derived from the Sun that will cure every disease.

Made in the USA
Columbia, SC
08 June 2020